HOSTILE TAKEOVER

By Derek Blount

This book is a work of fiction. References to real people, events, establishments, organizations, or locales are intended only to provide a sense of authenticity, and are used fictitiously. All other characters, and all incidents and dialogue, are drawn from the author's imagination and are not to be construed as real.

For information, contact Happy Prince Media, LLC at info@happyprincemedia.com.

Visit us on the Web:
happyprincemedia.com
derekblount.com

FIRST EDITION

Print ISBN 978-0-9967006-0-3

E-book ISBN 978-0-9967006-1-0

For Bethany...

PROLOGUE

THE THING IN THE DARK was getting closer. She couldn't hear it. She couldn't see it. But she could feel it. She knew it was coming, and she knew it was only a matter of time.

The woman's legs pumped harder as she increased her pace, the cuffs of her khaki pants slapping against her ankles. She silently cursed the light gray t-shirt she was wearing. Why couldn't she have had at least one item of dark clothing? Something, anything to help her blend into the desert night?

Because they didn't give you any dark clothing.

Only the locket on the thin gold chain hanging around her neck was her own—the single personal belonging she was allowed to keep. Everything else was part of the package. Part of the program. She had worn nothing but the gray shirt and khaki pants for the past three months, and now she was going to die in them.

At least she was wearing running shoes. Maybe that gave her some sort of chance. After all, she could have been barefoot.

The thought of running through the desert valley in her bare feet sent shivers down her spine. She had encountered far too many of the dangers of the New Mexico desert during the daytime. The tarantulas. The cactus. The scorpions. And the snakes. The thought of stepping on one of them in the dark added to the growing ball of fear in her stomach.

Please God, don't let me step on a rattlesnake.

A dark cloud crept in front of the silver quarter moon, shrouding its light and making the blackness palpable. It was difficult to see with the dim light supplied by the lunar reflection. Without it, it was like sprinting through traffic wearing a blindfold. She slowed her pace, fearful of stumbling in the dark or running headfirst into a large cactus. Her night vision had improved over the past three months, but there were limits to human eyesight. She wondered if the thing stalking her had any limits at all. She had come to doubt it.

The shrill echo of a coyote's howl traveled across the canyon floor. Could the coyote see her? Was it watching the hunt? A spectator? Anxiously awaiting the kill?

The grade of the rough path changed. She was running slightly uphill now. She had to get out of the valley. Over the mountains. She didn't know what lay on the other side. She had never been this far before, even on the forced runs, but whatever was on the other side of the mountains had to be better than this.

Even death would be better than this.

Goosebumps rose across her sweaty neck and arms. She tried to make herself believe it was the cool fall wind that had raised the chicken-flesh across her tanned body, but the words stayed with her, branded into her mind.

Even death would be better than this.

Wasn't that what she had convinced herself of almost two weeks ago, when she finally realized the truth? Wasn't that why she had risked everything to leave the writings? Wasn't that why she was committing almost certain suicide by running off into the desert alone?

The affirmation that she had made the right choice strengthened her resolve. She wasn't a coward. And if she came up short this one last time, if she failed, then she would die on her own terms. And that was worth something.

A branch snapped behind her and to the left.

She didn't stop. Instead, she quickened her pace just as the cloud passed away from the small sliver of moon. She risked a glance over her shoulder toward the noise.

She couldn't see anything. Only the dim outline of some bushes and rocks. The thing was playing a game. Toying with its prey. She knew how fast the thing was, knew that it could outrun her with ease. And it knew the desert. Knew it so much better than her. After all, this was its home. It was the thing's lair. How could she have ever hoped to escape it here?

The incline of the trail increased. It was steeper now, and the exhaustion in her calves was spreading into her thighs. Her legs were muscular. She had developed into a strong runner since joining the program, but the human body still had its limits. Everything had limits.

Except for the thing hunting her.

A flash of something to her right, just outside her range of vision. What was it doing? Why didn't it just come for her?

She listened, striving to hear its graceful, powerful footsteps. Praying she wouldn't. The only sound was the pounding of her own feet and the too-loud noise of her own heavy breathing. Her lungs were on fire. Each breath ignited the agony of cold air fusing into hot lung. Thinking about it made it worse.

The alternative thoughts were even less attractive. The questions pummeled her. *How far had she run? Ten miles? Fifteen? How far to go before she found some hint of civilization? Was there any civilization out here? Was she still in New Mexico? How far had she gotten before they realized she had escaped? How much of a head start did she have?*

A dry rattle erupted from the bush beside her right foot. Rattlesnake!

Instinct took over. She should have just kept running, trusted that the snake wouldn't strike unless it was provoked. But she couldn't help it. She bolted to her left, away from the sound. Away from the fangs and the venom and the terror. Her eyes stayed on the blackness where the sound was emanating. She should have been watching where she was running.

Her left foot struck the rock hard enough to split her big toe to the bone. The running shoe offered no protection from the violent blow. She fell forward into the thorny bush headfirst. The hard wooden needles buried themselves into her arms and scratched her face. One needle punctured the skin immediately below her chin and penetrated a full inch into her neck. Another settled deeply into her cheek, just below her eye. Her hands hit the ground and the rough combination of gravel and broken needles scraped the skin off her palms.

She cried out. She didn't mean to do it. She needed to stay silent, to avoid giving away her position. But the howl of pain escaped her lips before she hit the ground.

The woman didn't move for a moment. If there hadn't been so much pain, her stance would be almost comical. She was a sweating, bleeding statue in mid-push-up. She gingerly inched her toes forward, pulling her legs up until her thighs were pressing against the prickly branches. A couple of thorns pushed their way past the protection of the khaki material and poked her skin.

From this position, she was able to gradually lean back until her hands came off the ground, her body weight now supported by trembling, cramping legs. She felt a tug on her neck—her necklace had snagged on a branch—but she was unable to stop moving backward. The thin gold chain snapped and the woman pulled all the way back, away from the hateful thorns. The bush could have the necklace.

She slowly straightened her spine. She couldn't hear the snake anymore. Maybe it had slithered away to escape the commotion of her crash into the brush.

She reached up to wipe the hair from her forehead and brush it off her cheeks. Her hand came away sticky. In the dark, she didn't know if it was blood or sweat. As she looked closer at her palms, she realized her vision was blurry. Tears must be a part of the mixture, too. How long had she been crying?

Another sound behind her, barely audible. It was still coming. The fear rose once more in her stomach and she bolted into another run, only to stumble after one stuttering step. The blow against the rock had broken her big toe. She realized the same bloody stickiness on her hands was also inside her shoe. The rock must have split her toe wide open. The pain, unrecognized in her fear, now came in waves, racing up her ankle and leg and into her hip. The tears came harder now, unsuppressed.

This wasn't how she wanted it to end. Not like this.

Another sound, this time in front of her. Movement. The woman wiped her eyes with the back of her hand, the only part that didn't seem to be bleeding. She saw two small stars in the blackness, moving in parallel paths. Twin shooting stars. They were beautiful.

The noise. More of a hum. Distant, but growing louder.

Not stars. Lights. Headlights.

There was a road ahead. She had found a road. And a truck was coming.

For the first time that night, hope sprang into her heart, inching the fear aside. She risked a glance behind her. She was afraid the thing would be there. Waiting for her to get close, playing its game, allowing her to smell her freedom before it pounced on her.

There was nothing but blackness.

She spun toward the approaching headlights. How far off? Impossible to gauge in the desert at night. Yards? Miles? She had to find the road.

She began to hobble forward again. Still uphill. She took big steps with her right foot, then pivoted on her left heel, staying off the toe. The blood was beginning to collect in the heel of the shoe.

She moved faster, taking quick, fearful glances behind her with every third step. Still nothing. Was it ever back there? Had it ever been chasing her?

A black cloud crawled over the moon even as a dark certainty crept over the woman's mind. The thing was still out there. And it would never, ever let her reach the headlights. It was going to win. Because it always wins.

Fuck you.

The thought sprung into her mind as an act of defiance. She wanted to live. She had made so many mistakes in her life. The mistakes were why she had wound up here in the first place. But she had tried to make up for some of them. She had left the writings. And if she didn't succeed, someone else would. She took little solace in the knowledge. She just didn't want to die.

She quickened her pace again in the blackness of the cloud cover. She couldn't see her hand in front of her face. But she could see the headlights.

In her haste, she failed to pivot completely, bringing her weight down on her mauled toe. The pain was excruciating. Her head pounded with the agony. But she could see the headlights.

Her arm brushed against a tall cactus, opening new gouges and cuts. She walked on, maintaining her quick, limping pace. Big right step. Pivot. Swing the left foot to the front. Walk on the heel. Big right step.

She dragged her injured foot across a dead stump, sending fresh waves of pain as the front of her running shoe tore open, spilling blood on the gravel and sand. But the headlights were there. She had to reach them in time. She didn't want to even consider what would happen if the truck passed by before she reached the road.

Another rattlesnake began to hum a few yards away in the utter blackness. She didn't care. The dry rattle wasn't between her and the headlights. It didn't matter. Big right step. Pivot. Swing the left foot to the front. Walk on the heel. Big right step.

She was going to make it. She was sure of it. The thing wasn't going to win. Not this time. Big right step.

There was nothing there. Her right foot fell into empty space. Having no anchor from her injured back foot, her body followed the step.

The drop off was steep, but short. She had discovered what lay on the other side of the mountain. This part of the valley had risen gradually upward at an awkward angle, permitting full view of the road that began to the north and then proceeded to run to the southeast, on the other side of the hill.

The woman had stepped off a flat face, which dropped down about seven feet. From there, the decline was less steep. A person would be able to walk down the sloping descent if she was careful and moved slowly. The woman had neither option.

The initial seven-foot drop bounced her off a series of rocks jutting from the slope and carried her tumbling down the side of the mountain toward the road below. It was an unreal sensation. She felt like a child rolling down a grassy hill, but there was no grass, only unforgiving rock. She pushed her arms in front of her in an attempt to regain control. Her bloody palm glanced off a rock and the loud snap that accompanied it left no doubt of a severe break in her wrist. As she fell, she vaguely realized she could no longer move that hand.

She didn't care. In the midst of the fall, she still caught glimpses of the approaching headlights. Her body landed awkwardly on a large boulder, fracturing two ribs. She continued to tumble down the grade.

Her chin glanced off another rock, splitting her lip and snapping her teeth together. Her head filled with a bright light as her body began to go numb from the concussion.

How much further could she fall? How far down was the road?

The truck was close.

The cloud continued its slow trek across the heavens and pulled away from the moon. The dim light filled the valley once again. The woman was almost all the way down the cliff face. Her painful journey was nearing its end.

What she couldn't know was that the road was cut out of the base of the cliff so the asphalt didn't have to be poured on an incline. The cut ran about ten feet, straight down. Ten feet of smooth vertical face on that side of the highway. A long, final piece to drop.

She tried to use her good arm to break her fall. She needed to slow down. Needed to stop.

She couldn't.

Milton Polk had been driving fourteen hours straight. It was against regulations, but everybody did it. He had to doctor his log to show he never drove longer than ten hours without a break, but no one ever really checked the logbook. All anyone cared about was whether the shipment made it on time.

It was a lonely stretch of road through the desert. No good radio stations. No traffic. Only his books on tape. Milton was learning all about the millionaire next door and how he could be one too as his truck approached the cliff. He had just learned why he should invest a little bit every month—dollar cost averaging, they called it—when the woman crashed into the road ahead of him.

Milton slammed on the brakes as the woman struck the ground. A thousand thoughts flew through the disarrayed panic of his mind, but one stayed with him—*Thank God I'm running half*. If the trailer had been filled to capacity, he could never have stopped the truck before hitting the woman. As it was, the truck came to a screeching halt just five feet from her unmoving body.

Milton opened the door and climbed down from the cab. His heart was pounding in his ears and his eyes were wide as quarters. He raced to the front of the truck and knelt next to the woman. All he could see was blood. Her eyes were closed.

Milton didn't know what to do. He started to shake her, but thought he remembered that you weren't supposed to move people who had fallen like that. He glanced up the cliff face. She had fallen a long way. But what was he supposed to do? His radio wouldn't be any good out here, and he hadn't had a cell signal for hours. There wasn't a town for miles. Sonora was the closest one, and it was way too small to have a hospital.

He placed his fingers on her neck, not sure if he even remembered how to find a pulse. He noticed the spreading pool of blood on the asphalt beneath the woman's head.

Oh no.

Milton bent down, placing his hand behind her neck but afraid to lift her head, knowing what he'd find. When he got close, the woman's eyes opened. Just barely. Just enough so Milton could see they were brown in the white glow of the headlights.

Her lips were moving. He bent close to her.

"I'm right here, ma'am." He tried to sound calm. "Help's coming. You'll be fine." A lie, but a good lie. It seemed like the right thing to do.

"Help me," she whispered. Her eyes closed again, and her breathing stopped. The blood continued to spread on the gray asphalt beneath Milton's fingers.

Milton looked around, desperately wishing someone else was here. Wishing someone could tell him what to do. He had never been in a situation like this in his life.

He glanced up the cliff face again, wondering what she had been doing. Where this poor woman had come from.

He lowered his chin to his chest and said a prayer for her. He knew she was dead. And though he didn't know what else to do, this at least felt like the right thing.

If the night sky had been any brighter, Milton would have realized that he was not alone. Standing atop the cliff, another pair of eyes watched.

The figure was huge. The man approached seven feet in height and carried in excess of two hundred and eighty pounds on his muscular frame. He was shirtless, with sweat glistening in the dim moonlight. His massive chest moved up and down as he took in great breaths watching the idiot truck driver fawn over the dead woman.

He flexed the fingers of his right hand, balling them into a fist and then straightening them again. The twin blades strapped across his wrist and the back of his right hand were heavy, aching to be used. The six-inch daggers extended over his fingers, giving him the claws that had not been provided to him by God even though he so richly deserved them.

Perspiration ran down his face and dripped from the end of his nose. When the salty drops hit the ground, they were greedily absorbed by the parched earth. The hunt had been so good. So exciting. And it had ended too soon. With no satisfaction.

Now he stood there, the thing in the dark, staring at the pathetic man kneeling over the woman's body and wringing his hands. The truck driver was weak.

It would be so easy.

The thing waited in the cool blackness of the desert night for a very long while, debating what it should do next.

And somewhere in the darkness, the dead woman's necklace dangled from the branch of a desert bush. The gold locket hanging from the thin chain swung back and forth in the night breeze. There it would stay for many months, unnoticed, until the day it would save the life of a man currently over two thousand miles away.

Part I:
AWAKENINGS

CHAPTER 1

THE MAN'S ARM reached out from beneath the sheets and switched off the alarm five minutes before it was set to sound.

Dawn's earliest rays had yet to creep into the sky. The streetlight was still shining just past the tree outside the window. The soft glow cast amber shadows into the quiet bedroom.

John Michaels lay in bed with a blank stare, the back of his head pushed deep into the pillow. He had been awake for many hours but the endless rotations of the ceiling fan and the cream finish of the ceiling had provided none of the answers he longed for. Nothing had changed since he pulled the blanket up to his chin the previous evening. Nothing at all.

He eased his body into an upright position and swung his feet to the floor, cautious to minimize the disturbance. There was no sense in waking Sarah. Not now.

He glanced at the numbers burning red on the digital clock.

5:25 A.M.

His gaze shifted back to the window, the tree and the streetlight beyond. It was a long drive into downtown. He would get caught in traffic. Just like he did every day. His thoughts drifted. He wondered what time the streetlight ceased its glowing. Was it well into the morning? Or did the city set the lights to switch off at the first hint of dawn to save precious budget dollars?

Odd. He had lived in the same house and stared at the same streetlight every night for a decade. And he had never seen it go out. Every now and then on a weekend, he had seen the light first flicker to life, when the coolness of dusk was just setting in, but he had never been home to witness the light shut off in the morning hours.

He sighed as he eased off the bed. What difference did it make now anyway? He walked toward the bathroom. He would wait until the door was shut behind him before turning on the light, just as he did every morning. He didn't want Sarah to wake up, not this early.

A soft voice from the bed stopped him as his foot first encountered the bathroom tile.

"Did you sleep okay?" Sarah mumbled the question from the side of her mouth. The other half of her face was pressed into her pillow.

"Yeah," John said, staring at the dark patterns on the floor rather than facing the shadowed figure on the bed.

There was a long pause. He didn't go into the bathroom, but he wasn't sure why he remained standing in the doorway.

His wife spoke again, her voice more clear this time. "I love you."

Another long pause.

"Do you love me?" Tentative. Still soft, but more awake.

A strange emptiness pervaded John's mind. He wanted to think about it, to really consider the question, but he had already thought too much.

"Yeah," he said as he closed the door behind him and switched on the bathroom light.

He was looking at the large mirror over the sink as the harsh bulbs surrounding it sparked to life. For a brief moment, before the temporary blindness that always accompanies the first bright light of the morning, he saw himself. And in that brief flash of light, he felt no recognition for the man on the other side of the glass.

Eyes half-closed, he reached into the shower and turned on the hot water. He would give it a minute to warm up as he relieved himself. Standing in front of the toilet, listening to the water splash in the shower and in the bowl, the same emptiness stayed with him. There were no thoughts. No lingering doubts or worries from the night.

He stepped into the shower and cringed as the water scalded his shoulder and chest. He eased the knob a quarter turn and relaxed as the stream grew comfortably cooler. He pushed his face into the water and allowed the pressure to massage his cheeks and forehead. He kept his eyelids closed tight as the tiny jets bounced against them.

This wasn't right. He had to think. Had to allow himself at least that. But he had spent the entire night, his entire life, thinking. What else was there to think about?

Sarah.

It wasn't unusual for her to wake up when he made his way to the bathroom, but that was usually the fault of the alarm clock. The alarm hadn't sounded in weeks so why had she been awake today?

To speak to him? To ask him how he slept and if he loved her?

He reflected on his answers. He had spoken two words to his wife this morning, and he had lied twice.

Shit.

John looked into the bathroom mirror, evaluating the length of his tie. It looked right. He reached into the closet and removed his suit jacket from the hanger. The jacket was charcoal gray with classic pinstripes. His favorite suit.

He adjusted the knot on the red tie, his jacket cradled in the crook of his arm. How long had it been since he cared what he looked like? And why today? Of all days, why should he care today?

He shook his head at the man in the mirror. The man with the first hints of gray creeping into his dark brown hair. As a child, he would have considered thirty-five far too young to have gray hair, but it didn't seem so unreasonable now. His brown eyes were bloodshot. Curse of the insomniac.

He turned away from the mirror and switched off the bathroom light. Unaccustomed to the dark, his eyes saw white spots in the sudden blackness. He gently opened the bathroom door. The streetlight's amber glow still fought the darkness beyond the bedroom window.

John paused. He could hear Sarah's light breathing. Asleep again. That was good.

He crept past her sleeping form and closed the bedroom door behind him. He considered going back inside and planting a kiss on her forehead, but the gesture seemed too contrived. Instead, he walked down the hallway and proceeded down the stairs.

He entered the kitchen and turned on the light. The white tile seemed to absorb the light rather than reflect it. The floor was dingy. Sarah had always rejected the notion of a housekeeper in favor of cleaning the house herself, but she rarely made the effort anymore. John wasn't certain how long it had been since the kitchen had been mopped, but he guessed that didn't matter either.

He walked to the refrigerator and grabbed the container of orange juice. He leaned against the open door as he unscrewed the cap and downed several swallows. The acid in the juice burned his throat. He lowered the bottle and placed it back in the fridge. He left the cap on the counter.

Just as he started to close the door, the six-pack of beer caught his eye. Sarah must have gone to the store. He reached inside with both hands and grasped all six bottles, clenching their necks in the spaces between his fingers.

He had almost forgotten about this part. But it was important. At least, it had seemed important in the darkest hours of the night.

He opened a drawer next to the sink and removed the bottle opener. Deftly, he popped the caps off all six bottles and replaced the tool in the drawer. Holding a bottle in each hand, he upended them over the sink. The beer poured out in uneven glugs. The smell of it reached his nostrils. Even at six in the morning, the temptation was there to have just a sip, but he found that he could resist the thought with surprising ease. Man on a mission.

He tossed the empty bottles into the trash then grabbed the remaining four, two in each hand in a duplication of his trip from the refrigerator. Upending all four bottles into the sink, some of the beer splashed off the porcelain and landed on the counter.

John stepped back and extended his arms, careful not to allow any to splash on him. He didn't want to smell like beer. Not today. His tie dangled precariously close to the sink, but it remained clean.

He tossed the empty bottles into the trash. They clinked loudly against one another. John winced at the noise, but he knew the house had thick walls. The noise in the kitchen would not wake Sarah, which was good since his task wasn't finished yet.

He walked into the living room and opened the liquor cabinet beside the bookshelf. A dozen bottles of various sizes, colors and labels stared back him. The temptation was there. Stronger this time. The scotch would be exceptionally satisfying. The bottle was half empty anyway.

He shook his head. Not today.

He reached into the cabinet, extracted four bottles and walked to the kitchen sink.

The dark brown bourbon swirled down the drain as John turned on the faucet to wash the smell from the sink. He dropped the final bottle into the trash, now so full the neck of the bourbon protruded from the top. Satisfied, John switched off the kitchen light and walked towards the front door.

He glanced at his watch when he stopped in front of the hall closet. Emptying the liquor bottles had taken longer than expected. He was going to hit the worst of the morning traffic. Might even be late for work.

Oh well.

He opened the closet door and stood on his tiptoes, reaching to the very back of the top shelf. His fingers encountered a blanket, searched beneath it until he touched the cool metal and then reached further until he was able to grasp the handle at the top.

He pulled his arm back and flattened his feet on the floor, the small tin box now in both hands. One end of the blanket flopped over the lip of the shelf and came to rest on the shoulders of the jackets and winter coats hanging there. He considered pushing it back into its original space but instead closed the door. What were the odds Sarah would open the closet that morning? After all, it was spring. No more need for winter coats, no more need to open the closet door.

He looked at the metal box in his hands. It looked cheap, but that didn't really matter. Not much mattered today. Not anymore.

John Michaels opened the front door and walked to his car, metal box in hand.

CHAPTER 2

THE WARM TEAR ran into her ear and tickled the tiny hairs there. She hated the feeling. Lying on her back, head pressed into the pillow, the tears always trailed down from the corners of her eyes and fell into her ears. She knew that if she sat up, the tears would run down her cheeks. That would be preferable, but she couldn't bear the thought of sitting up. So Sarah Michaels lay there crying, soft sobs punctuated by a loud snort every few minutes.

That was even worse than the tears falling into her ears. The crying always made her nose run, but the tissues were in the bathroom, so the snot just crept into the back of her throat until she either sat up or snorted the vile stuff. It was awful. But not awful enough to make her sit up.

So she lay there and cried. The tears eventually clogged her left ear, resulting in a high-pitched whine on that side. The ceiling fan continued to make its circles in the newfound daylight. The wooden blades looked blurry through her moist eyes.

Another new day.

Sarah stood in front of the bathroom mirror. She was naked. The constant noise of the water running in the shower behind her was comforting. The image presented in the glass was not. She was ugly. Fat. A bloated cow.

No wonder John had stopped loving her.

She stretched her arms above her head. When she did that a year ago, she could see her ribs and her breasts pushed out in a perky tease. This morning, she could only see the fat. And her armpits hadn't been shaved in two weeks. She felt hideous.

A part of her knew she wasn't really that fat. She wasn't obese by any stretch of the imagination. The rational side of her mind reminded her that she was only about thirty pounds heavier than when she and John were first married. But she had always been thin. Now, all she could see was her bulging belly. The flabby skin under her arms. The miserable dimples of cellulite spreading across her ass.

She was hideous. There was no denying it.

She stood in the kitchen doorway wearing only her pink robe. The collar was frayed. It was the most used piece of clothing in her wardrobe. Just about the only thing that fit anymore. She had tried to buy new clothes a few weeks ago. She had gone to the department store by herself and ventured into the women's clothing area. And there was that smiling, eighteen-year-old, size two employee who asked if she needed any help. Her tone had sounded sincere, but Sarah knew the girl was laughing at her on the inside and would be smug when pointing out the plus-size clothing for her. Skinny bitch.

She had left the store and wandered in the mall until she reached the hot pretzel dealer. The pretzel had been good. Buttery. It made her feel better.

As Sarah stood at the kitchen window looking at the neighborhood, she reflected on her actions. She was not a dumb person. She had graduated in the top twenty of a high school class of over two hundred. She had come within a year of completing her degree in American history in college. She knew what an eating disorder was. She knew what depression was. And in some part of her mind, she recognized she was suffering from both. But that rational portion of her consciousness was quiet these days, and the intellectual recognition it whispered of her condition didn't make it any better.

She opened the freezer door and pulled out the box of Eggo waffles. She plugged in the toaster. It was a big, four-slot toaster. Family size. She should have thrown it away by now. Instead, she slid four of the round waffles into the slots and pressed the lever until it clicked.

Sarah replaced the box and opened the refrigerator door to pour a glass of milk. The orange juice was open. She glanced to her left. The bright orange cap sat on the counter. John hadn't bothered to replace it before he left for work.

She ignored it, and removed the carton of milk from the fridge. She checked the expiration date. Two days past. And she had just been at the store yesterday. Why was she so stupid?

She opened the carton and sniffed. It smelled like milk, but she couldn't really remember what fresh milk was supposed to smell like. Either way, if it wasn't bad enough to make her wrinkle her nose, it couldn't be too sour. She set the carton on the counter and opened the cabinet above the toaster. She reached for one of the plastic cups then hesitated. Why did she always drink from the cheap cups? She glanced at the crystal glasses lined up and sparkling on the other side of the cabinet. They had four nice juice glasses. Never used. What was the point of having them?

She grabbed one of the fancy glasses and held it up to the window over the sink. The morning light shimmered in the etchings along the sides of the glass. These glasses were purchased to be used. She might as well use one for breakfast.

The waffles popped up from the toaster with a loud springing sound, startling her. She flinched just enough to lose her grip on the glass. It fell into the sink, shattering when it impacted the porcelain.

Only the base of the glass and part of one side remained intact, the rest was in a thousand tiny shards. The family of glasses was ruined. She had made them an incomplete set. She knew she would never buy another to replace the broken one. It just wouldn't happen.

Tears came. Sudden and powerful. She gripped the front of the sink where it met the counter and squeezed her hands tight, leaning back as her knees became weak.

She no longer tried to contain the sounds of her sobs. What was the point? No one was home. No family. No friends. No life. She wept and shook as the sobs wracked her body, until finally, like an ebbing wave, the tears stopped flowing. Her sides ached from the sobs, but the pain was accompanied by something else. A sudden sense of clarity. Certainty. And that certainty bore an overwhelming sense of relief.

Sarah released her death grip on the sink and tore off a paper towel. She wiped her eyes and cheeks, then blew her nose into the rough paper. When she threw the towel in the trash, she didn't notice the mountain of empty liquor bottles. She was too enveloped by the new thought, the new feeling.

She opened the pantry and retrieved the maple syrup. She knew what she had to do, and she would do it right after breakfast.

CHAPTER 3

JOHN MICHAELS stared across the desk. His face showed no feeling, no emotion whatsoever. The effect was disconcerting for Reginald Nichols. He didn't know what else to say. Fortunately, John spoke next.

"One more time," he asked, his eyes betraying no impact of the news Reginald had just delivered.

"I'm sorry, John, I really am, but we think this is for the best. For the company and for you."

Reginald fidgeted behind his desk as he spoke. He had never been good at firing people, and the fact that it was *the* John Michaels sitting in front of him certainly didn't help matters.

"I helped build this company, Reginald. And now you're pushing me out the door." John's words were matter-of-fact in tone. He was not being argumentative. By the expression on John's face, Reginald couldn't read any degree of concern at all.

"I'm not pushing you out the door, John. Hell, this wasn't even my decision," Reginald lied. It had been his decision in the end, but this was much harder than he had expected. He had almost hoped for a fight, for John to be upset so Reginald could play his trump card, come off as the good guy. Oh well, might as well use it anyway. "And we do recognize the immense contribution you made here. That's why we want to give you one year of paid salary."

John's eyebrows arched at the statement. It was the first hint of facial expression he had given since Reginald had asked him into the office. "One year? That seems rather generous considering you're firing me. Why not keep me on and get some work in exchange for the money?"

Reginald sighed. "John, we just feel that it would be best for you and the company to part ways as amicably as possible. Now. The salary is just our way of saying 'thank you' for all the hard work you've put in these past ten years."

"Twelve." John's voice was soft, but clear.

"Sorry, twelve," Reginald said. "Of course, we would need you to sign a non-compete contract as part of the agreement." Reginald did his best not to say the words too quickly, to do anything to arouse John's suspicions. After all, there was no way in hell the *old* John would let something like this slide, but the old John wouldn't have been sitting in front of Reginald's desk getting shit-canned either.

Reginald sat in silence, waiting for a response. Nearly two minutes went by without one as John Michaels stared out the window behind Reginald, looking through his former employer. Reginald fidgeted more as he endured the unbearable quiet until finally, an almost imperceptible nod.

"Okay," John said, still looking out the window. "One condition."

"What have you got in mind?" Reginald asked, uneasiness churning in the pit of his stomach. He grew wary of the man in front of him. Was there still a spark somewhere in that hollow shell that used to be John Michaels? What could he possibly want that would make this deal any easier to swallow?

"I want the documents in writing, and I want the deposit in my account within the hour. I'll be packed and out of the building before lunch."

Reginald held his breath, waiting for more. When John said nothing else, Reginald had to suppress a smile. The papers were already in his drawer, freshly prepared by the attorneys the previous day. Making a wire transfer of that amount of money within the hour would require a couple of signatures, but that would be easy to manage. He held his hand to his mouth and coughed to make sure the grin didn't emerge while he spoke.

"All right, John," he said. "I'll have the papers to you in half an hour, and the money will be transferred once you sign."

John nodded and stood. The same blank expression on his face. He turned and opened the office door, walking out without a handshake or a goodbye.

As the door closed, Reginald Nichols leaned back in his chair and propped his feet on his desk. A broad smile spread across his face. He couldn't believe how easy that had been. He was a management god. He should write a book on how to handle touchy terminations with style.

Reginald laced his fingers and put them behind his head. The whole encounter with John had lasted less than twenty minutes. And he had been able to avoid mentioning the accident, the one thing that could have given John any ammunition in a wrongful termination suit.

In a way, it was sad. He had always considered himself a sort of friend to the consultants, and John was no exception. Well, a little exception. John was the only subordinate Reginald had that should have been promoted and made partner years ago, but John didn't have the same pedigree as the rest of the firm. There was no Harvard or Yale on his resume, just a list of successful deals that would make any CEO drool. But name recognition still counted for something at the firm, and there was, of course, the ugly practicality of promoting John Michaels that also created a glass ceiling over his head. John had been just so damn good, nobody wanted to pull him off the front lines. In the world of hostile takeovers, John Michaels was the generalissimo of guerrilla warfare. He was the ringer that clients asked for by name, and the name acquisition targets learned to fear. He was too hot to be promoted into some bullshit management job. And John hadn't wanted to go. He had been so good before the accident.

But that was then, and in the now, Reginald couldn't afford to lose any more clients. If shooting stars burned brightest before extinguishing, then John had erupted into a supernova after the accident. And his clients felt the heat. There was nothing but charred embers there now. Nothing of use to the firm.

Reginald considered the stoic expression on John's face throughout the meeting. He had been worried at first that John might slide back into his old self and manipulate the terms of the non-compete agreement. That he might return to form just long enough to take the firm's money and steal away some clients. And he could have done it. Reginald wasn't so arrogant to believe that he could have out-maneuvered John Michaels. But that had been a pointless concern. The man who sat across the desk was empty. There was nothing left.

The thought of John's uncaring eyes filled his mind. He had just sat there, staring past him out the window. Reginald spun his chair to take in the view from his office.

The blinds were drawn in front of the window.

The smile dissipated from Reginald's face, and a cold shiver ran up his spine as those empty eyes stared at him from his memory.

There was nothing left. Nothing at all.

CHAPTER 4

SARAH MICHAELS ran the brush through her hair a final time and looked into the bathroom mirror. That looked right. She reached for the hair spray and shielded her eyes with her other hand as she sprayed. Setting the can back on the counter, she leaned forward to peer closer at her reflection. Lipstick? Why not?

She reached into the little basket that held her makeup essentials and selected a light shade of red. She puckered and applied the hue, blotting her lips with a tissue when finished. She turned to look once more at the woman in the mirror. It was the first time she had fixed her hair or worn makeup in more weeks than she could remember. It didn't change anything. She now looked like a fat girl wearing makeup.

She shook her head but denied herself any more tears. She was wearing mascara, and there was no sense in making it run with more useless waterworks. Instead, she walked to the closet and perused her wardrobe. She removed the loose-fitting blue dress she hadn't worn since she was...since the accident. The dress was one of the few things in the closet she knew would still fit.

She slid the garment over her head and wiggled her arms through the sleeves. She faced the mirror as she buttoned the dress, then turned away. She couldn't look at herself. Not in the dress. There were too many memories.

She opened the medicine cabinet. It didn't take long to find what she needed. The pills were in the same place as always. Top left. She shook the bottle. More than half full. Should be fine. She closed the medicine cabinet and left the bathroom, turning off the light on the way out.

Sarah wandered around the house. Room to room, she went about the decision of where to sit. What would be the best place? Finally, she decided on the sofa in the living room. It was the most comfortable spot in the house. Besides, she could turn the television on if she wanted, although she doubted she would choose to do so.

She placed the bottle of pills on the coffee table then proceeded to the kitchen where, without hesitation, she grabbed one of the crystal glasses and filled it with water from the faucet. She raised the glass and pressed the smooth crystal against her lips, taking a small sip. The water was tepid. She didn't care.

Sarah took the glass of water back to the living room and placed it next to the pills on the coffee table. She sat back and took a deep breath, assessing the items in front of her. A cold chill ran through her and goose-bumps broke out on her arms.

A blanket. She would need a blanket.

She walked to the hall closet and opened the door. The dark green blanket was hanging off the shelf, part of it resting on the winter coats below. Odd. She grabbed the blanket and lightly pulled, freeing the remainder of the material from its perch on the shelf. The blanket fell to rest in her hands and on her shoulders. She closed the door to the closet with her foot and marched back to the sofa, pulling the blanket around her shoulders as she sat down.

She picked up the brown prescription bottle. *Xerenon*. Anti-depressant. Side effects include drowsiness, increased appetite and weight gain. The doctors had been kind enough to provide an ample supply of the pills after the accident. Always good to swap one set of problems for another, especially if the new set is covered by insurance.

She popped the cap off the bottle and tapped the side until a small pile of the medication formed on the table. She set the bottle down and lined up the little blue pills. Twelve in a row. That sounded about right.

She picked up the first pill and rolled it between her fingers. Over the lips and through the gums, watch out stomach, here it comes. She placed the pill on her tongue and swallowed a gulp of water.

How many of these things had she taken since that day on Sixth Avenue?

She put another pill in her mouth and swallowed.

What was John doing right now? Would he be the one to find her? Of course he would. She hadn't spoken to a friend in months, and she didn't have a family anymore. John would find her. It would just be a matter of time. Would he think she was pretty in her makeup and her dress?

She picked up another pill and repeated the procedure. For the first time in weeks, she allowed her thoughts to dwell on that afternoon.

Why had her father done it? The light was red. He had always been a good driver, had never even gotten a ticket. Was it because her mother was arguing with him?

Sarah closed her eyes as she swallowed another pill.

The argument had been about John. Why was he being so stubborn? What was wrong with giving the baby a family name? Why was he so opposed to using Sarah's maiden name as the baby's middle name? All they really wanted was some consideration. After all, they had given birth to the baby's mother.

Another pill.

Sarah defending John. They hadn't decided on a name yet. It just depended if it was a boy or girl. But why should it matter? It's just a middle name.

Another pill.

Sarah leaning back in the back seat, tugging at the seatbelt that was so damn uncomfortable under her growing belly. Pulling it up from her waist so that it rested across her belly. Just for a minute. The blaring horn. The jarring impact. Bright color becoming her only reality as her head smashed against the side window. The pain. Minutes that felt like hours.

Another pill. The glass of water now half-empty.

The voice of the sweet teenage boy asking if she was okay, telling her help was on the way. Asking if anything was broken, could he move her away from the car? His girlfriend in the background screaming something unintelligible through her sobs. The other voice, the van driver, saying it wasn't his fault. The light was green. He just couldn't stop.

Another pill.

Sarah mumbling something to the boy. She was pregnant. "Shit," the boy had said. Followed by, "don't worry, help is on the way." Still unable to see clearly. Everything so bright, so out of focus. Reaching out to touch her mom, to let her know she was okay. Her fingers brushing something warm and sticky. The boy grabbing her wrist and pulling her hand away. Taking the chance and lifting her from the back seat anyway. Getting her away from the car.

Another pill. The memories growing fuzzier, coming in gray waves.

Lying down on the asphalt, the boy's sweatshirt a pillow. Facing away from the car. Everything still fuzzy. Her body feeling wrong. The van driver's voice again, was she okay? He was so sorry, but it wasn't his fault. Blackness.

Another pill. Harder to swallow this time.

Waking up in the hospital. Her body still feeling wrong. Empty. John beside her. Tears in his eyes. Not able to tell her. Reaching down to hug his wife. Pulling up the blanket to cover her shoulders.

Everything starting to fade.

The blanket. Why was the blanket pulled down in the closet?

Dull realization.

Oh, John...

CHAPTER 5

JOHN MICHAELS slid the gearshift into Park and slumped back in the driver's seat. The radio was off, as was the air conditioning. He sat there for a moment, listening. It was too quiet. He touched two switches on the door, and both front windows slid open. The distant sounds of traffic and a slight breeze filled the vehicle.

That was better.

He turned off the car's engine. The sedate rumblings of the V6 ceased. John stared out the windshield and the open windows at his surroundings. It was nice for a public park. A few picnic tables. Good view of the bay. Plenty of parking. Boston was a good town. He supposed he'd miss it.

This park was, in fact, one of his favorite places in the city. There was no housing nearby so the park was virtually unused. Just some extra land the city had to do something with, he guessed. Every day, there would be a few businessmen like himself who would eat lunch by the water. Sometimes they spoke. Most of the time they didn't. John figured it would be deserted this time of the morning. He was right.

He sat there for a long while, gazing out over the water. A couple of commercial fishing boats were tooling around the harbor, heading back to the dock for repairs. At least, that's what John assumed. After all, no one ever brought in a full catch without spending at least twelve hours on the water. His father-in-law, the retired fisherman, had always let John know how hard it was to work on the boats for a living. That was man's work. He came home with blisters on his hands and stinking of fish. He earned his money the hard way.

The memories of Morty Simmons made John grimace. When it came right down to it, it was all Morty's fault. For all his bitching about his son-in-law, it had been Morty who had screwed up in the end, and John would never forgive him for it.

A sigh escaped his lips as he gazed at the boats floating on the dark waters.

He and Sarah had been so happy once. She was the first woman who ever understood him. Ever since they met in college. Two opposites. He was always alone. She was always with friends. But somehow, they fit together. And they were happy. Except for Morty and Estelle. Except for the fact that nothing John did was ever good enough. Nothing.

He worked hard, but it wasn't a real job since he showered before work instead of after. By the time he was thirty, he earned more money in a year than Morty had made in a lifetime as a fisherman. He took Sarah on exotic vacations and bought great presents for her parents every Christmas. He did everything he could to give their daughter the best life possible, and all he ever heard was that it wasn't good enough.

The remarks cut like a knife. He never told anyone, not even Sarah, how much it hurt. His own father had abandoned John's family when he was only six years old, and he was forced to become the man of the house. He had worked all his life to provide for his mother and older sister. He missed his senior year of high school to nurse his mother before the cancer finally took her. He then aced his GED and scored in the ninety-eighth percentile on the SATs. He worked and studied twice as hard as anyone in college, and his grades reflected it.

He had spent his entire life trying to prove something, but he never knew to whom. And when he finally met Sarah, when he hoped that maybe her father could be the dad John never had, all he received was criticism.

He would laugh it off, and Sarah would tell him not to worry about it. It was just the way her father was. But the seed of resentment had been planted, and it had years to grow deep roots. By the time the accident occurred, it exploded. He and Sarah never recovered. Her parents meant the world to her. She missed them. He blamed them. The communication stopped. There were no lifelines for either of them, and their love had drowned in the storm. It never stood a chance.

But Sarah would get better. He knew that, deep inside. She was always a strong person, and she would recover. Someday.

A small speedboat cut a wake through the harbor, weaving its way between the larger ships. Someone must be on vacation.

John touched the papers inside his coat pocket. It was the contract from Reginald, and the receipt for the wire transfer into his account this morning. The papers needed to be on his person. They would be entered into evidence, and Reginald wouldn't be able to try to take back the money as an erroneous transaction, a bank mistake.

He glanced down to the passenger seat. The small metal box sat there, unopened. He touched his fingers to the lid. Despite resting in the sun, the box was cool. Almost cold.

John pulled his fingers away and placed both hands on the steering wheel, closing his eyes and leaning his head back against the seat. He thought about Sarah. The way her hair looked in the morning. The sparkle in her eyes when she laughed. The laugh that had been silent for so very long. He wanted to love her again, but there had been too much. Too much pain. Too much distance. Too much blame to recover. The flaming passion that had once been their love had been reduced to ashes, and there was nothing left to stoke the fire.

But she would be okay. It would take her a while, but in the end, she'd be all right. After all, she was strong.

John opened his eyes, staring at the car's gray ceiling. He had always considered himself to be strong. Tough. Able to handle anything life could throw at him. He had already survived abandonment by his father, the painful death of his mother, and the estrangement of his sister. He still missed Jennifer. His greatest regret had been those last, harsh words he had spoken to his sister before she stormed out. He briefly wondered where she was now. Was she okay? Would she ever hear about this? How he had failed?

Because when all was said and done, it was the failure that had sapped his strength. The only thing that every really mattered to him, and he had failed to protect it. To protect her.

He didn't want to remember. He wanted to close his mind off to the thoughts. He had already spent so many hours allowing himself to be haunted by that day. But this was his time, and this was his penance. So he let the memories flood him.

The meeting with the board of directors from Park Brothers. John running things like a field general. Detailing the game plan for taking over their third-largest competitor. The company would be able to acquire it for less than half of what was expected, and it would be able to complete the transaction in less than three weeks. It was brilliant. John was brilliant. The clients were all smiles.

Then the phone rang.

It was his cell phone. The number was only to be used in absolute emergencies. Sarah knew that, she knew how important the meeting with Park Brothers was. Excusing himself from the table. Hitting the green button as he was leaving the room. Answering the call by asking, "What?!"

The nurse from the hospital saying there had been an accident, could he get to County General as quickly as possible? Not even bothering to hit the "end" button on the phone as he ran for the elevators. The drive to the hospital. Lucky he didn't kill himself or someone else. Never considering it in his panicked state of mind.

Rushing to the admissions desk. The attendant on the phone. The conversation not as important as the information he needed. Running down the hall, checking rooms for his wife. Another nurse finally chasing him down, explaining what happened. He could see his wife in a few minutes, but there was somewhere else he should go.

The harsh, antiseptic smell of the infant intensive care unit. No place for children. Too cold. Five incubators. Three occupied by babies. So small. The nurse leading him by the hand to his daughter.

Four months premature. Two pounds, six ounces.

Hot tears on the side of his face, not sure when they started. Asking the nurse the only question he could. Sympathetic eyes. A shake of the head. Zero possibility of survival. Organs not developed enough to sustain life. He could hold her through the incubator if he wanted.

His hand shaking. Trying to fit it into the glove. Having to stop. Breathe. Finally reaching his fingers into the cool latex. Barely touching his daughter on her side. No reaction. White gauze covering eyes that would never see.

Other hand in the second glove. The nurse standing nearby, watchful. Slowly, carefully reaching his gloved hand under the tiny body. Slight warmth from the blue lamp over the bed.

Her whole body fit so easily into his palm. So small. So fragile. His precious daughter. They were going to name her Chloe.

Zero possibility.

Vision blurring. Blinking the tears away since both hands were inside the incubator. The little foot moving slightly. The ugly, horrible IV line moving with it. The tube was too big for that tiny foot. Everything looked too big.

The sudden, constant tone from the machine next to him. The movement in his daughter's small chest stopping. The nurse not moving. Zero possibility. She was in her father's hands. It was the best thing possible.

Little Chloe, all of two hours old, lying limp in those too-big hands.

The shudder starting in his stomach, working its way into his chest. His whole body shaking. Everything except his hands. His hands statuesque in their stillness. Holding his baby girl.

The nurse with an arm around him. She was so sorry. So sorry. She smelled of antiseptic, too. His baby had died without ever smelling a rose. Or the ocean. Or fresh baked chocolate chip cookies.

Easing the tiny body onto the bed. Pulling his hands out of the gloves. Shrugging the nurse's arm away from his shoulders. Walking calmly out the door of the ward. Stepping into the stairwell. The tears. So many tears. All of them silent.

His baby was dead. All he had ever wanted. All he had ever hoped for. To have a family. To be the father he never had. To protect them at all costs.

And she had died in his hands in a cold room without even a whimper.

He was a failure.

John inhaled deeply, taking the salty breeze into his lungs. His head was pounding, a splitting headache behind his eyes. The memories always did that to him. But not for much longer.

He reached into his jacket pocket and removed his cell phone. The power was on. He had continued to keep it on and had religiously charged it every night, but it hadn't rung since that day. Only Sarah had the number. His clients had a number that went to his alternate smartphone. He never answered the business phone, requiring the caller to leave a message. This ensured John would always be in control of the communication.

The business phone was now sitting on top of the filing cabinet in his old office. Not that it really mattered. That phone hadn't rung in almost three months. His clients didn't seem to need him these days. Maybe it was the drinking. Maybe it was the attitude. Reginald had been right to let him go. He wasn't in the game anymore. One more instance of failure. But how could he play the game once he realized how utterly and completely pointless it was? A lot of rich men feeling self-important as they made decisions for a multitude of faceless investors with John calling the shots for all of them. Hundreds of millions of dollars changing hands. But when it came right down to it, what difference did it really make?

He set the cell phone on the passenger seat next to the metal box. He considered a note, but that seemed rather ridiculous. Who would read it? What could he possibly say that wasn't obvious to the only person who mattered?

She would find the liquor bottles. He was sure of that. She would know that he wasn't drunk. That was important. A note was pointless. Sarah would know, and if she couldn't understand, she would at least have an idea. And she would survive. Someday she would find happiness.

John flipped open the clasp on the metal box. He looked around the park once again. Still deserted. He wondered who would find him. He had never seen any children at the park. That was important, too. It would be one of the businessmen who would find him. It would ruin the guy's lunch, and John was sorry for that, but this was the only thing he could do. It was his last option.

He had failed his daughter, and he had failed his wife. Sarah deserved better. She deserved a man who could love her, and John could not. And so he would finish it, in the surest way he could imagine.

He opened the lid to the metal box. The .38 revolver gleamed in the sunlight. It had not been fired in over a decade. Sarah had given it to him as a gift when he first joined the company. Some of the other guys belonged to a gun club, and he was trying to fit in. He joined them at the club one evening, fired the gun several times and then left. He never returned. He just didn't enjoy it. It was just as well. Work took up all his time eventually. And the gun sat in the closet, forgotten.

It was still loaded. He remembered that fact vividly. He stared at the gun in the box for several minutes. He had to consider the details now. Placement. Timing. Once the gun was in his hand, he knew he would have to do it fast, or he might not do it at all.

He considered his last thoughts. He decided against saying a prayer. It seemed too hypocritical given the action he was about to take. He thought about his mother and his sister. Then, he thought about Sarah. And he did say a prayer, not for himself, but for his wife. He prayed that God would take care of her after he was gone. He hoped the Lord was listening.

John took one last look at the dark waters of Boston Harbor. He steeled himself as he inhaled deeply. He reached for the gun.

The cell phone rang.

CHAPTER 6

"WHY can't I see her?"

John's question was one of frustration. It was the same nightmare repeated. The reception desk attendant on the phone. Being led to an empty room by a nurse. Finally, the doctor coming in after fifteen agonizing minutes of pacing the floor.

"Take it easy, Mr. Michaels." The doctor's voice was calm. "Your wife is going to be fine. You can see her in just a minute, but you and I need to talk first."

"Just tell me what happened. Please."

"Mr. Michaels, it looks like Sarah intentionally overdosed on Xerenon. When we pumped her stomach, we found ten partially digested pills...more than enough for a lethal dose."

John couldn't comprehend the words. It didn't make sense. Not Sarah. She would never...

"Fortunately, she aborted the attempt," the doctor continued. "She dialed 911, and the paramedics did an excellent job. There shouldn't be any long-term physical effects from the experience, but there are obviously some pretty serious emotional issues at work here. That's why I wanted to talk with you before you saw her."

John was nodding. He didn't know what to say. How could he have been so stupid? So selfish?

The doctor reached into the oversized pocket of his white coat and pulled out a slip of paper. "She was clutching this in her fist when she was brought in," he said as he handed the paper to John. "Just thought you should know."

John looked at the item in his hand. It was his business card. He flipped it over. His cell phone number. Large black letters above it. *FOR EMERGENCY USE ONLY.*

He was such an asshole.

John stood with the doctor in front of Sarah's bed. The curtains had been pulled on either side to afford some privacy even though only one other bed in the emergency room was in use. While leading him into the room, the doctor had said the majority of the ER work occurred at night. John had simply nodded, not listening.

Sarah's eyes were closed, but John couldn't tell if she was asleep. She looked pale. The IV bag was dripping a clear liquid into the tube in her arm. John didn't move. He stood at the foot of the bed, staring at his wife. Seeing her again for the first time in a long, long while. She had put on weight, but she was still beautiful.

He walked to the side of the bed and kneeled down. The doctor remained at his post. John wondered if the doctor was afraid to leave him alone with his patient. Maybe it was hospital policy on suicide attempts.

Even thinking the phrase sent a shiver down John's spine. How could he have let it come to this?

He reached out and took Sarah's hand, cradling it gently in both of his own. Her eyes opened. They were bloodshot, but alive. They widened as she focused on the man kneeling next to her, holding her hand.

"John," her voice was raspy, the result of throat trauma from the violation of the stomach pump tube.

"Shhh," John whispered. He reached one hand up and brushed away a strand of hair from her eyes. "It's all right. I'm here."

"You're okay," she said.

It pained John to hear her voice like that. "I'm fine. And you're going to be fine. We're going to work this out." He paused, looking for the words. "I'm never going to leave you again. I promise."

Tears filled Sarah's eyes as she nodded. "I love you." Her lips mouthed the words, but no sound came out.

A tear ran down John's cheek, but he was smiling.

"I love you, too."

It was the truth.

CHAPTER 7

"SO THE PAST FEW MONTHS have been a state of almost total isolation. Is that correct?" Dr. Cornelius Luther raised one eyebrow from behind his half-glasses. It was a gesture John and Sarah had come to know intimately in the past week.

"That's correct," Sarah said. John nodded.

"No more family. No more friends. And essentially no longer having each other." The doctor did not phrase it as a question, but the eyebrow rose once more.

"That's right," John said. He distrusted doctors, too many of them assumed they were smarter than they really were, a condition medical school encouraged and society reinforced but was quite dangerous in practice. On the other hand, John was still committed to his promise to Sarah, and that meant working with Doctor Luther. "But we're willing to do anything to make it work again. We've got nothing left to lose." This time, Sarah nodded in time with his words.

"I see," Dr. Luther said softly. He removed his glasses and placed the earpiece into his mouth as he reviewed the notepad on his lap. His brow furrowed, as if he were studying something inscrutable on the pages in front of him. Finally, he raised his gaze to the couple.

"Over the past several days, I have learned a great deal about the two of you," he began. "We have discussed your pasts and the events leading up to the incident two weeks ago."

Sarah's eyes went to the floor. Doctor Luther always referred to it as *the incident*. She and John referred to it as *that day* in all their conversations. And they had had a lot of conversations in the past week. More than in the past six months. When John revealed to Sarah what he had been about to do when the hospital called, it was the hardest thing he had ever done. And Sarah knew it. It was an emotional leap for their relationship, but there was still a long way to go. They had fallen very far. Now, they were building slowly. Doctor Luther's sessions were a start.

"You have both been very committed to coming here every day," he continued. "That shows that you are indeed willing to work at resolving these issues, but before we continue with our sessions, I would like to discuss something else with you."

Sarah and John waited as the gray-headed man rocked back in his leather chair, silent, as if he were intentionally creating suspense.

"Yes?" John finally asked, prodding.

"What we are dealing with is a form of depression. Severe depression. In both of you. Many of my colleagues in the psychiatric profession would choose to treat this depression with medication and weekly therapy sessions for an indefinite amount of time. Call me an old fool, but I do not believe in such things. The secret to ridding one's self of depression is quite simple. One must find happiness. You never see a happy person throwing himself off a bridge, eh?"

John furrowed his brow. He found the reference inappropriate, but Sarah seemed unfazed. And, truth be told, John kind of liked the idea of a psychiatrist who didn't hide behind a curtain of clinical bullshit.

"Ah, but how does one find happiness? It is the question all people should ask themselves. Because really, what else is there? Offhand, I would guess both of you have forgotten the secret to happiness. Correct?"

Sarah nodded. John nodded as well, brow still furrowed.

"Well, I'll tell you. The secret of happiness is priorities. You determine what means the most to you in life, and focus on that. Find your center. Your top priority. For some, it's religion. For others, it's family. It's unique for every individual, but it's not always easy to figure out what that priority is. There are so many things the world gives you to focus on—bills, terrorism, getting the perfect body, drinking the right beer—it's no wonder so many people run around not knowing what's really important and sacrificing their own happiness because of it."

John rubbed his chin between his thumb and forefinger. The doctor sounded like a self-help personality trying to hock a new book, but the diplomas from MIT and Princeton hanging on the wall behind his desk belied that impression. The fact was, Doctor Luther had a point. A good point. John realized he had become so wrapped up in his view of himself as a failure that he had taken his eyes off everything else that mattered.

"So what do we do?" Sarah asked.

Doctor Luther sat in silence. The suspense building once more. After almost a minute had ticked off the clock on the wall, he appeared as if he had resolved a mental debate within himself and had reached a conclusion.

"I'm going to make a suggestion," he began. "This is not something I normally recommend, but I feel your unique circumstances may warrant this sort of treatment. There is a specialized program run by a colleague of mine, Doctor Lilith Regen. She's a clinical psychiatrist who has pioneered an extraordinary approach to the treatment of depression. Her program cannot be entered into lightly. She operates a retreat in New Mexico. It's located in the desert. Isolation by design. The retreat quite literally removes the intrusions of society. Doctor Regen uses this to facilitate the ability of her patients to find that inner truth, so to speak. To find what makes them happy."

Doctor Luther leaned forward in his chair. "She's had unbelievable results, but as I said, it takes a great deal of commitment. The program lasts three months. That's a long time to be away. Moreover, the cost is substantial. This sort of therapy is generally not covered by insurance so if you choose not to follow this course due to financial reasons, I will certainly understand. It's not an easy decision. If you go, you'll be leaving behind your lives here. Of course, you can stay, and we'll continue to meet as frequently as you both like. The choice is yours."

When he finished, the doctor leaned back in his chair and folded his hands across his lap. It was John and Sarah who now sat in silence. John was skeptical. Three months in the desert? But then, what did they have left in Boston? No job. No family. He looked at his wife. Sarah was staring at him, and there was a look in her eyes. It took John a moment to recognize it. *Hope*. Finally, John spoke.

"We don't really have lives here. Not anymore," he said. "And money isn't an issue. We can personally cover any costs involved."

"We promised ourselves we would concentrate on what was important, Doctor, and that's what we're going to do," Sarah said. "How do we apply for the program?"

A smile crossed Doctor Luther's lips. "To be truthful, there is a quite rigorous screening process. Doctor Regen only accepts a very limited number of patients every year. However, in your case, I'm happy to report I've already spoken with her. Our first few sessions have covered a great deal of the screening. I wouldn't have recommended you if I didn't feel you were both ideal candidates for the program. In fact, the next session begins next week. I believe you'll be able to make it."

John looked at his wife. Sarah was smiling for the first time in a long while. This was the right decision. Whatever it takes. He had promised himself that.

They shook hands with Doctor Luther and left the office. He told them he would provide more information the following day, and they should begin to wrap up any matters in Boston before they left.

Doctor Luther watched the door close as the Michaels exited his office. He sat behind his desk, savoring the moment. Finally, he picked up the phone. He knew the number by heart. It rang three times before a female voice answered.

"Lilith? It's Cornelius." The corners of his mouth turned upward in a horrible grin and his eyes danced with a wicked light as he spoke.

"Inform Mr. Kane that we have them. They'll be in New Mexico by the end of the week."

Part II:

SONORA VALLEY

CHAPTER 8

THE FIRST SIGNS OF CRIMSON LIGHT peered over the mountain ridge, slowly illuminating Sonora Valley. Earl "Cutter" Valentine adjusted the worn cowboy hat on his graying head and squinted in the direction of those first rays of dawn. The squint was unnecessary. The sun was at least half-an-hour from achieving true brightness, but the squint was instinctual.

A cool breeze filtered through the valley from the north, the night's final attempt to claim the desert for its own. The wind blew into Cutter's open denim jacket and chilled him. He leaned back against the side of his old Chevy pickup and sipped lukewarm coffee from a plastic cup. It was one of those cups that screwed onto the top of a thermos, and it could never keep even six or eight swallows of coffee hot for more than five minutes. Cutter flicked the cup forward. The black liquid splashed onto the earth next to a busy anthill. The ants scurried back and forth, avoiding the coffee puddle.

"You got lucky," Cutter mumbled to the insects. "Next time, I might not miss."

He walked to the open door on the driver's side of the truck and retrieved the thermos. He shook the plastic cup twice more to shed the last traces of the coffee and screwed it back onto the metal cylinder. He never could make coffee worth a damn. Just one more reason to miss Maggie.

Cutter tossed the thermos into the truck and walked to the back of the vehicle. Resting his hands on the edge of the pickup's bed, he looked over the contents in the dim light of the morning. Thirty-five six-foot posts. Three rolls of number four barbed wire. Post-hole diggers. Twenty pound sledge hammer. Four-foot crowbar. Flat blade shovel. Nails. Staples. And a mangy mutt named Walker.

Walker looked up from his position on the stack of wooden posts and opened his mouth just enough for his tongue to find its way out. He wasn't panting. It was too early in the day and not hot enough for that reflex yet. It was just his way of smiling at Cutter.

Cutter smiled back. He supposed Walker was pretty worthless as a dog, but he couldn't think of anything that would make a dog really worthwhile in the desert of New Mexico anyway. But Walker didn't chase cattle, and he would warn his master of the occasional rattlesnake before Cutter could hear it. That probably earned him the right to the dog food and water he was provided. Besides, Walker was the only friend Cutter had out here. And that made him worth something.

He had found the dog scavenging through the garbage cans at a rest stop near Odessa. Cutter had been on his way to his new home—if you could call it that—and the last thing he had counted on was picking up a furry hitchhiker. Still, he had offered the mutt part of his sandwich and had a friend for life. He had named him Walker after that television show with Chuck Norris. Cutter had found that funny as hell during a time when nothing seemed very amusing in his life. Strange how things like that work.

He faced the sunrise. The first third of the burning sphere had emerged over the ridge. Soft streaks of red and orange lit the azure morning sky. The sight was spectacular. It was also a portent of what was to come. It was going to be hot today. And bright.

Cutter reached under his jacket and felt the left breast pocket of his shirt. His sunglasses were there. His hand lingered for just a moment. It still felt odd. For thirty-five years, when he reached for his sunglasses, his hand touched the badge situated over that pocket. That same badge now sat in the glove compartment of his truck, just as it had for the past six months. His shirt still felt barren.

He withdrew his hand and glanced down at it. The first age spots were apparent on the back. Two just under the middle knuckles and one near his wrist. The constant exposure to the sun wasn't going to make them any better. But what are you going to do?

He turned toward Walker and reached to scratch his ears. The dog surprised him and jumped up, trying to lick his face. Cutter pulled away with a slight smile. The dog's rough tongue had just managed to catch part of his mustache. He wiped at his lip with the denim sleeve of his jacket. The mustache was almost completely gray now. He considered shaving it, but he had worn it while it was black, he could wear it now that it was gray.

As Cutter scratched Walker's ears, he turned east once more, his habitual squint shielded his piercing blue-gray eyes from the growing sunrise.

It was going to be hot today. Time to get to work.

CHAPTER 9

"HERE IT IS, folks. Lovely Sonora Valley."

John Michaels surveyed the town from his vantage point in the taxi's backseat. He couldn't tell if the cab driver was being sarcastic or just optimistic.

The town of Sonora consisted of a handful of businesses lining either side of the highway with houses extending away from the road in uneven residential clusters. Extending beyond the houses was the great nothingness of the desert, broken by the occasional mesquite tree and the distant low-lying mountains surrounding the valley like uneven teeth biting down on the only morsel of civilization for hundreds of miles. John had noted the population statistic on the sign as they entered town – 487.

Lovely Sonora Valley.

"We're supposed to meet at the community center," John informed the driver as he took Sarah's hand into his own. She was staring out her window as well. John wondered what his wife was thinking. She gently squeezed his hand and turned to look at him. Her eyes were full of hope. He squeezed her hand in return. Whatever it takes.

"So what do you know about this place?" John asked the driver. The taxi had slowed and was now creeping along the main street as the young Hispanic man peered at the signs in front of each building, searching for the community center.

"What are you talking about, man? Nobody knows anything about this town. It's a hole in the wall. A few houses out in the middle of a bunch of dirt and rocks. Why didn't you ask me about El Paso when we left the airport, man? That's my city. I could have told you all about it instead of sitting in silence the past two and a half hours." The last sentence trailed off until it was merely muttered under the driver's breath.

John narrowed his eyebrows. He had heard every mumbled word, but another gentle squeeze of his hand by Sarah prevented him from saying anything.

The cab pulled into a dirt parking lot in front of a small, gray building. A weathered sign hung beside the door – *Sonora Community Center, Established 1986*. The two windows on either side of the front door were filled with large air-conditioning units. John could hear them running even before the driver turned off the taxi's engine.

John opened the door and got out of the cab, stretching his back and legs. It had been a long ride. The driver walked behind the car to meet him, but the trunk stayed closed. Following the instructions they had received, the couple had brought no luggage.

"That's three-hundred dollars for the ride," the driver said. His eyes wandered toward Sarah as she bent at the waist to tie her shoe. His lips curled into a tight grin.

John's eyebrows narrowed once more. "My contact told me the fare would be two-hundred. Is your company quoting me the wrong price? We can give them a call..."

"No, man. I just figured you'd want to include a generous tip. After all, it's a long way out here, man."

John extracted a pair of hundred-dollar bills from his wallet and held them up. "You figured wrong."

The driver snatched the bills from John's hand and got back into the cab. "Shit, thanks for nothing, *cabrón*."

John put his arm around Sarah as they watched the taxi leave a trail of dust out of the parking lot as it headed back to El Paso.

Lovely Sonora Valley.

"Well, I'm glad you two made it safely. You're the last to arrive."

Doctor Lilith Regen was a tall woman with jet-black hair. She had a firm handshake, which she delivered to both John and Sarah as she greeted them at the door. Doctor Regen's dark eyes were a stark contrast to her pale complexion. John mused over the irony of a woman who lived in the desert appearing as if she had never seen the sun. Welcome to a new age, he thought. A world where even the desert-folk avoid tans.

There were six people sitting in the semi-circle of folding chairs behind Doctor Regen. John performed a cursory mental profile on each of the attendees based on their individual appearance. It was something he always did, an exercise he had long ago mastered in countless corporate board meetings. Size up the room. Figure out where you stand in relation to the other people.

In this case, John was surprised at the individuals populating the community center. There were three men and three women. A tall and thin black man somewhere in his late thirties sat next to a very attractive young white woman who John guessed couldn't be more than twenty years old, if that. Sitting to her left—his chair edged a bit closer than it should have been—was a young man in his early twenties with a short-cropped crew cut. To his left sat a short middle-aged woman wearing a lime green tube top far too small for her portly frame. A gaunt young woman with very dark hair and equally dark circles under her eyes sat next to her. John's immediate appraisal of her condition was that drugs had to be involved. Finally, to the thin woman's left—his chair sitting apart from the rest of the group—sat a short man in his late twenties. He fidgeted as his small eyes darted from one member of the group to the next.

Although he was reluctant to admit it to himself, and would never tell Sarah, John was a little disappointed at the cross-section of America that would be sharing the program with him and Sarah for the next three months. In the back of his mind, he had assumed the retreat would be populated with other people in his own demographic. Similar in income and standing. Instead, he felt like an immediate outsider in his Marc Jacobs shirt, navy trousers and five-hundred-dollar Salvatore

Ferragamo shoes. Everyone else in the room was wearing jeans and t-shirts, except for the noted exception of that classy lady in the tube top.

But there was one thing he and Sarah shared with every other member of the group. On each of their faces was a look of weariness and of guarded hope. They were all here for similar reasons, and John's reason was holding his hand, pulling him toward the two open seats next to the black man.

"Well," Doctor Regen began, "Now that everyone is present, we can get started. I'd like to begin by saying how much I'm looking forward to working with each of you over the next three months. We've made some extraordinary progress with a lot of patients since the inception of the program, and I'm certain this group will meet with equal success. We're going to have a brief meeting here, and then we'll proceed to the retreat."

John wondered what the retreat would be like. Doctor Cornelius hadn't been able to give any descriptions beyond "isolated in the New Mexico desert." Of course, how much more isolated could it possibly be than the building they were sitting in right now?

"First things first," Doctor Regen continued, her words crisply enunciated. "We're going to take some time this morning to get to know one another. We're all very different people, but we're also each working toward the same goal. We need to rediscover ourselves. We need to find out what it is that makes us happy and learn to shut out the rest of the world and focus on that happiness. Now, we're each going to spend a few minutes introducing ourselves and describing the circumstances leading up to attending this retreat. This may make some of you uncomfortable. Don't be. Starting today, we're a family. No one is going to judge anyone else. Everyone here has experienced some problems."

Doctor Regen's eyes moved from one person's face to the next, completing the semi-circle as she spoke, and then reversing direction. She pulled up a folding chair of her own and sat facing the group as she continued.

"To save the suspense, each person here has tried to take his or her own life. There's nothing to be ashamed of in that. We're not here to judge or to waste time regretting the past. We're here to work for the future. But it is important to recognize the events that brought about those decisions, those feelings, and to understand them. What is said in this room now, or at any time during the program, is absolutely confidential."

John surveyed the participants once again. He and Sarah had signed documents pledging their commitment to the confidentiality of the program, and he assumed each of the people seated in the folding chairs had done the same. He was instinctively wary of revealing too much to strangers, but this was a new situation. Before they ever left Boston, John had braced himself that aspects of the program would make him uncomfortable. He would get through it. For Sarah.

"Each of you already has my respect," Doctor Regen said. "By coming to this retreat, you've taken the first step toward recapturing your lives and your happiness. Now it's time to take the next step, introduce yourself and tell us about your life, about how you came to be here. Who'll be first?"

John glanced around the room. Who would be first to reveal their darkest secrets to a group of absolute strangers? He was starting to perspire in the coolness of the community center, but Sarah's hand remained in his, a constant reminder that this was worth it.

The first to speak was the young man with the crew cut. His name was Chance Martin, originally from Benton, Kansas, but after his parents died when he was ten, he went to live with his aunt and uncle in Oklahoma. When that didn't work out, he bounced across three different foster homes in the state. During that time, he clung to one goal. He wanted to be a Navy SEAL.

Chance had watched every documentary he could find on the SEALS, and read all the books. For a kid who had no family, the total loyalty and commitment of a team like the SEALS was inspiring. They had a firm code – no SEAL had ever been left behind. Even if a soldier fell in the line of duty, his teammates would ensure his body left the battlefield to have a proper burial befitting of a Navy SEAL. Nobody is left behind. Everyone goes home. That sense of family touched Chance, and he wanted it more than anything in the world.

Chance spent his summers at whatever pool or pond he could find wherever he was living. Every day, he would go underwater to see how long he could hold his breath. Most people thought he was crazy.

He enlisted in the Navy as soon as he graduated from high school. Chance was then crushed when he wasn't accepted into the SEAL program due to his low scores on the intelligence tests. "My Ma and Pa weren't very smart, so I guess I ain't either," he said. When his four-year contract was up, the Navy declined his reenlistment. Military cutbacks, they said.

And just like that, Chance had nothing. He had no family, no friends, and the only thing he had ever wanted to do was no longer an option. So he put a pistol to his head and pulled the trigger.

But the angle was wrong, or Chance's head was exceptionally solid. The bullet glanced off his skull and knocked him unconscious. When he woke up, he checked himself into the hospital and received twenty stitches for a laceration in his scalp. He pointed to the scar evident through his crew cut.

John smiled to himself as Chance wrapped up his story. Twenty stitches. Not bad considering he had just been shot in the head.

Everyone in the room nodded at the young man, a few mumbled words of encouragement were passed. John realized this was the closest he had ever come to a support group. It was going to be a long three months.

The next to speak was the thin young woman. Her name was Teri Mendoza. She was from Reseda in California, and John's profile had been dead-on. Teri had gotten into drugs when she was in high school. First marijuana, then ecstasy. Meth was next, followed by heroin. She stole to support her habit. Her parents kicked her out of the house at the age of nineteen, and she spent the next six years on the street. In and out of shelters. Living occasionally with friends until they caught her digging through their purses for cash in the middle of the night. She spent two years as a hooker on the streets of Los Angeles. All the money went for drugs.

She had been strung out for over a week when five teenagers from a gang agreed to give her an 8-ball of coke in exchange for some favors. She had sex with each of them in an alley, and when they were finished and she was finally alone, Teri scooped up the white powder from the baggie with the long nail on her pinkie finger, and snorted a burning nostril full of what turned out to be baking soda.

Teri had hit bottom. She walked into a pharmacy and shoplifted two bottles of aspirin. She found a water faucet in the alley behind the store and proceeded to down one bottle and almost half the next. She had already passed out when the pharmacist stepped outside for a cigarette break. After a trip to the emergency room and a stomach pumping, Teri was checked into a hospital detox program and put on suicide watch. The psychiatrist at the hospital recommended her for Doctor Regen's program.

More nods and mumbles emerged from the group as Teri finished her story. A few dim smiles of encouragement.

The middle-aged woman in the tube top volunteered her introduction next. Her name was Maude Krandel. Maude was from Oklahoma City. She and her husband had lived in a mobile home there until he ran off with a waitress from Hooters, leaving her with a stack of bills and a self-worth of zero. It was while watching a movie late one night on TNT that she found inspiration for what she had to do. The next day, she borrowed a length of garden hose from one of her neighbors and duct-taped it to the exhaust pipe of the '96 Buick parked in front of her trailer. She cracked one of the back windows just enough to slide the hose into the car, then she sat in the driver's seat, turned the ignition and waited to die.

A passing UPS deliveryman happened to notice the oddity of a garden hose sticking inside the window of a Buick. He thought a kid was pulling a practical joke, trying to fill up the car's interior with water, so he went to investigate. He found Maude and rescued her from the poisoned vehicle. She spent the next few weeks in the hospital receiving treatment for the damage to her lungs. She also received a pass into the hospital "suicide recovery" program, followed quickly by a doctor's recommendation to come to New Mexico.

The tall black man began to speak as soon as Maude finished. He spoke quickly, his eyes on the floor. Bill Jackson preferred to be called "BJ." He was a trucker by profession, at least until he was pulled over by an Oklahoma highway patrol officer who ticketed him for driving while intoxicated. BJ had been less than five miles from home.

Nothing destroys a trucker's career faster than a DWI charge. He couldn't find other work. His wife left him, taking the kid. She never wanted to see him again. He had lost all hope. That's when he jumped from the roof of a ten story building in Oklahoma City. He hadn't counted on landing on top of one of the few trees planted along the front of the building.

He pulled back his sleeve to show where one of the branches pierced his arm, entering just beneath his shoulder and exiting midway down his bicep. A second branch pierced his scrotum, a scar he didn't show. The tree broke his fall, allowing his final drop to the pavement to do no more damage than a broken arm.

Chance, the Navy man, interrupted the story with a quiet whistle. "Ten stories and you lived? That's pretty damn lucky."

BJ offered a pained smile. "Call it luck if you want, but you never had a tree branch sticking through your sack before."

The hospital admitted BJ to the same program that Maude attended, and the same doctor recommended him to the program. "Although," BJ admitted, "I believe this is the first time I've made Ms. Krandel's acquaintance."

John glanced around the room, wondering if anyone else was from the Boston area. There were still four who had not spoken, including he and Sarah.

The attractive young woman began to speak next. She had a small voice, and the group's participants all leaned closer to hear her. Chance seemed quite interested. He appeared to John to be almost close enough to smell the girl's blond hair. John wondered if that was what the young Navy man was trying to do.

Denise Claiborne was originally from Boston. Her father died when she was in middle school, a tragedy triggering a domino effect for the rest of her troubled childhood. Her mother was a waitress who couldn't live without male companionship, and after her husband's death, she began a string of bad relationships with a string of even worse men. She would frequently move in with the men, bringing her daughter along.

Denise attended six different high schools in three years. Her mother's boyfriends often began to enjoy Denise's company more than they should have—a fact that Denise's mother blamed soundly on her daughter being a whore, even though she always fought off any advances. Soon, Denise began to believe it herself. Her beauty became the focus of her life. Her mother was never going to love her so she would find a substitute for that love through the lustful looks from men. She began to diet, then took to throwing up after meals. She wanted to be loved. And being thin and beautiful was the best way to win that love.

The day she turned eighteen, Denise dropped out of high school and used what little savings she had to purchase a bus ticket to Los Angeles. She was going to be an actress or maybe a model. And she was going to be loved.

Within a month, Denise was working as a waitress at the same type of crummy diner in which her mother used to work. The only audition she had received resulted in her being told to "take acting lessons" and "lose the baby fat." One day, a man came into the diner wearing an expensive watch and a flashy suit. He struck up a conversation with Denise about her acting career. He said he was a movie producer and invited the eager young woman to participate in his next film.

When Denise arrived at the "set" the following morning, she encountered six men standing around a bed with bright lights and two video cameras. The producer from the diner informed her the movie was an adult film. He told her she needed to take off her clothes so he could see whether or not she was pretty enough for the movie. Denise was humiliated, but found she couldn't bear to say no.

She went into a small room with the producer and took off her shorts and t-shirt for him, followed by her underwear. She stood there, shivering despite the warmth of the room, as the producer slowly walked around her, gazing at every inch of her naked form. Finally, he told her that she was not pretty enough for the movie, that she couldn't handle it. She should get dressed and go. Another actress would be along shortly, and they could use her for the lead role. Embarrassed and ashamed, Denise pleaded with the producer to let her do the movie. She was pretty enough. Please?

Tears welled up in Denise's eyes as she told the story to the group in the community center. She was the first of the group to cry during the introductions. It was as if everyone prior to her had come to accept their lives and, because of that acceptance, shared details of the situation leading up to their own suicide attempts in an almost detached manner, as if it had all happened to somebody else. Sooner or later, everyone learns that shit happens, and sometimes it happens to you.

But Denise was still young, and it was obvious she couldn't understand, much less accept, why such horrible things had happened to her. John could tell, in a very real way, that Denise was the only dreamer left in the group sitting in the Sonora community center. She was the only one still young enough to hate the evil in the world rather than just accept it. As she told the tale of the movie in California, John felt genuine sympathy for her.

Through her tears, Denise explained she didn't want to make the movie. She didn't want to have sex with men she had never even met before, but she had to prove she was pretty. She had to hear someone say it. And she talked the producer into letting her star in the movie. She had sex with four different men over the course of three hours. She did things she didn't want to think about, and definitely couldn't speak of. Not yet. And when it was over, her body sore and her self-worth vanquished, the producer told her she had done okay and handed her a check for four hundred dollars.

Denise went back to her dingy studio apartment and stood in the shower for more than an hour, long after the hot water was exhausted and the freezing jets of ice chilled her to the bone. Still, she scrubbed more soap onto her raw skin and cried warm tears that burned against her freezing cheeks.

She finished her shower and sat at her small card table, the four hundred dollar check in front of her. She stared at it for a long, long time. Then, she went to the pawnshop and cashed it. She used the cash to rent a room at the Hilton, and she drew a nice hot bath. She left the hot water running as she sat in the bathtub and pulled a razor blade across each of her wrists. Then, she fell asleep.

The water soon flowed over the edge of the tub and accumulated on the floor, eventually soaking through to the ceiling of the bathroom downstairs. The man in the lower unit complained to the front desk, and when no one answered the phone in Denise's room, a maintenance man was sent to check the plumbing. He found Denise and called 911.

A short stay in the hospital garnered a psychiatric visit, and a recommendation to the program by the same psychiatrist Teri had mentioned.

Denise sniffed as she finished her story and drew her forefinger beneath her nose, wiping away a trace of glistening mucus. John couldn't help looking at her wrist, and he noticed definite scars, the stitches only recently removed. Chance sat next to her, looking unsure of what to do. He started to put his arm around her, to maybe offer some comfort, but Denise shook her head at him. She was polite, but she wanted no part of it. John felt sorry for Chance. The kid wasn't all that bright, but his heart was in the right place.

To John's surprise, Sarah began speaking next. Riding the wave of group revelation, she described the accident with her parents, the death of their premature daughter, and the ensuing heartache from the months of emotional separation that followed.

Under normal circumstances, John would have been mortified at such sensitive information being passed to complete strangers, but it was somehow different now. Hearing the stories of the others in the group had changed things. He wasn't exactly experiencing a feeling of family, as Doctor Regen had promised earlier, but there was a greater sense of acceptance. He was different from the others in the group, but there was also a feeling of familiarity. They all had something very basic in common.

John listened as Sarah told their story, never interrupting. He watched the faces of the others in the group. Maude, sympathetically nodding and hanging on every word. Chance, eyebrows furrowed as he followed the events of the tale. Teri and Denise, each watching Sarah speak, listening intently. BJ, his eyes remaining on the floor most of the time, only occasionally glancing at the speaker. And the short man on the end, still an unknown, with his small eyes darting around the room.

As Sarah finished their story, John was amazed at how simple it now sounded. Six months of hell leading up to a dual attempt at suicide, all neatly encapsulated into a ten-minute speech. Just like all the others in the room. Unbelievable, but undeniable.

John squeezed Sarah's hand when she stopped speaking. She had done well. Her eyes had grown misty at times, but no tears fell. She was treating this like a step, exactly as Doctor Regen had said. The first step toward the healing promise of the program. Don't regret the past, learn from it and move on.

John surveyed the room. All eyes were on him. It was his turn, but there wasn't much left to say.

"Well," he said. He had begun to perspire once more. "My wife essentially covered it all. We both made mistakes. I was lucky enough that Sarah stopped mine. Now, we want to make it better. We want to find our source of happiness and never look back. And we both feel very fortunate to be a part of the program."

He offered a slight smile. It was the kind of effortless, self-effacing move he had practiced to perfection in his corporate negotiations. Tell them what they want to hear and never show all your cards.

Shit.

John mentally chided himself. He had promised himself he would work at this, do it the way he was supposed to, do it the way Doctor Regen intended. They had been in the program for less than two hours, and he was already slipping back into old form. He couldn't allow himself to try to control the room. This was for Sarah. And if it meant giving up control, exposing his own weaknesses for her benefit, then it would be worth it.

He glanced at Doctor Regen and noticed a distinct look of skepticism etched on her face. She knew. John realized that of all the people in the room, Doctor Regen was the only one perceptive enough to read his motivations, and his tactics. He had to correct it, to try harder. For Sarah.

John opened his mouth to speak again, to attempt to open up more, when he was interrupted by a staccato voice.

"All right, so here's what happened." The words were spoken by the short man in the farthest seat. He had dark hair that was slicked back, making it appear wet. Or greasy. His small eyes were complemented by pointed facial features, giving his face a rat-like quality. He fidgeted as he spoke, his eyes darting around the room, further accentuating the rat comparison.

"So I met this girl, right?" he began. "Anyway, we hit it off, and we go back to my place. I want to take some pictures of her, and she lets me. I make the mistake of emailing her one of the pictures, you know, because I like her and all. But then her parents find the fucking picture, and the next thing I know, the father's busting into my place and takes a fucking nightstick to me. Turns out he's a fucking cop, and he tries to beat me half-to-death. And I'm not gonna fight back, right? Because then he might really kill me. And I don't know what the motherfucker is doing in there in the first place. Why should he care? I mean, all I did was take pictures, and I guarantee you that whore was fucking every guy in her school. The cop shoulda been going after them. And she was fifteen. A girl knows what she's doing when she's fifteen, right?"

John stared at the man as he spoke. He couldn't believe what he was hearing. Everyone else in the room had made bad decisions, had some bad luck, but this guy was a genuine criminal. How could someone like this possibly get into the program?

"Anyway, so this guy starts poking through all my stuff and finds some more of my pictures. And it was none of his fucking business what kind of pictures I had, but then he starts beating on me again. He knocked a tooth out." The man hooked a finger into his mouth and pulled his lip back to reveal the gap of the missing tooth before continuing.

"Then he tells me that I've got one hour to get out of town, and that's when I realize he can't kill me cause he's a cop, but he can't arrest me cause everyone would know what kind of slut his daughter is. But he tells me he's coming back with a pair of scissors, some gasoline and a match. Says he's gonna burn my shit up and that he'll cut my nuts off if I'm still there when he comes back. But I can't go to the cops and tell 'em, right? I mean this guy *is* the cops. And that was my stuff. And I couldn't leave my stuff. And then I realize there's *always* gonna be cops after me after this. I mean, this guy has friends. So I don't want to have to take this kind of shit for the rest of my life, right? So I go to the bridge downtown and jump off."

The ferrety man sat there in silence. His eyes still moved quickly from one person to the next. John wondered what he was looking for. Acceptance?

Finally, Chance spoke. "So what happened? When you jumped off the bridge, I mean."

The man looked at Chance as if he was crazy. "What do you think happened, man? I didn't die. The bridge wasn't tall enough. I just hit the water, and it was fucking cold. I can't swim, and I didn't want to drown, man. That ain't no way to die. So I started screaming and this lady jumped in the water and pulled me out."

A loud fit of laughter erupted from BJ. He was no longer looking at the floor. He was staring straight at the child pornographer who couldn't swim and laughing as if he just heard the best joke in the world. The laugh was unique, and BJ's deep voice made it boom loud and clear. The other members of the group couldn't help but smile at the outburst. Even John released a quiet chuckle.

"What the fuck is so funny, you asshole?" the short man screamed. His face was turning red. John wondered if he was insane. Even sitting down, John could tell BJ was at least a foot taller than the rat-man.

Doctor Regen got to her feet. A stern look crossed her face as she spoke. "Mr. Jackson, I'll ask you to please show more respect to your fellow program members."

BJ's laughter died down as he regained his composure. "I'm sorry, Doctor Regen. But, you know, jumping into the river but not wanting to drown? I think the shit is funny." A lingering chuckle fluttered from BJ's throat.

"It ain't funny, motherfucker!" The man was standing up now, his hands clenched into tight fists at his waist.

"Calm down, Vernon," Doctor Regen soothed.

John looked at the fuming man with the greased-back hair. So Vernon was his name. Vernon the child molester. Vernon the drowning rat. Vernon the Vermin.

"Vernon joins us from Los Angeles as well," Doctor Regen said. "And while the circumstances leading to his participation in the program may be different than your own, I would like to remind each of you that *everyone's* situation here is different. Remember, we are all working toward the same goal. In order to reach that goal, we must accept each other...that includes Vernon." She placed her hand on Vernon's shoulder as she spoke, and the rat-man gave BJ a smug look.

"The program starts now," Doctor Regen continued. "We'll be loading the truck to proceed to the retreat in a few minutes. Once there, your new lives will begin. You can forget the past, the weariness, the shame, the hurt. You can begin anew."

John took a deep breath. Begin anew. A new life with Sarah, and three months with his new "family." For Sarah. It would be worth it.

"Some ground rules before we leave." Doctor Regen's eyes met each of the participants as she slowed her speaking pattern. This was important.

"The beginning of your new life requires a break from the old, a release from the world's hold on you. Everything you have is part of your old life. Your clothes. Your jewelry. Your pictures. Your money. It's all irrelevant now. I have your new clothes in these boxes." She pointed to a set of boxes lined up along one wall of the community center.

"You provided your clothing sizes during your registration, and each box has an appropriately sized set of pants, shirts, shoes, and even underwear and socks. Your name is labeled on the box with your assigned clothes. As for your current belongings, we have a set of safe deposit boxes at the Sonora Valley Bank and Trust which will hold all of them. At the end of the program, your belongings will be returned to you."

John listened to the speech, not really surprised. He had suspected something like this when they were informed not to bring any luggage to the retreat.

"Excuse me," John began. "I don't want to be a dissident, but this is a really comfortable pair of shoes. Would it be all right if I held onto them?"

A small frown turned the corners of Doctor Regen's mouth downward. "I know this may sound strange, Mr. Michaels, but it is very important to the program to disassociate yourself from the outside world. I assure you the shoes and clothing we have provided are both comfortable and appropriate for the environment. However, since you brought it up, the program does permit each participant to bring along *one* personal item to the retreat, *if* you feel the need. It may be a picture or a piece of jewelry," she glanced at John as she spoke, "or even a pair of shoes."

Sarah elbowed John in the side and shot him a look. He was in trouble. So much for working harder to do it Doctor Regen's way.

John kneeled over his box and examined the contents. The men had gone into a separate room from the women to change, and Chance, BJ and Vernon were each inspecting their own boxes as well. Inside each box was four pair of khaki pants, four light gray T-shirts, eight pairs of gray athletic socks, and eight pairs of gray briefs. Two sets of white athletic shoes sat on the bottom of the box. They looked to be designed for running.

"Damn," the curse was spoken softly by BJ.

John looked at the man kneeling next to him. "What's the matter?" he asked.

"Looks like they hooked us up with some briefs, and I'm a boxer man, myself," he said as his lips parted into a broad smile.

John smiled back. "Yeah, that's a tragedy, all right."

He glanced down at the second box in front of him. It also had a label with "John Michaels" stamped across the top, but it was empty. This box would apparently be spending the next three months in a safe deposit vault at the bank. He pulled off his shirt and folded it as he set it in the cardboard container. He removed his shoes and pants, rolled the trousers into a tight ball—his wallet still in the back pocket and a tiny black jewelry box in the front pocket—and placed the ball into the cardboard box. He pulled out a set of the new clothes from the other box, and laid the underwear on top.

When was the last time he had stood naked in front of a bunch of other guys? John maintained the rules of the men's locker room. He kept his eyes on his own business, but his peripheral vision permitted him glimpses of BJ and Chance.

Chance was obviously at home with communal undressing. His time in the Navy had eliminated any traces of modesty. The young man even told a joke while they were getting ready. It was dumb, but funny, similar to the overall impression John had of Chance.

"Hey guys, how does a blonde turn on the lights after sex?" he asked, already smiling at the punchline about to be delivered.

Both BJ and John offered shoulder shrugs, encouraging the joke to continue.

"She opens the car door!" Chance said and laughed at his joke. BJ burst into another fit of laughter, sounding the same as he had earlier. Deep guffaws cut short by quick breaths. John joined in. He had heard the joke before, but he knew he needed to make friends with these men. They were going to be spending a lot of time together over the next few months.

"Bunch of faggots."

The words were spoken just softly enough that Vernon could deny saying them.

John turned his head. Vernon's back was to the other men as he pulled on the new pair of gray underwear over his impossibly white ass. Once the briefs were in place, he turned to face John.

"What are you looking over here for? You some kind of faggot?" Vernon said louder this time. The rat-man then glanced over at BJ and Chance, seeking support. It was a juvenile move to embarrass John and an attempt for Vernon to squeeze himself into the group at the expense of someone else. John had met Vernon's kind before.

BJ glanced at John as he pulled on his new khaki pants. "Just ignore him, my friend. Just ignore him." Chance nodded in agreement.

John allowed himself a small smile as he continued to get dressed. These guys were okay. Different, but okay.

He looked back at the boxes. The box with his old belongings was almost full. He was completely dressed except for his shoes. His pair of brown Ferragamos lay in front of him. Casual Italian leather. Well broken in. They were the most comfortable pair of shoes John had ever owned. And he had always hated athletic shoes, just as he had always hated running.

He closed his eyes for a moment. Three months. He could only keep one thing. The decision wasn't even close.

John followed the other men out of the changing room back to the main hall. He saw Sarah placing her box of personal belongings onto the cart by the door that would be taken to the bank. It didn't take long to notice which item she had chosen to keep, it was the same as his, and John smiled. The decision wasn't close for either of them. A good sign.

He could see the van waiting outside to transport them all to the retreat. There it would begin. The program was about finding happiness, and that was what he was going to do. Focus on the most important thing in his life.

He set his box on top of the cart and noticed his shoe had come untied. He reached down to secure the fresh white laces of the new running shoes into a better knot. A ray of sunlight from the open door glinted off his wedding band as he worked.

CHAPTER 10

MARCUS KANE grimaced as the metal bar touched his chest. He held it there for ten seconds, his body tensed from the exertion. Three iron plates were secured to either side of the bar, each plate weighed forty-five pounds. The bar was reinforced steel and weighed fifty pounds by itself. It was his twentieth repetition.

Kane lay on the bench and breathed in short bursts through his nose. Sweat glistened on his bare chest and arms. His abs were clenched tight and stood out in chiseled relief. The bar itself scraped against his massive chest, leaving a vague red line across the straining muscles.

He took one more short breath and began to push. His arms were shaking from the effort, but the bar continued its upward motion, the speed the same as it was for the first rep. Perfectly controlled. Absolute power.

The muscles in Kane's chest were rock-hard and individual striations could be seen through the skin as he forced the weight up, up, until finally, his elbows straightened and the bar fell back into place on the rack supports of the bench.

He sat up, concentrating on controlling his breathing. Deep inhale through the nose, slow exhale through the mouth. He glanced behind him at the metal bar with the iron plates. They meant nothing. There was no triumph in the workout. The weights were merely a tool.

He stood and looked around the weight room. It was small and dark, lit by a single bare bulb hanging from the ceiling. It housed only the weight equipment and a hundred pound heavy bag suspended from the ceiling. The heavy bag was wrapped in layers of duct tape to maintain its integrity from the countless, bruising blows it sustained on a weekly basis. The room also housed the only mirror in the complex. Kane gazed at the reflection in the glass.

Despite the dim light in the room, he could see the blue veins crisscrossing his chest. His pectoral muscles were pumped with blood from the workout, and the veins were pulsing through the skin in an effort to keep up. His brown hair was dripping with sweat, and his forehead was covered with beaded perspiration. Another blue vein stood out there as well.

He lifted his hands to shoulder height and extended them outward until he took the appearance of a man on a cross. The lat muscles in his back flared out into a wide V-shape. His neck was a course of layered muscle and pulsing veins. His shoulders looked like soccer balls imbedded beneath his skin.

But he could be so much more.

And he would be.

He glanced at the clock affixed to the wall above the mirror, the only clock in the complex. 10:00 AM. He needed to shower and prepare. The new sheep would arrive within two hours. And soon it would begin again.

Kane smiled at the reflection in the mirror.

Very soon.

CHAPTER 11

IT WAS ALMOST TEN-THIRTY in the morning when Walker let out a quiet bark from his station beneath the pickup, alerting Cutter Valentine to the sounds of the approaching horse. Cutter jammed the flat blade of the well-worn shovel into the dirt and released the handle. It remained upright, embedded in the earth.

The horse and its rider were roughly two hundred yards away, moving at a slow trot along the fence line Cutter was repairing. Their proximity surprised him. Cutter's property was miles outside the small town, and the sounds of an approaching automobile in the vacant desert landscape would be detectable some time before the vehicle actually arrived at its destination. But a horse moved more quietly than an automobile. Of course, Cutter supposed he didn't really know whether or not he could hear an approaching vehicle that clearly. One had never come out here. In fact, the man on the horse marked Cutter's first visitor since he made Sonora Valley his new home.

Cutter walked to his truck, removing leather gloves as he went. The gloves were soft and pliable after a morning's work. He tossed them into the open passenger window and reached in to retrieve his plastic cup. He moved to the truck's tailgate and held the cup beneath the white spigot of the bright orange cooler that rested there. Cutter pressed the button. Cold water filled the cup as he raised his eyes to the approaching figure.

Still over a hundred yards away, too far to shout out a greeting, particularly considering he didn't know who the man was.

Cutter drank from the cup and the cold bit into his jawline, the icy water in his mouth a stark contrast to the mounting heat of the morning. He bent down and poured the remaining contents of the cup into the small plastic dish next to the truck tire. Walker took his eyes off the horse just long enough to register what his master was doing. The dog inched his way out of the shadows beneath the truck and stood next to Cutter but did not drink from the dish. For now, Walker was on guard.

Cutter shook his head at his furry friend. *Dumb dog.* He scratched Walker's ears as the canine stood on alert to the approaching figure. *But a good dog.*

The horse and rider were now only fifty yards away, close enough for Cutter to make out some details. The rider was an older man, a categorization that had evolved for Cutter as the decades had passed. He looked to be somewhere in his seventies or perhaps even eighties, but was obviously in good enough shape to be riding alone. His cowboy hat was only slightly weathered, and his clothes were nicer than necessary. He wore pressed jeans and a bolo tie on his white shirt. The old man was a cowboy, but he was a cowboy with some money.

Cutter took his eyes off the stranger for a moment to refill his cup, prompting Walker to emit a low, soft growl at the horseman.

"Cut that out," Cutter said as he nudged the dog with his shin. "I don't think he's the dangerous type."

The growl went silent, and Cutter smiled. It was nice to have someone worry about him, even if it was just protecting him from a senior citizen out for a morning ride.

"Howdy," the voice of the rider carried the last twenty yards.

"Howdy," Cutter replied, tipping his hat with his finger. The gesture brought a smile from the old man as he closed the remaining distance and pulled lightly on the reins.

"You'll excuse me if I don't dismount," the man said through his grin. He had a thick Southern drawl to his voice, even more so than Cutter. "Fact of the matter is, it takes me a hell of a lot of effort to get up on one of these things anymore, and I don't want to bother you with having to help me back on. It's a pain in the ass, but I plan on riding till the day I die."

Cutter returned the smile. "Helping wouldn't be a problem, but I certainly understand. Can I get you some water? I've got an extra cup in the truck."

"Oh, that'd be mighty fine."

Cutter stepped to the cab and retrieved a second plastic cup, identical to his own. Returning to the tailgate, he filled the cup and glanced down at Walker, who stood in his same position, eyes never wavering from the visitor. The fur on the back of his neck stood up ever so slightly.

Cutter furrowed his eyebrows as he looked at Walker. *Dumb dog, all right.*

"Here you go," Cutter said as he reached up and handed the old man the plastic cup.

The rider took a long, slow drink and drained the cup, not showing any signs the cold water affected him. "Much obliged," he said as he passed it back down to Cutter.

Cutter accepted it and offered his hand to the old man. "Name's Earl Valentine, but most folks call me Cutter."

"Cutter, eh?" the rider said as he shook the proffered hand. When he said the name, his drawl dismissed the 'r' – pronouncing it *Cuttah.*

"I used to do a bit of competitive riding myself in my youth," the old man continued. "Took first place in cutting horses at the Midland Rodeo back in the day."

Cutter smiled. "That's great," he said, not bothering to correct the old man on the origins of his nickname.

"Friends call me Cal," the rider said. "Although some of the widow ladies in town still call me Calhoun. Last names don't matter much in a town this size so I won't concern you with mine." He paused to glance at the sun, slowly climbing toward its apex. "I see you're doing some fencing. That's good. It's good to see young folks still taking an interest in ranching. How's it suit you so far?"

Cutter dropped his head for just a moment, the brim of his hat shielding his broad smile from view. How many years since he'd been referred to as a "young folk"?

"It suits me fine," he said. "Another few weeks of fixing the fence line, and I should be able to open up this part of the property. Just in time, too. The cattle have just about cleaned out the east side."

"Boy, not like it was in the old days. We used to brand 'em and let 'em roam free. Had to spend a month at a time to round 'em up. Course, if we could have afforded fences, we would have done it that way," Cal grinned at his own joke.

"So what brings you out, Cal?" Cutter asked. "You just in the mood for a ride on a sunny day?"

"No," Cal began, "I actually wanted to talk to you." He paused for a moment, obviously debating how to continue. "Have you met many folks in town yet, Cutter?"

"Not really. I go to Mercer's every couple weeks to get building supplies and groceries and what-not, but I haven't really met anybody." Cutter averted his eyes as he spoke, uneasy about what he suspected was coming next in the conversation. Cutter had come out here to be alone. He considered himself a friendly guy, but this was a time in his life when socializing with people from town was the last thing he wanted to do. He dreaded the invitation to whatever social event had brought Cal all the way out here.

"Can't say as I blame you," Cal remarked. "With the unfortunate business you had to go through, I imagine you just came out here to get away from folks. Or am I wrong?"

Cutter's head snapped back to face the rider. Cal's words had caught him off guard. Somehow, he had expected that no one from Sonora Valley would know about him. His new home suddenly seemed a lot less friendly.

"Oh, don't worry about it, son," Cal said soothingly. "I don't think anyone else in town knows. Not many folks read the big city newspaper out here since the news don't really affect them none. It's a quiet town, and I can promise you this – even if folks did know about it, they would be in your corner one hundred percent. Fact is, there ought to be more people like you in law enforcement."

Cutter sat on the open tailgate and swallowed a drink of water. "Well, I appreciate it, Cal. But the fact is, I'm not in law enforcement. I'm a rancher now. Got some cattle. Got some fences. Even got a dog." He glanced down at Walker and noticed the mutt still had not moved. He continued to stand unrelenting, but unnecessary, guard for his master.

"Well now, that's what I came out here to talk to you about, Cutter." Cal's eyes narrowed as he sized up the man sitting on the back of the truck. "Fact is, I came out here to ask you a favor."

"What might that be, Cal?"

"It seems Sheriff Albright's wife has taken ill. Francine was such a lovely woman, but she's taken to the Alzheimer's in the past year, and I'm afraid it's just gotten worse. Jim has requested an indefinite leave of absence from his position to care for her. Can't blame him, but it has left me in a bit of a situation. You may not know it, but I'm the mayor of our fair town, and as such, I'm responsible for keeping the town of Sonora and the greater area of Sonora Valley in working order."

"The answer's *no*, Mayor," Cutter interrupted. He didn't need to hear the sales pitch.

"Well now, don't be so hasty there, Cutter Valentine," Cal said. "The post won't require any actual work. You see, our town population is just shy of five hundred people. There's not really any crime to speak of, and my nephew, Dwight, is an official deputy. The problem, you see, is that Dwight is only nineteen. Fresh out of high school, you know? He can do a fine job minding the crosswalk at school and keeping the sheriff's office in working order, but he doesn't exactly command respect. And respect is one thing a sheriff has got to have. Otherwise, it might prompt folks who would normally obey the law into maybe tempting fate a little. And we don't need that."

"So what are you asking, Cal?"

"All I'm asking is for you to *say* you'll be the new sheriff. Let Harriet put an announcement in the newspaper. It's a one-page sheet she makes on her computer once a week, but it only costs a nickel and everyone in town reads it. The point is, when folks read that a former Texas Ranger is the new sheriff, there will still be respect for the law. You don't even have to come to town. Stay out here and tend to your ranching. Let Dwight handle the work. He'll only call you if there's an emergency, and we haven't had us one of those in six years. Not since Billy Bob Swynnerton got drunk and shot Mrs. Escobar's Great Dane. He thought it was a bear." Cal chuckled softly at the story before continuing. "So you see, it's not too much to ask, is it?"

Cutter sat on the tailgate in silence. He didn't have to consider the proposition. He already knew his answer, but he wanted to give it some time so Cal would know he was serious.

"The answer's *no*, Cal," he said firmly. "I appreciate it, but I'm not in law enforcement anymore. You'll just have to find someone else."

Cal sat on his horse and stared at Cutter, a look of obvious displeasure on the old man's weathered face. "I understand," he said. He reached into the breast pocket of his white shirt and withdrew a slip of paper. "Here's my card. Got the numbers for my house and my office. If you change your mind, you give me a call."

Cutter shifted off the tailgate and reached up to accept the card. "It was nice meeting you, Cal. Best of luck on finding someone. I'm sorry I couldn't help you."

"Much obliged for the water," Cal said as he pulled one side of the reins and clicked his heels into the sides of his horse. The animal turned and trotted back in the direction it had come.

Cutter watched the old man ride into the distance. When he was just a speck on the horizon, Cutter raised his cup and drank the last of his water. He looked at the white business card he held in his hand. It was a generic card with *Mayor of Sonora* printed across the top in bold, black lettering. A line was printed beneath the title with a single word written in blue ink – *Cal*. Two phone numbers were written beneath the name in the same pen. It was a small town indeed. Cutter glanced down at Walker. The dog still hadn't moved.

"Well, what do you think?" he asked his companion. "Did we do the right thing?"

Walker turned away from the disappearing rider and looked up at Cutter's face. He let out a small bark and walked to his water dish. His tongue shot in and out of his mouth as he lapped the water.

"Yeah," Cutter said under his breath as he stared at the horizon Cal had just passed over. "I thought so."

CHAPTER 12

JOHN MICHAELS gripped the top of the seat in front of him as the van struck another bump in the road, violently jolting its passengers. His hair had actually brushed the van's ceiling that time. He pushed his feet forward, farther under the seat in front of him, hoping to use his legs to stabilize himself.

He glanced to his right. Sarah's hands were clamped to the bottom of her seat, just under her thighs, attempting to hold herself in position. Her face maintained that small, determined smile.

John looked to his left for the hundredth time. The black paint covering the window was still there, and for the hundredth time he felt like a hostage, or perhaps a victim of a polite kidnapping. All of the windows in the large van were blacked out, and a curtain was pulled between the rear passengers and the front seat, where Doctor Lilith Regen and the young man driving the van sat.

Unable to gauge their whereabouts, or the upcoming condition of the road, John and the other passengers were continually caught off-guard by the potholes and rocks in the road. And it seemed like they hit a bump every two minutes. The van continued to drive at a fairly quick speed, or so it felt to John based on the rapid rumblings of the dirt road beneath the tires.

Doctor Regen had explained the purpose of the blackout before the van departed the community center. The retreat was to be a new home, one designed to cast off the grip of the outside world. By blacking out the windows and preventing the participants from seeing the route to the complex, it would be easier to accept it as home and purge any sense of longing for the outside world.

The speech had made sense to John. It fit perfectly into the description of the program, but it was still difficult for him to accept. The immediate thought flashing through his mind after Doctor Regen's speech was simply – *what if we need to get out?* While the theory made sense, John couldn't help but see the danger in not knowing where they were going. If some situation occurred in which one of the participants would have to drive out of the complex—a medical emergency, for example—it would be prudent for everyone to know the route back to town.

But John had said nothing. It was difficult, but he remained silent and accepted the terms of the van ride without question. He gave up control. Knowingly and willingly. For the next three months, he would live in a place that was an utter geographical mystery. They could be in Mexico for all he knew. But he could accept it. For Sarah.

His gaze turned again to his wife. They had not spoken since the ride began. No one in the van had spoken. Sarah offered him a smile and a raised eyebrow. *Was he okay?* He nodded and shifted his eyes to the other passengers.

John was still digesting the personal revelations of his fellow program participants from the meeting at the community center. He supposed he and Sarah had been lucky to get into the program on such short notice. The others had been on waiting lists for weeks or months. They were quite a group of people.

He and Sarah sat in the center of the three passenger benches in the van. BJ sat on the other side of the bench from Sarah, next to the sliding door with its own blacked-out windows. BJ sat at an odd angle, allowing his long legs to stretch out in the extra space permitted by the step just inside the door.

Maude, Denise and Chance sat on the front bench, staring at the curtain which separated the passengers from the driver and Doctor Regen. Maude's gray t-shirt fit her considerably better than the tube top she was wearing earlier, and Denise was pretty enough to make even the drab new clothes look better than they actually were. She kept her arms crossed in front of her, still self-conscious of the pink scars running the length of her wrists. John half-expected Chance to attempt to put his arm across the back of Denise's seat during the trip, maybe make the first ill-conceived romantic move that John knew would occur at some point. After all, Chance was still young, too. But the bumpy ride made any subtle attempts at romance impossible.

Teri sat on the bench behind John alongside Vernon the Vermin. The little guy had been the last to enter the van, and apparently Teri had drawn the short straw. John could easily appreciate her reasons for leaving a wide gap in the seat between herself and Vernon and sitting slumped against the window, even though there was no view to be seen.

John glanced at his wrist out of habit, but there was no longer a watch there. He wondered how long they had been in the van. It felt like at least an hour, possibly longer. He wondered how much longer it would be until the van came to a merciful stop and the door was opened once again.

"So are you a lawyer?"

The question brought John's head up. It was the first time anyone had spoken since they entered the van. Denise had turned around in her seat to face him.

"Excuse me?" John asked.

"I said, 'Are you a lawyer'?" Denise repeated.

"No, not exactly," John said, shaking his head. All eyes in the van had turned to the conversation. "I worked with a lot of attorneys, but I'm not one myself. I just used them for paperwork and contract law, that sort of thing."

Denise didn't respond. Her blue eyes maintained a hard glint while she assessed him. The young woman looked as if she was angry with John, but he couldn't figure out why.

"Back in the center, your wife said you worked with 'mergers and acquisitions'. That's just lawyer talk for taking over businesses, right?"

"Yeah," John nodded. He wasn't sure if they were supposed to talk about their pasts anymore once they left the community center, but there was no sense in lying. "Hostile takeovers were my specialty."

"Really? So what did you do? How does that work?"

John's eyebrows furrowed. He didn't mind talking about his work, but he had no idea why an eighteen-year-old girl who had never spent a day in the business world would be interested.

"Well," he began, "it works like this. I would represent a company that wants to buy another company. If that target company wanted to stay independent—to not be purchased—then the company I represented would undertake a hostile takeover. The takeover itself is pretty complex. I mean, there are a million different issues to consider on that front, but I'll keep it simple."

John debated just how simple to keep it. Denise's expression hadn't changed, and everyone else was still staring at him. *Hell*, he thought, *even a lecture on business must be more interesting than listening to the crunching of rocks under the tires for an hour*.

"Okay. Excluding intellectual property, there are basically two parts to every business," John continued, "the stuff that a company works with and the people involved. The *stuff* is everything that appears on the balance sheet – the factory, the offices, the trucks, the machinery...pretty much everything. And that stuff is usually what the buying company is interested in. But there's another component to every company – the people. The employees, the management, the owners, the customers, the suppliers – all the people involved. Follow me so far?"

There were several subtle nods from John's peripheral audience, but Denise made no indication whether or not she understood. He assumed she did. He was, after all, keeping it pretty simple.

"Anyway, when the target company didn't want to be purchased, it was my job to figure out where the weakness in that company was and to exploit it. Sometimes the weakness was in the balance sheet—in the stuff and any debt associated with it—and sometimes it was with the people involved. Every business has a weakness, and I would find it and manipulate it into an opening for a takeover strategy. Then, like it or not, the company I represented acquired the target company. End of story."

John took his hands off the seat in front of him and raised them up. His career, his entire life, in a nutshell. He noticed a few additional nods from the van's passengers. Denise didn't move. She simply maintained the same steely glare on John. It looked odd on her sweet face, framed by her golden hair.

"Interesting job," she said. "Here's another job – brake pad inspector. That was my father's job. He used to inspect the brake pads at Solo Auto Parts in Boston. He worked there for twenty-five years, never did anything else. So when the factory was taken over by another company and he was let go, he couldn't find another job. The bastards who bought Solo didn't care about brake pads, they just wanted to sell off the *stuff* and make a quick buck."

Denise's expression grew harder as she spoke. "It was men like you who wore their expensive suits and ties and didn't give a rat's ass that my father and hundreds of other guys just like him were left without jobs or hope. And it was men like you who sat up in your fancy offices and never even heard about it when my father sat in our own backyard one afternoon and put a shotgun in his mouth and pulled the trigger. I found him when I came home from school. He must have been out there for hours because there were ants." Her voice grew softer. "There were a lot of ants... But that's not the sort of thing that makes it into your simple presentation, is it?"

John looked into the cold blue eyes of the young woman and found he didn't have any words for her. He hadn't had anything to do with the Solo Auto Parts acquisition, he wasn't even sure which company handled it, but that didn't really matter. He was part of the faceless enemy to Denise. He was a Nazi who never manned a concentration camp, but was no less guilty because of it.

He started to open his mouth, to say something, when Denise thrust her arm over the back of the seat and held her wrist inches in front of John's eyes. The scar hadn't healed well. It looked like a chubby, pink earthworm had burrowed beneath the soft flesh of her wrist, and it was lined with small pink dots on either side. The emergency room attendant who stitched it together hadn't done a very good job. John felt a sharp sting of guilt when he realized that he or Sarah, if faced with such lacerations, could afford a plastic surgeon to handle the job. Minimal scarring. An option Denise never had.

"I was eleven years old when I found him, but I learned something. I learned that *this* could be easy." She shoved the scar forward until her wrist almost touched John's nose. A lingering scent of inexpensive perfume touched his nostrils.

John didn't know what to say. In ways the young woman had no comprehension of, she was right. This was a battle he knew he wouldn't win. It didn't make any sense to even try and fight it.

"I'm sorry," he said.

A disgusted look crossed her face. "You're sorry," she said, as she pulled her hand and the horrible scar back behind the seat. "How do you sleep at night?"

Denise turned away from John and slumped into her seat, not waiting for an answer to her question. John gave one anyway. There was no sense in lying.

"I don't."

CHAPTER 13

AFTER ANOTHER HOUR of turns and bumps on unseen dirt roads, the van drew to a merciful stop. No one had spoken since John's uncomfortable conversation with Denise, and the ride had seemed to stretch for an eternity.

"We're here," came Doctor Regen's voice from the other side of the curtain. The sound of the front doors opening was followed by the clack of the sliding door's handle being pulled. BJ leaned forward to help ease the door open, and the powerful light of the desert sun filled the vehicle. After spending two hours in the dark interior of the van, the white rays were painfully bright.

John shielded his eyes with one hand while reaching into the pocket of his khakis with the other. He fished out the pair of dark, wrap-around sunglasses and placed them on his face. John noticed Sarah and most of the van's other passengers doing the same with their own.

Identical sunglasses for everyone. Just another part of the program.

Only BJ stepped out of the van without eye protection. John surmised the man's years of driving trucks had desensitized his vision. There was no telling how many hours BJ had spent staring into the rising or setting sun while he drove coast to coast. Now, the tall black man stepped gratefully into the light and stretched his long legs.

John followed the other passengers out and surveyed his surroundings. The desert of New Mexico was not what he had imagined. It was desolate, but not barren. Dry, but not sandy. Mesquite trees and short bushes blended with the cactus and the rocks. Small tufts of grass dotted the rocky landscape. The ground was comprised equally of loose dirt and a coating of gray pebbles that reminded him of the piles of gravel seen along construction sites.

The heat was impressive but by no means overbearing. He finally understood the concept of "dry heat." The temperature was probably in the low nineties, but it was not nearly as oppressive as a temperature of eighty degrees in the humid city of Boston. And it was phenomenally quiet. John had never heard such nothingness. Not in Boston. Not anywhere.

John spun in a slow circle, looking at the various bluffs surrounding the valley. They were spaced irregularly, some a short distance away and others lining the distant horizon. About half a mile from the complex was a peculiar rock formation. To one side of a normal looking bluff, three columns of rock rose at least forty feet. The effect of the natural formation reminded John of a pitchfork or a triton. It was spectacular.

The van was parked in a clearing about twenty yards from the complex. John could barely discern the road upon which they must have driven in. It obviously wasn't used often.

The complex consisted of five buildings. Four of the structures were identical. The buildings were aligned in an X-pattern, with the front of each structure facing the center of the X. All four of these buildings looked like cylinders set on their sides and half-buried in the earth. Quonset huts, he believed they were called.

We're going to be living in a community of big, concrete toilet-paper tubes, John thought as he evaluated the retreat.

Each of the buildings was completely windowless, with only a door in the front. On the roof of each structure was a giant gray metal box. Some sort of cooling system, John assumed.

The fifth building was only half the size of the others and looked to be a sort of garage or shed. This normal, square structure sat behind one of the cylindrical buildings. A garage door was visible on one side, and John wondered if the shed housed a generator for the property.

After all, they were a long way from civilization. Two large, white tanks stood behind the shed, presumably fuel storage, and a thirty-foot windmill stood farther behind the tanks, its blade endlessly spinning in the desert wind.

Doctor Regen directed the group toward the center of the complex, but John hesitated. The young man responsible for driving the van had opened the rear doors and was starting to unload the boxes containing the participants' new clothes. John began to walk over to offer his assistance when the young man looked up and smiled, waving him good-naturedly back toward the rest of the group. He continued to carry the boxes from the van to a spot a few feet away in the shade of a larger mesquite tree, one box at a time.

John turned and walked to join the rest of the group. He hated not to help the young man. When the kid had waved him on, John noticed his left hand was deformed. The young man's perfectly normal arm ended in what could only be described as the hand of an infant. The small, pink fingers curled into a useless claw. John resisted the impulse to feel sorry for him. He had known plenty of people with birth defects or handicaps in his lifetime, and the last thing they ever wanted was to be pitied. Besides, John figured the young man could handle the boxes without too much of a problem. He didn't look to be much out of high school, and as such, John figured he had to be pretty resilient.

When John rejoined the group, he saw something that had escaped his notice from his position by the van. In the center of the complex sat a giant sundial. The sundial was fashioned from a large rock rising about three feet from the ground. The rock was perfectly circular, perfectly flat, and roughly five feet in diameter. A groove had been cut into the flat surface of the rock where a triangular sheet of iron half-an-inch thick was set, like the emerging dorsal fin of a massive shark. It was quite impressive even though John had no idea how to tell time with such an apparatus.

Doctor Regen stood on the opposite side of the sundial, facing the group. She smiled as she addressed them.

"Welcome to your new home," she said. "Here, you will find the emotional comfort that has eluded each of you throughout your lives. Here, you will find sanctuary. Here, you will cast off the shallow influences of society and learn to focus on the truth. Your truth."

"It may sound corny, right now," she continued, "But the truth will set you free. All I ask of you are two things. First, keep an open mind. The activities and discussions during the next few weeks may seem odd to you. You may not understand the reasoning behind them, but there is a purpose to everything in the program." Doctor Regen steadied her gaze on John as she spoke. "And if you are to benefit from the program, you must trust us and follow our instructions. Only an open mind will lead you to the happiness you are seeking."

John grew uncomfortable as Lilith Regen's eyes remained on his own. He was being singled out for a reason, and he wondered if his comments at the earlier meeting in the community center had created the tension with the doctor.

"Do you trust us, John?" she asked.

It was an unfair question. Since the day his father had abandoned him and his sister, John had only trusted a handful of people, and each had taken years to earn that trust. But with Doctor Regen's gaze on him, he realized this was the first test of the program. How far was he willing to go against his own nature? How far to make this work for Sarah? For he and Sarah both?

"I trust you, Doctor Regen," he said. He heard a barely audible sigh of relief pass Sarah's lips as she stood next to him. "But may I ask who the other part of 'us' is?"

Doctor Regen smiled broadly at John's response. "I'm glad you trust us, John. It will pay off for you both," she said, indicating Sarah with a nod of her head.

"As for your perceptive notice of my using the term *us*, that leads us to the second thing the program asks of you. Allow me to introduce Marcus Kane." Doctor Regen's hand lifted toward the building behind her—the Quonset hut with the shed behind it—and as if on cue, the door to the structure opened.

Marcus Kane stepped from the building onto the small concrete slab in front of the door. The slab was about eight inches high, permitting easier access to the raised doorframe and adding a perception of additional height to the man. The perception was unnecessary. Kane stood almost seven feet in height – a full head taller than any other man in camp with the exception of BJ, and he clearly outweighed the trucker's thin frame by a hundred pounds.

Kane wore a black t-shirt that stretched tight against his massive chest and seemed to absorb the rays of the desert sun. There was an outline of something protruding beneath the material, something that hung from a chain around Kane's neck. Dog-tags? John couldn't tell. The sleeves of the man's shirt rode above his biceps to just beneath his shoulders. Even there, the cuffs appeared in danger of splitting wide open if Kane flexed his arm. The man was impressive.

John corrected his thoughts. *Intimidating* was the word.

As Kane stepped off the slab and walked toward the group, Doctor Regen continued speaking. "The program is multi-faceted in nature. As you know, it's designed to encompass all aspects of your lives over the next three months. An important part of the therapy is the individual counseling and group discussions. I will be coordinating and managing these sessions. The rest of the program involves your physical wellbeing and day-to-day life. For these matters, Marcus Kane is the final authority. The second thing the program asks is this – *follow the rules set by Mr. Kane*. For the next three months, he will be your guide and protector in the desert. Listen to him carefully."

Marcus Kane stepped beside Doctor Regen to address the group. Although the doctor was a tall woman, she was physically dwarfed by her partner. The top of her head aligned with the base of Kane's chest.

Kane stood with his hands on his hips in a posture that reminded John of the drill sergeants in old war movies. He wondered if Kane would begin to shout at the crew, informing them "their mamas ain't here to clean up after them."

Instead, Kane spoke softly, his deep voice rumbling in low tones over the eerie quiet of the desert. "Everyone take a look around you." The heads of the program participants began to sweep the area around the retreat, following the instructions of the giant. John considered the reaction, he had seen it only a few times before. It was rare for an audience to fully obey the words of a speaker. Many people took a minor amount of pride in ignoring instructions, forging the smallest triumph of independence wherever they could. John guessed that was never a factor when Marcus Kane spoke. He had a commanding presence, and people instinctively followed the wishes of a commanding speaker. John wondered if the man knew the sort of power he held. He suspected Kane knew very well.

"The desert is a place of beauty," Kane continued as the eyes of the group returned to his own. "It is also a place of death. How many of you have ever spent time in a desert environment?"

No hands were raised. For the second time, John was struck by the quiet of their surroundings. No street noise, no radios in the background, no mindless chatter, no traffic. Just absolute silence broken only by the deep voice of Marcus Kane.

"There are certain rules you will follow while you are in my compound. The first rule is to drink plenty of water every day. We have a well tapped into an underground aquifer. It supplies all the water for the complex, and the water is there in abundance. It is exceedingly clean – cleaner than the city water you've been drinking all your lives. Since we have plenty of water, you will be expected to shower daily and keep your clothing washed. I don't think this will be a problem, but it never hurts to mention."

One corner of John's mouth turned up in a half-grin at the comment. He wondered if they had, indeed, had a problem with that at some point in the past.

The sound of a starting engine interrupted the thought, and John turned his head to see the van pull away from the compound. The young man with the deformed baby-hand was returning to town.

Kane's voice increased in volume as he spoke over the departing vehicle.

"The second rule is to always wear sunscreen. Inside the barracks, we have an ample supply of sunscreen as well as toothpaste, deodorant, and all the basic toiletries. Sunscreen is critical. It's very easy to burn out here, particularly if you haven't spent much time outside lately, so be careful."

"The third rule is to never go out alone. Part of the program involves a regimen of physical activity – primarily running. This activity is critical to your development. 'Sound mind, sound body' is not just an expression. It is a truth. You will run, but you will never run alone. Is that clear?"

Kane raised his eyebrows, indicating a desire for a response. Heads nodded, including John's. The thought of daily running didn't appeal to John in the least, but he could do it. Besides, he could stand to lose a few pounds, and a regular exercise routine was something he hadn't considered in years.

"The fourth rule is not to leave your barracks at night. The desert comes alive after dark. Snakes, coyotes, mountain lions...all are primarily nocturnal. The danger of any of these things wandering through the complex at the exact moment you would be outside is not high, but we are too far away from medical facilities to allow any sort of risk. This is for your safety."

"The fifth and most important rule is to drink your supplements. Every morning, before you run, we will supply a beverage specifically formulated for desert activity. It replaces vitamins and provides essential nutrition for your stay at the compound. Without these supplements, you will begin to feel weak and you will thus not be able to maximize your benefit from the program." Kane leveled his gaze at each of the participants as he concluded his speech.

"These rules are in place to assist you in accomplishing your individual goals. They are for your safety and your health. If you do not abide by these rules, you are endangering yourself and possibly others in the program – something that will not be tolerated. Are we clear?"

Heads nodded again including John's, though he didn't feel entirely clear. He was wondering what Kane had meant by the phrase "will not be tolerated." At the same time, he was certain Kane had never been questioned on it, just as he was also sure no one had ever broken one of the rules before.

John pushed his thoughts aside. There was nothing in the rules that wasn't simple and easy enough to abide by. Even the running.

"Now we're going to take quick tour of the compound. You'll see your barracks and the dining hall. The remainder of the complex doesn't concern you. Doctor Regen will escort the ladies, the men will be with me. So grab your gear, and we'll get you moved in."

As the group dispersed to retrieve the boxes under the mesquite tree, John craned his neck and watched the last cloud of dust settle from the van departing over the horizon. That was it then. The isolation had begun. Three months.

They belonged to the program now.

Sarah took his hand and smiled. That same hopeful smile she wore at the community center in Sonora. He faced her, shutting out everything else around him. He tried to look beyond the dark sunglasses she wore, to stare into her green eyes and share in her hope. He offered a smile in return and gently kissed his wife on the lips. He could handle the program. He could handle anything as long as they were together.

He couldn't have noticed Marcus Kane standing on the other side of the sundial, his face devoid of any expression, staring at the couple for the longest time.

CHAPTER 14

JOHN LEANED BACK against the cool wall of the dining hall and inhaled the crisp air. The tour of the compound had been very brief. There wasn't much to the complex to be toured. Two of the structures were the barracks. One for the men and one for the women. Apparently, John and Sarah were going to have separate quarters for the duration of the program. John held his tongue. The matter could always be addressed later.

The barracks faced each other in the compound—one line of the X-pattern with the buildings separated by the sundial—and both were identical. Like all the structures in the complex, the barracks had no windows. The only entry was through the heavy front door, a fact that initially concerned John before he reasoned there was likely no danger from fire since the structures were composed completely of concrete and metal.

Upon entering, each barrack's first room consisted of four sets of bunk beds, two on either side of the room. Full-length lockers sat between each set of beds to store their clothes. It reminded John once again of how he had always imagined boot camp to be like for the military. Chance would be right at home. And because the four sets of bunks meant there were eight individual beds, at least each of the four men would have his own space and not literally be right on top of each other.

A large skylight provided the majority of lighting for the quarters, but John could also see four bare bulbs hanging from power cords in the ceiling for evening use.

A door led from the sleeping area to the restroom facilities. A sink, a toilet stall, and a shower lined each wall – each side perfectly symmetrical to the other. He noticed that the shower stalls had neither curtains nor doors. But that was the lesser of two evils, he supposed. John was grateful that at least the toilet stalls had doors. There would be some modicum of privacy over the next few months.

A second skylight located in the ceiling between the showers supplied ample light for the bathroom. Four more bare bulbs would provide illumination at night.

A final door at the back of the barracks opened into a large supply closet. As Kane had described, the barracks were well-stocked with boxes and crates of all sorts of supplies. Everything from razors to toothpaste to sunscreen to band-aids.

But no telephone and no television, John thought. *Don't want too much of that outside world creeping in.*

The greatest oddity of the bathroom was the lack of any mirrors. Vernon actually voiced a quiet question to Kane about their absence to which the giant replied, "Vanity is a product of society. Looks don't matter here."

And just like that, the issue was dropped. None of the other men said anything although John wondered if the same question was being raised in the women's barracks.

The men had placed their boxes of clothes they retrieved before the tour onto their selected bunks. John had drawn the proverbial short straw this time around. Vernon dropped his box onto the bed next to John's bunk and shot him a sneer. The look made John want to throttle the rat. It was going to be a long three months.

The tour then made its way into the dining hall. The building was more impressive than the barracks. A small office with three comfortable-looking chairs sat just inside the front door. John assumed the room would be used for the individual meetings with Doctor Regen. On the other side of the entryway was a small library. The dining area was beyond the two smaller rooms and consisted of a single large table with eighteen folding chairs – eight more than required by the current population of the compound by John's calculations. A large opening in the wall with a counter and another door provided access to the kitchen facilities.

The kitchen was the most impressive part of the dining hall. Two big ovens sat next to a large refrigerator with stainless steel doors. Stacks of plates and utensils and a multitude of shiny silver appliances populated the metal shelves of the room. The back of the kitchen consisted of a huge walk-in freezer next to a giant pantry stocked with countless cans of food and boxes and bags of dry goods. A gray washing machine sat in the far corner with laundry detergent lining a shelf above it.

If there was a nuclear war, we'd be set to live out here for a year, John thought. He considered the random nutcases in the news who constantly anticipated the end of the world. "Y2K". The Mayan apocalypse. Some big comet scheduled to pass by soon. Whatever. This place would be their fantasy. A self-sufficient, isolated compound.

Now, John stood against the wall of the dining hall with Sarah seated in a chair in front of him. Marcus Kane had returned from his and Doctor Regen's quarters (a building the program participants were not invited to tour) with a clipboard. Lilith Regen sat at the end of the table, apart from the group.

"This is a list of assignments that will need to be carried out by members of this group during the program. The list consists of essential chores such as cooking and cleaning. These chores need to be assigned so we have no arguments or disagreements as the program progresses. Everybody works. Whatever you're assigned today will be your responsibility for the next three months. Are we clear?"

Heads nodded, but John found himself again second-guessing the program. Why not rotate jobs on a weekly basis?

He chided himself for the thought. Why did he have to be like that? Just roll with the system.

Kane surveyed the group until his eyes stopped on Vernon. He held the clipboard out for the smaller man to take. Vernon, perhaps smelling work, was slow to accept the sheets, until Kane spoke. "You,

Vernon, why don't you handle assigning work responsibilities for the group?"

A quiet murmur passed through the other program participants at the statement. A grin creeped across Vernon's face as he took the clipboard and surveyed its contents. His teeth were a dingy gray.

John shook his head. He couldn't help himself. The child molester was being given responsibility. Not much, mind you, and it shouldn't have mattered, but it did. A guy who took pictures of naked little girls was being given a nod of acceptance and would be controlling part of the rest of the group's lives. But John held his tongue. If nothing else, because he knew the rest of the program members were just as put off by this action as he was. He would let someone else say something. But no one did.

Vernon looked up. "Okay, somebody has to be responsible for cleaning the bathrooms in each of the barracks. Drug-girl, you handle the chick dorm and lawyer-boy can handle the men's. That should be fun, scrubbing toilets and shit like that."

The rat man giggled, and John was once again overwhelmed with the urge to leap over the table and wrap his hands around the man's throat. He couldn't believe that Doctor Regen didn't say something to Vernon about his comments. Was her earlier "be civil" admonishment not applicable to criminals in the program?

"Let's see, kitchen and meal clean-up. We'll let army guy and the truck driver handle washing dishes."

"I served in the United States *Navy*, Vernon," Chance's statement was louder than necessary. He was clearly restraining the same violent feelings as John, yet John was almost grateful for Vernon's last comment. In the back of his mind, he had been sure the rat-man would address BJ with a racial slur. The guy with the clipboard was just stupid enough to do it. John found himself wondering if that comment would have been enough to force Doctor Regen into quieting the rodent. Nothing else seemed to.

"Yeah, Navy, whatever," Vernon continued. "Meal preparation. Why don't you two chubby chicks take care of that? I bet you can both cook," he said, indicating Maude and Sarah.

This time, John took a step away from the wall toward Vernon. The vermin could insult him all day, but bringing his wife into the matter forced a protective instinct into play. For just a moment, the rational part of John's mind gave way to hatred. He was going to strangle Vernon. It would be quick. No one would care.

All at once, three things occurred. Vernon noticed John's movement and stepped back, shrinking away from the encounter. Sarah reached out her hand and grabbed John's arm, silently asking him not to cause trouble, she'd be fine. And Marcus Kane's eyes shifted from Vernon toward John in a slow, watchful movement. His head cocked to the side as he observed John's reaction.

This time, Doctor Regen stepped in. "Vernon, that's enough. I shouldn't have to remind you there is no need for degradation here. Respect for one another is a critical aspect to making the program work."

"Yeah, sorry," Vernon said, warily eyeing John.

John stepped back to the wall as Sarah's grip loosened from his arm.

Vernon went back to studying the clipboard, its contents suddenly holding the greatest fascination for him. "Let's see. What's left? Looks like there are two spots for maintaining the garden. Who doesn't have a job yet? Oh, Denise, right?"

He glanced up from the clipboard to the young woman. She nodded her head, and her nose slightly wrinkled, as if her subconscious smelled something it didn't like very much. Vernon smiled in response, dingy teeth on full display.

"Okay. And I don't have a job yet, so I guess I'll do that, too." Vernon nodded, agreeing with himself that gardening was the job for him, and handed the clipboard back to Marcus Kane.

Kane took the clipboard and held it behind his back as he addressed the group. "We're about to take a break, after which Doctor

Regen will provide you with a basic schedule for the coming week. Your new lives officially begin with our first run tomorrow morning. Does anyone have any questions before we break?"

John had a thousand questions, but he said nothing. It was all a part of giving up control. Doctor Regen had asked John if he trusted them. He had said yes. That had been a lie, but if there was one thing he had become quite good at over the last year, it was lying.

The truth was that he loved his wife. And he would make this work.

And if that meant giving up his control for the next three months, he could do it. Even if he couldn't trust the good doctor or her muscled partner, he could at least follow directions. And he could follow them well. Even if he didn't care for them.

His new life would begin with the first run tomorrow morning.

And nothing would ever be the same again.

CHAPTER 15

"I'M GOING TO MISS sharing a bed with you."

Sarah looked into her husband's face as he spoke the words. She knew he meant them. She also knew that "sharing a bed" and "sleeping with" were two distinct categories, and John had chosen the one that fit him. She had never encountered anyone else who measured his words with such precision.

That was the significance of "sharing a bed." John had suffered from insomnia for years, as long as Sarah had known him. Sarah would occasionally wake to feel John rolling over, adjusting the blankets, shifting his pillow. He would try to be careful, try never to wake her, but she had often lain in the darkness, wondering what demons kept John's slumber at bay. She had asked him about it once, only a couple months after they had started sleeping together in college. John, in his measured way, said he was thinking, and he left it at that. She did, too. And she never brought it up again, even after they began sharing the same bed in marriage. Some things are just personal, even between a husband and wife. But she could imagine what had occupied his thoughts since the accident, why the insomnia had grown even worse after losing their baby, and she longed for the day when they could both put those demons to rest.

"I'm going to miss sleeping with you, too," she said. Her words held their own meaning. She would miss sleeping in the same bed with him, even if she knew he would spend most of the night staring out the window or watching the ceiling fan spin. But she would miss *sleeping* with him, too.

They had made love the evening she came home from the hospital, throat still sore from the tube used to pump the overdose of pills from her stomach. It was not a night of torrid passion. It was awkward. Sarah felt fat. John told her she was beautiful, and the look in his eyes told her he meant it, but she still opted to turn the lights off. They held each other. Sarah cried against her husband's bare shoulder. They went through the motions.

The love was there that night. Dim, barely remembered, but there. They could only hope that passion would someday follow. For that night, love was all they could ask for, even just an ember. It would grow over time. It would regain its strength.

Now, sitting on the raised concrete slab in front of the door to the dining hall, Sarah felt the love again. She knew how hard this was going to be for John. So many things in the program went against his very nature, but he was handling it with a smile. And Sarah truly believed in Doctor Regen. She liked the idea of the program. She loved the notion of escaping the world. Escaping the pills and the size-zero models on television. Escaping the set of crystal glasses that were now incomplete. Escaping the memory of her parents and her baby girl. Maybe not ridding herself of the memories, but pushing them away long enough to let the pain subside, long enough to remember the good, not just the hurt.

"Are you going to be okay?" she asked John. He leaned forward, picked up a small rock and tossed it back and forth in his hands while he considered the question.

"Yeah, I'm going to be fine," he responded. He sat in silence for a few moments, tossing his rock and watching the action in the center of the compound. Chance and BJ had developed a game, a riff on basketball's "around the world." They were standing on the concrete slab in front of the women's barracks. Each man had a rock about the size of a fist, and they were attempting to throw the rocks onto the flat surface of the sundial. To make it challenging, they decided the rock had to be thrown overhand, basketball style, for the "basket" to count.

Once you made a basket, you advanced to the slab of the next building and tried again. The first one "around the world" would win.

The two had started playing half an hour earlier, after finishing their assigned responsibility of kitchen clean-up. John had pitched in even though his designated duty was bathroom maintenance. It didn't take long for the three men to finish. Vernon had been missing since dinner was over, presumably in the barracks but no one seemed to care enough to investigate.

Chance and BJ had started the game outside the men's building, and had now progressed three baskets to the women's barracks. Denise and Teri joined in the game midway (once the guys were in front of Kane's building). Chance generously altered the rules to allow for underhanded "girl-throws" to count. Denise had scored the first basket (throwing her rock basketball style despite Chance's gesture) and moved to the women's building, but Chance and BJ soon caught up, with Teri struggling, still standing in front of Kane and Doctor Regen's quarters.

Sarah recognized that John was now playing with a rock of his own because subconsciously he was in *the game* as well. Her husband had been a competitor for as long as she had known him. She smiled to herself. She knew him so well. It was kind of scary, but kind of nice. That familiarity also told her John had something else on his mind, something serious, but wasn't ready to bring it up.

"The sunset's beautiful, isn't it?" she asked, hoping to prod his conversation. John sometimes needed prodding.

He looked up from his rock to see the desert sky alive with reds and oranges settling against feathery waves of clouds. It was different than the sunsets of Boston, but comfortably familiar at the same time, the way all sunsets are.

"It's amazing," he said. John glanced at Sarah then back to the sinking red sphere. He drew in a slow breath.

Sarah braced herself. Here it comes.

"Can I ask you something?"

Sarah nodded.

"And I don't want this to upset you. It's just a feeling." John's cadence was slow. Measured. "Do you feel out of place here?"

Sarah released a breath she didn't realize she had been holding. This particular question was not unexpected, as some of John's insights were. She could handle this.

"Of course I feel out of place. I think everyone probably feels out of place here. We're all surrounded by people we just met, far from home, trying to get over...stuff. I think it's only natural to feel out of place."

John seemed to consider this for a few moments. "But that's just it. We're not all surrounded by people we just met. You and I know each other. There aren't any other couples here."

"Well, that's probably because most of the people who try to kill themselves don't have anybody, or they've just lost someone. Look at Maude and BJ. You have to admit our situation is pretty unusual."

"Exactly," John countered. "Our situation is *very* different from everyone else. I mean, the fact is, everyone else here survived their suicide by sheer coincidence. Practically an act of God. But we had each other."

Sarah sighed. "And you wouldn't say coincidence or an act of God had something to do with us? Me getting the blanket from the hall closet? You leaving your personal cell phone turned on even though you never get calls on it? We're just like these people, John. Just like them."

John's eyebrows narrowed. He wasn't angry, but Sarah could tell he was trying to make a point she just wasn't getting. "That Vernon guy is a child molester, Sarah. *Don't* say we're just like them."

"I didn't mean him. I was talking about everyone else. Don't you like BJ and Chance? And Maude seems nice. I know that Denise is going to take some time."

John nodded. "Tell me about it. I think she'd rather talk to Vernon than me. And I *do* like everyone else, I'm just saying something doesn't feel quite right." He paused.

"Let me ask you this. Before we left Boston, I liquidated part of our portfolio so we could send a check for a hundred thousand dollars to

Doctor Regen to cover our admission into the program. That's quite a bit of money. Now how did Maude afford that? Or Teri? Or Chance?"

"Is that what this is about? The money?"

John shook his head. "No, the money's only part of it. I'm just saying something doesn't feel right."

"Excuse me, folks," the deep voice startled them both as BJ walked toward them from the sundial, rock in hand. "But I need to finish schoolin' the youngsters on how this game is played."

John smiled at BJ as he rose. Sarah could tell he really did like the trucker. John moved from the front of the concrete slab to the side, sitting next to Sarah and leaning against the building. "Maybe we can talk about this later," he said.

Sarah nodded. The truth was, she did feel out of place, but that wasn't going to stop her from trying. The program would work. She was sure of it. It would work if they both believed in it, but John already seemed to be wavering. And it was only the first day. The thought scared her.

She looked into John's brown eyes as they reflected the last of the day's sunlight, and she hoped for the best. It was all she had left.

Her gaze shifted as movement by the door caught her eye, and before she could catch herself, Sarah screamed.

The shrill cry made John leap to his feet and caused BJ's throw to overshoot the sundial by ten feet.

Sarah scrambled off the slab and backed away as a second leg emerged from the small space between the foundation of the dining hall and the concrete slab in front of it. The leg was black and hairy. Jointed in three places.

John leaned in closer as another leg sought the top of the slab. Chance raced over as a fourth emerged. By the time the body of the tarantula fully ascended from the inch-wide space between the slab and the building, the whole group had assembled in front of the dining hall. Even Vernon had come out of hiding.

"Son of a bitch," BJ said.

The tarantula was huge, as large as the rocks the guys had been tossing onto the sundial. It looked like something you would see on the Discovery Channel.

"Somebody kill it." The order was given by Denise, shuddering as she said it.

John took a step forward onto the slab. The spider might be big, but it wasn't big enough to survive a good stomp.

"Be careful, John," Sarah said as he lifted his foot.

A massive hand clamped onto John's shoulder. The fingertips extended past his collarbone even as he felt the thumb press into his spine. It could only be one person.

"Step back," Kane's voice rumbled. He must have emerged from his quarters at the sound of Sarah's scream. His grip on John's shoulder was firm, but not hard. John guessed that grip could be very hard if it wanted to be. He stepped back off the slab.

"Listen up, people," Kane said, his voice still soft as he addressed the crowd. All eyes and ears were on him. Even the spider seemed to stand at attention on the slab just in front of the door.

"This is a good time to educate you on three of the most common dangers you will find in the desert. The first is scorpions. They look scary, but the species of scorpions found in this part of the world have a sting that isn't much worse than a wasp. Benadryl cream will take care of it, but if you avoid a scorpion, you won't get stung in the first place. Problem solved."

"The second danger to be aware of is rattlesnakes. Forget what you think you know about them. A rattlesnake has a simple mind. If you're smaller than the snake, he thinks you're food. If you're bigger than the snake, he's afraid of you. I guarantee that you are bigger than every snake in New Mexico. If you encounter one, you will know it. A rattlesnake rattles when he is frightened. When you hear the rattle, walk away from it. A snake will not attack you or chase you. It will only strike if provoked. So just leave it alone. We do have anti-venom in case of an emergency, but I do not plan on having to use it, so don't fuck with the reptiles. Understood?"

The heads of the group nodded in unison, but this time they were not looking at Kane. Their eyes were affixed to the brown and black spider on the slab, looking like a mutated giant compared to the house spiders and garden spiders they had seen in their lifetimes. The tarantula's body was bouncing on its hairy legs, bobbing to music only its spider-ears could hear.

"The tarantula is just as simple. A tarantula is not very poisonous, contrary to what you may have thought, but they're also not exactly clean creatures mulling about in the desert. A bite from a tarantula can cause a nasty infection so do not get bit. A spider lives by the same rules as the snake, so it is afraid of you. You may think that because of its size, you can step on the spider and kill it."

Kane levelled the comment at John, but the message was for the whole group, all transfixed on the bobbing arachnid.

"Do *not* attempt to step on a tarantula. This particular spider jumps. And when I say 'jump', I mean that if a spider panics, it can clear three feet. A big foot coming toward its head can make a spider panic. It can jump. It can land on you. And since it's panicked, it might bite you. Do not let this happen. If you really feel the need to kill it, use a rock, or a long stick. Just keep your distance."

John's eyes narrowed. A jumping spider? He had never heard of such a thing. Of course, he had lived in the city his entire life, but a quick scan of BJ's and Chance's faces indicated he wasn't alone in his skepticism.

Kane must have sensed that.

He turned from the group and stepped onto the slab. He lifted his other boot as if he were going to step on the spider, and as he brought his foot down, the bobbing motion of the tarantula turned into a giant leap. Like a blurred jack-in-the-box, the spider shot up over two feet. In a fluid motion quicker than John thought humanly possible, Kane clenched his fist and drove it forward, striking the spider in mid-air and transforming it into a pulpy smear of red and black on the door of the dining hall.

A collective gasp rose from the group followed by scattered swear words whispered in awe. A thin line of dark blood flowed down the door into the crack between the building's foundation and the concrete slab.

As Kane walked back to his quarters in the growing darkness, John was certain of what he had just witnessed. One predator was destroyed by another. Obliterated.

He and Sarah stood in front of the slab a few more minutes as the rest of the group began to disperse to their barracks. After all, no one was supposed to be out after dark. It was one of the rules. And no one was about to break a rule after witnessing the display with the spider.

Sarah didn't say much. Neither of them wanted to reenter their earlier conversation. Instead, they lightly kissed each other goodnight and headed toward their opposite buildings. The program wasn't going to be easy. John would have to deal with running and cleaning toilets. Sarah would have to deal with tarantulas that would jump if you panicked them.

Lovely Sonora Valley.

CHAPTER 16

JOHN MICHAELS lay in his bed and stared through the skylight at the stars above. He was sleeping on the bottom bunk, but if he angled his body on the bed, he could see past the top bunk and through the glass fairly well.

Due to his sleeping habits—or lack of them—John had considered sleeping on the top bunk so he could watch the sparkling desert sky all night, but Vernon was sleeping on the top bunk of the beds next to John. Since there were four sets of bunk beds, each man had his own. John, Chance and BJ had each elected to sleep on the bottom bunk, as almost all adults would, but Vernon had scrambled to the top bed of his bunk set. It was apparent to John that Vernon wasn't much of a people person. He questioned whether that was a conscious choice or if the rat-man just didn't know how to relate to others. Probably a bit of both. Or maybe Vernon just wanted the top bunk for some privacy.

The thought sickened John. Sharing a room with an admitted child molester was bad, sharing a room with a child molester who wanted some evening privacy was much worse. Regardless, it had been a quick decision for John to bypass the easy view of the stars from the top bunk in favor of sleeping as far away from Vernon as possible.

John had lain awake for a couple of hours when the moon began to creep into the frame of the skylight. He let his mind wander.

What a first day it had been.

Leaving Boston on the red-eye the prior night seemed a lifetime ago. The events of the week leading to their arrival in Sonora Valley were even more distant. Putting his investment portfolio on auto-pilot.

Arranging matters with a bill-pay service to manage monthly expenses while they were out. The final meeting with Doctor Cornelius, where he explained they wouldn't need to bring any luggage to New Mexico.

So much had happened since then.

Now, he was lying in a bunk bed (his wife in another building, no less), unsure of his geographic location, wary of the program administrators, disgusted by one of his roommates, and wondering how close the coyotes were that had begun to howl about an hour earlier.

The howling had disturbed him at first. It was the sound of the unknown, the sound of the wild. John had heard it before in western movies and on nature shows, but listening to the coyotes in real life had been disquieting. Only after logical assessment ("I'm inside concrete walls with a very heavy door separating me from the animals...") was he able to relax once again. Soon, the sound became comforting. The coyotes were simply fellow insomniacs, keeping John company on the first of many long nights.

John considered the events of the day. The meeting in the Sonora Community Center that morning. The insufferably long ride in the van. The confrontation with Denise. The spider. Kane.

John's mind replayed the image. The spider jumping. Kane's blurred fist smashing it into the door. *Just another friendly reminder you're not in Boston anymore. It's a whole new world out here.* The scene was on a mental auto-playback loop, and each time, it was just as unreal.

Alongside the mangled tarantula, other thoughts coursed through John's mind, fighting for attention. This was his usual mental state each night as he struggled to find slumber. The equivalent of watching an entire wall of television screens with each displaying something unique. John's attention would stay with one, then shift, always absorbing the cacophony of media a little at a time. Tonight, Denise routinely returned to center stage. The look in her eyes when she turned in her seat to confront him in the van. So angry. So alone.

It reminded him of his sister. The last time John had seen Jennifer, she had only been a couple of years older than Denise, and she had that exact same look in her eyes at their mother's funeral. She had been angry. John knew the look well. Had seen it in his older sister's eyes for years. But that last time, after the burial, after the obligatory post-funeral visits from the well-wishers, after everyone had left the house and only John and Jennifer remained, she had started to speak.

But John hadn't let her. He had cut her off.

He hadn't been in the mood to listen. He hadn't been in the mood to forgive. He had been in the mood to unload. And Jennifer was the only target left.

Lying awake, as he had so many other nights, John could try to justify it to himself. He had just been a kid at the time, eighteen but feeling eighty. And the one person who should have been there to help him had run off. It was John who sat with their mother. The long days. The longer nights. And when his sister had just happened to call, right out of the blue, he begged her to come. It had been months since she had been home. John had told her the time was close, and the cancer was going to finish things very soon. Come home. But Jennifer had hung up the phone.

And when she did arrive at the house, three days later, it was too late. Their mother had succumbed to the weight of the sickness twelve hours earlier. Twelve lousy hours.

His mother hadn't said anything that night. She hadn't spoken coherently since John had checked her into the hospital, when things got so bad he finally had to accept assistance, but he knew she wondered where her daughter was. John wondered, too. And he was furious.

And so that last night, after the funeral, he had unleashed that fury on Jennifer. He never gave her a chance to speak. He didn't care about whatever excuses she may have had. She had abandoned them. She had fallen short, and he had to take up the slack. And he was sick of it. He had done it his whole life.

When he had finally asked her what she had to say for herself, when her angry eyes were awash in tears thanks to her baby brother's tirade, she answered by walking out the front door.

He hadn't seen her again after that. And he had always wondered. What would Jennifer have said? What would she have talked about if he had just let her speak?

John decided he would speak to Sarah about Denise more tomorrow. He couldn't abide the thought of seeing those eyes every day for the next three months and not trying to help. He wouldn't let anything more happen to her.

And he would find Jennifer. The notion had struck him before, but he had always pushed it away, still carrying the lingering shreds of resentment. Those shreds were gone now. Banished by the phone call he had received sitting in his car in the park. The extraordinary call that had stopped him from putting the barrel of a gun to his temple. In the clarity following that day, the grudge against his sister seemed beyond petty. It was childish. And it was now firmly in the past.

Outside of his wife, Jennifer was the only family John had left. A firm resolution set in. He would begin his search in earnest as soon as they finished the program. No more waiting. No more wondering. He would do it.

The satisfying thought tugged John's mind a different direction. Something about family. John's thoughts returned to the Sonora Community Center, to the meeting earlier in the day, to the information the other program members had revealed about themselves.

When John was voicing his concerns to Sarah sitting on the spider-hiding concrete slab earlier in the evening, he hadn't told her everything. He could tell she was beginning to get upset, and he was still determined to make this work for her. But lying in bed, he allowed himself to replay his analysis, to be his own sounding board to determine whether the ideas were crazy or not.

The other members of the group were from a vastly different financial bracket without a doubt. John was almost positive no one else had paid a hundred grand for the right to be here. But that in itself didn't really bother him. Perhaps the cost of the rehabilitation program was need-based. It wouldn't be the first time John had seen something handed to others while he worked for it, and he had always tried to avoid personal resentment at the fact. But the other differences between him and Sarah versus the rest of the program participants *did* bother him, and no matter what Sarah may have thought, they *were* different from the others. The simple fact that John and Sarah were in the program as a couple created that rift. Everyone else was alone.

The thought sharpened John's focus on what had first occurred to him in the van ride after Denise accosted him as being an accessory to her father's death. The statement had conceived something in his mind, an idea that was present, but seemed to skitter away each time he tried to pinpoint it, hiding in the dark recesses of his brain. As John relaxed his mind and listened to the coyotes sing and watched the moon emerge into the skylight above him, those dark recesses began to open.

What was it about this group of people that bothered him so much?

A cloud floated past the moon, and the room grew black. BJ snored softly and Chance kicked at his blankets.

The idea finally slipped into the light.

It wasn't the people that bothered John. *It was the circumstances.*

It was what had crossed his mind in a flash when he took a step toward Vernon in the dining hall after the rat-man had insulted his wife. He had wanted to strangle him. It would have been easy. And it would have felt good.

The idea hadn't given John any lingering guilt. It was just an angry impulse that he wouldn't have ever acted upon. And John had no problem with the loathing he felt toward Vernon. After all, the man was a criminal. No one would miss him.

And that was it.

The reason he and Sarah stood out from the group was they had each other to cling to. The rest of the people were absolutely, positively alone. No one cared they were in the desert trying to rediscover their happiness. In fact, no one would care if they just disappeared from the face of the earth.

And no one would know.

John pulled the blanket up as a chill ran down his spine and into his legs. His feet twitched as the shiver passed his ankles. The desert night was cold, even in the barracks.

The coyotes continued to howl. BJ continued to snore. And John continued to stare out the skylight as the cloud passed away from the moon, the lunar light again filling the room.

No one would know.

CHAPTER 17

CUTTER VALENTINE was immersed deep in sleep and sweating bullets beneath the cool white sheets. The dream had come again. His legs kicked as the memories flooded his unconscious. He had driven almost a thousand miles to escape the hell, but at night, he could still see the demon's smiling face.

On the back porch, Walker sat up on his haunches. He pawed at the back door, and a small whine escaped his canine lips. Walker knew his master was suffering. And it always happened at night.

Cutter experienced everything all over again. The same maddening series of events. The same fateful day.

Hector stood across from him in the hallway, his forehead beaded with perspiration.

"We need to wait, Cutter," he said, his English perfect, but his accent thick. Hector spoke Spanish at home but English at work.

Cutter looked to his right and left. The hallway was deserted except for the dust and the occasional rat scampering away from the intruders. It had taken the department three months to learn of this abandoned warehouse and the evil it held within its decaying walls. The search had not been easy. It had crossed agency lines and been fought over by the police and the FBI, but in the end, the Texas Rangers had the right mixture of intimidation and street connections to lead them to this door.

Hector spoke again, forcing his voice out with each breath, a directed whisper that could be heard clearly but would not travel far.

"We need to go back out to the truck and call for back-up. Then we can search the rest of the offices."

But Cutter didn't need to search the rest of the offices. This was it. The door in front of the two men was all that separated them from the target of the largest manhunt Texas had ever seen. And Cutter Valentine was not about to walk away from it.

"If he knows we're here, there's no telling what he'll do," Cutter whispered in his own low voice. "We've got to take him down now."

Cutter twisted the sheets in his hands. He knew what was coming next. It was the same thing that always happened.

They were going to open the door.

Hector's eyes were wide as he glanced from his partner to the door and back again. They had worked together a long time, and Cutter could tell that Hector knew he was right. The man behind the door was insane. If any hesitation on their part permitted another innocent to die...

Hector nodded. Cutter narrowed his eyes and nodded back. This was it. There would be no turning back. Once the door was opened, Cutter would never be able to un-see the atrocities that lay inside. But he had no choice. He was a Ranger. And that meant more to him than anything in the world.

Cutter knew better now, knew he didn't want to see what was behind that plain wooden door. He tried to tell himself that it was only a dream, a dream he'd dreamed a thousand times. It didn't have to be this way. He didn't have to open the door. Not in the dream. It wouldn't matter anyway.

Hector's hand went to his forehead, then to his chest and each shoulder. He was one of the few Catholics on the force, and it always made Cutter nervous when his partner crossed himself. It also made him a little jealous. He could use all the help he could get right now. But it wasn't his way.

Hector nodded again, shotgun held in the ready position. Cutter raised his pistol in front of him, elbows cocked, ready to charge into the room when his partner kicked open the door.

Hector raised his boot then brought it crashing into the door next to the doorknob.

Cutter bolted upright in bed. He didn't want to see what was behind that door, even if it meant never sleeping again.

He looked to his left and right, determining his whereabouts. He was at home. In his bedroom. He was sitting up in his sweat-soaked sheets on his sunken old mattress. He could hear Walker crying from the back porch. He'd have to step outside and check on him in a minute.

He swung his legs over the side of the bed and rested his bare feet on the cool hardwood floor. He took deep, slow breaths. The grip of the nightmare already loosening its hold on his exhausted mind.

How much longer? How long till the dreams went away? How many more nights would he see the Baptist's smiling face? How many times would he hear the terrible, irreversible retort of his pistol, signaling the end of everything he held sacred?

Cutter shifted his gaze out the window. The stars were bright in the black desert sky. A million shimmering reasons not to give up hope. He had to believe there was more to life than this. That he still had some purpose.

But perhaps he was denying himself the only purpose he ever had.

Cutter switched on the lamp beside the bed. The phone was on the nightstand, and so was the card. He picked up the receiver and dialed the number scrawled in blue ink.

"Cal? This is Cutter Valentine," he said. "Yeah, I'm sorry to wake you, but I needed to call now. About that position we discussed this morning? Well, I've reconsidered. Tell her to put my name in the paper. I'll be your sheriff. And just let your nephew know he can call me out here if he needs me."

The conversation ended, Cal's sleepy gratitude received, Cutter returned the handset to its cradle.

That hadn't been so hard. He had done the right thing, even though it wasn't much of a thing at all. But it was a start. And maybe it was a good enough start to begin chipping away at the power of the dreams.

He marched to the back door and opened it, permitting Walker the rare privilege of coming inside the house. He hugged the dog's neck and roughly scratched his back while Walker licked his face, happy to see his master was okay.

It was a start.

CHAPTER 18

"LADIES AND GENTLEMEN, you are about to start your first run. Prepare to begin your new lives."

Marcus Kane stood on the concrete slab in front of the dining hall as he spoke. He again wore a taut black t-shirt and dark gray fatigue pants. Kane's black combat boots (as opposed to the running shoes worn by the rest of the group) reinforced John's impression of a drill sergeant from the previous day.

John glanced to the bluffs toward the east. The sun was hazy and red having just emerged from behind the farthest ridge. It was beautiful. John had seen many sunrises over the years from behind the wheel of his BMW on the way to the office, but it wasn't the same as being out here. Here it was real. There was no pane of curved glass separating him from the sight, and no need to observe it through hasty glances while negotiating traffic. Here, he could appreciate it for what it was.

He knelt to tie his shoe, double-knotting it this time and then doing the same for his other foot. He wasn't sure what the first run would be like, and the last thing he wanted was to trip over his own shoelaces.

John felt butterflies in his stomach and wondered if they were caused by the anticipation of the impending run or the glass of green liquid he'd just consumed. He assumed it was the former. The feeling was similar to what he used to experience prior to strategy meetings for new acquisition cases. Exhilaration and fear, always commingled with the sense of confidence necessary to make the nervousness work for you rather than against you. Each time you conquered the butterflies, you won a victory over yourself and emerged a stronger person.

John couldn't deny his nerves now. He had never enjoyed running. Not even as a kid. Well, that wasn't entirely true. Kid-running was fun. The excited galloping of a child on his way to the ice cream truck or playing tag with friends. But it was in fourth grade gym class that all the kids were required to run around the football field four times. Some kind of physical fitness test. It was just under a mile, not an unreasonable distance, but it was purposeless running. No game. No scoring. Just running. Every kid had to do it. There was no choice in the matter. And John hated it.

Ever since then, the very idea of running for the sake of running alienated John. In his mind, jogging was what people did to exercise only when they had no other creative options.

But he could handle this.

After all, he did need to get in shape and there probably wasn't a better way to do it (at least, not out here). Months of sitting in the office and drinking his dinner more times than not had begun to play havoc with John's body, and it was time to lose the love handles.

And, in a way, there was a purpose to the running. The running was part of the program, and succeeding in the program meant everything to Sarah. So he would be running for Sarah. If he looked at it from that perspective, he could handle it.

"A few tips on running," Kane continued, the bass tones of his voice clear against the hush of the morning. "First, a note on geography. Does everyone see the pitchfork here?" He pointed toward the three-pronged rock formation that sat half a mile from camp, rising almost high enough to reach the sun at this time of morning. "Never, ever lose sight of the pitchfork. As long as you can see the pitchfork, you can find your way back to camp."

"Now, on the opposite side of the compound," Kane pointed beyond the women's barracks, "about two miles in that direction is a cliff. It's about a fifty-foot drop, straight down. There are two reasons you are not to run in that direction. First, the ground near the cliff is not stable. If you get close enough to see over the drop, you'll probably get to experience it firsthand when some rocks give way. Second, the area around the cliff is also home to one of the larger rattlesnake dens in the area. Remember what I said last night, rattlesnakes don't want to bite you, but they will if they have to. If you walk into a den of them, you're likely to panic. And when you panic, they'll panic. And then you'll get bit. So no one runs in that direction, are we clear?"

Heads nodded. Sarah nodded vigorously. John smiled. He was fully aware they were all city dwellers, and while some of them might dare to chance an unstable cliff side just to see the view, none of them would consider chancing a den of angry rattlesnakes.

A cool breeze swept through the compound causing John to shiver. He was wearing light gray sweatpants and a light gray sweatshirt he had found in the lockers in the barracks. Everyone else was wearing the same thing (except Chance, who had elected to forego the sweatshirt in favor of his t-shirt, it was the manly thing to do).

The temperature of the desert night had surprised John. He had expected the cooling units to run all evening, but the temperature dropped quickly after nightfall. He estimated it was in the low sixties right now as night gave way to morning. He wondered how much of a shift in climate there would be once spring phased into summer.

"Other running tips, this is not a contest. I suspect Chance can run circles around all of you, so do not gauge your progress against anyone else in the program."

John noticed Chance look at his shoes when the remark was delivered. It was the first compliment they had heard Marcus Kane give, and John doubted the man gave out many. Chance must have known it, too. The kid was smiling.

"Having said that, I do expect each of you to push yourselves. We reviewed your medical histories prior to your acceptance to the program. There is no asthma, no joint problems, no chronic ingrown toenails in this group. So I don't want to hear any excuses about not being able to run."

John scanned the group as Kane spoke. Chance was obviously fit to run. His time in the military had prepared him for it. But John really wondered how well a truck driver like BJ would do. Or an overweight woman like Maude. Or a rail-thin drug addict like Teri. Or a business consultant who drank too much, slept too little and was soft in the middle. It was going to be an interesting show.

The nerves in his stomach quieted. He may not be in great shape (or even in good shape for that matter), but John was certain he could hang with most of these people.

"The trail we'll be using is two miles in length. It curves around the pitchfork bluff, then turns back and rejoins itself a quarter mile from camp. The trail is marked with rock cairns – flat limestone stacked in piles every fifty yards. Everyone uses this trail today. Going forward, you're welcome to leave the trails and explore other areas. Just remember to avoid the cliff area and keep the pitchfork in sight so you don't get lost."

John noticed Vernon had begun to run in place, warming up. His head rolled from one shoulder to the other like a boxer getting ready for a fight. He looked ridiculous.

"I expect everyone to complete the length of the trail this morning. It's only two miles. You'll be going a lot farther than that before the program is over. I don't care if you walk or run...today. But within two weeks, I expect everyone to be *running*. Clear?"

More head nodding. John wondered whether he would be able to run the length of the path. He wondered how far Sarah would go. She hadn't said anything, but John suspected his wife was worried about the running as well. She had put on quite a few pounds since the accident, and this would probably be the first exercise she'd had in almost a year. The fact she hadn't said a negative word about the required runs emphasized to John her commitment to the program.

"I'm going to be leading the run this morning. This will be the only time I will lead a run during your stay here. You're all adults. You should be able to motivate yourself and be motivated by your fellow program participants. You don't need me shouting encouragement at you. And remember, from this day on, you are never to run alone. If you're on the trail, you don't necessarily have to run side-by-side with someone because we know where you are, but you will have someone else somewhere on the trail running at the same time. If you choose to run off the trail, you must have a running partner within sight at all times, just in case. Clear again?"

Nodding. Crystal.

"One last thing. There will be no puking on your runs. The only thing in your stomach at the moment is your supplement drink. It should give you plenty of energy to run without making you nauseous. If you push yourself too hard, if you feel like you're about to vomit, start walking. Do not keep running. If you do, you will throw up. Do not sit down to try to catch your breath. If you do, you will throw up. Just keep walking. The supplement beverage is important to your health, and the last thing you need is to leave it lying beside the trail somewhere."

There was some quiet laughter among the group. Marcus Kane had made a funny, even if he wasn't smiling.

John considered the beverage they had all drunk just a few minutes earlier. Sarah and Maude (since they were in charge of kitchen duty) had poured it from an unlabeled plastic container into cups and handed it out to the group. It was green and looked like dark, syrupy Gatorade. There was a lime flavor that succeeded fairly well in masking the under-taste that was both salty and metallic. John had drained his cup, per Kane's instructions.

John didn't really believe in the necessity of vitamin supplements. He considered the industry of over-the-counter vitamins to be one of the most prolific sucker deals in the history of retail. But he doubted it would hurt. And Kane and Doctor Regen probably had their reasons. After all, John had never spent any time in the desert before, so perhaps they knew something he didn't.

He looked toward the building opposite the dining hall and wondered where Lilith Regen was. He supposed she wasn't going to join them in the morning workout (if Kane wasn't joining them after today, why should she?), but he also wondered if she was still in bed.

Sleeping peacefully while her patients were about to set out on the first of their runs.

Still, the sunrise was beautiful, and it was the start of a new day. Two miles. He could handle that.

"Let's go." Kane delivered the order and began a light jog toward the pitchfork.

Two miles.

John, Sarah, and the rest of the group started after him.

The beginning of the trail was about twenty yards from camp (roughly the same spot the van had parked when dropping the group off the prior day). From the trail's entrance, Maude was able to jog a hundred yards before slowing to a walk. Teri made it an additional fifty yards before walking. Despite his elaborate warm-up, Vernon never broke into a jog. He loped along at the back of the pack, hands in the pockets of his sweatpants.

Sarah jogged almost to the half-mile point before her breathing became so labored she had to slow to a walk. John slowed to match his wife's pace. By this time, Kane and Chance were both a quarter mile in front of them with BJ and Denise—her short legs pumping double-time to keep up with BJ's long gait—slightly behind the frontrunners.

John stayed with Sarah even though he imagined he could have kept up with BJ and Denise, but when Sarah slowed to a walk, she waved John on.

"Go ahead," she said, speaking between labored breaths. "I'm fine...I'll see you on the way back."

John was hesitant. He didn't like the idea of leaving his wife behind, but he could see Teri and Maude in the distance, moving up the trail at a steady walk. Sarah would have company.

He took off again at a quicker pace.

Barring short sprints through the airport trying to make a connection, it was the first running John had done in years. While part of him still hated the idea of it, another part of him felt pretty good, like his body was remembering a long forgotten primitive joy.

The buzz started about a hundred yards after he left Sarah. A low buzz in his head, different from the hazy comfort felt after two martinis. Instead of pleasantly dulled, his senses felt sharp. He increased his pace, determined to catch up to BJ and Denise. He wondered if this was the "runner's high" he had read about from time to time.

It wasn't bad.

John was perspiring by the time he neared the halfway point of the trail. It had circled around the pitchfork and curved away from the edge of the bluffs. The path then looped around and continued back toward the compound, running parallel to the first part of the course. It would rejoin the original trail somewhere around the quarter mile mark. John suspected Kane and Chance were already at that junction.

John continued running around the loop. He could see BJ and Denise up ahead. They were both still jogging, but their pace had slowed. Apparently, BJ's career of sitting for hours on end was much like John's own.

John's lungs were burning. There was a dull ache in his thighs. BJ and Denise were so close, less than a hundred yards away, but he couldn't keep up the pace. John slowed to a walk. He pressed his hand into his side even though there was no cramp there. He wasn't sure why he did it. Who was he trying to convince?

The simple truth was that he was out of shape.

He didn't like admitting it to himself. Even though he knew his physical condition wasn't great when he came into the program, he still *wanted* to believe he could run a couple of miles if he had to, but that notion was wrong. He *couldn't* run two miles. He barely made it past one before he had to stop.

John shook his head as he walked. It felt like losing. Maybe only losing to himself—his optimistic perceptions falling victim to crushing reality—but it still felt like losing. He was going to do better tomorrow.

He glanced ahead of him. BJ had slowed to a walk, and Denise was walking about ten yards ahead of him. She must have continued running just a little farther than he did. Maybe she proved something.

Maybe we all just proved something, John thought. *But what?*

CHAPTER 19

"I'M TELLING YOU, he didn't even break a sweat."

Chance spoke as he was drying one of the metal plates BJ had just washed. Sarah and Maude had cooked an excellent breakfast. Eggs, bacon, oatmeal, toast. It was healthy, more or less, and the group had been starving after the morning's run. John offered once again to help his new friends with their assigned cleanup. He was now listening to Chance as he wiped off the stainless steel countertops in the kitchen.

"I mean, we ran a lot in the Navy, even went fifteen miles one time, but that guy is amazing. We must have finished the course in under twelve minutes, and I could have run farther, but I was definitely breathing hard. Kane just looked around to make sure everybody was still on the trail, nodded to me, and walked back to his quarters. Not out of breath. Not sweating. Nothing." Chance finished by shaking his head while breathing a low whistle to indicate how impressed he was.

"Well, let me tell you something," BJ began, "This old body hasn't seen much activity lately. I thought I was going to die out there. Figured Jesus was just going to come down and snatch me out of these running shoes."

"Oh, come on," Chance stacked another clean plate onto a shelf, "It's only a couple of miles. That's not so bad." He grinned. "Even for you old guys."

John smiled at the comment. "Fifteen or twenty more years and a mile will seem a lot longer to you, too."

Chance clapped a hand across John's back. "Don't worry about it. If there's one thing basic training taught me, it's that *anyone* can learn to run. We had guys in there that had done nothing but play video games their whole lives, then they graduated high school and had to do something else. Basic was tough on them, especially that first couple of weeks, but they came around. You guys will, too."

"I hope so," BJ said. "I didn't come all the way out here to die from a damn heart attack."

John grinned as he wrung out the dishcloth and hung it on the small rack above the sink. BJ, the man who jumped from a building and ended up with a tree branch impaled through his scrotum, didn't want to die of a heart attack in the desert. The program must be working already.

Doctor Regen stepped into the kitchen from the dining area. "If you gentlemen are almost finished, we'll be starting the morning's group session in about five minutes."

"We're done," John said as he and the other two men walked toward the door. Time for more togetherness.

John glanced at his wrist and for the tenth time remembered his watch was sitting in a safe deposit box in Sonora. He had yet to see a single clock in the entire complex, excluding the big sundial.

He shifted his eyes to the chair next to him. Good. Sarah hadn't noticed him check his wrist. Two hairs past a freckle. The same time as when Doctor Regen opened the session although John felt certain at least two hours had passed.

The topics of the first group session had been pretty benign. Doctor Regen began by discussing how hurtful the outside world could be (occasionally substituting the word "society"), and eventually, group members began chiming in with what they disliked about the world outside Sonora Valley.

Maude hated how thin the women on television were. BJ hated how people judged you for your past. Teri hated the way salesclerks followed her around at department stores thinking she was a shoplifter (even though, she revealed, many times she was). Denise hated how you couldn't trust anyone. How people were only out for themselves.

And so it went. John listened intently, but didn't join in. He watched Doctor Regen. He noticed she was wearing make-up. Not much. Just a little. And her hair was fixed.

The rest of the female population looked very different from the previous day. Life without make-up and mirrors in the women's barracks had taken a toll on their personal appearances. The rules were different for the working class, it seemed.

Still, John hadn't heard a single complaint. The ladies were troopers. And though he wouldn't have expected it, John liked the natural appearance. Sarah looked good. The earlier run had left her with a subtle glow, a pinkish hue that remained on her cheeks for the rest of the morning.

The male participants, on the other hand, looked very much like they had the previous day. Men were easy. Wash this. Shave that (it was easier to shave "by feel" than John would have thought prior to trying it). Brush this. Comb that. And you're done.

He hadn't even minded sharing the bathroom. Chance was quick and efficient (John would have expected no less), and BJ was always pleasant to be around.

And Vernon. The rat-man stayed outside until the other three men were finished. Vernon liked to shower in private. But it worked out okay. The women took longer than the men anyway. And John got to practice his technique on the "around the world" game (he found a perfect rock after the run and managed to shoot it on the sundial fairly well). Besides, anything that kept Vernon away from the rest of them suited John fine.

"How about you, John?"

Doctor Regen's query snapped John out of his reverie. He had been caught not paying attention. Damn. Now he had to recover.

Three more months.

CHAPTER 20

SARAH WRAPPED THE TOWEL around her, tucking the corner into place just above her left breast. The towel was gray, like everything else here, but it was soft. She and John had plush, Egyptian cotton terry towels at their home in Boston, and Sarah felt a twinge of homesickness rising before banishing it away. A shattered crystal glass had triggered her attempt to kill herself. A stupid glass. She wasn't about to let a towel stand as a barrier between her and the road to recovery.

"Thanks again for your help today."

The voice came from the shower stall behind her. Denise was tucking her own towel into place, though her towel wrapped further around her body. The tuck was almost under Denise's arm, where Sarah's had once been before the accident. Before the antidepressants and the eating problem.

Sarah repressed her jealousy. It wasn't that difficult. She liked Denise, and she felt sorry for her. It's hard to be envious of someone you pity.

"Don't worry about it," Sarah replied. "I needed something to do."

Sarah had helped Denise in the garden for almost two hours earlier in the afternoon. The "garden" (which Sarah hadn't even noticed prior to Doctor Regen showing it to her) was located on the other side of the windmill. It was a patch of ground thirty feet wide by fifty feet long with its perimeter surrounded by a chicken-wire fence at waist height. There wasn't much to it, and it appeared to have been left unkempt since the last group in the program. Denise and Sarah had spent their time pulling weeds and nursing some of the plants by removing dead leaves and watering the roots using a hose attached to the pump at the windmill. It had been hard work, but it had felt good. And neither of them had been sunburned after Doctor Regen had again reminded the group to wear sunscreen earlier in the day.

Sarah had decided to join Denise for a couple of reasons. After her and John's individual session with Doctor Regen (which was technically a "couple's session"), Sarah wanted to get out and be active, and gardening was something she and her mom had done in her childhood. Beyond that, Sarah simply couldn't tolerate the thought of leaving Denise alone in the garden with Vernon.

The garden was shielded from view of the courtyard by the interspersed scraggly brush that populated the landscape, and Sarah didn't like the idea of any of the women being left out there with Vernon, particularly Denise. John had asked Sarah if she wanted him to join them, he didn't have anything else to do, but Sarah had declined. She didn't think now was the best time for John to be around Denise. The incident in the van was barely twenty-four hours old, and Sarah didn't want to push the girl too hard. She didn't mention it during their gardening nor while they shared the bathroom in the barracks.

That was what made Denise's next words to Sarah so surprising.

"I owe you an apology," she said quietly.

"For what?" Sarah asked as she removed the rubber bands from her hair, letting it fall to her shoulders. The second shower of the day felt fantastic after spending the afternoon sweating in the garden, but she hadn't felt like washing her hair again. It was after dinner, and it was almost dark anyway.

"For John," Denise replied, setting her own hair free from the rubber bands holding it. "I got upset yesterday morning, telling my story to everyone. I kind of relived it, you know? And it wasn't any better the second time around. Anyway, I wound up taking it out on John in the van, and that was wrong of me."

Sarah smiled. This was good news.

"I saw him this morning after the run," Denise continued. "We all went to the kitchen to get some water, and he came in and got a few bottles. You know, when he brought it out to you and Maude and Teri? I watched him. He didn't take a drink for himself until the rest of you were finished with the run and had your own bottles. That's really nice. So like I said, I think I was wrong."

Sarah touched Denise on the arm. It was something that would have merited a hug had they not both been wearing towels. "He *is* nice, and he'll be really glad to hear you think so. He's been worried about you."

Denise blushed. Sarah suspected no one had worried about Denise in a long time. Denise's eyes moistened, and she changed the subject before real tears could begin.

"So what do you think so far?"

"About the program?" Sarah began. "It's good. Different, but good. I got a little light-headed during the run this morning, but it wasn't really a *bad* kind of light-headed."

"Yeah, I felt the same thing. I guess that's just from running." Denise paused. "So what's the deal with Doctor Regen and Marcus? Are they, like, a couple? Way weird, right?" She giggled with the question, banishing the tired eyes of the adult who had suffered through more than her eighteen years deserved and reverting, however momentarily, to a sparkly-eyed teenager engaging in locker-room gossip.

The change was welcome. Although she was an only child, it made Sarah feel like a big sister. Whether the feeling was the result of displaced maternal instincts, or just the happiness of finding a friend, Sarah didn't care. Talking with Denise felt good.

"I doubt it. She's a psychiatrist. He seems more like GI Joe or something."

"But they stay in the same building. And don't even tell me you don't think Marcus has a killer body."

"Yes, Marcus does have an, um, impressive physique, but not really the kind I'm interested in. He's a little scary."

Denise rolled her eyes, the teen coming out in full force. "Tell me about it. That thing with the spider last night? Gross."

"Gross is right," Sarah said. "I'm just wondering how long until someone cleans that mess off the door."

"That is some repugnant shit."

John nodded at BJ's observation. They were standing in front of the dining hall, staring at the remnants of the tarantula carcass on the door. A small swarm of flies was circling. They would land on the meat, one at a time, then fly away, allowing more to land.

"You know what's really bad?" John asked. "Those flies are going to lay eggs in there. And those eggs will turn into maggots."

BJ's eyebrows rose. "Seriously? Man, that is gonna be some *seriously* repugnant shit."

"I'll clean it tomorrow," John said. "It probably falls under my assignment one way or another. It shouldn't take too long."

A rattle came from the other side of the door, then it swung outward toward the men. Chance emerged with three bottles of water for the men. They had all been drinking a lot of water. Just like they were supposed to.

"Stupid doors," he said. "I keep forgetting they open to the outside. I keep trying to pull when I should push and vice versa."

John nodded. He had done the same thing several times since they arrived. The doors were thick and heavy. He assumed they opened outward to combat excessive wind. Better to have the wind keeping the door closed than blowing it open all the time.

"I tell you what I don't get," John said. "Those giant air-conditioners." He pointed to the big gray unit sitting atop the women's barracks. "I would have thought they'd want something small and efficient since this place runs off a generator."

BJ shook his head. "Those things *are* efficient, man. That's a swamp cooler. I used to drive a route through Nevada and those things were all over the place. A buddy of mine in Reno showed me how they work one time. The reason they're so efficient is they use water to cool. See those panels on the sides?"

John looked. It was getting dark but he could make out the vented sides of the unit.

"Those are louvers, and behind the louvers, water is being pumped over a bunch of filters. The wind cuts through the sides, cools the water, and the filters transfer the cold into the system. It only uses a little bit of electricity, but it works really well in a dry climate. Keeps the place frosty."

John nodded appreciatively. "Learn something new every day." He glanced toward the west. The clouds were still pink. John picked up his rock. "We've still got about fifteen minutes, how about you two learn how to throw your rocks?"

Chance grinned and picked his own rock up from beside the concrete slab. BJ did the same. Let the game begin.

CHAPTER 21

VERNON KNEELED TO TIE HIS SHOE but remained crouched behind the mesquite bush for several minutes. It was at a slight angle, but he could see the back of the building perfectly from here. The women's barracks were less than fifty feet away. Easily close enough to make his calculations.

He grinned.

Calculations.

Yeah. This sort of thing wouldn't be easy. It would take calculations. It would take all sorts of calculations for him to do it right. And he had to do it right. Doing it right was the most important thing of all.

He remembered his father kicking over the sandcastle at the beach when Vernon was only five. He had stopped using the bucket and was pushing the little castle turrets together with his hands when something had set the old man off.

If you can't do something right, don't do it at all.

Later that same day, Vernon's father had tried to teach him to swim. The Pacific was probably a bad place to learn. A swimming pool would have been much easier. Fewer waves. And Vernon could have seen the bottom. That would have been nice, too.

When his father picked him up and walked him thirty yards from shore, the water had come to the man's chest. Vernon knew he couldn't touch bottom. When his father let him go, he told him to kick with his feet and stroke with his arms, just like he had shown him on shore. But Vernon had struggled and tried to grab back onto his father.

Of course, he *had* learned to swim. He'd never forget his father grabbing his head and shoving it under the water. Five seconds. Ten.

Pulling him out by the neck and saying, "Swim. Kick and stroke. If you can't do it right, don't do it at all."

The water was salty. It burned his eyes and hurt the inside of his nose. He cried and begged. He thought he was going to drown.

But he learned to swim.

The next weekend when they went back to the beach, Vernon had brought his new kitten with him. He was going to teach it to swim.

It kept trying to grab on to his arm with its tiny paws. The kitten's claws cut Vernon's arm and the salt water made the cuts burn, but he didn't give up. He did it exactly as his father had done. He held the kitten underwater until it learned to swim.

But the kitten didn't learn.

He buried it in the sand while his father went to buy more beer. When he returned, Vernon told his dad the kitten had run away. But when Vernon didn't even try to look for it that afternoon, his father knew the truth. Vernon wasn't allowed to have any more pets after that.

But that had been a long time ago. Vernon had been young. He didn't know what he was doing. He had gotten caught. Because he hadn't made any calculations.

Vernon cocked his head as he saw the light flick on in the women's barracks. The skylight near the back of the building had gone from dark to yellow. Someone was in the bathroom.

He shifted his gaze to the giant air conditioning unit at the center of the roof. He made his calculations.

He moved his eyes to the back of the building. There were ten wooden pallets back there, aged and gray. They had probably been sitting there since this place was built. Sitting there waiting to be put to use.

Vernon licked his lips. Calculations.

If you can't do something right, don't do it at all.

CHAPTER 22

DOCTOR LILITH REGEN leaned against the worktable, and it shifted slightly. The beakers and test tubes lightly clinked against each other, but she knew the table was stable. The compound had been built to last.

"So what else have you observed?"

The deep voice was coming from the other side of the room. Marcus Kane sat in front of the computer, but he wasn't using it. Seven brown folders lay on the keyboard, and he was scanning the contents of the eighth, which he held in his hands. He was wearing only a towel that clung loosely around his hips.

Lilith took a deep breath. "I observed enough to confirm what I told you last week. This is too dangerous."

Kane gave no indication he was listening. His back was to her, and he continued running his finger along the notes Lilith had scribbled in each file from her afternoon sessions.

"Marcus, I understand the need for progress, and I realize the importance of incorporating certain random variables into the sociological equation, but this is too much. There is no way we can adjust our controls to match this group as it stands."

Kane closed the folder in his hands and set it aside. He picked up the next one from the keyboard. It was labeled "*Michaels, John.*" The corners of Kane's mouth turned up slightly as he opened the file. Lilith noticed his expression through the reflection on the computer monitor.

"And *he's* the biggest concern. I know we have to incorporate the family element into the program at some point, but this is too soon. And we shouldn't be starting with people like John and Sarah Michaels."

Kane continued to face the wall as he read.

"Marcus, please. We should ask the Michaels to leave. Let them go now before we advance too far. You have to listen—."

Lilith was cut off as Kane shifted in his seat, raised his hand and wagged his index finger. His eyes remained on the file as he spoke. "Tut-tut, *Doctor* Regen. John Michaels is here for a very good reason, and I will not let him go just because you lack faith."

The words cut like a knife. "You know I don't lack faith, Marcus. I just think we need to proceed carefully. Slowly. Like the plan..."

Kane lowered the file and turned his chair to face her. "I *know* the plan, Lilith. And you seem to be forgetting your place in it."

She spoke more carefully now. "If we're going to keep John Michaels, at least let me dismiss Vernon. He doesn't need to be here."

Kane shook his head. "Oh, short-sighted Lilith. John Michaels' presence is the very reason we *need* Vernon. That perverted simp has his place in the plan, too. And when it's time, he will fulfill his role. Now go to bed. It's only the start, and you need your rest."

He lifted the folder and turned to again face the wall. Lilith stared at his back for several moments. A few droplets of water from his earlier shower still clung to the muscle layered over his shoulder blades.

"Are you going to join me?" she asked.

"No. I'll see you in the morning." The response was curt but not agitated. Thank God it wasn't agitated.

Lilith Regen stood in the doorway for a few more seconds, then walked up the stairs from the basement and proceeded down the hall to her quarters. Kane was right. She did need her rest.

After all, it was only the start.

Part III:
THE WRITINGS

CHAPTER 23

JOHN MICHAELS witnessed several interesting developments during the first month of the program. There was, of course, the improvement in the general fitness level of the entire group. It took John two weeks to be able to complete the entire two-mile trail without slowing to a walk. BJ accomplished that feat the same morning with Chance running alongside both men, offering encouragement and generally looking like he could run all day. The very next morning, the three men left the trail to begin exploratory hikes. Sometimes running, sometimes walking, they had spent the past two weeks venturing out a bit farther each time, but always keeping the pitchfork rock formation in view.

Their hikes were no longer limited to the designated pre-breakfast running times either. There wasn't much else to do at the compound. John had checked the small library in the dining hall and found nothing to his liking. There was no television or radio. Not even a deck of cards or a Monopoly game. So the three men had begun to go hiking in the afternoons as well, arranging the hikes around their individual private therapy sessions.

After a month of the program, the physical appearance of the participants was noticeably different as well. Everyone sported deepening tans on their faces and arms (all except Doctor Regen, who never seemed to venture into the sun beyond walking across the courtyard from her quarters to the dining hall). Chance's crew-cut was no longer trimmed. His hair grew unevenly over the long pink scar from the bullet that had once glanced off his skull. John supposed his own hair was getting longer as well, but without mirrors, it rarely crossed his mind. In an odd way, it was remarkably freeing.

And hair wasn't the only physical change. The light buzz John felt during that first run had begun to dissipate less and less during the course of the day. His "runner's high" was staying with him longer each time. It felt good. John felt good. His stomach felt tighter. His energy level had risen. And he was starting to sleep a bit more at night, not much more, but finding slumber was growing easier. The running was becoming more tolerable, and though he hesitated to admit it, he was actually beginning to enjoy the morning outings.

John noticed the change in other group members, too. Sarah had already lost an impressive amount of weight. There were no scales in the camp to confirm it, but he could tell, and so could she. When they said goodnight, she hugged him tighter than she used to.

John's resentment at not being able to sleep in the same building with his wife grew stronger each day, but he held his tongue. This was the way things had to be, and it meant everything to Sarah. Besides, they would have their entire lives to spend together after the program. After the healing was complete.

And John could see healing taking place. If the program had succeeded in nothing else, it had undoubtedly begun to whittle away at the pressures of the outside world. The lives of the participants were simple now. They consisted of eating, sleeping, running, cleaning and talking. Some of the talking was in the morning's group therapy sessions, some of it was in the private afternoon sessions with Doctor Regen, but the most therapeutic talking took place amongst themselves. Relationships were forming, friendships.

Despite their differences, John had grown to respect Chance and BJ. They were both genuine people, something John had not encountered in a long time. As he lay awake in the evenings, he considered the irony of his past priorities. He had worked so hard to elevate his and Sarah's lifestyle. It had meant so much for them to have a nice home and to drive nice vehicles. To exist in the social strata John believed Sarah deserved. And yet, John had despised most of those around him. His colleagues, the guys who drove overpriced cars and went snow-skiing three times a year and played golf at Pebble Beach every summer, the ones who couldn't stand even the thought of their kids going to public school (with *public* spat out like a swear word), they were all alike. Pretentious. Fake.

There was nothing fake about either BJ or Chance. They laughed when they thought something was funny. They were serious when the situation called for it. They said what they meant. And John had developed more respect for these two men than for every Reginald Nichols clone he had ever met at his company.

Moreover, he liked BJ and Chance. He enjoyed running with them. He liked playing the around-the-world game in the evenings. And if the program's path to healing was simplicity, then finding enjoyment through throwing a rock onto a sundial surely proved some level of effectiveness. Sarah's optimism had been well founded. John was beginning to believe in Doctor Regen and her concepts.

John wasn't the only one to make friends. Sarah had grown close to Denise. They spent a lot of time together. John wondered if his wife's interrupted maternal instincts had been subconsciously redirected toward the troubled teenager. Denise was too old to be her daughter, but John could tell Sarah was protective of the girl. And, by nature, John took upon himself a part of that responsibility.

When Chance began to ask him for advice on how to approach Denise, John responded much like a father would to a potential suitor for his little girl. Fortunately, John liked Chance, and today the young man's patience had paid off. Denise had agreed to run with Chance that morning. Only on the trail, and only for two miles, but it was a start.

Of the other three participants, John hadn't been able to gauge the effects of the program. True to the impression she gave early on, Teri was sullen most days. She no longer wore the black clothes she had sported in the Sonora community center (she was now decked out in gray and khaki just like everyone else), but her attitude seemed to remain dark. John wondered if Doctor Regen was having any success in their private sessions.

Maude seemed the perfect mimic. If the mood surrounding her was light, Maude was all smiles. If she was spending time with Teri, Maude looked depressed. And on the morning runs, Maude looked tired. Of all the participants, John knew the physical rigors of the program had to be toughest on the overweight, middle-aged woman. But she was doing her best, which was admirable, despite the comments by Vernon.

Twice John had heard Vernon remark about Maude's weight, twice John had verbally reproached the rat-man and walked toward him, and twice Vernon had dropped whatever he was doing and left. Fleeing the scene seemed a skill at which Vernon was quite adept. John had begun to see the Vermin less and less. Vernon went for long "walks" by himself (something technically against the program's rules, but the only person John saw less than Vernon was Marcus Kane, so this particular rule was becoming easier and easier to ignore). Vernon went to bed early. He took his showers late and always alone (a fact that reminded John to use rubber gloves while cleaning the bathroom). The rat-man was a creature of isolation, and that was fine by John.

There were many interesting developments indeed during the first month of the program, but none quite as interesting as the one John and BJ were now staring at.

They stood about two miles from the pitchfork, far north of the primary trail, the compound itself no longer in view. They had stumbled upon what appeared to be a little-used trail and had followed it to this point. Both men were sweating and still breathing hard despite having been standing in place looking at the same spot on the ground for several minutes.

The writing was created using a collection of rocks, each relatively flat and about the size of a frying pan. The rocks has been used to form letters on the ground inside a clearing slightly larger than an automobile and clearly visible from the trail. The writing was crude and consisted of two words.

NO DRINK.

BJ moved his gaze from the ground to his running partner. Neither of them had spoken. “What do you think it means?”

John shrugged, studying the rocks. “Don’t drink, I guess.”

BJ turned his attention back to the clearing. “Yeah, I got that, too. What I meant was, how do you think it got here?”

John kneeled down and held his hand over the “D” in “drink.” He didn’t touch the rocks. For some reason, tampering with them didn’t feel right.

“I don’t know. Maybe it’s part of the program. Something we haven’t reached yet. *Go out and write your goals in the desert*, something like that,” John offered.

BJ nodded. It made sense. “Could be. But why haven’t we seen more of these?”

John didn’t have an answer. “No telling. Maybe everyone else wrote theirs in the dirt with a stick and they blew away. I guess this woman wanted hers to last.”

BJ’s eyebrows furrowed. “Woman? How do you know it was a woman?”

John smiled at him. “Because guys are too lazy for stuff like this. I don’t know. It just feels like a woman did it.”

BJ chuckled. “Yeah, could be, I suppose. I’ve known plenty of women who drank too much in my time.”

John stood from his crouch and shook the tightness from his legs, preparing to run. “Well, you’re looking at a man who drank too much. Before Sarah and I came here, I was about two steps away from becoming a full-blown alcoholic.”

BJ smiled, but the smile didn’t reach his eyes. “Then I guess I was about three steps ahead of you,” he said.

John stopped stretching. There was something there, something behind BJ’s eyes. “What’s the real story, BJ?” he asked. “I know you lost your job because of a DWI, but I’ve got be honest, from what I’ve seen, you’re not the type of guy to pack it all up over a job.”

BJ lifted one big hand, stopping John's comments. "It wasn't the job. My wife left me, took the kid, said she never wanted to see me again." His voice trailed off.

"Bullshit," John said, surprising himself even as he said it. "You're a good man, BJ. I can't believe your wife left you because you couldn't find a job. What really happened?"

BJ stared at John, then shifted his eyes to the desert landscape around them. John could tell this wasn't easy for the man, but this was important. Finally, BJ's gaze returned to his friend.

"It is bullshit," he began, shaking his head. "Simone didn't leave me because I couldn't find a job. She left because I was treating her like shit. I was drinking every day, man. Three beers at breakfast, and so on. She said I hit my boy one night when he didn't turn the television down quick enough. I don't remember that, but I don't remember a lot of stuff. It's still hard for me to believe I could do something like that, but deep down here," he patted his chest, "I know it's true. Anyway, one night I told Simone she should just pack up and leave if she didn't like it, and she took me up on it. It was all my fault, John."

BJ's eyes grew moist as he spoke, but no tears fell.

"The thing is, I promised myself I would stop. *I promised myself.* See, the DWI was nothing but a trigger, man. Two weeks before I got pulled over by that cop..." BJ hesitated, John wasn't sure if he would continue, but he did. "I almost killed a kid."

John was taken aback by the statement, but BJ kept talking. He was on a roll now, and he was going to get this out.

"I was coming home from a long haul, and I had had a few beers that afternoon. I was driving through my neighborhood, when a kid ran out in the street with his dog. I saw the kid. I saw the dog. I hit the brakes, but everything was in slow motion. You ever have those dreams where something's chasing you and you try to run but you can only move real slow?"

John nodded.

"Anyway, I hit my brakes, but it's not fast enough. The kid sees me and jumps out of the way, but Deion wasn't so lucky."

"Deion?"

BJ absently nodded. "Deion was the dog. Just a mutt, but he could run real fast like Deion Sanders used to, so that's what we named him."

Despite the heat, a shiver ran down John's neck as he saw where the story was going.

"Deion was my dog. And the kid was my son," BJ said. A single tear escaped and made its way down his cheek. BJ ignored it. "It was *my son*, John. If he hadn't jumped out of the way... I killed his dog right in front of him. He loved that dog. Hell, I loved that dog."

BJ wiped away the tear and seemed to mentally return from the place he had just gone. "Anyway, I swore to myself right then that I wouldn't ever drink again. Not another drop. And two weeks later, I had a DWI and lost my job. Shit. If you can't even keep a promise to yourself, what kind of man are you?"

John put his hand on BJ's shoulder, squeezing it as he spoke. "I'll tell you what kind of man you are, BJ. In the past month, I've seen you work without complaining. I've seen you compliment Sarah on her cooking every day, even though no one else remembers. I've seen you rub aloe-vera on Maude's neck that day she got sunburned. I saw you go out and kill that rattlesnake in front of the women's barracks when Denise ran into the kitchen screaming. And I've heard you talk about how proud you are of your son at least a dozen times... People make mistakes, BJ, but your son is still alive, and so is your wife. You're a good man. You can't let this thing beat you."

BJ reached his hand up and gripped John's forearm. "I almost did. It was real close. I wish I could say that I've got it licked now, but man, every night I lay there and think about how good an ice cold beer would taste."

John smiled. "I hear you. But you've gone a month now. After three months, you'll have a solid head-start on it."

BJ returned the smile and released John's arm. "I hope so. Listen, John," he hesitated, "Don't tell anybody about this all right? I haven't even told Doctor Regen about it yet. It's just not something I can really talk about, you know?"

John nodded. “It’s in the vault. What do you say we head back to the compound?”

“Okay,” BJ agreed. “And, John...thanks. Really.”

John nodded again and began jogging back down the same, almost indiscernible trail they had come in on. BJ matched his pace.

They had traveled a quarter mile when they heard the screams.

CHAPTER 24

TERI HAD YET TO CALM DOWN half an hour after it happened. She alternated between screaming at those standing around her and sobbing into Maude's shoulder. At the moment, she was screaming.

"I hate this fucking place! How are we supposed to live like this?" Tears streaked down her red face. Her pants were still covered in dirt from her fall, and her hands bore small cuts. Her tirade was deafening in the dining hall.

"Calm down, Teri. You're okay," Doctor Regen attempted to soothe the young woman, but the task was formidable. "You're not hurt."

Teri sat on a folding chair next to Maude, her thin frame exaggerated against Maude's larger body. Teri leaned against her once more, and Maude put an arm around her, trying to help calm the hysterical girl.

John turned from the distraught woman to speak to Chance. "So what happened?"

Denise didn't let Chance answer. "He saved her. I mean, we were jogging on the trail, and we heard these screams, so he left the trail and took off toward them. And Chance can really run fast." Chance blushed as Denise unfolded the story. "Anyway, he gets to Teri and these coyotes are all around her. So he starts yelling and throwing rocks at them, and they run away. I mean, they're gone before I even get there."

Chance offered a humble grin. "That's pretty much what happened. But it didn't take much to scare those coyotes away. They were pretty skittish. I think they just started chasing Teri because she was alone, and then when she fell down..."

"Teri, why were you running by yourself?" The question came from Doctor Regen. Her tone was no longer soothing.

Teri raised her head from Maude's shoulder, leaving the gray fabric of Maude's shirt dark with tears. "I wasn't," Teri stammered. "I mean, I thought it was okay to run by ourselves as long as we stayed on the trail."

"Denise and Chance said you weren't on the trail," Doctor Regen pressed. Chance looked down at his shoes, embarrassed.

"So I wandered off the fucking trail, so what?" The tears renewed as she defended herself. "So what if I got off the trail? I hate it here! This place sucks! I want to go home." Teri sank back into Maude's shoulder.

Doctor Regen nodded. At least the girl wasn't throwing things anymore. "We'll discuss it this afternoon, Teri. In the meantime, no one is to leave the compound for the rest of the day." She gave a harsh look to the rest of the group, all of whom were in attendance. Even Vernon had come to witness the show.

"Our group meeting will begin in one hour," Doctor Regen said as she walked out the front door of the dining hall.

John glanced at Sarah, who was staring at Teri, a mixture of pity and sympathy in her eyes. He would later wonder if it had been Teri's outburst that sparked Doctor Regen's divisive comments in his and Sarah's private session that afternoon. After all, why else would she have chosen that day to break them apart?

CHAPTER 25

WALKER BARKED FROM THE BACK of the pickup truck as it came to a stop in front of Mercer's Grocery and Feed Supply. Cutter Valentine emerged from the driver's door and reached into the bed of the truck to scratch the mutt behind his ears. He lifted the handle on the tailgate and let it drop into place as Walker jumped out. The dog winced and let out a soft cry as his front paws hit the dirt of the parking lot.

Cutter shook his head. "You stay by the truck. I'll ask Red about it. Be back in a minute."

Red Mercer was stacking fifty-pound bags of cattle feed when Cutter found him at the back of the store. Although he stood about the same height as Cutter, Red probably outweighed him by a hundred pounds. Red had a gigantic stomach that distended the front of his overalls, but he also had solid arms, the result of years of this sort of labor. An ancient green cap with an almost-worn-off "Skoal" logo covered his hair, and bits of grain and dust stood out in his bright red beard. Cutter liked him a lot.

"What do you say, Red?"

"As little as possible," Red said as he looked up from the growing mountain of feed sacks. "Best way to keep out of trouble, Sheriff."

Cutter smiled. So word had gotten out. "Yeah, well, keep that 'sheriff' business to a minimum, will you? I'm just doing Cal a favor."

Red nodded. "So the mayor himself rode out to see you, huh? Important man." He dropped the bag of seed in place and held out his hand to Cutter.

Cutter's hand was enveloped in Red's meaty paw for a hearty handshake.

"Good to hear it anyway, Cutter," Red smiled. "Best to get back on the horse."

Cutter's smile faded. "What do you mean?"

Red noticed the change in expression. "Aw hell, Cutter, I didn't mean to get personal or nothing. It's none of my danged business, that's why I never said anything before. But just so you know, I think you did the right thing."

Cutter pinched the bridge of his nose between his thumb and forefinger, an attempt to abate the onset of a headache. Damn it all to hell.

"Cal?" He asked.

Red shook his head and grinned. "Nope. Come on, Cutter, this is the twenty-first century. I've got me an Apple computer in the office. Pretty thing. It's shiny. Internet ready and all that shit. Use it to keep my records for the store and to read the news." Red's eyebrows arched conspiratorially. "And I look at some girlie pictures on occasion, too. But don't go telling my wife."

Cutter allowed himself a small smile but continued to rub the bridge of his nose. "I just didn't expect..." he began. "Dammit, Red, I came out here to get away from it. That's all."

Red nodded. "You *are* away from it. This ain't Dallas and it's not Fort Worth. Folks out here are your friends, if you want them to be."

Cutter pushed his hands into his pockets. He liked Red, but this wasn't a conversation he wanted to have. Especially since the big man could be right. Maybe he couldn't run from it after all.

"So what'd you come in here for?" Red broke Cutter's introspective. "I sold you enough lumber and fence to last you plenty last time. Least I thought I did."

"No. I just came in to get some groceries and ask you a question. Last time I was in, did I hear you say you delivered a calf at the Hancock's ranch?"

Red hooked his thumbs into his overalls and nodded. "Yep. A baby girl. About seventy pounds. Momma and daughter are doing fine." He grinned.

"So you do some vet work then?"

Red arched one eyebrow. "Cutter, do you see any diplomas on my wall?" he asked, pointing to the dirty wall of the storeroom.

Cutter shook his head. All he saw were some screwdrivers and wrenches hanging up and a "Snap-On Tools" calendar where Miss April was proudly displaying a fine looking ratchet set.

"Well, since there are no diplomas on my wall," Red continued, "that would make it illegal for me practice veterinary medicine in the great state of New Mexico. But since we don't have any vet to speak of in these parts, people do tend to ask my advice from time to time."

Cutter grinned. "Well, suppose I was to ask you some advice about my dog. Do you think you could give us a hand?"

"Walker? What's wrong with him?"

Cutter and Red began to walk through the store toward the parking lot, where Walker lay in the shade of the porch.

"He's favoring his right front paw, and he keeps trying to bite at something in it. I thought a tick might have gotten between his toes, but I can't find anything."

Red nodded, and detoured toward his office at the side of the store. "I'll bet you dollars to donuts he got a bit of cactus stuck up in there and buried it beneath the skin. I see it all the time. It's tough to spot because once the needle breaks off the fur conceals it. Let me grab some tweezers and antibiotic cream in case it's infected."

He returned a minute later with a black case full of professional grade medical instruments and a white tube of cream. When Cutter raised his eyebrow in question, Red merely smiled. "What can I say? People around these parts have been asking for my advice on their animals since I flunked out of Texas A&M's College of Veterinary Medicine twenty years ago. Guess I learned more than they thought."

Cutter steered the truck down the dirt road. He was almost home. He was grateful Red was able to get the cactus needle out of Walker's foot (and the dog had licked Red right across his beard in appreciation), but he was still bothered by Red's knowledge of his past. If everyone in town knew about him, what was the point of staying here?

A dry breeze gusted through the open windows of the truck as Cutter observed his surroundings. The afternoon sun shone on the desert landscape. Rocks. Cactus. Brush. Dirt. It wasn't much to look at, but one thing was certain, as far as the eye could see, there were no people.

No matter what the people in town knew about him, they weren't here. Out here, it was just him and Walker and a few head of cattle. And that was how it needed to be.

For now.

CHAPTER 26

JOHN MICHAELS was furious. Everything had been going so well. He had been trying so hard. And now, after all their work, he and Sarah had taken a giant step backwards. Thank you, Doctor Regen.

Why would she do something like that? She was a doctor. You would think her first responsibility would be to help people. Not this.

John clenched his fist and punched the metal door of his locker in the barracks. The sound of the impact filled the cement room, as did the string of swear words John shouted as he pulled his injured hand back and clutched it into his crotch, bending forward at the waist and marveling at his own stupidity. He hopped beside the bunk bed, trying to stomp the pain away from his knuckles and into the gray concrete floor.

He was grateful that at least no one was present to witness the scene. BJ was in the midst of his own private session with Doctor Regen, and Chance had been invited by Denise to assist in the garden work with her.

John inspected his hand in the illumination provided by the skylight. His knuckles were bright red, but when he flexed his fingers, nothing appeared to be broken. But there would be bruises. John glanced at Vernon's empty bunk. Hitting him would have hurt a lot less than the locker. It would have felt better, too.

But the vermin was in the garden with Chance and Denise. And Sarah. John wondered what she was thinking about right now. Did she regret what happened? Did she question Doctor Regen's agenda in the least?

John walked into the bathroom and thrust his hand into the sink, holding it beneath the faucet, letting the cold water sooth his swelling knuckles.

Who was he kidding? Doctor Regen may have set it up, but he walked right into it. He should have known better.

He leaned forward and rested his head on the front of one of the shelves above the sink, a space normally occupied by a mirror or medicine cabinet. John realized he hadn't seen his own reflection in weeks. Odd. He hadn't really missed it.

And it was all part of the great and mighty program.

Society says we have to look good. Society tells us to worry and fret about our appearance. Society tells us happiness will result if we wear the right make-up and perfume. Let it go. Let go of society's rules and focus on yourself, the inner you.

John dipped his face toward the sink and splashed cold water onto his cheeks. The program and its tenets. *Halle-fucking-lujah.*

Did the program include manipulating you into a fight with the one person you truly care about? Did the program involve rubbing salt into old wounds? Why did she have to ask about his feelings toward Sarah's parents?

It was his fault. He should have lied. They had this same fight the week after the accident, after they had lost their daughter. It had been the aftershocks of that argument that had eventually laid waste to the remnants of their relationship. Yet for some reason, John thought he could be honest about it in the therapy sessions.

But why did Doctor Regen have to bring it up in the first place? He thought they had progressed beyond the accident. For the entire first month of the program, their private sessions had been focused upon the present. What mattered *now*. Not searching for blame in the past.

But today, thanks to Doctor Regen's timely questioning, the same fight had ignited, and this time it ended with Sarah's whispered words, the statement that had spun John into a quiet fury in the therapy room in the dining hall, and into a loud rage in the barracks fifteen minutes later.

"I think maybe we should have separate private sessions from now on."

And just like that, he and Sarah were separated. They already slept in different buildings. They ran with different groups. They worked on different chores. But at least John knew that every day, he and Sarah were committed to an hour together with Doctor Regen. They could steal time for themselves every now and then during the day, but there was always that hour that was *their* time. Their time to work toward a common goal. Their time to heal.

And now it was gone.

John turned off the water and left the bathroom. He stopped in front of the locker. There was a substantial dent in the center of the door.

Hooray for the program, he thought. *I probably couldn't have done that before.*

He decided to lie down. There was nothing outside but heat. At least the air-conditioning was keeping the barracks cool. He needed time to gather his thoughts. He needed to figure out how to make it work.

It was pure chance that John decided to stay in the barracks.

If he had walked outside at that exact moment, he would have seen Marcus Kane opening the door to the women's quarters and walking inside.

CHAPTER 27

TERI LAY ON HER BED in the women's barracks. She was on the bottom bunk with her knees pulled to her chest. She heard the door open and close, but she continued facing the concrete wall. She didn't want to talk to anyone. Footsteps approached and the bed across from hers creaked under the weight of her visitor.

"I understand you had rough day." Marcus Kane's deep voice cut through the stillness of the room. Teri startled at the sound. She turned for just a moment, long enough to see him sitting, his massive frame too large for the space between the bottom and top bunk so he was leaning forward with his arms resting on his knees.

She rolled back to again face the wall. Her first impulse was to tell him to leave her alone, but she couldn't bring herself to say it. Not to him. She wasn't sure if it was fear or something else.

"I had a very rough day," she said. There were no more tears. There hadn't been for a few hours. She had reached a new resolution. She knew what she wanted. And it was a *good* thing Marcus Kane was here. She could just tell him.

"I want to go home. I don't like it here anymore." Her voice was soft. A child asking a parent for a favor.

Kane made a noise that sounded like a woodpecker striking a tree. Three short clicks of the tongue. It was a chastising sound. Teri used to hear it from her teachers all the time.

"Teri, Teri. You don't want to leave," he said.

"Yes, I do," she replied. She held her pillow tightly.

"Teri. Look at me." His voice was more forceful now. She rolled over and complied, the pillow clutched beneath her chin.

"There's nothing for you out there. Nothing," he said. "That's why you're here. Out there was death. Here is life."

"There are coyotes here. They almost attacked me today. I could have been killed."

"Teri, what did Doctor Regen tell you about my role in this compound on that first day?"

Teri strained to remember.

"Come on, what was it?"

"That...that you would teach us about the desert. That you would protect us." Her voice trailed off, not sure if this was the answer he was looking for.

"That's right. I'm here to protect you, Teri. And I will protect you, but only if you stay. I can't protect you if you leave. Do you understand?"

Teri nodded into her pillow. "But I don't like it here. I don't."

This time Kane nodded. There was sympathy in his eyes. "You know, the whole point of the program is to find happiness. Are you saying you're not finding happiness here, Teri?"

She nodded again.

"That's bad. I *want* you to find happiness here, Teri. I want you to be able to be honest with me. I want you to know this is your home. I want you to be able to tell me exactly what it is that would make you happy."

His tone was authoritative, but soft, soothing. Teri realized she hadn't blinked while she was staring into his eyes.

"Tell me, Teri. What's the one thing you *really* want to do?"

Teri forced herself to blink, and this time the tears did come. No sobbing, just trails of moisture down her cheeks. She realized she needed to tell him. She needed to tell somebody.

"Come now, Teri. What do you want to do?"

"I want to get glassed." A whisper. The words left her mouth before she could stop them. And this time, more tears did come.

Kane placed his hand on her thin shoulder. His palm completely covered it. He was nodding sympathetically.

"That's what I thought." His other hand reached behind him and pulled a zip-lock baggie from his back pocket. He held the clear bag in front of Teri's wet eyes. She blinked away the tears. There were five small, red pills inside the bag.

She blinked again. She couldn't quite believe what she was seeing. It was so beautiful.

"Now listen closely, Teri. I'm going to give these to you right now." He shook the baggie and the red pills danced inside. "You're to keep them hidden. No one else is to know. Not even Doctor Regen. Do you understand?"

Teri nodded. Transfixed. So beautiful.

"You will stay here and participate in the program. You will do everything I say. And I will continue to provide you with these. Are we clear?"

Teri cocked her head to one side. She licked her lips.

"Teri, are we clear?" Kane lowered the bag and Teri's eyes returned to his. This time, she nodded.

"Tell me what you're going to do," he said.

Teri swallowed. Her throat was dry. "I'm going to hide the pills. No one will know about them. I swear."

Kane nodded. "What else?"

"I'm going to stay here. And I'll do whatever you tell me." She reached toward the baggie resting on Kane's leg, but her hand wavered. "Please," she whispered.

Kane handed her the baggie then extended his hand to her face. He held her chin between his thumb and forefinger and leaned in close to her. Teri could feel the heat of his breath on her forehead.

"One more thing," he said. "I want you to talk to Maude. I understand you got her upset this morning. Tell Maude that you're fine, and that she's fine. Tell Maude how happy you are here."

Teri nodded, her face hot in Kane's grip. "O-okay."

Kane released her chin and stood. He walked to the door, speaking as he went. “Oh Teri, things are going to work out just fine.”

CHAPTER 28

VERNON SET HIS TRAY on the counter in the kitchen and walked toward the front door of the dining hall. All part of the plan.

"I'm going for a walk." He spoke to no one in particular, but it was important to say. It was important for people to know he'd made a routine of being away from the compound after the evening meal. Out of sight, out of mind.

Once outside, he stood in front of the sundial, looking around. He put his hands in the pockets of his khaki pants. Just a guy with a full stomach, debating where to walk for his evening constitutional.

He counted to one hundred. No one emerged from the dining hall. It was usually at least five minutes before the first of the other program members walked outside. And by then, Vernon would no longer be in front of the sundial. Nope. He'd have already started on his evening stroll.

He walked past the men's barracks and proceeded about two hundred yards before beginning his circle. The brush was excellent concealment if you walked far enough out. And he could do that. He could walk quite a ways out and still see what he needed to see. Vernon had excellent vision.

He found his spot behind the low mesquite tree and sat cross-legged, his back against the trunk. From this vantage point, he could clearly see the door of the dining hall and a good portion of the courtyard, but he would be completely obscured by brush if someone were looking out from those areas.

Vernon couldn't believe how well everything was working out. All according to his calculations.

Because that was all it took. Calculations and time. Patience. Getting beaten up by that cop in LA had been the worst thing that had ever happened to him, and it wasn't going to happen again.

Not if he was careful. And not if he was patient.

And he had been patient. Oh, he had been so patient. And now, at last, everything was developing according to his plan. According to his calculations.

The door to the dining hall opened and a figure stepped out. Skinny. It was Teri. And she would be followed by Maude. Just like she was every night.

Teri would walk around the courtyard for about twenty minutes, until Michaels (Vernon couldn't bear to think of him as "John") and his two flunkies finished cleaning the kitchen. And once the guys finished, they would spend the remaining hour or so of dusk playing their stupid game. They would stand around like retards throwing rocks at the sundial and think they were enjoying themselves.

Bunch of assclowns.

But they didn't really concern Vernon. As long as they stayed in the courtyard, that was part of the plan, too.

The door opened again and Vernon watched Maude walk out, right on queue. The fat bag would follow Teri around for a while, at least until Teri offered whatever excuse it was that got her back in the dining hall and away from Maude. Then Tubbo would just sit outside, watching the men's game or staring into space.

Vernon grinned and ran his fingertips lightly through the dirt. He knew the routine so well. Maude was outside now. The guys would stay in the dining hall for at least another twenty minutes to finish their cleaning. And that meant...

Bingo.

The door to the dining hall opened outward once again as Sarah and Denise emerged. They were talking together and laughing. Well, Denise was laughing. Sarah had seemed a little put-off about something all afternoon. So had Michaels. They must have had a fight. At dinner, they had sat together away from the rest of the group. It was uncharacteristic for them. Must have been having a talk about something important. Whatever it was, they worked it out. Neither of them seemed happy about it, but both seemed in a better mood than when they walked in for dinner.

Of course, it didn't matter to Vernon either way. The two rich people could fight all they wanted. Neither of them concerned him. Well, the chick wasn't too bad looking, but she just wasn't really Vernon's type, not unless she lost some more weight. And even then, she was still too old.

Old wasn't any fun.

Besides, Sarah Michaels had complicated his plan. He had to adjust his calculations for her presence in the garden. But that was okay. These were the little setbacks that just made you try harder. Make sure you did it right.

Because if you can't do something right, you shouldn't do it at all.

And Vernon was doing it right. And it was working out so well.

He watched as Denise and Sarah walked from the dining hall straight to the women's barracks. No standing around and talking. No chatting with Maude or Teri. Straight to the barracks, just like they were supposed to.

CHAPTER 29

THE THING CROUCHED IN THE DARKNESS at the base of the cliff. Waiting.

The thing refused to think of itself as a man. Not tonight. Tonight he was beyond the constraints of humanity. He was far more than just a man.

He drew in a great breath of air, sniffing at the wind, searching for the scent. He detected nothing. Perhaps there was nothing there. Or perhaps his senses were not as sharp as they should be. Not yet.

His prey would arrive soon enough. The coyotes were stupid animals. Stupid and predictable. And tonight they would meet their death at the hands of a superior predator.

The thing tilted his head to one side, just far enough to stretch the corded sinew of muscle, but not far enough to pop his neck. Popping it would result in noise. And the noise could frighten his prey.

For the coyotes were cowards. Only immense hunger would drive them to attack a human. And attacking humans was something he could not permit.

The thing realized he was partly to blame for the attack. In a way, he had taught the animals that human flesh could be eaten. That humans were vulnerable. And the coyotes had learned their lesson too well.

A cloud passed overhead, blocking the three-quarters moon. It didn't matter. If the thing's nose was not acutely sensitive to the desert yet, his eyes and ears were more than adequate. The prey would enter in front of him. There was no other entry point. There was nothing behind him but the cliff-face and his rappelling rope. The thing had smiled when he tied the rope to the boulder before lowering himself over the sheer edge of the cliff and down the fifty feet to its base.

Rattlesnakes. He had told them there was a den of rattlesnakes.

The sheep were so gullible. So easy to frighten.

He relaxed his vision, peering into the dark. That's where they would come. Not from behind. Not from the cliff or the rope or the skeletal remains.

And the prey would come soon. This was where they had found their food so many nights before. On the full moon.

The thing glanced skyward as the cloud shifted once more, revealing the silver orb. Not full, not yet. And it would be two more cycles until the reckoning.

But the coyotes couldn't know that. All they could know is the cliff had provided food in the past. And the thing suspected the beasts routinely ventured to the cliff just to check. Just to see if perhaps tonight was the night.

And tonight they would find him. It shouldn't have had to come to this. But they never should have attacked one of his sheep.

Oh well.

The thing in the dark smiled.

CHAPTER 30

THE COYOTE HAD NO NAME, but he was as self-aware as any animal could be. He knew his place in the world. He was the runt. He was born the smallest of the pack, and he had never grown in size to match any of his brothers or sisters.

He had lived among his own kind his entire life. He had never made a kill on his own. While the coyote is by nature a scavenging breed, the runt lived the life of a parasite. Always last to the kill. Always forced to eat whatever remains his siblings deigned to leave of the carcass. He had lived that way since birth.

But he was not unintelligent. As the smallest of the pack, he had learned to pay close attention to his surroundings. He had learned to take careful heed of his senses. Otherwise, he would not have survived as long as he had.

Tonight, he was aware that something was wrong.

His two pack brothers were walking ahead. Hunger had driven them to immense courage earlier in the day. They had been bold enough to threaten one of the upright creatures. That was unheard of. The upright creatures could kill without moving. Earlier in his life, the coyote had seen a sibling drop in her tracks when an upright had made a loud noise. The noise hurt the runt's ears, and the noise had killed his sister.

Although communication was limited among their kind, it was an understanding that the upright creatures were to be avoided at all costs. But it had been weeks since the pack had eaten. Hunger drives desperation. And desperation drives courage. So they had advanced upon the upright earlier that day. It had been the smallest of those they had observed, the sickliest, and even the runt could taste the fear in the air as his siblings had approached it.

But then the other came. The arrival of another upright would surely signal more on the way so the three coyotes had retreated. They had gone back into hiding. Back out to search for rabbits or fallen cattle. They had found none.

So tonight, they had returned to the place. It was instinct. It was here they had found immense feasts before so it was natural to return, to hope for more bounty. Most nights, the base of the cliff held only the bones of previous meals. But tonight, there was something else.

Tonight, something was wrong.

There was a presence at the base of the cliff. A whiff of the air indicated an upright's scent, but there was something unusual about it.

The coyote whined, indicating his reluctance to his two pack brothers ahead, but the larger coyotes never even slowed. They were accustomed to the runt's timidity. They kept advancing, step by step, toward the thing in the dark.

The runt finally stopped. He knew what was wrong. He could tell not only by the scent, but by the manner of the creature his brothers were advancing upon. The thing at the base of the cliff may have been an upright, but it had no fear.

The fear from the smaller upright had been palpable earlier in the day. The scent of terror had been so thick, each of the three coyotes in the pack could taste it. But not this one. This upright, this *thing*, had no fear. And the thing knew they were coming.

The runt voiced another whine, louder. It was ignored. The larger coyotes were within ten feet of the crouching upright now. The runt cocked his head. There was something on one of the creature's paws. Two silver blades reflected the moonlight. This upright had claws.

The runt took a tentative step forward, torn between his hunger, his desire to help his brothers, and his own growing fear of the thing in the dark.

The larger coyotes were almost upon it now. Five feet. The thing still hadn't moved. It remained crouched. Ready.

The runt turned and ran. He ran back the way the three of them had come. He would spend the night hunting rabbits or looking for fallen cattle. He would not face the thing that had no fear. The thing with the claws.

He was a coward. But he was a runt. That was his nature.

And he would live.

CHAPTER 31

"MAN, I'VE SEEN A LOT OF SHIT in my day, but I think that takes the cake."

BJ was speaking in short bursts as he ran. His statement pretty much summed up what John was thinking as he and Chance jogged alongside him. The breeze in their faces was still cool, but the mornings were getting noticeably warmer as spring progressed toward summer. And each morning was bringing a new surprise.

Teri's encounter with the coyotes during the previous day's run had created some nervousness among the group. Enough anxiety that after drinking the green supplement beverage at dawn, no one left the compound. The group instead milled about the courtyard. Some stretched. Some jogged in place. But no one was leaving. Kane (who John now saw only during the morning supplement ritual) stood at the door of the dining hall with his massive arms crossed over his chest.

After a few minutes of silent observation, Kane spoke.

"Running is part of the program. Run."

John expected Teri to say something, but she remained silent. Chance instead ventured to speak. "It's just that, well, with what happened to Teri yesterday..." His sentence trailed off. Kane continued to lean on the doorframe, expressionless.

John took up where Chance left off and began to address the group. "Why don't we all run together today? We'll stick to the trail and—"

Kane took a step forward, interrupting John's idea. "That's not necessary." His voice was low and soft, as always. "You'll continue to run just as you have previously. The problem has been dealt with."

With that, Kane walked past the assembled members, through the courtyard, and into the doorway of his quarters. As the rest of the group stared after him, Teri began walking toward the opening of the main trail.

"Marcus said we should run like always," she said. Maude began to follow, then the rest.

They noticed streaks of crimson stained into the dirt as they walked, but it was at the entrance to the trail that they all realized what Kane meant when he said the problem had been "dealt with."

The two coyote heads had each been neatly severed at the base of the neck. One was laid on either side of the trail entrance. The dirt around the heads was stained a deep maroon in an uneven circle. Flies gathered in the wounds. John noticed one fly walking across the open, vacant eye of the coyote on the left. The animal's tongue drooped out of its mouth, the tip touching the blood-soaked earth.

John had been reluctant to leave Sarah after that, to go run with BJ and Chance, but their fight the previous day lingered, and she wanted to run with the women so John had not pressed the issue. He just let it go. That was becoming easier and easier.

Now, the three men were well into their morning run. They had taken the same barely discernable trail that John and BJ had used the previous day since they wanted to show Chance the stone writing. Adrenaline still coursed after the surprise of the coyote death display, and after looking at the writing for a few minutes (Chance didn't know what to make of it either), they elected to press on for another half mile before turning back.

The mostly pleasant buzz in John's head was constant. He had worked up a serious sweat, and all three of them were breathing hard, even Chance. At times, John could have sworn he could actually hear the buzzing in his ears. He felt good. The run felt good. But something wasn't quite right. Something besides the severed heads that had greeted each of them before breakfast. There was something else.

The discovery of the second writing interrupted his thoughts.

This clearing was larger than the first. Located beyond a slight bend in the trail, the writing was comprised of rocks similar in size to the first. It stood half in sunlight and half in the cool shade provided by the surrounding brush. The writing consisted of only one word.

REMEMBER.

CHAPTER 32

VERNON WATCHED through the myriad of mesquite thorns and leaves as the last glimpse of the sun dropped beneath the horizon. He had been stationed at his position for roughly five minutes. At least that was his best guess since Teri had just emerged from the dining hall. Right on schedule.

Vernon was so excited he could no longer sit still. He rose to his knees and began gently rocking back and forth. Just enough movement to calm himself, but not so much as to attract any attention from the courtyard.

Of course, there was no true concern about anyone in the courtyard seeing him. Teri was the only person out there right now, walking around the compound like she had the jitters, like she was waiting for a cab or something. Freak.

And when Maude came out, that wouldn't be a problem. She was old and stupid. Vernon was pretty sure her eyesight wasn't good enough to spot him. And it was all a moot point anyway because today had been laundry day for Sarah and Denise. And while washing the clothes was easy enough with the washing machine at the back of the dining hall, drying the clothes was done the old-fashioned way. In fact, it was after that first week, when the women began hanging the laundry on the clothesline behind their barracks, that Vernon fully realized his vision. That was when he really began making his calculations.

And now it was working out so well.

The laundry hung on lines that would make him virtually invisible from the courtyard. Between the scattered brush on the ground and the shirts and pants flapping in the breeze, no one could possibly notice him.

And there were other benefits to laundry day.

Vernon raised the light gray panties to his face once again and inhaled deeply. All he could smell was detergent. But he knew, he knew, that somewhere in that fabric were traces of Denise. He inhaled again, harder. Hard enough he could have released his grip and the panties would have clung to his face by virtue of the suction alone.

She was there.

Vernon manipulated the underwear in his hands until he found the sweet spot, the inside of the fabric that rested between Denise's legs. So perfect. Just a little hourglass of cotton sewn into the panties. So beautiful.

Vernon raised the panties to his mouth and licked his tongue from the front of the hourglass to the back. It tasted like cotton. But that didn't matter. He would replace the underwear on the line before he left. Leave them right where he found them. And when Denise wore the panties later on, she would wear a little part of Vernon, too.

He smiled.

The door to the dining hall opened again and fat Maude walked out. She headed straight for Teri. Poor skinny bitch. What had she done to deserve Maude?

Vernon glanced at the place in the sky where the sun used to be. It would still be light for another half hour or so, but it was approaching full dusk. He wished he had a watch, something with which to measure his progress, but his watch was sitting in a safe deposit box in a Sonora bank. When Doctor Regen told them they could each take one personal possession into the program, there was no way Vernon was going to hang on to a stupid digital Casio. He had something much better.

But watch or no watch, there was one thing about which Vernon was certain—today was the latest the group had ever eaten dinner.

All according to his calculations.

In a way, the fact that Sarah had taken such an interest in the garden (and in being friends with Denise) had worked to Vernon's advantage. Sure, he didn't get to spend the kind of quality time alone with Denise he had anticipated when Kane allowed him to assign jobs that first day. But this was going to be so much better. Talk about serious quality time.

The seeds of the desert weeds he had been scattering and watering while everyone else was running were finally beginning to take hold. Denise and Sarah (and Vernon, for appearance's sake) were forced to spend more and more time in the garden pulling weeds and trying to keep the growth from spreading. That meant longer hours. More time in the sun, sweating. That also meant the dinner hour was getting pushed back further and further (thanks to the cook, Sarah, spending her time in the garden). It was all so complex and so perfect.

The door to the dining hall opened again. Vernon's rocking quickened. Denise and Sarah walked out the door. Vernon vaguely realized he was rubbing his erection through the material of his khaki pants.

Please let tonight be the night, he thought. *It's been such a long month.*

Denise and Sarah walked straight to the women's barracks, just like they were supposed to. Vernon shifted his sights. The back of the women's quarters was directly in front of him. All clear.

He had worked so hard, planned everything so well. The pallets in the back of the building. He had moved one every other day, just to make sure no one ever noticed the difference. That was the genius of it all. His calculations were subtle.

Now, everything was ready, he just needed that one last thing. That one last piece of the puzzle for everything to be perfect.

He stared at the roof of the women's barracks. The giant swamp cooler air-conditioning unit stood out in a dark profile against the sky. And Vernon knew the rear skylight of the dorm sat just this side of it. Just like in the men's barracks.

One last piece of the puzzle.

It was getting dark. Darker than it had ever been when they finished dinner. Later than it had ever been. All thanks to Vernon. All thanks to the plan.

The skylight turned stark yellow as the glow of the electric lights inside the dorm were flicked on. Perfect. Vernon licked his lips and smiled.

If you can't do something right, don't do it at all.

CHAPTER 33

JOHN MICHAELS lay in bed, hearing only the breathing and occasional snores of his bunkmates. During his time with the program, John's nights had always begun like this, but eventually, the night would be pierced by the howl of the coyotes. Tonight was different. Even though John estimated he had lain awake for at least two hours, there was no howling. Nor would there be. John's fellow insomniacs were dead. There would be no more singing to the traveling moon. There would be no more hunting. There would only be flies marching across dead eyes.

The execution of the coyotes haunted John. The visage of the animals' severed heads now replaced the spider-killing incident as the screensaver on John's mental computer. As he tried to shut down the activity of his brain, as he tried to force himself into slumber, the picture of the coyote heads at the trail entrance continued to play. It was primal. Something straight out of *Lord of the Flies*.

But is that what we're coming to?

John tried to redirect his thoughts. He needed sleep. And sleep had been coming easier in the last few weeks. Maybe it was the running. Maybe it was the "healing effects" of the program. Whatever it was, he had found it was taking less and less time to achieve slumber each night. Granted, that still meant John was awake two or three hours later than his roommates, but that also meant he was going to sleep closer to midnight or one in the morning. Practically a personal record.

But the sleep wasn't coming tonight. Try as he might to shut down the mental grinding of the gears, he could not. There was too much. Too much gnawing at him. The death of the coyotes had triggered it.

It wasn't so much that John hated to see them die. He wasn't sentimental enough to imagine they had formed a special bond just because he had listened to their nightly performances for the past month. The coyotes had attacked Teri, and it was better the problem be solved than risk the safety of the rest of the group. In the grand scheme of importance, a coyote's life (even if it did provide John a musical distraction) was nowhere near the value of a human life.

No, what bothered John was something else. Something that had begun to trouble him during the run. The discovery of the second writing had interrupted his thoughts on the matter, but lying in bed, John realized the writing also provided the answer.

REMEMBER.

The writing itself was a mystery. Whereas, "NO DRINK" was a reasonable resolution to record in the wilderness as part of the program, "REMEMBER" didn't make much sense. In fact, it essentially refuted one of the main premises of the program—to concentrate on the present and forget the past. That was one of the few tenets of the program John had wholly embraced. He was tired of remembering. He loved his baby girl so much, but the memory of holding Chloe in that ICU ward had devastated him for too long. He wanted to put some distance there. To forget for the time being, so perhaps he could remember later without the pain.

Still, there had not yet been any mention of the writings by Doctor Regen so John suspected that particular activity was a later part of the program. It was why John mentioned to BJ and Chance that maybe they shouldn't mention their discovery to anyone else. If it was part of the later stages of the program, they probably weren't supposed to know about it yet. BJ and Chance had agreed, and John had been impressed with himself. Despite his fight with Sarah, he was still doing his best to make the program work.

REMEMBER.

A logical program resolution or not, the writing did spark John's realization of what disturbed him that morning. He relaxed his mind and fanned the spark, letting his memory guide him to the answer.

Strangely enough, he remembered more dead animals. He remembered driving down a country road late one Saturday night. He and Sarah had attended a football game while they were still in college. John hadn't cared much for football, but Sarah had a lot of friends back then and they were all attending. It was an "away" game at the stadium of the rival university. The game had been fun for Sarah and tolerable for John, and it was well after dark when they began the trek back to the city.

The road was deserted as they drove with the exception of a pair of tail lights from a vehicle a mile in front of them. Occasionally, the red lights would meander to the right or left. The driver of the vehicle had probably been drinking.

But it was when the brake lights suddenly flared and the red streaks swerved violently to the left and then back into the lane that John knew there was a problem. He slowed even though the other vehicle was still at least half a mile in front of them. The other car didn't stop. The brake lights extinguished, replaced by the normal running lights, and the vehicle continued on its way.

Moments later, when John and Sarah came upon the cat in the road, it was obvious what had happened. Sarah begged John to stop, and he did, even though he knew it would be bad. The cat was near the center stripe in the road. The back half of its body had been crushed, and the animal was attempting to drag itself forward using its front paws.

Sarah got out of the vehicle, kneeled in front of the cat and reached her hand down to touch it, to offer it comfort, when John yelled for her to stop. He told her the animal was dying, and it might bite her out of fear. But she had done it anyway. John had been wrong. The cat didn't try to bite her. It didn't try to scratch her. It just looked up at her with confused eyes.

And Sarah stayed there. For fifteen minutes she sat in the middle of the road as John stayed alert for approaching traffic. None came. She knew it was hopeless. John knew it was hopeless. And the cat knew it was hopeless. So for fifteen minutes, Sarah sat on the cold pavement, stroking the cat's head and speaking softly to it.

When the cat finally stopped breathing, she had John carry it to the side of the road and lay it in a soft patch of grass. She cried for the remainder of the drive back to the city. For almost an hour she had cried. Quietly. And John hadn't known what to say.

Sarah had always been like that. She had a gentle soul, and she couldn't bear to see an animal suffer.

So why didn't Sarah look upset in the slightest when she saw the severed coyote heads at the entrance to the trail?

Or Denise? Or Teri? Or Maude? Or BJ or Chance? Why weren't any of them upset that two animals had been violently slaughtered the night before?

The forefront of John's mind offered the obvious answer—*because the coyotes had attacked Teri.* John had already acknowledged this to himself and surely everyone else in the group could see things with that logic. A human life was worth a hundred coyotes.

But that wasn't it. Not entirely. That didn't explain why Sarah wouldn't instinctively be horrified at seeing decapitated animal heads.

And why were the heads left out there anyway? Why the *Lord of the Flies* act?

Kane could just as easily have informed the group he had eliminated the coyotes so the program members could run in peace. He could have explained he was looking out for their safety. He could have done so many things besides leaving the remains of his kill at the trail with the message that the problem had been "dealt with".

John believed he knew the answer to that as well. Even if he refused to acknowledge it in the daytime, the brutal honesty that accompanied his insomnia forced John to recognize why Kane had elected to show the group what had happened to the coyotes rather than just telling them. A picture is worth a thousand words. And Kane had a story to tell.

The story was simple—actions carry consequences. The coyotes had attacked Teri. Simply put, they had fucked with the program. And the coyotes had reaped the consequences of those actions.

John pulled the covers up to his chin. He was cold. He never thought you could be so cold in the desert, but he was shivering.

He lay there for another hour. Sleep beyond his grasp. He dwelled on the lack of reaction of the group towards the incident that morning. Had everyone immersed themselves so fully into the program that their former values were completely forgotten?

He thought of his wife, and why the resentment of their fight the previous day continued to linger. Why had Doctor Regen ever asked those questions in the first place?

He considered the stone writings. What was it about them that continued to bother him so much?

And as he lay there, searching for answers he couldn't be sure even existed, he heard it. It was soft, mournful, but it was there. The howl of a single coyote. One was still out there. Its cry was not as powerful as the others John had heard, but a coyote still roamed the desert night.

In that cry, like the gentle singing of a mother's lullaby, John began to drift off. And in that cry, a single thought ran through John's mind as slumber stole over him.

It had lived. Something had fucked with the program and lived.

CHAPTER 34

THE NIGHTMARE was upon Walker's master once again. From his place on the back porch, the dog let out a howl that blended with the cry of the lone coyote miles away. The effect was eerie, but not enough to awaken Cutter Valentine.

Cutter writhed in bed, sweating despite the coolness of the room and despite having kicked off the last of the sheets and blankets at the onset of the dream. He wanted to wake up, wanted to find himself lying in his bedroom in the small ranch house, but he knew he would not. Not tonight. Tonight, he would face the demon again. Like it or not.

In the confines of the dream, Cutter heard Hector's whisper in the hallway of the rat-infested Fort Worth warehouse.

"We need to go back out to the truck and call for back-up. Then we can search the rest of the offices."

But Cutter knew then just as he knew now—searching the other warehouse offices was pointless. The evil for which they had spent the past three months searching was right behind the door. The plain wooden door right in front of them. The door that the DFW police departments, the FBI, and thousands of local volunteer task forces had been searching for as well. The Texas Rangers had found it. And Cutter wasn't about to walk away from it.

Cutter could hear his own voice in the dream. A brusque and urgent whisper.

"If he knows we're here, then there's no telling what he'll do. We've got to take him down now."

Cutter shook his head in his sleep, trying to communicate with his dream self. *Don't do it. Don't open that door.* But he knew they would. He saw Hector cross himself and watched his partner raise his boot.

Cutter's gun rose in front of his face in the dream. He was in the ready position. The same position he had learned more than thirty years earlier, long before he became known as "Cutter" to a group of new recruits he helped train later. He had learned so much over the years but not a single thing that would help him deal with what he was about to see. Cutter groaned in bed, loud enough for Walker to hear. The dog scratched at the door, leaving marks in the wood from his claws.

Hector's foot smashed into the black door.

Cutter angled his body as the frame splintered and the door flew open. He took three steps into the room and stepped to the side, gun lowered into position and swinging back and forth as he assessed the situation.

It would haunt him for the rest of his life.

The thin man sat in the middle of the room. The cult leader. The one they called The Baptist. He had a habit of selecting his prey from the playgrounds of Baptist churches and then using a unique and terrifying method of water torture to indoctrinate the children into his cult. After a few weeks, he became their master. Their new god.

Now, The Baptist sat on his knees on the bare floor of the decaying office. He was completely naked and seemed to be lost in a world of his own, staring at a spot on the floor two feet in front of him.

The Baptist's flock lay scattered in a semi-circle around him. Fourteen children. All nude. Some piled on top of one another. And the blood.

Oh mercy, the blood.

Hector bolted into the room, shotgun at the ready. His eyes grew wide at the carnage contained within the gray plaster walls. One hand came off the barrel of the gun and made the crossing motions once again.

"Madre de Dios," Hector whispered, his voice betraying the nausea creeping into his body.

Cutter had not moved. His .357 remained trained on the forehead of The Baptist. Only his eyes divulged the revulsion and rage at the scene in front of him.

One man had done this. To the children. And Cutter had been too late to save them.

The Baptist appeared to become aware of the Rangers' presence within the room. He raised his head to face Cutter. He cocked his head and straightened his back. The action was enough to cause his erect penis to sway back and forth. A few drops of blood splattered onto the floor. The rest remained coated on his loathsome member.

Movement!

Cutter's eyes flashed beyond the thin man in the center of the room. One of the kids had moved. She looked to be an older child, in her early teens. A survivor. A small and pained moan escaped her lips. She shifted her body and raised her hand a few inches before it dropped back to the floor.

The Baptist slowly moved his head to peer over his shoulder, following Cutter's gaze. He remained on his knees. Statuesque in the midst of his handiwork.

Then, he turned his countenance back to Cutter. There was a deadness in those eyes. Cutter had seen it on the faces of drug addicts deep in the spell of heroin. People who knew the world around them, who understood their own actions, but could care less about either. The Baptist knew it was over. He knew, and he wanted Cutter to see his handiwork. To see his sacrificed flock.

Cutter stood unmoving. Sick to his stomach at the carnage around him. Sick to his soul at the revolting beast that knelt before him, so proud of the carnage he had wrought.

The Baptist smiled.

The boom of Cutter's .357 was deafening in the enclosed quarters. An opening the size of a quarter appeared in The Baptist's forehead, and a hole the size of a grapefruit blew out the back of his skull. Gray matter and more blood spattered onto the children behind the cult leader.

The Baptist's smile transformed into a slack-jawed expression of confusion, but the eyes remained the same. Dead. He slumped forward and cracked his emptied skull onto the dusty floor.

Cutter's gun was still raised, smoke rising in small blue tendrils from the barrel. For a long moment, he didn't move. He simply stared at the monster that lay on the floor in front of him.

Hector was already in action. He crossed the room to the far corner and picked up the long, curved dagger the demon had obviously used on his victims. Blood still coated the blade just as it had coated the killer's engorged penis.

Hector kneeled in front of the dead man and placed the dagger into his hand, curling The Baptist's fingers around the ornate handle. When Hector stood, he wiped his hand on his pants, as if absent-mindedly attempting to rid his palm of whatever evil it had just encountered.

Cutter lowered the gun and stared at his partner, his friend. He could not believe what was transpiring. Couldn't believe what he had just done.

"He came at you with the knife, amigo," Hector said. "I saw it. You had no choice, man."

Cutter shook his head, mouth agape, in shock at the events that had just transpired. "No, we can't do this. It's not right."

Hector moved to within a foot of his older partner and spoke directly into his face. "Look around you, man. This *isn't right. He came at you with the knife, and you shot him. There was nothing else you could do."*

Cutter again shook his head. "There's got to be another way."

Hector put his hand on Cutter's shoulder and looked into his eyes. "I tell you what. There's a little girl over there that's still alive. One little girl out of fourteen kids. Why don't we get her to the hospital, and if you think of another way in the meantime, you just let me know."

Cutter lowered his head. The blood from the demon's head had spread across the floor. It had reached the toe of Cutter's boot.

Walker's bark was loud enough to reach his master, who sat up in bed with a gasp. Cutter looked around him, confirming his surroundings as the bedroom of the ranch house. The clock read 2:15 AM. Walker continued to bark and scratch at the back door. Cutter decided to let him in.

He walked to the door and let his friend inside. Walker nuzzled his head against Cutter's chest as his master kneeled to pet him. The cool breeze from the back door chilled the sweat still standing on Cutter's shoulders and face.

How much longer?

He walked to the living room and sat on the sofa. Walker promptly sat on the floor at Cutter's feet. The dog knew better than to get on the furniture, although tonight, Cutter wouldn't have cared.

Cutter was still breathing hard from the nightmare, still fighting the image of The Baptist back into his subconscious. Back where it belonged.

What else could he do? How do you exorcise a demon of your own creation? How do you return to the man you once were?

The answer stunned him in its immediacy.

You become that man once again.

Like it or not, Cutter was a lawman. He had been for his entire life. He supposed he knew that, deep down inside, when Cal had offered him the position of sheriff. He had felt it a little stronger the night he accepted the job. But Cal wasn't looking for a real sheriff, just someone to put in the newspaper while Dwight kept the town in order.

Well, Cal was going to get more for his money. Cutter couldn't stay out here forever. Sooner or later, he would have to take his first step to become the man he once was. To become the man Maggie had married, and hopefully, the one she still waited for to return to her. The first step would be small. Like all first steps, it would be a baby step.

Cutter scratched Walker behind the ears. He only lacked about three weeks until he finished the remaining repairs on his fence line.

Three weeks. That wasn't so long, and it would give him time to prepare.

Three weeks and he would take that first step.

Three weeks and he would take an active role as Sheriff of Sonora Valley.

And maybe, just maybe, he could walk the path that would make him Cutter Valentine once again.

Part IV:
DESCENT

CHAPTER 35

IT WAS PURE COINCIDENCE that John Michaels ever saw the key. He spotted it a couple of hours prior to his hike with Chance—the hike in which they would find the arrowhead.

It felt like a very long time since the eternal van ride from Sonora that had brought the group to the program's compound, where the young man with the deformed baby-hand had left his driver's seat to help with the luggage.

It was about three weeks after the severed coyote heads had been placed at the entrance to the jogging trail. The heads had been removed sometime the following night, leaving only fading maroon circles in the dirt to mark their former presence.

It was the day before Denise disappeared, and at least two weeks before John realized she had been murdered. The nightmare with Vernon still lay in the future. And Marcus Kane was still seen only during the early morning hours, when the group drank their vitamin supplements. The spiritual awakenings had not yet begun.

John noticed the key during his private session with Doctor Regen after lunch. His therapy now took place early in the afternoon, following Sarah's personal session (both his wife and the good doctor felt it best to continue keeping the sessions separate for the time being). He and Sarah would pass in the doorway of the private therapy room in the dining hall, and she would offer him that same tentative smile every day. Those moments were awkward each time.

John was afraid he might be losing her. He always wondered what Doctor Regen had discussed with his wife in her session. Were those conversations responsible for him and Sarah slipping further apart? Or was the gradual separation a natural occurrence stemming from the trauma their relationship had endured? He began to wonder if there was any hope left, and he hated himself for even contemplating the question.

But facts are facts. Sarah was growing more distant every day. Each evening they spoke less and less. And every night, as John lay staring at the stars through the skylight, he wondered what was happening to them.

His private sessions with Doctor Regen had become his personal hell. He had never believed in therapy, had never bought into the idea behind psychiatry. He had always looked at the profession as a means for the strong-willed to extract money from the weak-minded under the ambiguous guise of medicine.

But John had set aside those prejudices for his wife. He had sworn to himself that he would try to make the program work. And he had. He had kept an open mind, and he had run every morning, just like he was supposed to. He had even slept in the bed next to a child molester for the past seven weeks. He had paid his dues, and yet, Sarah still seemed to be slipping away from him. So what was the point?

Doctor Regen would spend the afternoons asking him question after question. *What was his childhood like?* Lonely. *How did he feel when his sister left home?* Angry. *Did he ever feel out of place in the world?* Daily. *Did he feel at home here? Did he trust Doctor Regen?*

Everything seemed to come back to those last two questions. The good doctor was pushing the program for all it was worth, and for the most part, John felt the influence. He wasn't so stubborn that he couldn't recognize his own change in attitude, as well as the attitudes of those around him. The program was chipping away at him, and it wasn't entirely unwelcome. He noticed himself thinking less and less about the outside world.

Going into the program, he assumed that after the first month, he would be immensely homesick for the basic luxuries of life. Television.

Fast food. A comfortable bed. But he missed none of them. They were trappings of a life he had moved beyond.

If the program was about forgetting the pressures of life and focusing on yourself, it had worked in spades. Even his restless nights were becoming shorter and shorter. His mind was plagued with fewer thoughts, fewer worries.

There were no reminders in the barracks. No bills. No pictures of relatives. No small pink booties he had purchased as soon as they received the results of the second trimester sonogram. No worries or sadness at all.

And the ugliest truth, the one John had begun to hate himself for, was that he was not entirely upset that Sarah was distancing herself. He still loved her, he was sure of that much, at least, but if she was not willing to return his love, then perhaps the distance developing between them was for the best. Maybe the entire program was for the best.

John never revealed these thoughts to Doctor Regen during the private sessions, even though he could tell she was pushing for a personal revelation about those issues. But his thoughts on that particular matter belonged only to him. If it could be worked out, he and Sarah would work it out on their own. If the program could help, so be it.

It was in the middle of that day's private session that Lilith Regen accidentally dropped her pen. She had been jotting notes in John's file regarding his answers to the latest question—*did he blame himself for his father's abandonment?* She leaned down to retrieve the pen, and the key slipped out.

John had been gazing at the floor between them when the pen dropped (he didn't like looking at the doctor as she wrote in the file, it was awkward), and his eyes remained where they were when Doctor Regen leaned over to recover it.

John glimpsed cleavage revealed under the doctor's unbuttoned neckline. Though he didn't find the woman particularly attractive, the reflex of looking was as instinctive as drinking water when thirsty. As

Doctor Regen grasped the pen from the tiled floor, the key slipped from between her breasts, swinging toward the floor from the necklace she wore.

The key was silver, smaller than a house key. Although he thought nothing of it at the time, John would later recognize the key as belonging to a padlock—an identical key to the one Marcus Kane wore around his own chain and tucked into his black t-shirts (the bulge John had mistaken for dog-tags that first day).

John averted his eyes before Doctor Regen rose, tucked the key casually back inside her shirt, and then continued the session as if nothing had happened. Because really, nothing had. A pen had been dropped and retrieved. It certainly wasn't an earth-shattering event. It was nothing.

But John had seen the key. And later, he would remember.

CHAPTER 36

CUTTER VALENTINE gripped the steering wheel of his Chevy pickup. The engine had been off for almost a minute, but he remained in the truck. He glanced into the rearview mirror and his own blue-gray eyes stared back at him.

Come on. Take that first step.

Cutter opened the door and set his foot onto the dirt parking lot in front of the Sonora Sheriff's office.

When Cutter opened the front door to the building, a gust of cool air escaped the room and washed over him. It felt good. Stepping into the air-conditioned office wasn't so bad, even if it didn't feel quite right.

The room was occupied by only one person. A young man of about nineteen sat at the desk with his hands in his lap. The comics section of the *El Paso Times* was spread across the top of the desk.

"You must be Dwight."

The young man looked up at the sound. Cutter realized how quietly he must have opened the door to go unnoticed. Old habits die hard.

Dwight started to get up, and Cutter shook his head, walking to the desk.

"No, please, keep your seat," he said as he extended his hand over the top of the desk toward the deputy. "My name's Earl Valentine. Friends call me Cutter."

The young man's right hand emerged from beneath the desk to shake Cutter's. He had a firm grip. That was good.

"Deputy Dwight Owens. It's nice to meet you, sir. A lot of people call me Dewey." Dwight wore a sheepish grin as he introduced himself. Cutter could tell the kid was embarrassed to be caught reading the funnies.

"Do you like that?" Cutter asked.

"What?"

"Being called Dewey."

The grin grew a bit wider as he shook his head. "No, sir. Not really."

"Why don't we stick to Dwight then?"

Dwight's grin turned into a genuine smile, and he seemed to relax in his chair. His hand dropped back into his lap. "Yes, sir. That sounds fine. It really is a pleasure to meet you, Mr. Valentine...Sheriff. Uncle Cal said you wouldn't be coming in, that I should only call you if there was an emergency."

Cutter plopped himself into the wooden chair in front of the desk. He wasn't sure what he had expected, but this wasn't so bad at all. As far as first steps go.

"Well, I hadn't planned on it, Dwight. But I thought I might as well swing into town and at least see the place. Meet you. And by the way, please call me Cutter."

Dwight nodded. "Well, I'd show you around, but this is pretty much it. We've got the one holding cell right there." He nodded toward the tiny cell on the opposite side of the room. "And that's really all there is."

Cutter glanced around the office. It looked like a set off the old black and white Andy Griffith show. Not what he expected at all. And nothing like the Ranger offices in Garland that covered Dallas-Fort Worth.

"It's a nice place, Dwight. Looks like you keep it up well. I'll be honest, I wasn't sure I'd find you here. I noticed there wasn't a squad car out front."

"Yes, sir. The car needs a new transmission. Mr. Murphy's had it at his garage for about a month. He said he'd fix it when he had the chance. It's not a rush job since the town can't pay much. I'm just using my car in the meantime."

Cutter remembered seeing the lime green Ford Fiesta in the parking lot. It looked like the bastard child of a VW bug and a Yugo. Not exactly a rugged law enforcement vehicle, but he wasn't about to criticize.

"You mind if I ask you a personal question, Dwight?"

The young man shook his head.

"And I'm just asking because I'm curious. But your uncle seems awfully old to be, well, your uncle."

Dwight smiled as he interrupted Cutter's thought. "Yes, sir. I get that question a lot. Uncle Cal is my mother's brother. At least, he was before Mom died two years ago. You see, Uncle Cal told me he was a surprise for my grandparents. He was born when they were both still in high school. Anyway, times were tough on them. They couldn't afford more than one child so they didn't have another kid until Uncle Cal had already left home and was working in the oilfields. But he stayed close by and helped raise my mother."

The young man paused after mentioning his mother. "She used to talk about him all the time. When she passed on, he offered to take me in, let me finish up school here in Sonora. And when I graduated last year, he made me an official deputy so I could help Sheriff Albright. Unfortunately, it turned out to be a necessity a few months ago."

Cutter nodded. "Cal told me about Sheriff Albright's wife. I feel for them. Alzheimer's is a cruel disease."

"Yes, sir. I don't know her very well, but Mrs. Albright is a sweet lady. I hate it for her. I'm not sure when the sheriff will be back, the old sheriff, I mean, but we're awfully glad you agreed to help out. Oh, and as long as you're here..." Dwight scooted his chair back as he opened the middle desk drawer and retrieved something. He held it across the desk toward Cutter, clutching it in his right hand.

It was a badge.

Cutter took it from the young man. The badge was old and heavy. It was a traditional six-pointed star fashioned from polished iron rather than from the lightweight metal commonly used in the new badges. He glanced at the shield on Dwight's shirt. It was shiny and thin. A new badge for a new deputy, probably the first deputy a town the size of Sonora had ever had.

"I appreciate it, Dwight. But I don't need this. Like your uncle said, I don't plan on doing any more than being available for emergencies."

"Well, sir. Keep it anyway. That way, if you do need it, you'll have it. Oh and here's a spare key to the office here." Dwight pulled the key from the drawer and slid it across the desk.

Cutter smiled and put the heavy badge into his shirt pocket. The key went into his pants pocket.

"Mr. Valentine—" Dwight caught himself. "Cutter, can I ask you a personal question in return?"

Cutter nodded.

"Please don't think I'm being nosy, and if you don't want to answer you don't have to, but it's something I'd like to know—one lawman to another." Dwight raised one eyebrow. "Why'd you leave the Rangers? The jury acquitted you. You didn't have to retire."

Cutter sank in his chair and let out a sigh. Of course the kid knew. Everybody knew. In Sonora Valley, Cutter was as big a hit as Elvis.

He suddenly felt old. And the first step seemed a hell of a lot more difficult now than it had only a minute ago.

"Can I ask you a question, Dwight?" The deputy nodded in response. "Why'd you want to become a lawman?" He used Dwight's earlier nomenclature, but he was not mocking in any way. He was trying to make a point.

The young man seemed to consider the question carefully. "I don't know. I guess because I wanted to help people. I mean, there isn't much real crime out here. But I keep the kids safe at the school crosswalk. I check on the bank every day. Some nights I'll go check on the gas station just to let Mr. Johnson know someone's watching out for his place. It may not be much, but it means something. It means something to me."

Cutter nodded as Dwight spoke. "You became a deputy because you wanted to help people. You wanted them to know that as they slept at night, someone was out there keeping the bad guys away from them. You wanted them to trust you. You wanted them to know you were there to uphold the law."

Dwight's eyes grew larger as Cutter spoke, and he nodded enthusiastically. "Yes sir. That's exactly it."

"Well then," Cutter continued, "Imagine if one day you broke the law that you swore to uphold. What if you turned your back on the thing you had lived your entire life trying to protect? And what if you got caught? Would it matter if a jury told you it was okay, that it was justifiable? Would it matter that people said you did the right thing? Would it matter if your department completely exonerated you? Would any of those things change the fact that when it came right down to it, you violated the very principles upon which you had built your life?"

Cutter caught himself. He didn't realize he had been raising his voice, but the young man behind the desk had seemed to shrink in his seat as Cutter directed the questions to him. Cutter took a breath.

"I'm sorry, Dwight. I didn't mean to get off like that."

A tentative smile crossed the young man's face. "That's okay. I probably shouldn't have stuck my nose in it."

Cutter stood up. He had been in the office too long. He needed to get back to the ranch. Maybe work on fixing the pens. Something.

"It was nice meeting you, Dwight. Call me if you need anything."

"Cutter?" The deputy looked hesitant, hunched behind the desk. Cutter could tell the kid wanted to say something to make it better. "You did save the one girl, right? I remember reading that you saved a girl from that warehouse."

Cutter stopped at the front door. The girl. Of all the bad things that had happened, the girl was the worst.

"We took her to the hospital, and they saved her life. She was fourteen. Three days after they let her out of the ICU and moved her into a private room, her parents left to get some coffee. They thought she was asleep. When they got back, they found the note she left before she jumped out the window. It said, '*I'm going to join my love. I hope the Ranger burns in hell.*'"

Cutter adjusted his hat. The deputy didn't move. He sat there, eyes wide, hands still clutched in his lap beneath the desk, looking like he deeply regretted having asked the question.

"Don't worry about it, Dwight," he said. "Call me if you need anything."

Cutter opened the door and stepped into the welcome heat of the afternoon.

CHAPTER 37

"SO HOW DID you two meet?"

Chance voiced the question as he kicked a small rock off the edge of the low embankment. The two men had climbed about twenty feet so far.

"We were in college," John said. "I was studying in the library when I saw this beautiful girl walk past my table. I wouldn't have paid much attention to her—there were a lot of good looking girls in school—but she was reading a book on the Civil War and walked right into a bookshelf. Made a hell of a lot of racket."

John smiled at the memory, and Chance grinned in response.

"Civil War, huh?"

John braced himself with one hand as he stepped onto the next ridge. The men had ascended high enough they needed to be careful. A fall from this height might not kill you, but it would probably break a leg. And it was a long way to go for medical attention.

"Yeah. There was just something about her." John shook his head at the memory. "My mother was a history buff. She had a real thing for World War II. She had a bunch of recordings of Churchill's speeches. She used to play them to my sister and me when we were growing up."

John trailed off as he surveyed the view. The pitchfork rock formation loomed above them, and the compound spread in front of them. Not bad, but he suspected they could ascend one more plateau.

"Anyway, they say a man will often wind up marrying a woman like his own mother. I don't think Sarah is like my mother in very many ways, but the history connection is what started it. It was her sophomore year. She was having a hard time in a course on the history of the American West. I wanted to go out with her so I told her I had already taken the class and could help her if she wanted."

John paused. He hadn't thought about it in a long time. "Anyway, I bought a copy of the textbook and read the entire thing before that weekend. I failed an accounting test that Friday, but by the time our study session rolled around, I could at least pretend I knew something about it."

Chance lifted himself up onto the next set of flat rocks. They could make out the curved rooftops of the compound's Quonset huts clearly from here. They could even see the garden. Sarah was working out there now. So was Denise. Chance squinted into the light, and then glanced toward John.

"No kidding? You read an entire textbook in one week? For a girl?"

John grinned. "No kidding. But she was worth it. And the material was pretty interesting. Cowboys and Indians and all that kind of stuff. I read about train robberies and gunfights and the Texas Rangers. I used to love the Lone Ranger as a kid, so I thought that chapter was pretty neat."

Chance nodded as he bent over and picked up a small rock. John glanced upward toward the pitchfork. The triple rock formation appeared formidably tall when viewed from beside its base, but the climb had been easy. The base of the rock formation was a gradual series of plateaus, and Chance had assured John they could basically walk up it if they came at it from the right angle. John had agreed to give it a shot. BJ was another story. After his freefall from the building in Oklahoma City, he still had a thing about heights. Neither man had pushed him into coming.

But it didn't look like John or Chance would be ascending any further. The ridge was now almost a flat face. Straight up. There was no way to climb it safely without proper gear. Oh well.

"I used to watch the Lone Ranger on Saturday mornings growing up," Chance said. "I felt sorry for Tonto. He'd always go into town and get beat up by the bad guys." Chance threw the small rock into the distance beneath them. It landed near a cactus patch with a small puff of dust.

"Poor Tonto," John agreed. He began to pick up his own collection of small rocks to toss from the ledge—not the most intellectual of endeavors, but it was something to do—when he discovered the oddly shaped stone. John dropped the other rocks and focused on the unusual stone in his hands.

"I'll be damned," he muttered as he blew on the stone and rubbed his thumb over it, removing some of the packed dirt from its surface.

"Whatcha got?" Chance asked.

John held it between his thumb and forefinger and lifted it toward Chance, who furrowed his eyebrows in puzzlement.

"I don't get it. It's a rock."

John shook his head and rubbed his thumb harder on the rock, attempting to remove the compacted dirt. "No, look closer."

Chance did. The stone was oddly shaped, triangular and darker than the other rocks, but it still just looked like a rock. He shrugged his shoulders.

"It's an arrowhead, Chance. And it looks like it's fashioned from black onyx. This thing has probably been here at least a hundred years."

Chance reassessed the find. "Cool. I haven't noticed any of that black rock around before. I wonder how it got here." He seemed to ponder the question for a moment, and then shrugged it off, looking back to John. "So what are you going to do with it?"

"I don't know. I think I'll hang onto it, polish it up a bit."

Chance again squinted into the sunlight. John followed his sightline. Chance was looking at the garden. Denise and Sarah were kneeling on the ground near each other, pulling weeds and talking.

Chance's crush on Denise hadn't diminished. John smiled. He then noticed Chance's gaze shift. Something had caught his attention.

"Huh," Chance said. "That's weird."

"What's that?"

Chance pointed and spoke as John's eyes followed his finger toward the shed located behind the quarters of Kane and Doctor Regen. "The roof of the shed is sunken a couple of feet. There's a satellite dish on it that I never noticed before."

John cocked his head as he assessed it for himself. "You're right. There's no way you could see it from the ground, only from up here."

The thought reverberated in his mind. "Why would they lie about there not being any communication into or out of the compound?" John mumbled the question, speaking to himself, but Chance apparently heard it and shrugged.

"I don't know. I guess Mr. Kane likes to watch TV at night. I mean, he's not part of the program anyway." He shrugged again. "I guess it doesn't make any difference. I don't really miss it, do you?"

John was lost in his own world, staring at the roof of the shed in the distance. It took him a moment to respond. "No. I don't miss television. It just seems odd. That's all."

John held a hand to his forehead, further shading his eyes from the harsh sunlight even though he was wearing his sunglasses. He was straining to see something on the shed's roof.

"Chance, can you make out what that is next to the satellite dish? Is it blinking?"

"Yep, that blinking light is what caught my attention. What you see beside the dish," he said, speaking with authority, "Is an antenna for a XRT Satellite Phone. I used one a few times in Guam my second year in the Navy. They're pretty cool. You can use them anywhere on earth and get a signal. A lot better than a cell phone, but they're pretty expensive."

John absently nodded as he continued to focus his vision. "Why's it blinking?"

Chance started to throw rocks off the ledge again, his gaze returning to the garden and his thoughts most likely shifting back to Denise. "Blinking? Oh, someone must be making a call."

CHAPTER 38

LILITH REGEN poured the clear solution from the test tube into the beaker and swirled the contents. The mixture was in the proper proportions, but the color needed adjustment. She walked to the refrigeration unit and removed a vial of dark green liquid. She noticed Marcus was no longer watching her prepare the formula as he spoke on the phone. His concentration was elsewhere.

Kane was staring at his notes on the computer monitor as he conversed. The headset attached to his ear allowed freedom of movement in both hands so he could review the data on the screen as he answered the incoming questions. The call itself was being routed through half a dozen separate web-based centers. Free long distance was only one perk. The network system also allowed for different calling routes each time the contact was made. In theory, no authorities should be watching for these particular numbers, but caution was the watchword.

"Yes, we introduced R4 ten days ago and haven't noticed any negative results thus far. We're making the modifications for R5 now. We'll start the subjects on it in five days."

Lilith used the eyedropper to measure seven drops of the dark green coloring agent into the beaker. It dispersed into the solution as she swirled the beaker. R5 was almost the correct shade of lime.

"Yes, Subject-C is the only one with whom we've experienced a major malfunction. The doctor was ineffective with her."

Lilith stopped swirling as she turned her attention to the conversation. Kane was still focused on the computer monitor as he spoke.

"Negative, it wasn't the doctor's fault. An outside variable intervened. We reintroduced amphetamines to her three weeks ago. She's a lost cause."

Lilith began swirling the solution once more and held it up to the bright light provided by the lamp above the workbench. Perfect.

"Complications? Well, Subject-H is still proving a challenge, but that was expected. The rest of the group is progressing within standard parameters."

Lilith shook her head. *Subject-H.* She knew that Kane had not hinted at the true identity of Subject-H to the party on the other end of the phone, and the secrecy went beyond standard security measures. True identities were never divulged in electronic communication, and if all went well, hard copies of the files would not be transferred and inspected for another two months. Until then, Kane didn't want to admit that John Michaels was part of the program. Not until it was over, and he had proved his point.

"Affirmative. You'll have the night report at 1:00 AM Central."

Kane ended the call with a press of one finger and removed the headset. The calls always agitated him to a certain degree.

And agitated could be bad.

Lilith focused her attention on the R5 solution.

Kane stood and took a deep breath, clearing his mind of the conversation. Lilith felt him walk behind her and stop. She continued to hold the beaker to the light, inspecting the perfect shade of green.

His hands closed over her shoulders, gentle but powerful. Lilith's breath caught in her throat. The feeling never changed.

His deep voice whispered softly in her ear.

"Get undressed and meet me in the gym."

It suddenly felt too warm in the lab. She nodded and instinctively reached to the top button of her shirt.

The large hands released her shoulders. She watched his massive form walk down the basement hall and step through the door to the exercise room, removing his shirt as he went.

Lilith was sweating as she undid the first button.

It wasn't love, but it was Marcus Kane. And that was enough.

She undid the second button and walked down the hall.

CHAPTER 39

JOHN CLOSED THE DOOR to the small library in the dining hall and looked at Denise. She was sitting in one of the two folding chairs at the card table and unconsciously rubbing her hands over the long pink scars on her wrists. John had seen her doing that before in the group meetings, when the conversation turned to any subject that made her uncomfortable. The girl was nervous about something.

There were still sweat-stains on her shirt from the afternoon of work in the garden. John knew that she and Sarah normally both showered after dinner so they could each go straight to bed afterwards. But tonight, he had distinctly heard Denise tell his wife that she was going to stick around and talk with Chance after dinner. Later, she discreetly asked John if he would meet her in the library while BJ and Chance cleaned up after dinner. He wasn't quite sure what was going to come next.

"Do you want me to sit down?" he asked.

Denise nodded and pushed the other chair toward him as she began to speak. "I'm really sorry for catching you off-guard like this, but I've got a problem that I need to talk about with someone."

John's eyebrows furrowed. "Well, I'll do what I can, but why not talk about it with Doctor Regen? That's what she's here for."

Denise shook her head. "That's just it. I don't know if I should talk to her or not. That's why I wanted to ask you first."

"Um, okay, shoot."

She looked down, realized she was rubbing her wrists and slapped her hands into the lap of her khaki pants, making them stop. "And I would have talked to Sarah, but, well, everybody comes to you. You're kind of the leader. You know?"

A small smile touched John's lips. He didn't know, but he was flattered. "Is it about Chance?" he asked, taking a wild guess.

Denise shook her head. "No, no. Chance is nice and all, but it's not him. It's me. I haven't, well, I haven't been feeling right lately."

"What do you mean, are you sick?"

"No, although it almost feels like it. It's like I just feel wrong, you know? Have you ever been somewhere and you just started feeling *wrong*? Not sick, just like everything is out of whack?"

John wasn't sure what she was talking about. "So you feel out of place? Something's making you uncomfortable?"

"Yeah...I don't know. It's just that, well, that first week I started feeling a little light-headed, kind of *buzzy*, you know?"

John nodded. He knew the *buzzy* feeling well. Even sitting at the table, Denise was talking over the subtle buzz that had found a permanent home in John's head. "It's what they call a runner's high. I've been getting it, too. We all have."

Denise sighed and partially closed her eyes, as if she had been afraid of this sort of reaction. "That's what Sarah said when I mentioned it to her a couple of weeks ago, but it's more than that. It's like I can't even think anymore. Sometimes, when I look at something, I can't remember what it is. Yesterday at breakfast, I looked at my spoon and I couldn't remember what the name of it was. And earlier this week, Sarah and I were picking tomatoes from the garden, and I couldn't remember what they tasted like. I didn't know whether I liked them or not."

She looked at John with a hopeful expression, followed by disappointment when she could tell he had little understanding of what she was talking about.

"And people...just don't seem to matter. Right now, I'm looking at you, and I don't know whether I like you or not. And I try to remember, and I know I'm supposed to like you—you're my friend. But I can't remember *why* you're my friend. The word 'friend' doesn't even mean anything to me anymore. And when I look at Chance, it kind of hurts, and I don't know why."

John paid close attention as she spoke. Denise was so confused, she couldn't even express herself. He expected her to start crying—after all, this sounded like a serious problem—but her face gave the impression that tears weren't even an option, they were another forgotten emotion. It was a far cry from the teary girl first telling the story of her attempted suicide at the Sonora Community Center.

Although the girl's speech made little sense to John, in a very real way, he understood it. Didn't he lay awake at night, cursing himself for letting Sarah slip further and further away, yet he did nothing to try to bridge that distance when he finally saw her during the day?

Denise kept speaking. "All I know for sure is, it wasn't always like this. Now, I just feel wrong. I think there might be something wrong with my head. I—I think I want to go home."

John reached out and took her hands. He didn't entirely understand what Denise was talking about—he had found the runner's high to be mostly pleasant so he wasn't sure why it affected Denise so harshly—but he could tell she was upset. And he knew she needed help.

"Denise, why'd you come out here in the first place?"

Her face looked as if John had just presented her with a complex trigonometry calculation to perform. Perhaps her memory really was slipping.

"Denise, did you join the program to find happiness?"

She nodded. That was it.

"Are you happy?"

With no hesitation, she shook her head. "Not at all."

John nodded. The answer seemed simple enough for him. "Then the program isn't working for you. Go home. You're an adult. Do what *you* want to do."

A smile crossed Denise's face, a look of resolution. Had she been seeking John's approval before she told Doctor Regen she wanted to leave the program?

"Okay," she said. She stood and walked to the door, opening it slightly before turning back to him. "John?"

He looked at her from the card-table.

"I don't know what happened between you and Sarah, but I've heard her talk about you. She really loves you. Maybe it's getting hard for her to remember, too, but she does love you."

John didn't know what to say.

"Anyway, thanks. I'm going to go talk to Doctor Regen." Denise walked out, leaving the door to the library open behind her. John could hear the water running in the kitchen as BJ and Chance washed the evening's dishes.

"You're welcome," he said quietly. "And thank you."

CHAPTER 40

"WHAT ARE YOU getting at?"

Sarah Michaels gave her husband a harsh look. They were sitting on opposite bunk beds in the women's barracks. She had finished her shower and was wearing her sweat pants and t-shirt. She had been getting ready for bed when John knocked on the door and came inside. It was his first time in the female quarters, and he strongly suspected he was violating the rules by being there, but they needed privacy for this conversation.

"What I'm getting at is that Denise is in Doctor Regen's quarters right now saying she wants to leave the program, and I think we should, too."

Sarah's hard expression turned into one of surprise. And hurt? John thought he could see that, too. "Why in the world does Denise want out? She didn't say anything to me about it."

"She just feels wrong. And I do, too." John paused, trying to word his thoughts the right way. If his wife was angry, she wouldn't be able to assess the situation rationally. "Sarah, the whole reason we came out here was to rebuild our marriage, but right now, I feel like we're not even husband and wife."

"Why? Because we don't sleep in the same bed? You promised me that you would make the program work. You *promised* and now you're backing out."

This time, it was John's turn to be exasperated. "I *did* try to make the program work. It's just that—"

"No, you didn't," Sarah interrupted. "You've questioned it from the first day. You may not have said it, but you've always thought you could work it out on your own. Well guess what, John? You can't. You had the chance to work it out on your own, and you ended up with a gun to your head while I ended up getting my stomach pumped. There are some things you can't handle by yourself, and this is one of them."

She paused, adding emphasis to her point. "I *like* the program. I like Doctor Regen. And I feel better about myself today than I have in a long time. A very long time, John. So what does that tell me about you? Now that I'm finding happiness, you want to make me leave. Do you just not want me to be happy? Is that it?"

"Sarah, stop it." John was getting angry. This wasn't what he wanted. "Of course I want you to be happy. I want both of us to be happy, but right now we're drifting apart, and I can't just stand by and let that happen. I know I won't be happy without you. And I don't want to believe you'd be happier without me."

He didn't know what else to say. This wasn't what he wanted at all.

Sarah took a deep breath. "John, I love you. You know that. But right now, I need time to find my own happiness. Doctor Regen and I are making real progress in our afternoon sessions, and I've lost almost all the weight I gained after the accident. *I finally feel good.* Please, just let me feel good. The program will be over in few more weeks, and we can start over then, okay?"

John shook his head. "What if it's too late?"

The question seemed to trigger something in Sarah. "Oh, what is that? Is that a subtle ultimatum? Now or never? Don't do that, John. Please don't do that to me. If you need an ultimatum, then give one to yourself—stick with the program or don't. And when you make that decision, remember that I'm part of the program now. I believe in it, and it's helping me. I know it can help you, too. Please give it a chance, for me."

John put his head into his hands. So this is what it came down to? The program or life without Sarah? It wasn't even an option. He would stick with the program. He would do anything for her.

As John walked across the courtyard returning to the men's barracks, he glanced toward the closed door of Kane and Doctor Regen's quarters. His talk with Sarah had been a monumental failure. He wondered if Denise was faring any better.

CHAPTER 41

DOCTOR REGEN glanced up from the file labeled "*Claiborne, Denise*" and frowned at the young woman sitting on the bed across from her. They were in Doctor Regen's bedroom in the front section of the main bunker. Denise was sitting on the bed with the doctor in a chair beside a small desk. The entrance to the bedroom was immediately next to the front door of the barracks. The stairs leading to the basement sublevel could not be viewed from that part of the building.

That was good. It wasn't too late. The girl hadn't seen too much.

"Denise, I know how awkward much of this must seem, but you can't give up now. You and I are on the verge of a major breakthrough together. Things will get better, I can promise you that."

The girl slowly shook her head. She was resolute, as she had been since she first knocked on the door half an hour ago.

"It's not that, Doctor Regen, I'm trying to tell you I just *feel* wrong. In my head. It's like I can walk a perfectly straight line, but up here," she said, pointing to her head, "I feel like I'm about to lose my balance."

"I understand," Doctor Regen replied. "You feel wrong. You've said that. It's probably an inner ear infection. Why don't I give you a thorough exam, and we'll see what we can do to fix it?"

More head shaking. "No, ma'am. I'd really rather just go home. I'm tired of being out here. I'm tired of feeling weird. I—I think I'd like to try to find my mom."

Doctor Regen narrowed her thin black eyebrows and gave the girl a harsh look. "Denise, I shouldn't have to remind you about your mother. Have you forgotten that she used to call you a slut? A whore? That it's her fault you ended up in California? That she's the reason you wound up in the movie? That she's responsible for you being violated by three men at once in front of a camera? Have you forgotten what it felt like to have all those hands on you, inside you? Have you forgotten those things, Denise?"

Tears welled in Denise's eyes as the doctor reminded her of all the things they had discussed during their private sessions. The ability to cry hadn't been lost yet after all.

"I haven't forgotten," Denise said. "But I don't want to stay here anymore."

Doctor Regen pursed her lips. "Denise, what happened the last time you were on your own?"

Denise pushed her palms against her cheeks, wiping away the hot tears. "I don't know. I mean—"

"You slit your wrists with a razor blade, that's what happened," Doctor Regen interrupted. "You almost died Denise. I don't want that to happen to you again. I want to help you, but in order for me to help, you have to stay with the program."

"But I won't do it again. I promise. I'll be okay, I just need to—"

"What you *need* is to stay here, Denise." Doctor Regen was no longer prodding, her voice was now commanding. This had to be dealt with immediately. "Now if you don't feel well, then I'll examine you, and we'll treat your symptoms. But I cannot in good conscience allow you to leave the program. There's no telling what will happen to you out there."

Denise's eyes were awash in confusion. She closed them. Lilith held her breath. When the girl's eyes opened again, the look was resolute.

"Doctor Regen, I want to go home. I'm an adult, and I want to go home. You can't make me stay here."

The tears were gone. The manipulation had failed.

Lilith Regen sighed. Damn.

"Very well. I'll go get Marcus. He'll escort you back to the city tonight. Do you have any personal items you need?"

"No. I didn't have anything personal I wanted to bring out here. Everything is where we left it at the bank in Sonora."

"All right. I want you to stay in my quarters for now. The others here believe in the program, and it's working for them. If they speak to you, if they experience your negativity toward the program, it just may hinder their progress. You wouldn't want that, would you, Denise?"

Denise watched Dr. Regen leave the room. She sat on the bed and rubbed her wrists. She wanted to say goodbye to Sarah and John. And Chance. But she didn't want to hurt them. That was the last thing she wanted. She guessed it would be okay to leave without saying goodbye. It was for the best.

Marcus Kane's arms were folded across his chest, and a frown was etched on his face as he stood in the basement lab.

"You're certain we can't keep her in the program?"

Lilith Regen sighed. "I've tried everything. She wants to go home. It's not just emotional either, she's having some sort of physical reaction. It's happening too fast."

Kane nodded. "Contributing factors?"

"She's blood type A-positive. We've been hit and miss with A-positive so far. But I suspect it's more in line with genetic make-up. There's only one way to know for sure."

"It's a shame," Kane said. "It would have been preferable to attempt adjustments through ongoing observation. We're going to have to start from scratch again—find another girl her age and blood type. That won't be easy."

Lilith nodded. It wouldn't be easy, but if there was one thing she knew about the program—it had resources. Still, she hated to lose Denise. Of anyone in the program, the girl should have been the most susceptible to the private therapy sessions, not to mention the forthcoming spiritual awakenings. Lilith should have been able to talk

Denise into staying. The girl's refusal to remain with the program felt like a failure on her part. And failures were never good.

Kane walked across the room and retrieved the black duffel bag. The bag was almost three feet long.

"So one of our little sheep wants to go home?" He unzipped the bag and peered at what lay within. "Then I guess we have no choice but to see how fast she can run."

CHAPTER 42

CUTTER VALENTINE stood at the sink, scrubbing the iron skillet with the scouring pad. The grease was cooked hard. He had fixed fried potatoes and onions for supper again. He had let the skillet sit out too long again. Now he was scrubbing again. He figured he'd probably never learn. You just can't teach an old dog new tricks. And Maggie had always handled the kitchen duties.

It wasn't old-fashioned or sexist. Maggie liked cooking and didn't mind cleaning up afterward. Cutter was lousy at one and clumsy at the other so it had worked out perfectly. Through all the years it had worked out perfectly.

He missed her so much.

Cutter glanced at the clock on the kitchen counter. It was too damn late to be scrubbing dishes.

His gaze shifted to the old telephone next to the clock. It was definitely too late to call. Way too late.

"I'm sorry I woke you up, Darlin', really. I just needed to hear your voice."

Cutter sat on the ancient stool at the counter, cradling the phone to his ear with one hand while rubbing the bridge of his nose with the thumb and forefinger of the other. There was no headache, just the heart-wrenching sound of Maggie's voice.

"It's okay. I never sleep well when you're not here anyway...still." Her voice was tired. She had been asleep, even if she wouldn't admit it.

"Are you okay? Is Robert okay?"

"We're both fine. Robert just finished his midterms at Tech. He thinks he has all A's." She paused for a moment. "He misses you, you know. You should really give him a call."

"Yeah. I know. It's just that it's still hard. That's all."

Although he couldn't see her, Cutter suspected she was nodding her head at the other end of the phone. She understood. Maggie always understood.

"Is it getting any better? Is it worth it?" It was a hard question for her to ask, but Cutter knew it was a fair question. He had to be honest. God knew she deserved it.

"I don't know. I think it's going to get better. I kind of took a step today."

"Really? Anything you want to tell me about?"

Cutter shook his head, even though she couldn't see the reaction. He wouldn't even know where to begin explaining it.

"No. Not yet. But I'm getting there."

"I miss you, Earl." Maggie was the only person Cutter knew who called him Earl. She had loathed his nickname for as long as they'd been together, ever since it was bestowed upon him by the first freshman class of Rangers he had helped train so many years ago—a moniker one skinny rookie impulsively shouted after witnessing his instructor jokingly show the class a second option for taking down a criminal, if they had the talent. The rest of the class joined in, chanting the nickname that would stick with him for the rest of his life. Maggie had hated the alias from the beginning, but it was one more thing she tolerated. She always had.

Now, hearing her say his given name made his heart ache.

"I miss you, too. I just need a little more time."

There was a long pause on the other end of the phone.

"Don't make me wait forever, Earl. I don't know if I can." Her voice was shaking, but she was trying to be brave. He loved her so much for it.

"I'll be back, Maggie. I promise."

Cutter finished the rest of the kitchen cleanup and stared out the window into the desert night. Had he lied to his wife? Had he taken a step today, or was he kidding himself? When he went to sleep tonight, would it be any better?

Going to the sheriff's office today had felt like progress. And the kid, Dwight, had seemed nice enough. Cutter still felt bad for giving the deputy such harsh treatment in response to his innocent question, but the Andy Griffith jailhouse had started to close in on him. He had needed to get away.

But it had been a step, hadn't it?

Cutter glanced at the clock on the kitchen counter. It was too late to go into town now. Way too late to feel his way around the sheriff's office for himself. Way too damn late for any of that.

Cutter grabbed his hat off the table and walked out the back door.

CHAPTER 43

DENISE WAS GETTING TIRED. They had been walking for more than an hour, and they still hadn't reached their destination. Moreover, she had no idea where they were. Every so often, Kane had made a slight turn, deviating their course, and she now had no idea where she was in relation to the compound. They could be walking in a complete circle, and she wouldn't have known the difference.

The white circle of light from the flashlight bobbed in front of them, guiding the way. A quick, rustling movement sounded to her right. It was too fast and loud to be a rattlesnake—probably just a rabbit—but that fact didn't stop her from stepping closer to Kane.

Since the program had started, Denise had spent every night in her bed inside the women's barracks. This was her first time being outside in the desert at night. In the dark. Her shoulder brushed Kane's elbow, and she took half a step away. She was scared, but not that scared. Finally, she had to ask the unthinkable.

"Marcus, um, Mr. Kane? Are you sure you know where we're going?"

The cloudiness of the night sky covered the half-moon and afforded almost no light. Was he smiling? She couldn't tell.

"Don't worry, Denise. I know exactly where we're going. And we're almost there. The garage is up ahead."

Denise gave a sigh of relief. It was getting really late. And although she had been a night owl in her life before the program, she had become accustomed over the past seven weeks to going to bed soon after the sun had set. Doing this much walking during the time she normally slept was taxing.

"Why do you keep the Jeep way out here? Why not just leave it in the shed at the compound?" The question had been on her mind since leaving Doctor Regen's quarters and walking out of camp with Kane.

"Because, Denise, it's better to keep such reminders of the outside world away from people who are trying to find inner peace."

She nodded. The conversation was kind of surreal, like talking to a Zen master who happened to look like the Incredible Hulk.

"I understand," she said. "I appreciate you driving me back to town, Mr. Kane. I know it's kind of late."

"Oh, it's no problem, Denise. I enjoy it. Gives us both a chance to get some exercise." A break in the clouds increased the dim illumination provided by the moon, and this time, Denise was positive Kane was smiling. "Tell me, Denise, did you have a chance to talk with anyone else back at camp, about how you feel?"

The question was casual. Normal conversation.

"No," she said. "I pretty much keep to myself."

Denise had no idea why she lied. Mainly because Kane's question had been *so* casual, it felt wrong.

"Good, good."

Kane stopped. Denise pulled up next to him and scanned her surroundings. There was no garage to be seen. In fact, based on what Denise could see in the muted moonlight, they were standing in the middle of nowhere. She cocked her head and listened intently. She wondered if Kane had heard a rattlesnake or a coyote or something.

"What is it?" she whispered.

"*It?*" Kane repeated. "*It* is a game. A game you and I are about to play."

His voice remained in a normal conversational tone so there must not have been any danger about, but that didn't explain why the hairs on the back of Denise's neck were standing up.

"What kind of game?" she asked hesitantly, not sure she wanted to know the answer.

"It's a simple game," Kane continued. "Here are the ground rules. There is no Jeep. There never was. I have two four-wheeler ATV's in the shed at the compound. That's what I use for transportation."

Denise was confused. If that was true, why had they walked all the way out here?

The giant duffel bag Kane had been carrying dropped to the earth with a thud.

"There is, however, a town within five miles of this spot," Kane said. "Now, if I told you which direction it was in, that would eliminate a lot of the game's fun, so I'll leave you to guess at that."

The hairs on the back of Denise's neck were standing at full attention now, and nausea was creeping into her stomach.

"I will give you a full ten minute head start. That's a long time when you think about it. You're welcome to use the flashlight, although I'll be straight with you, that'll make it easier for me to find you."

A cool breeze blew, and Denise shivered more than she normally would have.

"Now, if you get to the town before I get to you, you win. But if I find you out here..." Kane swept his hand through the darkness. "You lose. Do you understand?"

Denise shook her head, tears in her eyes. This wasn't funny. She didn't like this at all.

"Then I'll make this real simple, cutey-pie." His voice lowered from its earlier, casual tone. It sounded rougher, almost growling. "You are going to die tonight. You can go down fighting and make it interesting, or you can just stand there and accept it."

Denise was shaking now. Her stomach hurt. "This isn't funny. Please don't—"

A long finger appeared in front of her face. Kane wagged it at her. "Shhh...don't do that. You need to conserve your energy. Use it for running, not for begging." Kane paused, his tone became one of sadness. "Poor Denise. You could have been part of something really special. Now, you're going to be nothing but a stupid whore who dies in the desert. What a waste."

Tears were falling now. Denise's nose was running. She couldn't believe what he was saying. Didn't want to believe.

"The game has begun, Denise." His voice was conversational again. "Your ten minutes just started. I strongly suggest you use them."

Denise turned and ran.

CHAPTER 44

CUTTER SLID THE KEY into the door and turned it. The lock clicked and the Sonora Sheriff's Office was open for business. He pushed the door open, the gust of cold air from within no longer as noticeable in the cool of the desert night. He stepped inside and felt for a switch on the wall.

Fluorescent lights illuminated the one room office with the sparse furniture and the single jail cell. Cutter helped himself to a slow look around the place. It was easier this time, without the kid here.

Cutter glanced at the desk. Its surface was almost completely bare. Only a lamp, a desk-set for two ballpoint pens, and a baseball sat on it. The kid was a neat-freak. Nothing wrong with that. Cutter had known too many officers who would leave sensitive materials out on their desks for weeks at a time. No common sense.

An old computer sat on a credenza behind the desk. It was dusty from lack of use. Not much need to check criminal references out here. And the kid apparently didn't spend his days on the internet. Good for him.

Cutter lifted the baseball from its little pedestal, holding it up for inspection. He hadn't seen it earlier in the day. Dwight's newspaper must have been covering it. The ball was signed by Ivan Rodriguez of the Texas Rangers. Cutter smiled.

Naturally.

Cutter had seen ol' Pudge knock a few out of the Ballpark at Arlington in his day. The Ranger's baseball team actually offered discounted tickets for all their games to the "real" Texas Rangers. It was nice.

Cutter tossed the ball from one hand to the other as he walked around the office. He took a deep breath and inhaled the scent of the place. It was clean. He glanced to the jail cell and wondered how long since it had last been used. Did Sonora have its own version of Otis the town drunk who checked himself in to the cell to dry out?

He smiled at the thought. This wasn't so bad. At night. By himself. The sheriff's office wasn't bad at all.

He set the baseball on top of a filing cabinet and opened the top drawer. A dozen files lined the inside. Cutter thumbed at the labels on the manila folders. *Drunk and Disorderly* boasted the most pages (somewhere around ten). *Vandalism* was close (with one perpetrator accounting for all eight of the pages inside).

Cutter shook his head. No violent crimes. Not even an assault charge anywhere. He wasn't naïve, of course. He guessed there were fistfights in Sonora just like everywhere else, but apparently nothing had ever gotten too far out of hand.

Cutter closed the top drawer and opened the other two. A few backdated files. Nothing extraordinary. Nothing violent (although he did find the folder where Billy Bob Swynnerton had mistakenly shot Mrs. Escobar's Great Dane). Apparently, Cal had been honest with him. The town really didn't need a full-time sheriff. If the bulk of the work was Dwight walking the kids across the street as a crossing-guard, then Cutter certainly didn't have a reason to come in from the ranch.

What in the world did Jim Albright do with his days while he still wore the heavy iron Sheriff's badge?

Cutter slammed the bottom drawer of the cabinet harder than he intended and a loud bang echoed through the office. The baseball rolled backward and dropped behind the cabinet. It fell with a clunk.

Damn.

Cutter maneuvered himself alongside the cabinet and reached his arm behind it. The baseball had to be back there somewhere. His fingers finally found it, and nudged something else alongside the ball.

He retrieved the baseball and sat up, carefully placing the ball back on the desk, sitting smartly upon its little pedestal. He reached behind the cabinet again.

After several attempts, he was finally able to grasp the item, freeing it from its hiding place behind the metal cabinet. It was another manila folder.

Cutter eased himself into the desk chair and set the file in front of him. He turned on the lamp and opened the folder, thumbing through the pages.

He couldn't believe what he was seeing.

CHAPTER 45

MARCUS KANE pressed one knee into the gravelly earth as he unzipped the black duffel bag. He scanned the horizon. The tiny white light was still bobbing, heading in a steady easterly direction. The prey would turn off the light soon enough. She was too afraid of the dark right now to extinguish the flashlight, but he felt this one had it in her to overcome the fear of the dark. She would choose to forego the flashlight to increase her chance of survival. When she made that choice, the light would flick off, and the real hunt would begin.

Kane pulled off his black t-shirt and wadded it into a ball. The shirt went into the bag, along with the chain and key from around his neck. He rolled his head from side to side, stretching his neck. The cool wind invigorated him.

This was where he could leave the shackles of humanity behind and become what he knew he should rightfully be.

Kane surveyed his surroundings, memorizing his current position by the alignment of certain landmarks. He would have to return for the bag later.

He reached into the duffel and extracted the twin blades attached to the double bands of thick leather. He held the knives against the back of his right hand and began securing the straps around his right wrist and palm.

The blades were heavy. They felt right. Kane had a gun in the storage room in the basement of his barracks—he had lots of things in that storage room—but he had no desire to use the .38 revolver. Not tonight. Guns were no fun.

He held the twin blades to his face and lightly ran the cool metal of one against his cheek. The serrations on one side of the blade scratched against his stubble. *This* was fun.

The serrations were new. He had painstakingly cut them into each blade after his encounter with the coyotes. The tearing action would be more efficient. It would be beautiful. He couldn't wait to try it out.

He peered into the darkness once more. The bobbing white dot of the flashlight had disappeared. Excellent.

Kane rose and looked up into the cloudy night sky. He raised his arms towards the heavens and let the glory of the moment wash over him.

Let the hunt begin.

CHAPTER 46

T*HIS WASN'T HAPPENING. It couldn't be.*

Denise fought the urge to switch on the flashlight as she ran. She needed the light. It was so scary in the dark. Scary and dangerous. Especially running.

And she was running. As hard as she could.

Where was the freaking moon?

She risked a glance away from the dark impression of the path she was taking and looked upward. Black clouds filled the sky. She could see a faint silver hue framing a portion of one, but the light ended in the heavens. None of it reached her.

Her arm brushed a thorny branch, causing her to cry out in surprise more than pain. Her voice was a timid yelp in her ears. She switched the flashlight to her other hand so she could press her free palm against her arm. Was she bleeding?

Her arm felt slick, but as much as she was sweating, the slickness could be blood or just perspiration.

Let it be sweat. Please.

It wasn't the thought of bleeding that scared Denise, but the unfocused fear that accompanied her thoughts of Marcus Kane. He had been so casual. And that smile.

Kane would be able to smell her blood. She was sure of it. He was going to hunt her down using her blood as a scent. And he was going to kill her.

This wasn't happening.

A rustling sounded in the brush to her left.

Shit.

It was small. Had to be a rabbit. Or a snake? A shiver shot down her spine as she ran. It was a rabbit. It had to be. All that mattered was that it was too small to be Kane.

Denise realized she was holding her breath. She gasped a quick burst of air. She had to keep running. Find the town.

Are you sure there even is a town?

The voice of self-doubt rang in her ears. Why had she believed Kane when he told her there was a town? If he was going to kill her, why be honest about something like the town?

No. There is a town. I can find it.

She had to believe. There had to be a way out of this. She had screwed up before. She had made some bad mistakes that led to her being in the program, but she hadn't screwed up so badly to deserve this. She didn't deserve to die in the desert alone.

What about Sarah? And John? And Chance? What about Chance?

They were her friends. Was this going to happen to them, too?

No.

She shook her head as she ran. She was no longer paying close attention to where she was going. She was just running. The buzzing sound in her ears was constant. It was the runner's high, but it didn't feel good.

Nothing felt good anymore. Everything felt wrong. Especially this. She didn't want to die. She may have wanted to before, in the hotel in Los Angeles, but she didn't want to die now. She just wanted to go home.

Tears streamed down her face as she continued to run. Snot clogged her nose and forced her to breathe through her mouth. Her lungs burned. This wasn't fair. Not at all. It couldn't be happening. Lilith Regen was a doctor. How could she let this happen? She was supposed to help people.

That's when the thought occurred to her.

She *didn't* want to die. Maybe this was all part of the program. Maybe Doctor Regen had planned for Kane to take her out and pretend that he was going to kill her. Maybe it was an extreme step in the program designed to scare her into wanting to live.

That bitch.

Denise blinked against the tears.

That dirty bitch. Program or not, how could she justify scaring someone like this? And how could Kane go along with it?

Her foot struck something that gave way and wrapped around her shin. She kicked her leg in a panic and the thing flew five feet in front of her and landed with a soft thump on the desert floor.

She altered her momentum and took three steps to the side, still unsure of what the thing was. She tried to peer at it through the darkness, but the thing was just a black lump on the black earth, lying among the low brush.

Denise forced herself to be still as she looked around. She tried to listen to her surroundings, but she could hear only her ragged breathing.

Was Kane around?

She sniffed at her leaking nose.

Did it matter? This was all just a cruel game anyway. Sick motherfucking bastards.

She raised the flashlight and pointed it toward the black lump in front of her. Her thumb trembled over the switch, hesitant to use the light.

It was just a game. Just a game.

She switched on the flashlight.

The harsh white glow of the beam illuminated the area around the object. It was a giant black duffel bag, lying on its side.

She had run in a circle.

She took a tentative step toward the bag. It was hard to move her feet.

Just a game.

She walked around the bag as if it were a snake. There was something protruding from the open zipper portion on the other side. Something that reflected the light.

Denise glanced around again. She saw nothing but blackness. Switching on the flashlight had ruined what little night vision she had developed over the past twenty minutes. She lowered the beam and knelt next to the bag, inspecting the object inside.

It was Styrofoam. A Styrofoam ice chest. It had fallen on its side when she kicked the duffel bag.

Her hands shook as she reached out and righted the chest, then removed the lid. There was nothing inside but ice and a folded plastic bag.

Denise realized she had been holding her breath again and let it out in a rush. Ice and a stupid plastic bag. Why in the world would Kane have that? What would he find way out here in the desert that needed to be put on ice?

She sniffed again, trying to clear her nasal passages. Her lungs burned from her terrified run. She raised her hand and wiped the tears from her cheeks. Then she put her palm to her forehead and closed her eyes against the raging, panic-induced headache.

Just a game.

She brushed the bangs from her forehead and ran her fingertips through her hair. Her head was killing her. How could something so small hurt so much?

Her eyes went back to the empty ice chest.

Oh shit.

She was reaching to turn off the flashlight when she heard footsteps behind her.

This wasn't happening.

CHAPTER 47

JOHN TURNED OFF THE SHOWER and waited a moment for the water to drain. The tile needed to be wet, or so the instructions read.

He pulled the sticky paper off the top of the new container of Comet and revealed the seven little holes in the top, like a big green saltshaker. It was the fourth can of the cleanser he'd used since the program began. He shook the cardboard cylinder over the shower in the men's barracks and watched as the green sand poured out in uneven waves.

Let sit fifteen seconds for most problems. Let stand one minute for persistent problems.

John began counting to sixty in his head. He heartily considered cleaning the shower a persistent problem.

It had been an interesting morning. Marcus Kane had greeted them at dawn with the news that Denise had elected not to remain with the program. He then followed the information with an announcement—there was something lacking in the program. Denise's departure had accentuated the need for it.

Spiritual development.

As the group drank their morning supplemental beverage, Kane informed them that they would begin a nightly time of spiritual awakening, starting this evening after supper.

John nodded his agreement to the idea along with everyone else. Spiritual development didn't sound so bad. He could probably use a little himself. Besides, it was part of the program, and John's mind was still quite fresh off his heated conversation with Sarah the previous night. He had never before seen his wife take such a vehement stand on any issue. The program was important to her. As much as John hated to believe it, perhaps more important to Sarah than her husband.

Maybe he couldn't blame her for that. After all, what had he done for her, really? Given her a nice house? A nice car? Nice vacations?

So what?

The house meant nothing when their newborn daughter lay dying in an intensive care unit. The car didn't seem to make Sarah feel any better when they had driven it to the funeral home for the services laying her parents to rest. Perhaps she was right to take her stand against him. Perhaps Sarah was right about the program.

So John would do as he was told. And if that meant finding his spiritual self under the guidance of Marcus Kane of all people, then consider his spirit ready and willing.

It was funny how easy that was. Turning it all over to someone else. In the back of his mind, John recognized the attitude was new for him. He was more accustomed to fighting something new rather than embracing it. But maybe that was why he had been wrong his entire life.

He knelt next to the shower and began to work the abrasive sponge against the tile. Cleaning wasn't so bad. You started and the shower was dirty, you finished and the shower was clean. It was *real*. There were no abstract numbers, no vague assumptions of stockholder value, no wordy legal documents that you paid for by the pound. It once was dirty, but now it's clean. Hallelujah.

He worked the green foam into the grout. Be clean.

John's mind flickered back to his childhood, a rarity these days. In truth, since joining the program, his mind didn't seem to flicker much at all anymore. But on this day, the Comet had reminded him of something. Some things are just too ingrained to change, no matter how loud the buzzing in your head.

He had been five years old when he learned the song. He had just begun kindergarten and his sister had been in second grade. Their mother had been cleaning the kitchen sink and had left the green can of Comet on the counter. Seeing it, Jennifer began singing the song she had learned in summer camp that year. It would be years before John recognized the notes as the whistled tune in the film *Bridge on the River Kwai.*

John smiled as he listened to the tune in his head while scrubbing the tile and grout in the shower. It was a silly song, a kid's song, but those are the kind that can stick with you for a lifetime. The voice singing was that of his sister.

Comet – it makes your mouth turn green.

Comet – it tastes like gasoline.

Comet – it makes you vomit.

So have some Comet, and vomit, todaaaayyyyy.

John closed his eyes. The buzzing was still there, but for just a moment, his sister's voice overrode it. It was his last memory of her as a happy child. Sometime after that, she had changed. Sometime after their father had left them.

Of course, Jennifer wasn't always unhappy growing up. There were times she smiled. And times she laughed. But there was always something not quite right. That something exploded sometime around the year she turned sixteen. That's when she became openly hostile. That's when she really started to hate the world around her.

That's when she seemed to give up on John and his mother.

And it was only a few years later when the cancer struck their mother. And Jennifer had stayed mad. And she hadn't come back to help John. Mad or not, she had fallen short just when he needed her most.

John realized he had stopped scrubbing and shook his head. Wow. How long since that had happened to him? It had been weeks since he'd become so lost in his own thoughts. Must be the fumes from the cleaning powder.

His thoughts changed direction, turning to Denise. So the girl had left. She was on her way home.

John hoped things worked out for Denise. He had grown fond of her while she was here. He supposed he'd miss her, but he hadn't really felt it yet.

But Sarah...

The connection sparked in John's buzzing head. When Kane told them that Denise was gone earlier that morning, Sarah had just nodded. It hadn't clicked at the time, but looking back, John was surprised his wife hadn't been more upset at the news. After all, she had become close friends with Denise over the course of the program. In fact, she was the first real friend Sarah had had since the aftermath of the accident.

So why wasn't Sarah upset at her sudden departure?

Had life calloused her before they ever arrived to the desert, or had the first several weeks of the program plied Sarah to a point of quiet apathy, the same vague feeling of uncaring that John now felt?

As suddenly as it had appeared, the thought dissipated into the green foam now swirling its way down the drain as John rinsed the shower. Most of his thoughts were that way now.

The program was doing a great job. John hadn't really felt sad about anything for weeks, and apparently neither had Sarah. But if it was working so well, why did John have that nagging feeling in the back of his mind, somewhere behind the buzzing, that he couldn't quite put his finger on?

CHAPTER 48

CUTTER STEPPED INTO THE SHERIFF'S OFFICE and glanced around. The room was empty. No Dwight at the desk. No Otis in the holding cell.

He had specifically arrived at the same time as his initial visit the previous day, hoping to catch the deputy in the office. No such luck.

Cutter opened the door to walk out when a toilet flushed. He paused and listened to the sound of water running in the sink on the other side of the bathroom door. Hands were being washed.

Cutter removed his hat and hung it on the rack beside the door. He took a seat in one of the wooden chairs in front of the desk. His same spot as yesterday.

The bathroom door opened and Dwight walked out, newspaper folded beneath one arm. It was open to the comics section.

"How you doing, Deputy?" Cutter's voice was casual. He didn't want to startle the kid too much.

It didn't work.

Dwight jumped at the sound and the newspaper fell to the floor in three sections. He was a mite skittish. Cutter smiled. He had been a skittish kid, too. A very long time ago.

"Mr. Valentine...Sheriff...uh, Cutter." The words came out fast as Dwight bent to retrieve the newspaper. Cutter felt bad for startling him.

"Have you been here long?" Dwight stood as he asked the question, the newspaper placed on the desk in crumpled wads. His face was red.

"I just walked in, Dwight. Take 'er easy. Even a lawman has to pinch one off now and again." He winked at the kid. Dwight smiled sheepishly, but seemed more together. That was good.

"I'm sorry, Cutter. It's just that I don't get many people in here." Dwight took a seat behind the desk. He moved the wadded pile of newspaper to the corner. Cutter wondered if the deputy would try to sort it out after he left.

"Don't worry about it. I hadn't planned on coming back in so soon myself, but something happened last night."

Dwight's ears perked up, and he leaned forward in his chair. Cutter wondered if the young man was expecting him to ask for help 'cracking a case?'

"I couldn't sleep, so I thought I'd mosey over here. Look around a little bit. Break in that spare key you gave me."

Dwight sat back in his chair again. The kid was disappointed. It wasn't going to be something big after all. "Oh, well that's great, Cutter. What did you think of the place? I try to keep it clean, you know, organized."

Cutter nodded and reached into his denim jacket. "Well the place looks great, Dwight. Very organized. But I did want to ask you about this." He pulled the manila folder from his jacket and laid it on the desk.

Dwight's eyebrows drew together in a quizzical expression as he opened the folder and reviewed the contents.

"You guys had a Jane Doe suicide seven months ago? Trucker said she just barreled onto the highway off a small cliff right in front of him. Said she was beat all to hell. That's pretty big news for a small town like Sonora. So I was just wondering, Dwight, why no one mentioned it to me."

Dwight shook his head as he looked at the papers in the file. "I'll be honest with you, Cutter. I didn't know we still had this file. Sheriff Albright took the trucker's statement and handled the arrangements for the body—that was just a couple of weeks before he left—but he told me the case was open and shut, that he could handle it himself."

Dwight paused. "Sheriff Albright liked to handle most things himself. I don't think he cared much for me being around. He just kind of put up with me since I was the mayor's nephew. But I'm good at my job, Cutter."

Dwight looked hopefully at him. Cutter wasn't sure what the kid wanted to hear, but he liked him, so he simply nodded. "I'm sure you are."

"Anyway," the deputy continued, "Sheriff Albright said we'd leave the case on file with the state authorities since it happened on a state road and outside of the Sonora Township."

Cutter cocked his head. "I assumed the Sheriff's Department handled all criminal activity in the greater Sonora Valley area. Why would this get transferred to State?"

It took Dwight a moment to respond. "Well, it's not *really* criminal activity. I mean, the woman jumped off a cliff in front of a truck. That's pretty much suicide. That kind of thing happens."

"But Dwight," Cutter paused, hoping this would sink in, "Where did she come from? I checked the map. There's nothing around that spot for ten miles. And the file says Albright didn't find an abandoned vehicle anywhere along the road. Something there doesn't add up. Did you do any follow up work on the case, find out what kind of research State did on it?"

Dwight shook his head. "No sir. That was about the time Sheriff Albright left, and I didn't think there was anything I could do on something like that anyway. So I just let the state people handle it. I wasn't wrong, was I?"

Cutter shook his head. He hadn't wanted to put the kid on the spot. "No, Dwight, you didn't do anything wrong. It's just not quite the way I would have dealt with it. But that's not a knock on you. Different strokes for different folks. I'm sure the state authorities handled it properly. Besides, it's seven months old, and that's getting pretty damn cold, especially for something that happened out in the middle of nowhere. Don't sweat it."

Dwight sank back in his chair. He looked relieved. Cutter could tell the deputy had been afraid of being chastised. He wondered if Albright had given him a hard time.

"Don't worry about it at all," Cutter continued. "It's just that I happened to find the file behind the cabinet there, and I thought it was awful peculiar for a file that important not to be in the drawers."

Dwight turned to look at the cabinet, as if expecting to see more manila folders poking out beside the wall. "I don't get it, Cutter. I'm usually real careful about keeping all the files in the drawer. But like I said, I didn't even know we still had that folder."

Cutter nodded and pushed himself to a standing position. The room was starting to feel small again. Too enclosed. But it was better than yesterday.

He extended his hand to the deputy.

"It's okay, Dwight, I just wanted to stop back in and let you know some paper had gotten away from you. It was good seeing you again. Call if you need me."

Dwight stood and shook Cutter's hand. He was a nice kid. The deputy even walked around the desk to open the door for Cutter as he put on his hat.

"I will call if I need you. But feel free to come in anytime you want. It's nice to have someone to talk to."

Cutter nodded as he walked to the parking lot and climbed into his pick-up. He could see the deputy still standing in the doorway.

The kid was polite, too.

Cutter watched as Dwight slid both hands in his pants pockets and leaned against the doorframe. It was a very natural, very practiced stance. Cutter turned the key in his ignition and put the truck into reverse.

It was the kind of stance a kid would be forced to develop at a young age. A subtle way to hide a birth defect the other kids might make fun of.

As Cutter drove out of the parking lot, he finally realized why he hadn't noticed it yesterday. Dwight had been sitting at the desk with his hands in his lap. Probably something else he always did subconsciously.

After all, the poor kid's left hand was horribly underdeveloped. It was the size of a baby's hand with the small, pink fingers curled into a useless claw.

Cutter felt sorry for him.

CHAPTER 49

VERNON PLACED HIS HANDS on the concrete in front of him and hunched lower. He knew the extra precaution was unnecessary. It was very dark now and the air-conditioning unit was almost twice his size anyway. But caution was the watchword.

Because if you can't do something right, don't do it at all.

The darkness was great. A gift from the most unlikely of sources. Kane's announcement earlier that morning about the need for "spiritual meetings" had concerned Vernon all day. If the meetings took place after supper, what would that do to his plan? How would it affect his calculations if everyone had to stay together after the evening meal?

But he had been worried for nothing. The first spiritual awakening lasted less than fifteen minutes. Everyone had sat in a cluster in front of the dining hall with Kane standing at the sundial. He had built a fire using dried brush and mesquite and the flames blazed between him and his audience.

He had spoken in general terms about the need for belonging. The need for a sense of greater purpose. The need to serve something larger than yourself. It was stuff Vernon had heard before. A buddy of his had been in Alcoholics Anonymous and Vernon had joined him for a meeting one time. It sucked. People preached and cried and all the women were too fucking old.

Tonight had been different though. Kane had definitely held everyone's attention at *his* meeting. And the stuff he said made sense (it also sounded a lot like the stuff Doctor Regen had been telling

Vernon in their private sessions). The group members had all nodded. Their eyes had all looked glassy in the dancing flames. Vernon had wanted to pay attention, listen more closely, but his mind had been elsewhere. It always was at that time of night.

But the best thing about the spiritual awakening was that after it had finished, the old rule about not being out at night seemed to vanish. Although both Kane and Doctor Regen went back to their quarters, the three assholes he shared a dorm with stayed outside to play their queer little "around the world" game by the light of the fire. Teri went back to the dining hall to be alone (like always), and Maude sat on the concrete slab in front of the women's barracks, staring off into space.

And now it was very dark. It was even better than Vernon could have hoped for. He had been worried for nothing.

In fact, things were better now than ever. Well, almost. Vernon already missed Denise. She had been so pretty. So tight. So firm.

But beggars can't be choosers, and there wasn't much choice right now. Vernon took one hand from the concrete to unbutton his pants. He lowered himself to his knees, but stayed hunched over. He didn't feel as if he were in danger of losing his balance, but the roof of the women's barracks was curved like all the buildings, and the last thing Vernon needed was to fall. That might attract attention. And that would be bad, very bad.

The skylight in front of him burned yellow from the electric lights inside, but there was nothing to look at. Not yet. It had only been a few minutes since the meeting had ended.

How could he be expected to concentrate on speeches about spiritual awakening when he had *this* on his mind? It was all so perfect. His calculations were impeccable.

Movement.

Vernon unzipped his pants and eased his hand inside. Quiet. Very quiet.

Sarah Michaels stepped into view beneath him. She was wearing a towel. She reached into the shower and turned the knob, waiting for the water to heat.

Yes, beggars can't be choosers, but if Denise was no longer around, Sarah wasn't a bad choice at all. She may be a little old for his tastes, but she was starting to look good. Vernon had noticed the changes. He had seen them every night. Her body was fast improving. And although his attention had normally been focused on Denise (she had liked to bend straight over to wash her toes, Vernon had spent his load several times to that gorgeous sight), Sarah had caught his eye more and more often.

Vernon's hand moved slowly. Quiet. Careful.

If you can't do something right, don't do it at all.

Sarah unwrapped the towel and hung it beside the shower. She still hadn't shaved down there. She was a wool heaven.

Vernon's hand sped up.

This wasn't a bad choice at all.

CHAPTER 50

LILITH REGEN paused her keystrokes on the computer when she heard Kane's footsteps in the hallway. She glanced at the clock. 2:00 AM. He stepped through the doorway into the lab.

"Have you e-mailed the relevant information?" The question was quick but not brusque. He was in a better mood tonight. He walked to the workbench as Lilith responded.

"Yes, they know what to expect and what to look for. They're anticipating the package tomorrow night."

"Excellent." Kane checked the taping on the ice chest for the fifth time. Lilith understood. The last thing they needed was for it to start leaking. "And did you make contact for tonight? Is he expecting me?"

She nodded. "Dewey will meet you halfway. He'll probably get there before you."

"Good." Kane set the ice chest into the black duffel. He zipped the bag and started to walk out when Lilith cleared her throat.

"Marcus," she began, her voice breaking slightly as she spoke, "I want you to reconsider John Michaels. We're at a very delicate stage in the program, particularly with the developments regarding Denise, and you starting the spiritual meetings a week early. I think Michaels will react poorly to it."

Kane set the duffel on the floor and walked to Lilith. He put his hands on her shoulders and gently massaged them as he spoke.

"Lilith, I told you about John Michaels. I want him here. And here is where he will stay. Are we clear on that?"

Lilith nodded. She was clear but that didn't diminish her conviction on the matter. She decided to risk it.

"It's just that he's a very unstable element. I don't have to remind you of the difficulties we've had in the past with dominant personalities. I don't want us to take any unnecessary risks. We can still get him out."

Kane's hands moved from her shoulders to her neck. She stopped speaking. He was still massaging, but the powerful fingers were so close to the tender flesh. He leaned near and whispered. She felt his hot breath inside her ear.

"Listen to me carefully. John Michaels stays. I have a plan for him."

Lilith closed her eyes. This had been a mistake.

"And if you ever question me again after I've already made my feelings clear on an issue, it will be your head I'm FedEx'ing to Texas. You're valuable to the program, Lilith, but not indispensable. Do you understand me?"

A fleck of spittle flew from Kane's lips and landed just inside Lilith's ear. It tickled the tiny hairs there. Her only movement was a slight nod of her head. She understood perfectly.

"Good." Kane released his hands from her neck, retrieved the black bag and walked out the door. Lilith stared straight in front of her until she heard the footsteps ascend the stairs and the front door close.

She exhaled loudly and slumped in the chair.

Why did she do it? Why did she bring it up again?

She pushed at the pile of folders beside the keyboard, and they spread out like a stack of cards. They were all identical, yet one stood out to her. It was labeled "*Michaels, John.*"

In the quiet of the lab, Lilith Regen contemplated her hatred for the man in the file, and considered how to get even.

CHAPTER 51

JOHN LAY IN BED and stared through the skylight at the clouds passing high above in the night. It had been cloudy all week, and he missed the sparkling stars that usually accompanied his insomnia. Still, it was getting better. In a way.

His hands found the arrowhead in the dark and unconsciously started doing what had become a habit in his waking intervals. He rubbed the stone with the blanket. The coarse fibers were already doing a commendable job whittling away the aged and crusted earth surrounding the black onyx. A few minutes with a wire brush would have worked just as well, but one could only work with what limited supplies one had in the desert, so John had begun to patiently polish the arrowhead at night.

A loud snort interrupted BJ's snoring, but it soon resumed again. The man really sawed logs after midnight. John was surprised no one else in the quarters had ever said anything to him. But it was just as well.

Random thoughts bounced through John's mind in the dark, but it was different now. In his previous life, his nightly struggle to find slumber would be interrupted by the need to analyze a particular concept. A transaction he was working on for his company. Something that Sarah had said over dinner. The accident. The hospital. The games that he would never be able to play with his daughter.

These were the thoughts that had plagued John's mind in the past. Once chanced upon, he would spend hours examining them. It was a mental reflex that had been with him his entire life. But that was no longer the case.

Sleep had begun to come earlier and earlier, but it was a fickle sleep. He awoke and then dropped back off several times each night. The thoughts he once dwelled upon would visit him just long enough to nudge his consciousness, then they would evaporate in the dark.

It was an odd sensation. On some level, John recognized he was no longer the man he once was—that he was no longer actively chasing the thoughts and ideas that had once seemed so important—but at the same time, he just didn't care. He hadn't really liked the old thoughts anyway.

Lying there that night, John encountered many of the same memories—his sister, his mother, the accident, Sarah's speech to him the previous night—but there were a few new ones as well. The satellite dish on the roof of the shed. The lack of reaction to Denise's departure. The strange introduction of Kane's spiritual awakening meetings. And that damn "Comet" song from his youth.

When taken together, something about the thoughts bothered John. At least, they bothered him enough to wake him several times, but never enough to force an analysis. Or keep him from falling back to sleep again.

As he buried his head into the pillow once more, he heard it. A sound that had become so foreign, it took him several moments to pinpoint what it was.

An engine.

It was loud for less than a minute, nearby for just that long, then it began to fade into the distance. It was a small engine. A motorcycle?

No transportation in or out of the compound. Another lie from Doctor Regen and Marcus Kane. But why? What was the point of covering up such trivial things as a satellite phone or a motorcycle?

It was just another flitting thought in his buzzing head. No analysis. Just a brief glance. John fell back asleep.

CHAPTER 52

CUTTER SAT UP IN BED and glanced at the red numbers of the digital alarm clock.

2:45 AM.

This was ridiculous.

He lay back into his pillow and gazed at the ceiling of his bedroom. It consisted of that white popcorn stuff that hadn't been in fashion for decades. Part of it had started to come loose in one corner. Cutter had been staring at it all night.

Why couldn't he sleep? He'd put in a full day constructing a new set of cattle pens. It was a big job, and he had just gotten started. He spent the entire afternoon hauling iron and prepping the mobile welder he rented from Red Mercer. He should be exhausted.

Cutter sighed. He *was* exhausted, but he still wasn't asleep. Something ate at his mind, and he had a sinking feeling he knew what it was. The reason you can't teach an old dog new tricks is because he's usually obsessed with the tricks he already knows.

And Cutter Valentine was feeling more like an old dog every day.

The kid seemed to be doing a fine job. And it's not like Sonora was a hotbed of criminal activity. Dwight's heart was in the right place, and he knew the number to the ranch if ever needed help.

But what the hell was Jane Doe doing out in the middle of the desert jumping off a cliff in front of an eighteen-wheeler?

It just didn't make sense, even if the state authorities were handling the case. With "if" being the operative word. Cutter knew that in a rural suicide case, the file had probably gotten less than an hour's attention from some clerk in the capitol.

So what? It's not like it was his problem. The last thing an eager pup like Dwight needed was an old fart nosing around and telling him how to do his job. The kid could handle the crosswalk, and he could grow into the rest of the job once Sheriff Albright returned to duty. It wasn't Cutter's responsibility.

But you can't teach an old dog new tricks. And as much as this old dog wanted to pretend he could concentrate on welding pipe into a new set of cattle pens, at night, his mind would wander back to the same old tricks. The only tricks he really knew.

Cutter would give the kid some more time. The pens were a good three weeks worth of work. He should give Dwight at least that long before he started showing up at the sheriff's office again. It was the right thing to do. Let the kid breathe.

Cutter stared at the white popcorn ceiling.

Why the hell was she out there in the first place?

CHAPTER 53

JOHN'S LEGS WERE ON FIRE. He squinted at the figure running ahead of him. Chance was a good half-mile in front. The kid was fast.

John increased his pace. He could do it. The fire was in his legs and his lungs, but it felt good. The buzz was palpable in his head, but that felt good, too. It was a new morning, and he was a running machine.

He cut left to dodge an outcropping of brush that protruded into the path. He and Chance were running on the same ancient trail that had the stone writings. John liked the old trail, and it was marked for a decent distance, though the markings were hardly noticeable if you weren't paying attention.

John sucked in great gulps of air as he ran. He never should have told Chance he wanted to race back to the compound, but he had been feeling cocky. The buzz was alive in him, and he really thought he stood a chance against the kid.

Big mistake.

Too bad BJ had decided to stick to the main trail that morning. He had been doing that lately. Every third morning or so the tall man had elected a slow jog on the primary two-mile trail, said he didn't want his knees to start hurting. Made sense, but the running felt too good to John to pass up the longer courses with Chance.

Now, Chance was so far ahead John could barely make him out. The kid was fast indeed.

John glanced to his left as he ran past the stone writing farthest from the compound.

REMEMBER.

They still had not encountered any more writings, and no mention of a "go-forth-into-the-desert-and-write" initiative had been made by Doctor Regen in either the group meetings or the private sessions. John wondered if perhaps they had misconstrued the purpose of the carefully placed stones. It didn't really matter. John's mind didn't dwell on much anymore, and the writings only went to the front of his thoughts when he jogged past them on the long runs.

REMEMBER.

That wasn't so easy anymore. But seeing the word triggered a few choice memories for John, just the ones that had been sitting on the surface. For some reason, Jennifer popped foremost into his mind. Her child's voice was still singing the same song.

Comet – it makes your mouth turn green.

Sudden, blinding pain shot through John's side as the cramp hit beneath his ribs on one side. It felt like he was caving in and was helpless to stop it.

Comet – it tastes like gasoline.

He pushed one hand against the pain, hoping the pressure would alleviate the searing agony. It didn't help.

Comet – it makes you vomit.

John slowed to a walk. With each giant breath, the pain increased. He knew he had pushed it way too hard. He glanced up from the trail. Chance was a light gray speck in the distance.

So have some Comet, and vomit, today.

John bent at the waist as he tried to breathe. He saw that he had reached the first of the stone writings. The one closest to the compound.

NO DRINK.

The cramp seemed to reach out and grab John's throat. Without warning, he dropped to his knees and heaved. Green vomit sprayed from his mouth and coated the gravel and dirt of the desert floor. Two of the large rocks were splattered as well. On his hands and knees, John watched as the bottom part of the first "N" in the writing was painted a dark green as he heaved. The vomit burned his throat and made his eyes water. The vile liquid had entered his sinuses. The inside of his nose hurt.

When the rush of acidic vomit finally ceased, John leaned back on his knees and let out a low moan. It had been more than five years since he had last thrown up, and it wasn't an experience he had missed.

He looked upward and tears ran down his cheeks. Oh, that had been bad. He shouldn't have tried to push himself that hard. Chance could do that sort of thing as much as he wanted. John had to be careful. He wasn't a kid anymore.

Comet – it makes your mouth turn green.

John shook his head. Stupid song. He wiped the back of his hand across his mouth. Green streaks of slobber shone on it.

Comet – it takes like gasoline.

He spit into the dirt, trying to rid his mouth of the last of the bile. His teeth felt rough, like some of the enamel had been dissolved. Potent puke. He needed something to drink. Something to wash his mouth out.

Comet – it makes you vomit.

He lowered his blurry gaze to the stones in front of him. The "N" was floating in a sea of the world's most disgusting lime Kool-Aid.

So have some Comet, and vomit, today.

And just like that, it started to come together. The thoughts that had flitted about John's mind the past few weeks began to meld, to become cohesive with one another. It all started to make sense.

The writings. The running. The mandatory supplemental beverage.

It wasn't locked down yet. His thoughts were still jumbled in an inarticulate mass, but for the first time, John was beginning to see the forest rather than the trees. He felt like the puzzle was solvable. Needed to be solved. And understanding was in his grasp.

The green vomit trailed in tiny streams from the main puddle. One of the rivulets made its way toward the place where John's hand was resting in the dirt. He pulled it away.

It didn't make sense yet, not at all, but now there was a glimmer. Now, there was hope. All of a sudden, he was beginning to feel like John Michaels again.

He stood and began walking toward the compound. Chance would be along soon. He would get near the compound and notice John was too far back to be seen, then he would backtrack and find him so they could return to camp together. He was a good kid.

John grabbed his waist and leaned backwards as he walked, stretching his abdomen. Little by little, the cramping pain beneath his ribs was subsiding. John knew it would be gone after he walked another quarter of a mile. And something else would have changed by then, too. For the first time in weeks, the buzzing in John's head would begin to grow quiet.

And he would remember.

Part V:
DISCOVERY

CHAPTER 54

JOHN SLOWED HIS PACE as he ran and squinted against the sunlight. What in the world had he just seen?

He dropped his speed to a fast walk and lifted his gray t-shirt to wipe the beading perspiration from his forehead. When he dropped the shirt, his hand grazed against his stomach. It was an unusual feeling. His abs had become tight since the beginning of the program. Nine weeks of daily running. His physical conditioning hadn't been this good since he was a teenager. Maybe not even then.

John reluctantly shifted his eyes from what he had just seen for a quick glance ahead of him. He didn't want to lose the spot, but he needed to check on BJ and Chance. The three of them had agreed to see how far they could run. Chance told them they would surprise themselves, said the three of them could probably do fifteen miles if they wanted. They had set their goal as the bluff that lay about a mile in front of where John now stood. It was the farthest point from the camp in which the pitchfork rock formation remained visible so they were still technically following the rules of the program.

BJ and Chance were nearing the far bluff. John had lagged behind. Fifteen miles was a long damn way regardless (and the bluff was actually the halfway point of seven or eight miles, since they would have to reverse direction and cover the same distance on the run back to the compound), but it was especially rough for John. His energy levels were no longer the same since he had begun sticking his finger down his throat to force himself to throw up every morning.

It was an ugly process, but unavoidable. Kane still stood watch each dawn to ensure everyone in the program drank the glass of green "supplement beverage," and John followed the rules, draining his glass every morning for the sake of appearance. He couldn't allow Sarah to know he had been regurgitating the stuff every morning for the past two weeks. He couldn't let BJ or Chance know either.

So John had begun to excuse himself before each run, telling BJ and Chance to start without him, he'd catch up. That was the nice thing about guys—all men respected regularity. They just assumed John had become a morning shitter.

John would go to the bathroom in the barracks, close the stall door behind him, kneel in front of the porcelain, and gag himself until the green puke splashed into the bowl. Then, he'd brush his teeth, drink a few handfuls of water from the faucet, and race to catch up with his friends. The process was disgusting, but necessary. Appearances were definitely necessary.

Purging the green drink from his system over the past two weeks was showing its effects. His energy level was decreasing, but John suspected that wasn't due to losing the benefit of "vitamins" from the drink. He was beginning to think the green liquid somehow stimulated the adrenal gland.

John wasn't a doctor, but he postulated that increased adrenaline could be responsible for much of the unusual behavior of the program participants. The growing urge to run. Farther every day. Pushing yourself. Not to mention the sense of apathy that now permeated the group. The vague "fight or flight" stimulus provoked by adrenaline was primitive. It superseded higher levels of thinking. That would explain why the thoughts of love or friendship that defined humanity were more and more difficult for the program members to grasp.

Adrenaline.

That's why BJ and Chance were so far ahead of John this morning. Two weeks ago, John could outrun BJ. Now, he was sucking wind while the other men were just catching their stride. Of course, John's new sleep patterns may have had something to do with his reduced energy levels as well, though "new" wasn't entirely accurate. The sleep patterns were, in fact, anything but new. His insomnia was back. With a vengeance.

As the buzz from the formula had dissipated, the apathetic malaise of his mind had vanished as well. No longer did John lie in bed dozing off and on, awakening just long enough to glimpse the night sky before returning to slumber. He now lay beneath the skylight, gazing at the stars, his eyes open for hours at a time. It was as if his mind was indignantly railing against the chemicals to which they had been subjected for so long.

If before, John's random thoughts flitted into his consciousness for just a moment before he banished them, never giving them the attention they deserved; now, each and every idea was pored over and examined at length. Nothing escaped John's notice and subsequent analysis. And with each examination, the nebulous sense of uneasiness increased. As the buzz that had accompanied his waking hours for so many weeks began to fade, an underlying feeling of dread began to replace it. But John hadn't yet been able to identify the root of the dread. That remained a mystery.

John veered from his current path and walked toward the bush he had pinpointed moments before. There was nothing overtly unique about the bush, but it had piqued his curiosity. He was positive he had seen something shiny catch the morning sunlight and reflect it. Unless he had imagined it.

John shook his head as he made his way through the cactus and brush. That wouldn't be farfetched. After all, his mind had been in overdrive since the day he vomited on the stone writing. The same day Kane had begun the nightly "spiritual awakening" meetings.

The meetings had made sense at first, even touched John in a way. Kane's words were powerful. Spoken over the blazing fire, his deep voice telling the group that in order to fulfill their happiness, they needed to find a higher purpose. John had accepted it as just another part of the program. Unusual, since Kane didn't seem to fit the mold of a spiritual leader, but the meetings were very much in line with what

Doctor Regen talked about in her daily private sessions with John. The sessions that still didn't include Sarah.

His wife had continued to distance herself from him over the past few weeks. Probably not intentionally—or so John hoped. The whole group was becoming more distant. It occurred to John that he hadn't spoken to Maude or Teri in more than a week. Not a word. Granted, John didn't consider himself close friends with either of them, but still, the program's participants were a small group. A lack of interaction like that seemed unusual. Plus, John had noticed BJ and Chance growing more distant as well.

No one in the group talked much anymore. Meals were often quiet. People had begun to skip the regular meal times and make themselves peanut butter and jelly sandwiches instead. The sandwiches were becoming a predominant part of the group's diet as the running increased their bodies' desire for carbs. Moreover, Sarah and Maude seemed less inclined to prepare more elaborate meals. Sarah continued to work in the garden every afternoon, but she harvested fewer and fewer of the fresh vegetables to include with the meals.

It was a far cry from the first weeks of the program, when everyone was trying to be friendly to one another. When the most common facial expression in camp was a timid smile of hope, of appreciation to be included in the program. That was all gone.

Now, John barely spoke to his friends, never saw Vernon (not something he would complain about anyway), and spent less than five minutes a day alone with his wife. Of more concern, Sarah had started to seem uncomfortable around him, like she was fulfilling an obligation she no longer wanted by spending time with him. It was becoming increasingly difficult for John to communicate with her.

He supposed that was why he hadn't said anything to her about the supplement drink. He knew there was something wrong with it, but he didn't know exactly what. He knew there was something wrong with the program, but he didn't know exactly what. If he went to his wife with "I feel uneasy about this whole thing, something's up," she might very well turn on him. The night Denise left had revealed a side of

Sarah that John had never seen. She was adamant about the program. She believed in it. If he was going to get them out of it, he had to have something concrete. Proof. Otherwise, John feared he would lose her forever.

As John approached the bush, he checked the progress of Chance and BJ. The men were almost to the bluff. John knew they would turn around and meet up with him on their way back. That was fine. It would give John a few minutes to find whatever had caught his eye in the brush.

Another desert mystery perhaps? His mind automatically conjured the stone writings.

NO DRINK.

They now occupied his thoughts quite often.

REMEMBER.

There was just something about them.

He was certain now that the writings were not part of the program. They were meant as a warning. A past program member had sensed something was wrong with the drink.

That had to be it.

So whoever it was ran into the desert and left the stone writings for future participants to find. To warn them.

What John couldn't figure out was why. Why not just report Doctor Regen to the American Medical Association after the three months of the program ended? Why not try to shut the entire program down if you realized it was force-feeding you medication without your consent?

And what was there about the whole thing that left him with that vague sense of dread that haunted him at night?

John stood in front of the bush and cocked his head. The vegetation had taken a beating. Large branches snapped in two. Broken thorns strewn about the desert floor.

John's eyebrows lifted as he noticed the odd coloration of the gravelly earth beneath the bush. He dropped to one knee for a closer look. It was familiar. The rocks and dirt were splotched in uneven patterns of maroon.

REMEMBER.

The image of the severed coyote heads flashed into John's mind. The open, vacant eyes. The fly walking across the black retina. The gnats gathered at the base of the wound. The pool of blood, greedily absorbed by the dry earth around it.

It was blood.

John reached his hand out and tentatively brushed his fingertips against several small pebbles baked a dry red. It was old blood. But it was blood.

A shiver ran down John's spine.

He glanced up and saw it. As he rested on his knee, the locket was at eye level. It hung on a thin gold chain, clinging to a thorny branch. The chain was broken.

He didn't touch it. Not at first. He simply watched it swing and turn in the breeze. This was what had caught the sun's morning rays and brought him to the bush. The locket was gold, shaped in an oval. It was old-fashioned. As it spun on the branch, John noticed a nondescript little design across each side of it.

It was the sort of jewelry that was familiar to everyone. Your grandmother owned one. Or perhaps your mother. There were thousands of these lockets in the world, but this particular one hung on a thorny branch in the middle of nowhere.

John's hand shook as he reached for the chain. He stopped and took a deep breath. It wasn't possible.

He closed his fingers around the locket and pulled. The chain slipped off the branch. It took him almost a minute to unclench his fingers.

"Yo, John! Where'd you go?"

The voice was BJ's, deep and echoing. John glanced up. The men were coming back, but they were still a good quarter-mile away.

"Yeah, over here!" He called out in return. "Just stretching a little. My legs felt tight."

His eyes returned to his closed fist. The chain extended from the top of his hand and loosely swung against his fingers.

He had to look before they got here. He had to know.

John opened his hand, and his thumb gently pressed the small gold clasp on top. The locket popped open.

John's world collapsed.

He fell backward, off his knees, and sat roughly in the gravel and dirt.

It wasn't possible. It wasn't possible.

The tears were there before he could stop them. Hot against his face. Burning with the same pain that crushed his heart.

It all finally made sense.

"John, you okay?"

This time, the voice belonged to Chance. It was closer than John expected, only a couple of hundred yards from where he was sitting. The guys were fast. He had to pull himself together. He stood and turned away from the approaching men, snorting to clear his nose before he spoke. He used his t-shirt to wipe the tears from his eyes and cheeks and continued to rub it against his forehead, feigning the motions of whisking away perspiration.

"Yeah, just got a little hot." He spoke into his shirt, still facing away from the men. "My legs feel better now." He turned from the bush and began to walk back. A quick glance showed his two running companions less than a hundred yards away.

"Well, I hope you got a good rest because we're only halfway there. Let's pick up the pace on the way back to the compound." Chance sounded upbeat. He did love his running.

"Shit." John could hear BJ's reply, somewhat less enthusiastic. "What are you, the Bionic Man or something?"

Seventy-five yards.

"Who?"

BJ glanced toward John and shouted. "We are old, John! We are old."

John forced a smile at the comment. He had never felt so old in his life.

The men were fifty yards away.

"Just don't ask him about *Gunsmoke*," John replied. "He won't have a clue who Marshall Dillon is." His voice sounded strange.

Thirty yards.

John glanced at his hand once more. He wanted to keep holding the locket. He wanted to look at it longer. He needed time to think. Time to figure out what the hell was going on. But time was almost out.

Twenty yards.

"Come on, guys," Chance was defending himself. "I know about *Gunsmoke*. It was a John Wayne movie, right?"

John closed his palm on the locket, snapping it shut.

Ten yards. They could see his hands through the brush if they were looking. Neither man was. The conversation continued.

"John Wayne?" BJ was incredulous. "Shit."

John forced another smile as he shoved his hand into his pocket, hiding the locket. He would open it again later. When he was alone. He would open it and look at the pictures inside once more. The tiny picture of himself as a young boy. And the tiny picture of his sister on the opposite side.

And he would try to figure out what the fuck was going on.

But for now, he had to run.

"Let me tell you about Marshall Dillon, Chance," John began as he moved his feet into a steady pace alongside the two men. "He was a lawman in the old west..."

His voice still sounded funny.

CHAPTER 55

VERNON RUBBED THE GRASSY WEEDS between the palms of his hands. Seeds and bits of shredded vegetation fell to the brown dirt of the garden. He threw the weeds over the chicken-wire fence and kicked the earth to bury his handiwork. He would be sure to water the seeds that afternoon.

All part of the plan.

Vernon had worried that after Denise left, Sarah wouldn't want to work in the garden anymore. If that happened, she wouldn't get all hot and sweaty in the afternoons. And if she didn't get sweaty, Vernon doubted she would continue to shower following the spiritual meetings after dinner. That would have been bad.

But he had worried for nothing. Even with Denise gone, Sarah came to work every day, pulling the weeds that kept coming back no matter how many times she cleaned out a particular section of the garden. It was her routine.

She and Vernon never spoke, and he would usually only work for an hour or so and then leave. No sense in having a heatstroke himself.

The plan was still going well. It was everything to him. His one outlet. The one pleasure that consumed his thoughts. Watching Sarah Michaels shower. Oh, he would love to get some of that.

He spent his mornings sprinkling the seeds while everybody else ran (Vernon walked to the trail then made a big circle back to the garden. No one cared about his running anyway. That was an old rule that wasn't enforced anymore). He would suffer through the pre-lunch group meetings and listen to everyone talk about how miserable the outside world was and how happy they were here and how thankful they were to Doctor Regen for allowing them into the program. Then he would sit in his private therapy sessions with the doctor during the afternoon. She would talk to him about his place in the world. That he was a follower, and there was nothing wrong with that. He just needed to find someone strong to follow.

And at night, he would listen to Marcus Kane speak over the dancing flames. Vernon would be torn between his anticipation of watching Sarah shower and the words flowing from Kane's mouth. The giant was right about a lot of things. He was right about needing to forget the past. He was right about embracing who you are. He was right about so much. And somewhere in the back of his mind, Vernon had decided that Kane would be the man he would follow. It was like Doctor Regen said—he needed someone strong. And no one was stronger than Marcus Kane. In the desert, Kane was the king.

That was why it came as such a shock to hear his deep, soft voice that morning.

"We need to talk, Vernon."

The rat-man's head shot up at the sound. Kane was standing by the windmill, hands behind his back, black shirt stretched tight across his shoulders and chest.

No one *ever* saw Kane outside of drinking the supplements at dawn and his speeches over the fire at night. And now he was at the garden, wanting to talk with Vernon. It was like being visited by Jesus. Or Satan.

Shit. Vernon was supposed to be running. Kane had seen him plant the weeds. How was he going to explain this? This wasn't part of the plan.

"Um," Vernon stammered, his eyes looking at Kane's boots, not at his face. "I was just checking on the cabbage before I started my run." His voice lifted on the last word. It had come out sounding like a question. Shit.

Kane took a step forward. He was standing by the chicken wire now. The fence that reached Vernon's navel stopped at Kane's thighs.

"Don't worry about the runs, Vernon," he said gently. "You don't need to run. And besides, you don't like to run, do you?"

Was it a trick question? Vernon kept his eyes on the black boots on the other side of the fence. How do you lie to a god? You don't. Vernon shook his head. He didn't like the runs.

"Vernon, look at me." The command was simple, but the rat-man's fear made meeting Kane's gaze a near impossibility. Finally, almost painfully, he raised his head and looked at the face of his master.

"Good. Tell me Vernon, what is the point of the program? Why are you here?"

Shit. More questions. Vernon's mind raced. He vaguely remembered jumping off a bridge. And the doctor at the hospital had signed him up for this program. Shit. What else? Why *was* he here?

"You're here to find happiness. Correct?"

Vernon nodded. *Of course*. Fuck. That's what they talked about all the time. Why couldn't he remember that?

"Tell me, Vernon. Are you doing all the things that make you happy right now?"

This had to be a trick question. He wanted to please Kane, wanted to give the right answer. He nodded his head, but he didn't take his eyes off of Kane's. Now that he was looking at him, he couldn't look away.

"Don't lie to me, Vernon." The low voice now had a hardness to it.

Shit.

"I want you to be all you can be," Kane continued. That tone had lost some of its edge and was lulling again. "You can't be happy unless you allow yourself to become the person you should be, and you can only do that by doing the things that make you happy. No limits, Vernon. No rules. Do it."

Vernon started to nod in agreement, then stopped. No. He couldn't do everything he wanted. He had never been able to. He had almost been killed by a cop in L.A. for doing the things that made him happy. He couldn't let that happen again.

Kane seemed to read his mind.

"You're worried, aren't you? You're worried that you can't do the things you want. *That it's against the rules*. Look around you, Vernon."

Vernon's eyes left Kane for the first time at his command. His head swiveled as he took in his surroundings. The garden. The fence. The windmill. The brush. The buildings. The desert. The nothingness.

"I make the rules here. And I want you to do that thing you want to do. I want you to be all you can be. Do you understand me?"

Vernon looked into Kane's eyes again. Could he? Yes. He could. Kane said so. He could do anything. And he knew how. In the back of his mind, he had been planning it all along. Maybe just as a fantasy, but he had been making his calculations.

His hand went to his back pocket. It was there. His one personal item he had chosen to keep for the program. The one thing he had brought from the outside world. And it was still sharp.

He had what he needed. He could do it. Kane said so.

"The others will be running for another hour or so. You have time. Think about what I said."

Vernon nodded again. Kane turned and walked slowly away. Vernon stood in place, not moving for several moments. Then it hit him. The clock was ticking. He needed to get to it. He had to make calculations. He had to do this right.

Because if you can't do something right, don't do it at all.

Fucking-A.

CHAPTER 56

CUTTER VALENTINE peered through the windshield at the fading name on the weathered mailbox.

Albright.

This was it. He turned the steering wheel and guided his pick-up truck down the driveway toward the white house. The Albright place was a couple of miles outside town off the main highway that ran through Sonora. The rooftops of their neighbors' houses could be just discerned in the distance. Spacious property was the norm in the Sonora suburbs.

Cutter stopped the truck at the end of the driveway. An ancient carport housed two vehicles. A pick-up truck much like Cutter's own and an aged Chevrolet Caprice. The car was a light brown color. Tan. Cutter figured Mrs. Albright had probably liked that color. She wouldn't have had to wash it very often.

Cutter opened his door, and the afternoon heat washed over him. He retrieved his hat and pushed it firmly onto his head.

What the hell was he doing?

The cattle pens weren't finished. He still had another solid week's worth of work before they would be useable, but something had been tugging at him the past few days. Something that wouldn't go away no matter how much iron he cut or how many tiny burns he got on his forearms from the welding sparks.

He needed to talk to Jim Albright. He wasn't sure why. And he really wasn't sure whether it was a good idea. If Jim was home caring for his wife, the last thing on his mind would be a suicide case from more than half a year ago.

Alzheimer's affected more than just those battling the illness. It shattered the lives of the victim's loved ones—the poor souls who had to remind their mother of their names, who had to reteach their husbands how to use toilet paper. At his age, Cutter had seen the effects of the disease in several of his friends' families, but thank God, never his own.

He walked up the wooden steps of the front porch and stopped. This was a bad idea. Jim Albright had his hands full as it was. There was no point in dragging up old cases.

But you can't teach an old dog new tricks. And Cutter couldn't get that nagging feeling out of his head. Something smelled funny.

He needed to talk to the former sheriff of Sonora. If nothing else, he just needed to meet the man.

Hell with it.

Cutter knocked soundly on the door three times. He turned from the door while he waited, looking out over the Albright's front yard. Like most folks in Sonora Valley, they had a rock garden. Clusters of bleached white stones were arranged throughout the yard and lined the driveway.

No one answered the door.

Cutter gave it another minute, then looked for a doorbell. Pressing the button, an electronic chime sounded inside. The bell was loud. That should do it.

Another two minutes.

Cutter rapped his knuckles on the door harder. Five quick knocks.

Still nothing.

He hooked his thumbs into his front belt-loops and descended the front porch steps. No one was home.

He glanced back at the carport. There was no way the sheriff of a tiny town like Sonora would have more than two vehicles.

Cutter made his way around to the back of the house, glancing into the windows of the home as he walked. None of the curtains were drawn, but Cutter didn't see any activity inside. No lights were on.

The back porch of the house was little more than a concrete slab under a tin roof supported by two wooden poles. An old freezer sat beside the back door. Cutter opened it. The wire shelves rested at angles on the bottom of the fridge, and a few ice trays were left there. It was hot.

Cutter looked between the freezer and the wall. Not plugged in.

He knocked on the back door loudly for several seconds and waited. A red wasp flew by his ear. Cutter looked up and noticed several nests hanging from the corrugated tin roof.

If you leave them alone, they'll leave you alone.

Still no answer at the door. He knocked again, and this time announced his presence.

"Mr. Albright? This is Earl Valentine. I'm working with Dwight at the sheriff's office."

Still nothing.

His thumbs returned to his belt-loops and Cutter took two steps toward his truck before stopping. Something smelled funnier now than ever. He just didn't know what.

Hell with it again.

Cutter turned around and reached for the doorknob. It was unlocked. He pushed and the door eased open with a soft creak.

"Mr. Albright?"

Nothing. Cutter hadn't expected a reply.

He stepped inside what turned out to be the kitchen. Green linoleum lined the floor, and the counters and appliances were a unique shade of avocado that Cutter hadn't seen since the seventies.

He took several steps into the kitchen and listened intently. No sound. No air-conditioning either. It was hot as the mischief in the house.

"Hello?"

Once more, just to be certain. The last thing he wanted was an irate (and likely armed) lawman who thought he was trespassing.

Still no answer.

Cutter began to walk through the house. He wasn't sure what he was looking for, if anything. He was just looking. It was what he did. One of this old dog's few tricks.

He glanced into the bedrooms. There were only two. One had a big old bed that had surely seen many a night with the sheriff and his wife. The other had a small twin bed and a smaller desk. An old file cabinet sat next to it. The sheriff had sometimes taken his work home, it seemed.

Cutter scanned the pictures hanging in the hallway. They were all of the same couple. In some, Jim and his wife were a dark-haired twosome that had apparently been to the beach and even smooched with the Statue of Liberty in the background on one occasion. In others, the hair of both had started to gray as they pointed to Mount Rushmore and posed in front of the Grand Canyon. One or two pictures showed the couple when the hair had turned all gray. They were still smiling.

No kids. Apparently, the twin bed in the other bedroom must have been for the sheriff when he got in trouble. Cutter smiled at the thought.

Standing in the hallway, he noticed the closet. There was no door, just a frayed brown curtain that hung from the frame, supported by several thumbtacks. Cutter pushed the curtain aside and reviewed the contents of the closet.

Jackets hung from a wooden pole. A few colorful blankets were stacked on a shelf above the pole. Three big Samsonite suitcases sat in a line on the floor. The luggage had decals and bumper stickers posted across their heavy black fronts touting the destinations they had seen, including the classic "I 'heart' New York." Cutter smiled again.

He let the curtain fall back into place and walked out of the kitchen and into the yard, closing the back door behind him. He wasn't sure what he had expected to find, but he had just walked through the house of a nice old couple who wasn't home. Maybe they had gone to stay with a family member. No kids, but maybe there was a sister or brother. Someone who could help Jim care for his wife.

Or if that was the case, maybe he had broken down and taken her to a professional facility. Sometimes that was the only option.

Wherever it was, it was for an extended stay. When you didn't want to pay for airport parking, you had a friend drive you, or you took a cab or a shuttle. Even from out here, it would be cheaper than the outrageous parking rates the airport charged. Two vehicles in the carport was no big deal. It was only natural.

Cutter shook his head. He felt sorry for the nice couple who had seen Mount Rushmore and New York City. Old age was a bitch, but what are you gonna do?

He opened the door to his truck and climbed inside. He needed to get back to work on the pens.

Besides, he had seen all he needed to see at the Albright place. What he had seen wouldn't strike him as really unusual until later that evening.

CHAPTER 57

VERNON LICKED HIS LIPS as he crouched in the dark, waiting. He was so hard, it hurt. This was so fucking cool.

The door to the supply closet was cracked about three inches, just wide enough that Vernon could peek through and see the showers, but not quite so wide that enough light would get into the closet to reveal his hiding place.

He tightened his grip on the handle of the four-inch switchblade knife then relaxed his fingers again. He had used the knife to loosen the screws on the skylight that morning, after his conversation with Kane. One screw at each corner. It had been so easy.

After that night's spiritual awakening meeting over the fire, Vernon had casually walked away from the group, then raced around the camp's perimeter to the back of the women's barracks. The wooden pallets were arranged perfectly. He was on the roof in ten seconds, and slipping in through the skylight within thirty seconds. That was the hardest part. The skylight was located between the two shower stalls, so Vernon had to carefully stand on top of the concrete partitioning walls of the showers and lower himself in. It was tough.

He had to go fast, or Sarah would walk right in on him. He had to be quiet, because he wasn't sure how soon Sarah would open the front door of the barracks and go to her locker to get her towel and get undressed. He had to be careful, because the last thing he needed was to fall and break his leg in the women's bathroom.

But he had made it. With plenty of time to spare. And now he was crouched in the dark supply closet, waiting. And it was so fucking cool.

CHAPTER 58

JOHN PACED BETWEEN THE BUNK BEDS in the men's barracks. The light from the four bare bulbs in the ceiling cast strange shadows on the gray concrete floor. Every now and then, he heard a comment from outside the door made by BJ or Chance. The two men were playing "Around the World" in the courtyard. The game had changed over the weeks, and it was no longer as fun. It was played mostly in silence now—just something to occupy the time, tossing stones onto the sundial—and at this moment, the game was the farthest thing from John's mind.

His thoughts raced. He was torn between his grief and the need to develop a plan. He had known the situation was bad, but the events of the day had made it exponentially worse. This was no longer a case of a warped suicide treatment program. Lives were at stake. And some lives had already been lost.

John clenched his hand around the gold locket. The day had been so hard. He had been forced to go through the motions, keep up appearances while he tried to sort things out. He had spent the afternoon alone, walking the compound, noticing things and remembering.

He noticed the garage door on the shed could only be opened from the inside. And he remembered the sound of the small engine he heard that one night.

He noticed the other metal door leading inside the shed was secured with a padlock. And he remembered spotting the key hanging from Doctor Regen's necklace, and the outline of a similar key beneath Kane's shirt.

He noticed the faces of the group that night at the spiritual awakening while Kane launched into a mighty tirade against the outside world. He noticed the blank expressions of acceptance as glassy eyes shined in the dancing flames of the campfire. He noticed Sarah carried the same expression. And he remembered the night Denise went missing, when his wife told him he had a choice to make, she belonged to the program.

How could he have ever let it come to this?

That was the worst of it. In the end, this was all his fault. He had blamed Sarah's father for the accident that killed his baby and almost ended his marriage, but John had been the one who shut his wife out for so long. John had been the one who chose to drown his sorrow in booze rather than share his feelings. He had been the one who couldn't see that the woman he loved was ready to swallow her death in the little blue pills. And he had been the one who, so many years ago, had driven his sister away. And Jennifer had landed in this Godforsaken program. And her blood was now baked into the dry and merciless earth of the New Mexico desert.

It was all his fault.

And he had to set it right. No matter what, he would get his wife out of this alive. He had let her swallow the pills once, but he'd be damned if he stood aside and let her worship a monster like Kane until her life was taken away, just like Jennifer's.

But he had to figure out a way to tell Sarah. He had seen her face tonight in the pulsing orange glow of the fire. He knew the power the program held over her. Her mind was caught in the chemical frenzy of that green bile being fed to the group. And the truth was, John didn't know if he'd be able to break through it. But he had to try. He had to find a way.

John held his closed fist to his lips and kissed the golden locket held within. He was so sorry. So sorry for what had happened.

It was all his fault.

CHAPTER 59

VERNON TENTATIVELY TOUCHED THE DOORKNOB, closed his eyes and quietly breathed in through his nose. He could smell the shampoo. It was the same shampoo they used in the men's barracks, but it smelled different here.

Sweeter.

He gripped the switchblade with his other hand. His palm was sweaty. He was sweaty all over. This was so great.

It was almost like a dream. Something he fantasized about when he was on the roof or lying in bed at night, but something he had known he would never do in real life. *Except he was doing it.* He was doing it right now. Kane said he could.

He opened his eyes and peered through the cracked door. The white lather of the sweet shampoo coated Sarah's hair and ran in little streams down her face. Her eyes were closed tight against the suds as she massaged her scalp with her fingers. She was facing Vernon. Her breasts jiggled as she shampooed. Water trickled down in a current between her breasts then formed an upside-down V at her navel. Two little streams ran to either side of that delicious black bush.

Vernon licked his lips again. Now was the time. He had planned it. He had made his calculations. This was perfect.

He pushed and the door swung open easily. He tiptoed out of the supply closet. A little noise would be okay, eventually. By now, Teri would be back in the dining hall by herself, doing whatever it was she did in there. Maude would be sitting on the concrete slab outside of one of the buildings, watching the men play that stupid game with their rocks.

He took a few steps toward the shower stall. Sarah was leaning back into the jets of water, the shampoo rinsing from her hair and landing in splatters on the tile floor. Vernon glanced down. A tiny circle of white suds was resting on the toe of his running shoe.

He smiled and raised the knife. Damn she looked good. This was going to feel fucking great.

Sarah turned and pushed her face into the water, rinsing away the last of the shampoo. Vernon was so excited he couldn't stand it. He shook his leg, hoping the khaki material of his pants would shift and not bind his erection so much. He'd need it in a second.

Sarah turned around and opened her eyes. Vernon saw the look of immediate shock on her face, then her instinctive reaction. Her hands were a blur of motion—the right lifting and covering the nipple of her left breast, while trusting her elbow to shield her right nipple (it didn't work, Vernon could still see half of that perfect pink circle) and her left hand going downstairs, covering her womanhood. She took a sharp, deep breath. She was about to scream.

Vernon had thought of that. It was a perfectly natural reaction. Of course it would take Sarah a moment to realize how much she wanted him. And she would. Vernon knew that once she thought about what was happening—once she saw the knife and realized the danger she was in—that she would get excited. It was every girl's fantasy. Sarah was going to like this. She was going to get wet.

Vernon lifted his finger to his lips and raised the switchblade to eye level.

"Ah, ah, ah," he said softly. "You scream, and I'll cut you."

The breath hitched in Sarah's throat. Her eyes were wide in terror, but she didn't scream.

He knew it.

"I knew it," he said, nodding in satisfaction. "Now, we're going to get down to business. You and me. Turn around and bend over, bitch."

Vernon never saw it coming. One moment, Sarah's bare foot was set in the puddle of running water on the tiled shower floor, the next, an explosion of pain erupted from Vernon's balls that he felt into his lower back. He leaned forward, clutching at himself and gasping for breath. He was raising the knife when he heard the scream, ear-splitting and echoing in the cement confines of the bathroom.

"JOHN!"

CHAPTER 60

JOHN HAD JUST OPENED THE DOOR of the men's barracks when he heard the scream. It was muffled by the walls of the women's quarters, but John knew his wife's voice.

BJ and Chance were standing on the concrete slab in front of the dining hall. Maude was sitting in front of the women's barracks, staring into the night. The fire still blazed in front of the sundial.

John bolted toward the sound of Sarah's voice and was halfway across the courtyard when the door to the women's barracks swung outward, banging against the concrete wall. A hunched over Vernon, brandishing a knife, ran out of the building. He didn't see Maude sitting there and collided with her, his knee ramming into the middle of her back. She cried out and Vernon flew over her, face first into the dirt of the courtyard.

John was past the sundial when Sarah appeared in the doorway. She was soaking wet, clutching a towel around her with one hand and pointing at Vernon with the other. No words came out of her mouth, just guttural noises of fear and rage. She held the towel to her chest, between her breasts, and it spilled open past her stomach, revealing her to the world. She didn't care. John didn't care.

He never broke stride.

John knew what the little bastard attempting to regain his balance had tried. And it was over.

He dove past the blazing fire and tackled Vernon from behind. Vernon lost his balance and fell face first into the ground. John concentrated on grabbing the knife.

First things first.

Vernon's hands were all over the place, struggling to free himself from the weight of the man on top of him, but John didn't let up. He managed to grab Vernon's wrist and forced it back as hard as he could. He wanted to hear a snap. He wanted the hand to come flopping back toward the vermin's shoulder.

The wrist didn't break, but the knife fell from Vernon's hand.

John didn't try to grab it. He didn't need it. Instead, he kicked at the blade and sent it flying into the darkness.

BJ and Chance were right there, but they didn't jump in. John didn't need any help. That was evident.

From the corner of his eye, John saw Sarah standing next to Maude. Dirt was clinging to his wife's wet legs.

John rolled the struggling rat-man onto his back and drove a punch with all the force he could muster into Vernon's face. He felt the cartilage in the nose give way under his fist. The punch also sent a wave of pain up John's forearm. He hadn't tightened his fist properly, and the blow had sprained his wrist.

He didn't care.

John rained punch after punch onto the squealing man. Vernon couldn't fight back. He kept trying to cover his face, but John would knock his hands away, or punch straight through them.

The group was in a circle around them now. Chance and BJ and Maude and Teri all watching John pummel the most despised member of the program. And Sarah. She was watching, too.

John landed a solid shot to Vernon's eye, and the rat-man let out a loud cry.

It wasn't enough.

All the pain, all the anger, all the grief from the program flowed from John's shoulders and exploded through his fists. He punched the vermin's mouth at just the right angle and Vernon's front teeth punctured his lip. The lip stayed in place for a moment, anchored by the incisor, then slipped away when the blood lubricated the tooth enough to permit it.

Out in the middle of nowhere. Sister dead. Force-fed fucking chemicals that did God-knows-what. And now this piece of shit child molester tries to rape my wife.

John stopped punching and dropped his hands to Vernon's throat. His thumbs positioned beneath the Adam's apple. Squeezing felt good.

Vernon's eyes were already swelling shut from the lacerations and the bruises, but John could see the look of desperation on his face.

Fucking child molester. Rat bastard rapist.

John looked up at the faces of those in the circle. Everyone was leaning forward, eyes wide. There was no shock. No indignation. Only...anticipation.

That's when he heard it.

"Kill him."

The voice belonged to BJ. John saw the reflection of orange flames dancing in his eyes. The effect was eerie.

He squeezed harder on Vernon's throat.

"Kill him, John."

This time it was Chance.

"Kill him."

Maude, echoing the others.

John lifted Vernon's head and banged it into the hard-packed earth of the courtyard as he continued to choke him.

"Kill him."

Teri joining in.

John tightened his grip.

"Kill him."

BJ repeating himself. Chance saying it with him.

An ugly gurgling sound from Vernon's mouth.

"Kill him."

A new voice. Sarah's eyes were wide as she said it. Expectant.

No.

A scream erupted from John's throat as he released his grip, letting Vernon's head drop to the dirt. The rat-man rolled away in a panic until he struck the base of the sundial, and he sucked in a huge, strained breath.

The group went silent.

"No." John stood and turned his back on Vernon to face the members of the program. "I'm not going to kill him."

Sarah looked incredulous. It hurt John just to see her face.

Vernon struggled to regain his feet. He planted one hand in front of him and the other on the side of the stone sundial for balance, then eased himself onto his knees. He was starting to take another gulp of air when a massive hand enveloped his tender neck and clamped down hard.

Kane jerked Vernon upright with one hand, using the man's throat as his only grip. He bent his knees and clamped his other hand onto Vernon's groin in a powerful blow. Kane stepped close to the smaller man and lifted him, holding Vernon horizontally against his chest like a powerlifter with a barbell.

With barely a grunt, Kane pressed his arms upward and raised Vernon over his head, one hand still wrapped around the vermin's neck and the other holding his crotch. Vernon's legs kicked weakly.

John couldn't believe what he was seeing. It looked like something out of professional wrestling, only this wasn't fake. This was as real as it gets.

Kane spun in a slow circle, turning toward each member of the group, holding Vernon above him as if the man was nothing more than a rag doll. Blood ran from Vernon's battered face and trailed down Kane's arm. John could tell he was trying to speak, but Kane's grip allowed no words to pass.

"This one has violated the sanctity of the family. He is a traitor."

Kane's voice was deep and resonant, but not excited. To John, the giant appeared perfectly calm as he displayed Vernon to his congregation.

"What shall we do with him?"

John shook his head. This couldn't be happening.

"Kill him."

No. The words were soft, but clear. John would know that voice anywhere.

Please God no.

Sarah's head was raised as she watched Kane. She wanted this.

Murmurs of agreement from the rest of the group.

Kane turned the circle once again as he locked eyes with each member of the group. Vernon squeaked. The rat-man knew what was coming.

Kane stopped at John. Their eyes met for a five-second eternity. It was dark in the ebbing flames of the fire, but John could have sworn he saw Kane smile.

Kane turned and brought his arms down with swift and unrelenting force. Vernon's torso smashed onto the iron blade of the sundial with a sickening thud. The point of the half-inch-thick blade cut between Vernon's ribs and shattered his spine.

From the force, John expected the blade to puncture all the way through Vernon's chest, but it didn't. Instead, it just left a peculiar shape to the rat-man's ribcage.

Vernon's body hung on the long, thin steel. His legs dangled off the end of the sundial while his arms fell to either side. It looked like the vermin had taken the Nestea plunge onto the massive stone.

John wanted to turn away from the body, but he couldn't. Everyone else was still staring. One of Vernon's feet started kicking, as if he was chasing rabbits in his sleep. It was the last thing he would ever do.

John looked at the rat-man's small eyes, but he was too far away. Even with the fire burning, they were just black holes in the night.

This couldn't be happening.

That's when it started. The first of the chanting. John wasn't sure who initiated it. It sounded like Teri. A single, lonely voice.

"Kane. Kane. Kane."

But it didn't take long for everyone to join in.

"Kane. Kane. Kane."

The chant was growing louder, faster, rising into the heavens with the smoke from the burning fire.

"Kane. Kane. Kane."

John looked at his wife. Sarah was still holding the towel. It was no longer gaping. It fully covered her nakedness. The flames made the remaining drops of water on her shoulders glisten. Her face was intense as she chanted. She was a different woman.

"Kane. Kane. Kane."

Marcus Kane lifted his arms, accepting his role as ruler of these people. John had no illusions about that fact. Though Denise had told him only two short weeks ago that everyone looked to John for leadership, the events of this night firmly shifted the balance of power to the giant in the black shirt.

The same son of a bitch that John was certain murdered Denise. And his sister.

"Kane. Kane. Kane."

John knew he should join in the chanting. It was important to keep up appearances, at least until he could figure out a way to get the hell out of there. But he couldn't do it. He couldn't chant his name. So he stood there, still breathing hard from the fight with Vernon, staring at the massive form of Marcus Kane.

"Kane. Kane. Kane."

Their eyes locked over the flames, and for the second time that night, John was certain he saw Kane smile.

CHAPTER 61

"CAL, I SERIOUSLY DOUBT THEY PAY YOU enough to keep these kinds of hours." Cutter smiled as he stepped into the office and addressed the old man.

Cal stood and walked from behind his desk, offering Cutter a hearty handshake with his bony fingers.

"Well, a mayor's work is never done. A fact I'm certain you're aware of, Cutter Valentine." The old man was grinning and wearing the same white, pressed western shirt with the bolo tie that he had worn when he first rode out to see Cutter. Or maybe he just had a closet full of them at home.

"Such is life," Cutter began, "I was glad to hear you were still at the office. I'll be honest, I just planned on calling and leaving a message."

The mayor's office was a white, one-room mobile home with a wooden plaque hung from a post by the sidewalk – *Sonora Mayoral Office*. The interior was mostly barren. An ancient yellow couch. A desk with two chairs in front of it. And a card table supporting a Mr. Coffee and some Styrofoam cups. Not a lot of frills with this job.

"Now Cutter, ever since the Missus passed on, I've lived alone. I never mind a phone call, but you can't leave me a message. No answering machines here or in my house. Don't believe in them. None of that voicemail stuff either. Life is far too complicated without all that new-fangled technology. Computers and answering machines and cellular phones and whatnot are nothing but trouble. Hell, I wouldn't have a television if it wasn't for that show with the girlie lifeguards on the beach."

Cal raised one eyebrow in a conspiratorial manner and grinned wide enough for Cutter to see his dentures.

"Well, thanks for waiting around after I called. I just wanted to drop by and ask you about—"

The door to the office swung open and Dwight stepped inside. "Hey, Uncle Cal. Hey, Mr. Valent—Cutter. I hope I'm not interrupting anything."

Cal shook his head at the young man. "Not at all, boy, that's why I asked you down here. Mr. Valentine called and said he wanted to talk to me about something, and I figured the Deputy Sheriff of Sonora Valley ought to be here, too."

"Actually Dwight," Cutter said, "I'm glad you're here. I was going to drop by the office tomorrow anyway."

The deputy's eyebrows narrowed in anticipation. It was an expression Cutter had come to expect from the kid whenever they spoke.

"Is something wrong?" he asked.

"No, not at all. It's really not anything important, that's why I hadn't meant to drag everyone out here in the middle of the night. It's just that I was thinking about Jim Albright earlier today and decided to go visit him."

Cal eased himself back into his desk chair. "Did you now? How's Francine? Doing any better?"

Cutter shook his head. "I wouldn't know. I'm afraid I didn't get the chance to meet her. They weren't home."

"Maybe they were at Mercer's," Cal offered. "Jim told me a while back that he can't leave Francine at home when he goes for groceries anymore."

"No. Both their vehicles were in the driveway, but they weren't home. The back door was unlocked, so I stepped inside and took a quick look around, just to be sure everything was okay."

Cal lifted an eyebrow at the remark. Cutter wondered if either man would call him on it. Without probable cause that sort of thing was basically unlawful entry, but this was a small town, and he doubted if either the mayor or the deputy would see a problem with his actions.

"Find anything?" Cal asked.

Cutter shook his head again. "Not really. Just your normal stuff. But it occurred to me this evening that I should probably talk to you two. Just to see if Jim has contacted either of you lately—told you they were going out of town or something."

Dwight shook his head and Cal responded likewise.

"No," the old man said. "But that doesn't mean much. Jim always kept to himself a bit, particularly after Francine went under. I think it embarrassed him a little. A man doesn't like to admit he can't protect his family, but sickness is something that none of us can stop. Especially hers."

Cutter nodded. "Yeah, I understand that. But neither of you have gotten any phone calls lately? Letters?"

"No sir," Dwight said. "But like Uncle Cal said, that's not so unusual. If they went to stay with family or something, we probably wouldn't hear from him until they got back."

"That's pretty much what I thought, but I did want to check," Cutter responded. "Sorry to keep you guys out this late."

He walked to the door but stopped with his hand on the doorknob.

"Course, one thing did strike me as funny," he said. "I told you I looked through their house a bit. They seemed like nice folks. No kids, but it looked like they traveled an awful lot. Some nice pictures on the wall from their trips, but they didn't have a lot of nice stuff. I imagine Jim and his wife lived pretty frugally on a sheriff's salary."

Cal and Dwight both nodded at the comment.

"I've known plenty of folks like the Albrights," Cutter continued. "People who don't have much, but what they do have they use."

He paused for a moment.

"So if the Albrights did go to stay with a family member, even if they caught a ride with someone else, why would their luggage still be in the hall closet?"

Cutter put on his hat and walked out the door.

CHAPTER 62

SARAH MICHAELS stared at the gold locket on the table.

"I don't understand, John. What are you telling me? That your sister's here?"

Her husband shook his head. It didn't move much. He was resting his forehead in his palms. He wasn't crying, but it was evident the story had taken a lot out of him.

The door to the library was still closed. That was good. She didn't want anyone else hearing this.

Of course, there wasn't much chance of that. No one had bothered them since Sarah had gotten dressed and the two of them had come in here. She figured everyone else was probably in bed by now, even after the excitement of the evening.

Everyone except Vernon.

"No," John began, "she *was* here. I found the locket in the desert. There was blood on the ground."

"John, just because you saw someone die tonight, it doesn't mean your sister was killed." She did her best soothe him. "If the locket was hers, then Jennifer was probably here at some point to get therapy. You told me yourself that she was a mopey, angry kid. She must have come here for help, like us. And I'm sure that Doctor Regen helped her, just like she's helping us."

"But she wasn't getting help. She figured out what was going on. That's why she left the stone writings out there. NO DRINK. REMEMBER. She wanted to warn others about the drugs and their effects in case she didn't make it out of the program."

Sarah rolled her eyes without thinking. John didn't see the expression. "John, there's no way you could know it was Jennifer who arranged those rocks. It could have been kids. And if the writings are so important, why didn't you mention them to me before, when you first found them? Why now?"

"Because I didn't know what they meant. I didn't know what was going on with any of this until two weeks ago when I started throwing up the formula."

Sarah's eyebrows shot up. "You started doing what?"

John sighed. "Two weeks ago I was running and got sick. After I vomited, the buzzing in my head started to go away. So I've been drinking the juice every morning to keep up appearances and then going to the bathroom to throw up. I couldn't let Kane know that I realized something was wrong with the formula."

"John, do you realize how crazy this sounds? Stone writings? Your sister's locket? Vomiting every morning on purpose? In secret?"

"Sarah, listen to me." John reached across the table and put his hands over hers. "I know this sounds crazy, and I know how hard this is for you to believe. Right now, it's hard for you to think straight. It's hard to remember. All you can hear is that buzzing. I understand, but I want you to fight it for me. Fight it for us."

Sarah sat in silence as she considered his words. *A buzz?* Was that what he called it? She runs, loses weight, and works in a garden just so she can finally feel good—and he chalks it up to a chemical *buzz*? Why did John have to do this?

"So all of this is one big conspiracy? Kane? Doctor Regen? Doctor Cornelius in Boston? All those other psychiatrists who recommended everyone else in the program? They're all in on it, too?"

John's head lowered at the comments. So he didn't have all the answers.

"And what is the big conspiracy? Illegal drug testing? Is that what you're accusing them of?"

"It's not just the drugs," John replied. "It's more than that. I think the entire program is geared toward some form of mind control. The drugs merely deaden the emotional nerves, make you open to it. That's why Kane started those 'spiritual awakenings' at night. It's the perfect set-up. Everyone in the group spends every waking hour together, getting to know one another, becoming friends, learning each other's strengths and weaknesses. *Except Kane*. He's the one person you never see. The unseen force. He comes out just long enough to tell us he's our protector and to smash a tarantula and decapitate some coyotes. He's hinting at his power. It's like a damn teaser at the movie theater."

He stopped. He always interjected pauses when he was in lecture mode. Sarah waited.

"You see, it's hard enough for people to take orders from a friend. It's damn near impossible to accept spiritual enlightenment from someone whom you've seen gripe about his petty problems in a group therapy session. But if you're the man behind the curtain—the man of mystery—then when you appear, everyone is open to following your guidance. We spent two months listening to how we needed to belong to a greater purpose, how we needed to accept the family of the program. Suddenly, right when we need it most, Kane steps out from behind the curtain. He's like Warren Buffett appearing to take over a troubled company, swooping in from the sky to turn it around and make it profitable. He's the hero."

Sarah cocked her head listening to the analogy. It was still unbelievable, but she got the gist.

"But something must have gone wrong with Jennifer, just like it went wrong with Denise. Maybe the drugs didn't react properly to their systems. Denise sat right there and told me she felt *wrong*. She told me she wanted to leave the program, and I told her she should." John's voice softened as he spoke. "Now she's gone."

Sarah squeezed her husband's hands. No matter how incredible the story, he obviously believed it with all his heart.

"But John," she said gently, "Think about it. If something funny really is going on, why hasn't anyone reported it? Why isn't Doctor Regen under some kind of investigation? Why wouldn't someone just go to the authorities after they finish the program? It doesn't make sense."

John closed his eyes before he spoke.

"Sarah, I don't think anyone *ever* finishes the program." His voice was quiet. Sarah let go of his hands and pulled hers away, leaning back in the metal folding chair.

"What are you saying?"

"Remember that first night of the program, I told you something didn't add up about the people selected as participants?"

Sarah nodded, only vaguely recalling the conversation. It was hard to remember.

"It wasn't just about the money—it was obvious no one else could afford to pay the same price for admission we did. What was unusual was the fact that nobody had anyone who would miss them. No one waiting at home, hoping the program went well. No one who would expect a phone call at some point. *No one...period.* Even you and me. It took me a while to realize that, but it's true. The only person in this world I care about—and the only person who cares for me—is you. And if something happened that caused us to disappear together, no one would ever stir up a fuss."

A chill ran up Sarah's spine. She didn't like this conversation. She had been humoring him at first, but this was getting serious.

"And if all eight of us were like that," John continued, "It's very reasonable to assume all the other program members before us could have been like that, too. There's no telling how many people have slept in our beds, or drank that same green formula, with Kane and Doctor Regen taking notes on the results. Tweaking the drug mixture a little each time to see how it affected the new group."

"Stop it, John." Sarah's voice was low, but clear. "What you're describing isn't possible. Doctor Regen is helping us. She's a psychiatrist. Psychiatrists don't go around experimenting on people. It's wrong."

"I know it's wrong," John said. "But that doesn't mean it's not happening."

Sarah shook her head. She didn't want to hear this.

"Even if you're right, even if they are testing drugs, that doesn't mean we're all going to die. There are eight of us. Too many to try anything like that. Even for Kane."

"There are only six of us now," John corrected. "And I don't know *what* is going to happen. But I think I know when."

"What are you talking about?"

John leaned forward. "I think we have less than three weeks until it happens. That's the next full moon. It coincides with the end of the program. See, there was a full moon the first night we were here—I remember because I didn't sleep and could see it through the skylight."

He paused again. He didn't need to explain his sleeping patterns to Sarah.

"The lunar cycle is approximately one month long," he continued. "Three lunar cycles would take us through the different phases of the program. By the end of the third lunar cycle, the next full moon, everyone in the program would have been on the drugs for ninety days. They would have been listening to Kane's nightly spiritual awakenings for an entire month. And the full moon is thought to alter the body's balance to a certain extent. That's when people do crazy things. By the time the next full moon rolls around, everyone here may be willing to do, well, anything. You saw what we were all like tonight."

Sarah caught the meaning of the comment. After all, John always measured his words. He had used "we" in that last sentence for a reason, and Sarah knew it. Because she had been paying attention in the courtyard, too. And she had noticed how everyone acted as well. Including her husband.

"John, I won't lie to you, most of this stuff sounds crazy, but I know you really believe in it and it does make some sense. I trust you."

She stroked his cheek with her fingertips.

"But tonight has been one of the worst nights of my life. I don't think I can handle much more of this. Let me think about this tonight. I'll skip working in the garden tomorrow. We can get together and work this out. Make a plan to get out of here. Together." She paused for a moment. "I'm not going to let anything happen to you."

John smiled. "You're right. Get some sleep. We'll meet tomorrow and figure something out." He squeezed her hand before pocketing the gold locket and walking to the door. He glanced over his shoulder on the way out. "We're going to make it through this. I promise."

Sarah watched her husband leave the library and open the door to exit the dining hall. She acknowledged his small wave before he stepped into the courtyard.

She couldn't believe the story she had just heard. John was losing it. It hurt to admit, but he was losing it.

Doctor Regen had been warning her of this sort of thing. For the past few weeks, she had been working with Sarah in her private sessions on understanding the issues that had gone wrong in her marriage. How John had tried to tear her away from her parents because he wanted to control her. How he wanted to keep her unhappy because it was easier to manipulate her that way. How, given time, he would even try to lure her away from the program.

She hadn't wanted to believe it, but it was now painfully evident. It was so obvious after what happened tonight.

Vernon had tried to rape her, and John had refused to kill him. He had refused to ensure Sarah's safety. Her happiness. Maybe he *wanted* her to be scared.

But Kane. Kane stayed true to his word. He had promised to guide the group, to lead them, to protect them. And in the end, Kane was willing to kill another man for Sarah's safety.

Sarah Michaels sighed and leaned back in her chair. It would be heartbreaking if she let herself think about it so she chose not to. Why go through the pain of remembering, of thinking, when you could just feel good with who you were? Sarah was thin and happy. She had a family again. The program had accepted her, and she belonged to it. And she felt good because of it.

It was too bad about John. She vaguely remembered being truly in love with him once, but it hurt too much to try to fully recall the emotion. Regardless, she couldn't let him endanger the program. Couldn't let him threaten her family, the people who really cared for her.

She would wait another few minutes for John to get to his barracks and go to bed. Then, she would march across the courtyard to Kane and Doctor Regen's quarters. She would knock on the door and tell them about John. She was sure they would find a way to help him. That was what they did. That was what the program was for.

It was for his own good.

CHAPTER 63

JOHN STOOD ALONE beside the sundial and stared at the broken body of Vernon the Vermin. The weight of his body had partially angled the blade of the sundial out of the groove cut into the face of the giant flat stone. If the blade were removed from that groove, the transformation of the sundial into a sacrificial altar would be complete. After all, that's what it was.

John gently closed the lids of Vernon's small, open eyes. He supposed it really didn't matter. John suspected the body wouldn't be here when they woke up in the morning. Just like the coyotes.

John also guessed the experience would be like an unsettling dream for everyone in the soothing light of dawn. Only an afterimage of Kane, his powerful arms lifting Vernon's struggling body over his head, would remain. But the blood would still be on the sundial. The blood would be there for a very long time.

John walked to the spot where he had kicked Vernon's switchblade and scanned the ground. It was missing. Damn. He thought he had seen Kane stoop to retrieve something when the giant went back to his quarters as the chanting died down, but John still wanted to check. The knife would have been good to have.

John glanced toward the fire. The flames were ebbing. Every so often, a spark would pop and rise from the heat, following the tendrils of smoke into the night sky. The stars were out tonight, but the moon was just a sliver. Three weeks until it would be full. They still had time. But not much.

John put his hands in his pockets and walked toward the men's barracks. His right hand encountered the small, smooth surface of the gold locket. His left fingers hit something sharp. He reflexively pulled the hand from his pocket and put his finger in his mouth. There was no blood. He wasn't cut. But it was definitely sharp. He had worked on that for days.

And he forgot.

Damn.

How could he forget?

He pushed his hands back into his pockets and turned back toward the dining hall. He needed to see Sarah.

CHAPTER 64

SARAH RAN HER FINGER along the paperback books on the shelf. She hadn't read a single book while she had been here, despite the lack of demands on her time, partly because she hadn't felt like reading for the past few weeks, but mainly because the selection in the small library was eclectic to say the least.

She didn't recognize the titles or authors of most of the books, and the ones she did know weren't very happy novels—George Orwell and William Golding had several titles. Come to think of it, Sarah hadn't seen anyone read much while they were here.

Oh well.

She turned and headed toward the door. She had waited long enough. It was time to talk to Doctor Regen.

She was three feet from the door when it swung open and John stepped inside. She gasped a quick breath in surprise.

"Hi. Didn't mean to scare you." He was smiling.

Sarah let out the breath and waved the air in front of her face with her hand. "It's okay. Just still a little on edge. I thought you were going to bed."

"I was, but then I realized I forgot to give you your present."

Her brow furrowed. "Present? What are you talking about?"

A hint of redness crept into John's cheeks. "Well, I know the timing couldn't be worse, but there's no way around the calendar."

He held out his hand, fingers closed and palm facing the floor. She cupped her hands and held them beneath his as he gently dropped something heavy into her palms.

"Happy birthday," he said.

It was an arrowhead fashioned from black onyx. Polished to a glossy shine and sharp. It was beautiful.

"John, I don't..."

He shrugged his shoulders. "I know. With everything that's happened tonight, the last thing on your mind was getting a gift. But today is your birthday, and remembering your birthday is one of the few things in our marriage I'm good at."

She turned the black stone over in her hands. It was incredible. She hadn't seen anything like it outside a museum. It took her back to college. She had been studying the history of the American West. She and John had read books and gone to museums. They studied the Indians and the ranchers and Texas Rangers. And he had done it for her.

"I didn't even know it was my birthday," she said softly.

But he did. Despite everything, John had remembered.

"I've been keeping track of the days in my head," he said. "Before we left Boston, I noticed your birthday would fall while we were out here. I actually bought you a great set of earrings, but the 'no personal items' policy threw that plan off. The earrings are sitting in a bank box in Sonora. I hope this is okay."

Sarah's head began to ache. It was painful to remember so much, but she couldn't stop. Holding the arrowhead, she recalled the days in college. She had begun dating a brilliant loner against the advice of her friends. They just didn't get the attraction. John had no friends of his own, but he was so sweet. He cared for her.

She remembered when he admitted to not having taken the history class they had been spending all of their nights together studying for. That was the night she fell in love with him.

Her headache spread. It felt as if her mind was struggling against the buzzing in her ears, and the buzz was growing unpleasant as it fought back. John was still talking—he couldn't see the battle raging inside her head.

"I found this weeks ago and polished it with my blanket every night to wear down the dirt that was caked onto it. Once I got that off, I used one of my t-shirts and some toothpaste to buff it. The shirt's ruined, but I think the arrowhead turned out pretty well." He smiled as Sarah continued to turn the stone over in her hands.

The pain was intense. It hurt to remember, but she wanted to. She had to. She remembered the day John proposed to her under the giant oak tree in front of the Academic Building on campus. He had gotten down on one knee and everything.

"I couldn't believe how sharp the thing was once I cleaned it off. It really retained an edge. I honed it a little with the metal on my bed post, but it didn't take much."

She remembered the first night they made love. John had cooked her dinner. Spaghetti. He was a terrible cook, but he had tried. He had always tried. He tried because he loved her.

And she loved him. *He* was her family. The realization tugged at the curtain that had been drawn over her mind. The curtain had made her feel good, but it had been covering up the true Sarah Michaels. She understood that now. The pain was still there. The curtain wasn't removed, but it was pulled aside far enough for her to remember the person she used to be.

"I know it's not much," John said. "But do you like it?"

Tears rimmed Sarah's eyes. Tears that hadn't been there when Denise had left weeks ago, and that hadn't even been there when Sarah had almost been raped this very night. She had hated her tears for so long. Now, she welcomed them as they began to stream down her cheeks.

It hurt, but it was going to get better. She and John would make it better.

"Sweetheart, are you okay?" There was concern in John's eyes.

She wrapped her arms around her husband and hugged him as hard as she could. She tried to pull him into her body, to make them become one. She had missed him so much.

"I love it," she said. "I love you."

John was hugging her back now. He finally knew. He finally understood.

"I love you, too," he whispered into her ear, his voice throaty. She couldn't see his face, but she suspected there were tears in his eyes as well. She considered pulling away to look at him, to gaze into those eyes that were a window into her own soul, but she couldn't bear to end the embrace.

The hug felt so good.

"What are we going to do?" she asked, her face pressed into his chest. She hoped he knew. She hoped to God he had a way out of this. She just wanted to go home.

"Well," he began. "I've been thinking about it. I've got a plan, but it's going to take both of us. Are you ready?"

Sarah nodded her head into his chest.

She was ready.

CHAPTER 65

JOHN SQUINTED INTO THE MORNING SUN as he ran. They had only been out for fifteen minutes, and he was already breathing hard. He lifted his shirt to his forehead. The light gray material came away with a dark patch of sweat.

BJ ran alongside him, John taking five steps for every four of his. BJ was a tall man with a long stride. He was also breathing hard. John wondered how he was feeling.

Chance had decided to leg out a faster pace that morning and was a quarter mile in front of the other two men. John would have to find time alone with Chance later in the day. He would need to talk to him, too.

But for now, John's focus was on BJ. He needed to determine how to broach the conversation. Saying anything at all wouldn't be easy. Not a word had been spoken since the group awoke earlier that morning. When they walked into the courtyard, everyone looked at the sundial. Everyone saw the dark maroon face of the flat rock that was previously a light brown. Yet nobody wondered aloud where the body of Vernon had disappeared to.

Then again, perhaps it was good that nobody had said anything that morning. That meant the first part of John's plan was working. For now.

John glanced again at BJ as they ran. The big man's eyes were centered on the path ahead of them.

John wished he could wait to enter the conversation. It had the potential for disastrous results if it went badly. He remembered the look on BJ's face as he stood in front of the fire the previous night.

"*Kill him,*" he had said.

Potential for disastrous results indeed.

But time was a luxury John didn't have. None of them did. And he couldn't risk waiting too long for the first phase of their plan to take effect. The simple fact was that John and Sarah needed BJ and Chance for the final phases of the plan. They couldn't pull it off without them.

Sarah would test the waters with Maude and Teri, but John didn't hold out much hope for them. If they were all drinking the same mix of formula, and in the same proportions (which they had been since the first day—one glass for each person poured by Sarah from the same set of plastic jugs in the kitchen), then John had to assume that body mass would be a factor. As thin as Teri was, John was certain the chemicals would be further advanced in her than in Chance or BJ, both of whom outweighed her by at least eighty pounds.

There was perhaps more hope for Maude given her size, but the psychological risk was much higher there. If John and Sarah had learned one thing from the previous night, it was that the mental barrier erected by the chemicals could be broken with the right incentives.

A powerful emotional response could force the person into confronting the buzz they had all mistaken for a perpetual runner's high. But John didn't know Maude very well, and neither did Sarah. Neither of them knew which mental buttons to push to trigger a reaction, and it would be tempting fate to risk pushing the wrong ones. Sarah had admitted to John how close she had been to turning him in to Kane and Doctor Regen. How much easier would that be for Maude?

John thought he could succeed with Chance and BJ though. It would have to be a process—a carefully orchestrated procedure to make them recognize the subtle effects of the program, to make them remember.

BJ and Chance were good people, and they didn't deserve what the program had in store for them. John had to stop it. He had failed so many times before. Baby Chloe. Denise. Jennifer. He wouldn't fail again. They were going to get out of the program. They were going to survive.

Somehow.

John glanced to the trail ahead. They would be coming up on the farthest stone writing in a few minutes.

REMEMBER.

He needed to open the conversation, prime the pump. It was a risky undertaking, but the plan required it. And John had faith. They would get through this.

"So BJ, what do you think your son's doing right now?"

Part VI:
RECKONINGS

CHAPTER 66

SPARKS FLEW as Cutter Valentine pressed the flat blade of the shovel against the spinning composite wheel of the bench grinder. He had spent the past hour sharpening his tools, and the shovel was the final piece of equipment. That was the problem with the ground in New Mexico, no matter where you decided to put up fence, there would be rock just beneath the loose dirt. After a while, it became a clear choice between regularly sharpening your tools or assuring yourself an extra hour a day of bouncing a dull shovel off an unyielding layer of rock.

He pulled the shovel across the grinder for one more pass. The corners were honed to points and the last half-inch of the blade was now a shiny silver, contrasting sharply to the dirt-encrusted remainder of the metal. Cutter flicked his thumb against the edge. Not bad.

He turned the grinder off and knelt to gather the other tools from the wooden floor of the shed. He absent-mindedly touched the hilt of the Bowie knife secured to his boot. Just another tool, one that never left his side, often as useful as the other tools he was gathering off the floor. Post-hole diggers, crowbar, pickaxe. Bundling them all into his arms was awkward. He nudged the door open with his boot and made his way to the truck. The post-hole diggers began to slip as he walked.

He knew he should have made two trips.

Cutter quickly took the final few steps, raised his arms and dropped the equipment into the back of the truck, where the tools landed with a series of clunks. He turned and leaned against the side of the pick-up, squinting into the morning sun.

Why was he in such a hurry? The day was just beginning, and it wasn't like he had any pressing matters at hand. He had just planned on driving to the north forty and checking the repairs he had made to the fence line a few weeks earlier, make sure they were holding up. There was no rush. None at all.

He turned his gaze to the small ranch house. Walker was sitting on the porch, panting in the shade and waiting for word to jump into the back of the truck.

Cutter smiled. The mutt wasn't in a hurry, he was just taking it easy, like Cutter was supposed to be doing. Taking it easy and forgetting about the past.

He hadn't had the dream in a week. That was a good sign. He had never gone that long before. Maybe his time in Sonora Valley was doing the trick. Maybe it was working out.

Maybe your mind's on something else.

Nothing like a little morning honesty. His mind *was* on something else. It was on her. Jane Doe. Dead in the middle of nowhere for no apparent reason.

And his mind was on Jim Albright and his wife. Away from home with their well-traveled luggage staying put in the hall closet.

He had pushed it to the back of his mind for the past two weeks, ever since he met with Cal and Dwight in the little mayoral office mobile home. He had decided there was nothing with which to concern himself. That his mind was sniffing at ghosts because he had been out of the game for so long. And the game had been the thing Cutter was best at for a long time.

But he was a rancher now.

And if you believe that, I've got some oceanfront property on the other side of town to sell you.

He couldn't kid himself any longer. Couldn't keep rushing through the chores at the ranch in an effort to relieve his antsy mind. If his brain needed assurances that everything was right in the peaceful town of Sonora, then he would go and double-check. Just in case.

Because there was nothing there. Nothing to kick up a fuss over.

He stepped inside the house and retrieved something from the kitchen counter, putting it inside his shirt pocket for now. Just in case.

He would drive to town and make another quick check, just to be sure, just to make himself feel better about the whole thing. Then, he'd drive out to the north forty and check that fence line.

Nothing to be concerned with at all.

Cutter stopped next to Walker on the back porch. He nudged him with the toe of his boot, and the dog looked up, lips pulled back in that canine grin.

"Come on. Let's go for a ride."

CHAPTER 67

MARCUS KANE used one arm to balance the plastic crate against his hip as he pulled open the door to the dining hall with the other. The crate contained four plastic jugs of the green supplement beverage. R7. The last formula for this group. It was potent—a significantly higher concentration than R6—but by this point the sheep wouldn't be able to notice the change in taste.

Kane checked the courtyard before walking into the building. He was alone. The sheep were on their morning run. How they had grown to love their morning runs, just like they were supposed to. And some of them had gotten quite good at it. From his occasional observations, Kane noted that Chance was fast. The hillbilly would have been fun as prey. It would have been a good hunt, but unnecessary, and it wouldn't have yielded the data they needed. The hunts were a last resort. A pleasurable perk, granted, but only a last resort.

Kane walked through the dining hall to the kitchen and set the jugs of R7 on the metal counter. He felt the enhanced formula was superfluous. The final surge of the chemical in their systems was overkill, a safety measure. His flock was ready. He could do it tonight if he wanted, but the full moon wouldn't appear for another five nights. And the orders were to give the sheep the new formula for all five days preceding the great event.

In the grand scheme of things, father knew best.

Kane opened the stainless steel door of the oversized refrigerator and plucked out a plastic jug, the container that was still full. Only two containers of R6 remained. The sheep had drunk the rest. Just like they were supposed to.

He set the full jug into the crate and grabbed the handle of the second R6 jug. It was almost empty. And that's when he saw it.

If he hadn't been paying attention, it never would have caught his attention. But as the plastic jug passed by the bright bulb illuminating the contents of the refrigerator, Kane noticed the sediment at the bottom of the container.

He lifted the container toward the skylight and gently shook the remaining contents of the jug, swirling the green liquid and stirring the tiny sunken particles. It looked like salt.

He opened the container, snatched a glass from the counter and poured it half full. He took a small sip. It wasn't the formula. The taste was similar, the color almost an exact match, but the liquid in the container was *not* R6.

He put his hands on the stainless steel countertop and closed his eyes, concentrating on the liquid in his mouth. Water. Lemon juice. Sugar. Salt for a familiar aftertaste. And just enough green food coloring to deceive the watchful eyes of Marcus Kane.

That son of a bitch.

There was no doubt in his mind who was responsible, but the question was—*how long?*

Kane took a deep breath and opened his eyes. He spit the imposter liquid into the sink, then put the four new jugs of formula onto the shelf in the refrigerator.

How long?

Kane grabbed the plastic crate and walked to the door.

He was going to find out.

CHAPTER 68

CUTTER SAT AT THE SMALL DESK and rubbed his temples. What had he expected? There was nothing different about the Albright's house today than when he had visited two weeks earlier.

As he sat, he swiveled back and forth. The chair was ancient, but it didn't squeak. Sheriff Jim Albright kept his house in working order. Cutter glanced around the small home office. It still had the twin bed, the desk and the filing cabinet. Everything was immaculate. Even the books resting in the corner were stacked with their corners in perfect alignment.

A place for everything and everything in its place.

Jim Albright would have been a fine military man, but none of the pictures in the hallway indicated he had served. Perhaps he had missed his calling by not entering the armed services. After all, the real world was rarely neat or tidy, a fact most obvious in law enforcement. The things people did to each other probably didn't make much sense to an orderly man like Jim Albright.

His wife's illness must have been especially tough on him. Alzheimer's was a chaotic and ugly disease where nothing made sense, for either the afflicted or their loved ones. Cutter looked at the small picture of Jim and Francine Albright sitting on the desk. They were on a boat, holding up a big tuna. Deep sea fishing. The hair was already gray by that point, but the smiles were big and white. How long had that been before she became ill?

Cutter pushed the chair away from the desk and stood. He didn't belong here. He should load Walker into the truck, go back to the ranch, and inspect the fence. If he still felt the itch tomorrow, he'd drive to town to see Dwight—maybe ask if there was anything else he could help with. Spend some time in that nice, clean Andy Griffith sheriff's office.

He glanced around the kitchen before opening the back door. All the dishes were stacked. All the cups were in perfect alignment. No wonder Dwight kept the sheriff's office so neat. He had learned from Jim Albright.

Cutter's hand slipped off the doorknob without turning it.

The sheriff's office in town *was* neat. Perfectly in order. Just like the house.

He turned on his heel and marched back into the home office. It was just a hunch, but that's what old dogs did—they stuck to the tricks they knew best. And something had just stirred this old dog's mind.

A place for everything and everything in its place—so what the hell was the Jane Doe case folder doing behind the filing cabinet in the sheriff's office?

Cutter put his hand against the old metal file cabinet and lowered himself to one knee on the carpet. He rested his cheek against the wall and closed one eye, focusing the other on that thin, dark space behind the cabinet.

There was something down there.

He retrieved a wooden ruler from the desk drawer and proceeded to fish the thing out. After a few tries, the corner of a white envelope emerged along the wall. Cutter grabbed it and sat at the desk. He opened the unsealed envelope and found another envelope inside. This one small and brown. Cutter removed it.

A tiny key fell out of the envelope. It looked like the kind of key that would open a padlock or a gate, but there was no *Masterlock* or *Schlage* brand name printed on it. Instead, a single word was etched into the rounded base—*LeFEBURE*.

Cutter had seen a key like this before. In fact, he owned one. His key opened a safe deposit box in the vault of a bank branch in Fort Worth, Texas.

He flipped the envelope over. There it was. Purple ink from a rubber stamp. *Sonora Valley Bank and Trust*. A number was written in black and circled. *518*.

Cutter stared at the key in his left hand and the brown envelope in his right.

A place for everything and everything in its place.

Why in the world had Jim Albright left these things here?

One way to find out. And he would. There was no turning back now.

He unbuttoned his shirt pocket, retrieving the thing he had grabbed from his kitchen counter earlier. He hadn't planned on needing it, but there had been that damned hunch.

Cutter walked out of the house and Walker joined him in stride from the porch. He let down the tailgate and the dog immediately jumped into the back of the truck, stepping around the long wooden handles of the tools. The dog licked at his face, and Cutter pulled away. The heavy iron sheriff's badge now thumped against his chest when he moved.

He slammed the tailgate and walked to the driver's door, taking a deep breath before opening it and sliding behind the wheel.

Time to go to the bank.

CHAPTER 69

JOHN MICHAELS put his hands in his pockets and glanced casually around him. There wasn't another person in sight. Good.

He slowed his walk and stopped in front of the main door to the shed. He had already checked the garage door, and he could discern no way to open it from the outside. That left the other.

BJ and Chance were still on a run. John had told the men he hadn't felt like running, maybe he'd just walk around the compound that morning instead. They didn't say a word. He suspected they knew exactly what he was doing, but they hadn't said anything. John didn't know if that was good or bad.

He and Sarah had been substituting the sugar-water concoction in place of the formula for the past two weeks. John knew it had to be working, but remembering his own experience, he realized it wouldn't happen overnight. He had tried to align his plan with the gradual eradication of the drugs from the group's systems. Slow and steady.

He had talked to BJ more and more about his son. BJ didn't care for the conversations at first—they seemed to give him a headache—but John had persisted, and as time went on, John thought the curtain was starting to come down. The discussions were getting better, and BJ was remembering more every day.

John had asked Chance lots of questions about the Navy SEALS. What they did. How they operated. What was that special SEAL code Chance had told them about that first day at the community center? The young man from Oklahoma struggled in the beginning but had started to recall more each day as John quizzed him on the subject.

Of course, exercising the memory banks of his friends was one thing, opening their eyes to the truth of the program was something else altogether. The risk factor there was incredibly high. Both men believed in the program, just like they were supposed to. And both men now revered Marcus Kane on an almost religious level, just like they were supposed to. It was disturbing to say the least.

When one of them would start to tell John how great Kane's speech was at the spiritual enlightenment meeting the night before, John would change the subject. Once or twice he had responded with a comment calling into question something Kane had said, just to test the waters, see what the reaction would be. Each time he had received a look of incredulity. How could anyone question Marcus Kane?

Each night, John looked through the skylight and gauged the progress of the moon's cycle as it grew fuller, and he would shut his eyes against the vision of Kane slamming Vernon onto the metal blade of the sundial.

He was playing a dangerous game.

He couldn't wait any longer. By John's mental calendar, the program would hit the three-month mark in five days. He couldn't take a chance on waiting until the last day. There was no way to know whether the program stayed on a specific schedule. Whatever it was that John feared could occur any day now.

He wished he knew what it was. He wished he knew what Kane and Doctor Regen had in store for the members of the program. It would make it so much easier to convince BJ and Chance if he had something concrete to present to them, something that would show them the truth about the program, and the evil of Marcus Kane.

The latter was something of which John had become certain. He was by no means a strong believer in the supernatural forces of good and evil, but he had come to understand that Marcus Kane was evil. There was no other description.

He had also become certain that Kane was the controlling force behind the program, not Doctor Regen. His private therapy sessions with the doctor had become a two-way interrogation. Lilith would assail him with her usual barrage of questions concerning John's childhood, his insecurities and his sister. John would answer in a manner he knew she would expect—always keeping up appearances—and then slip a question or comment of his own into the mix. He had carefully observed Lilith's reaction when he mentioned Marcus Kane. Power was something he had come to recognize intimately in the boardroom, where billions of dollars were sometimes at stake, and he could tell that Lilith was not the person wielding the power here.

John stood in front of the shed and ran his fingers along the padlock and the metal plate securing the door. It was solid. Very solid. That was bad.

John had yet to devise a refined plan on making their escape. He had developed what he hoped was a system for returning BJ and Chance to their former selves (Sarah had made an attempt to assess Maude and Teri, and found their devotion to Kane and the program unshakable), but the mechanics of the actual escape were proving to be nearly impossible.

Unfortunately, escape also seemed to be their only legitimate option. John suspected the satellite phone and reception dish on the shed connected to a computer in Kane's quarters. But even if they could get in—an unlikely prospect at best—who would they call? It wasn't as if they could give the police or FBI directions to find the compound and rescue them. None of them had any idea of their geographical position. The phone wasn't a landline so the call couldn't be traced. And if they broke into Kane's barracks, it would only be a matter of time before he found out. Then their problems would increase exponentially.

Escape was the only option.

John and Sarah had spent several afternoons exploring possible options. With Vernon gone, John had taken the opportunity to assume the rat-man's duties in the garden as it afforded him and Sarah a means to privacy without raising suspicion from Doctor Regen.

John had tossed out numerous ideas to his wife, but there were problems inherent in every one. Sarah offered suggestions, but they had many of the same flaws. It all came down to two central problems—the geographic isolation of the compound and Kane himself.

Without knowing where the nearest town or even highway was, they had no choice but to try to hijack whatever means of transportation were in the shed. Moreover, they had to recognize the strong possibility that—unless there was a van sitting behind that garage door—there wouldn't be a way to get all six of them out together.

That wasn't acceptable. Neither John nor Sarah could stand the thought of leaving Maude or Teri behind. Just because they were blinded by the program, it didn't mean they deserved to die for it. They were coming whether they liked it or not.

That was another reason they desperately needed Chance and BJ on their side. There was strength in numbers, and they would need all the strength they could get.

Because even if they could get to the transportation, there was still the issue of Marcus Kane. Barring a miraculous sneak attack, no one in the group was capable of physically defeating Kane. There were no weapons in the compound, and an ambush was risky in itself. If it failed, there would be hell to pay.

On the other hand, John had developed a plan for capturing Kane, at least temporarily, but there were complications in how to get everyone out of the complex before he could escape. Sarah couldn't see a way to make it work.

And time was running out. Rapidly.

That meant tonight was the night. It had to be. Tonight he would meet with BJ and Chance and lay his cards on the table. All of them. John suspected the two men were far enough along to accept the truth. At least, he hoped they were.

If only he had that proof. If only he could show them the true Marcus Kane.

But how to get through this door?

John closed his eyes, considering the dilemma. When he opened them, he saw a huge shadow on the door in front of him. He spun around just in time to see a black t-shirt and register an enormous blurred fist about to impact his face.

Light exploded in John's head as he fell backward against the door, then slumped to the earth. He could just make out the toes of Kane's black combat boots as the darkness closed over him.

CHAPTER 70

"RIGHT THIS WAY, Sheriff."

The middle-aged man in the powder blue shirt and yellow tie marched in front of Cutter toward the bank's vault.

Cutter smiled at the treatment. Small towns were great. In the city, everyone seemed to go out of their way to look for a violation of their rights by the police. There was no chance Cutter would have been able to walk into a bank in Dallas, introduce himself as the new sheriff, and ask to see the safe deposit boxes because he needed to check on something. A city teller or bank manager would have rolled their eyes and launched into a speech on warrants and private property.

But not the Sonora Valley Bank and Trust. He had simply smiled at the lone teller working the counter and asked if he could talk to the manager. She waved to one of only three other people working in the bank, and lo and behold, Mr. Powder Blue had shaken his hand and said how great it was to finally meet the new sheriff. They were all so glad Cutter had agreed to take on the job. He wanted to check the safe deposit boxes? No problem. Anything to help the sheriff.

Small towns were nice that way.

Powder Blue walked through the vault door and waved his hand with a flourish.

"Here they are Sheriff. You check what you need to, and I'll be at my desk if you need me for anything."

And just like that, the bank manager was gone.

Cutter couldn't suppress the smile. Too bad he wasn't a bank robber. He could have made a lot more money.

As it was, he ran his finger along the wall of metal faceplates, each shielding a separate safe deposit box.

518.

Cutter pulled the key from the pocket of his jeans and slid it into the slot. The lock turned easily. He pulled the box from its housing and set it on the large metal table that ran along one wall of the vault. The box was long and thin, designed to hold documents and the like.

He opened it.

Within was a manila folder closed inside what looked like a records book. He opened the cover of the book and glanced at its contents. Notes were scribbled on the white pages in black ink. Conservative block lettering. It was the penmanship of a man who likes things orderly.

Cutter closed the book. He didn't want to leave Walker sitting in the truck in the bank's parking lot for too long. He could look over the pages of notes and the contents of the folder in the cab of his truck.

He was certain Powder Blue Bank Manager wouldn't mind.

That was the beauty of the small town.

CHAPTER 71

THE SPLASH OF COLD WATER on his face brought John back to consciousness in a violent jerk. His vision was fuzzy. White spots floating in the darkness. His head throbbed in waves that hurt the backs of his eyes. It hurt to see.

It was too dark.

Water ran from John's hair onto his neck and down his shirt. He was standing. No. He was hanging. His arms were raised. He could feel the pressure of his weight on his wrists. His hands hurt.

He did his best to plant his feet on the concrete floor and straighten his legs. They were heavy. The pain in his head seemed to weigh down the rest of his body. It was like moving through molasses. Finally, he pushed his weight upward, regaining his balance. There was slack in his arms now, but he still couldn't move his wrists. They were bound tightly in place.

Why was it so dark?

He strained to focus his vision. He was in a room. A room he had never been in before. A single bare bulb hung from the ceiling. Dim wattage. There was no skylight.

He groggily moved his head to scan his surroundings. There was a low, padded bench in the corner. A metal bar with weight plates on either end rested on braces extending above the bench. A large punching bag leaned against one wall. Duct tape was wrapped around the center of it. John rolled his head to his right.

Someone else was hanging in the room. Another man in a similar position to John, arms above his head, wrists bound to a chain extending from the ceiling. The punching bag on the floor probably normally hung from the chain.

John squinted, trying to make out the other man. It couldn't be BJ. Chance? He turned his body, grimacing through the pain as he tried to get a better look.

The other man turned toward him, mimicking the movement. The other man was John. It was a mirror.

It had been so long since John had seen one, the memory of what he looked like had faded in the post-concussion awakening. He regarded his reflection. He had lost weight.

John saw another figure in the mirror and rolled his head the other direction to face him. Marcus Kane stood in front of an open door. An empty plastic bucket dangled from one hand, water dripping from it. That explained the water dripping from John's hair. His host wanted him awake.

He glanced down at Kane's combat boots, the last thing he remembered before losing consciousness. Another plastic bucket was there. That one still full of water. A large metal box sat next to it. There was something inside.

Oh shit.

"Welcome back, John."

Kane's voice was deep and soft. It echoed in the acoustical confines of the makeshift gym. It was cold in the room. Maybe that explained the gooseflesh that had erupted across John's arms.

"You're trying to figure out what happened, aren't you? Your head hurts. It's hard to think through that kind of pain, but a million questions are still running through your mind. Am I right?"

John looked into the eyes of the giant. Kane wasn't smiling, but he didn't look angry either. He was totally composed. John wished he could say the same for himself. He had started to sweat despite the coolness of the room.

"No answer? That's okay. I already know that one. How about we make a little trade? I'll answer one of the questions racing through that overactive mind of yours, and then you can answer one of mine. Fair?"

John didn't respond. He attempted to move his arms, testing his restraints. His wrists didn't budge. He couldn't protect himself. His abdomen was exposed and vulnerable.

"Right now, you're in my private workout room. It's in the basement of my quarters. You didn't know there was a basement, did you? That's okay. There's a lot you don't know. The basement's not big. Just this gym, a lab, and a supply room stocked with all sorts of things. Items you might think you'd never possibly need but are good to have on hand just in case."

John suppressed a shiver. He wouldn't let Kane see him crack. Any sign of weakness could be fatal. For himself and Sarah.

Sarah.

His eyes widened at the thought of his wife. If he was trapped in here, where was she? If this son of a bitch had hurt her...

"Ah, a change of expression. You're waking up now, and I'd be willing to bet you're thinking about your lovely wife. She really is pretty, you know? The program's done a lot for her. She's lost weight. Has a nice tan. *Found herself*, one might say."

John found his voice. "If you've done anything to her, I swear—" his words came out scratchy. His throat was impossibly dry. It hurt to speak.

Kane put a finger to his lips, indicating silence.

"John, John, John. Believe me, you've really got other things to worry about right now. We'll talk about Sarah soon enough. Maybe we'll consider that a reward for your cooperation, but you have to be cooperative first."

Kane stepped closer, his face only a few inches from John.

"How long have you been substituting my formula, Michaels? How long?"

Shit.

Kane's breath was hot. Putrid. It burned John's nostrils. John tried to push himself away, but the chains made retreat impossible. He leaned backwards, supported by his wrists, his abdomen feeling more exposed than ever.

John remained silent.

"Well, I really didn't think you'd make this easy. Hell, I was counting on it."

Kane reached into the metal box at his feet and pulled out Vernon's discarded switchblade. He thumbed the button and the blade popped out of the knife's black handle. He eased the knife toward John.

John attempted to push himself away with more force, straining against the chains. They didn't budge. He couldn't retreat.

Kane put his left hand onto John's struggling chest.

"Careful, John. If you keep jumping around like that, I might accidentally cut you." His voice was still soft. It was eerie.

Kane's right hand flashed upward in a blur of motion. The knife was a silver streak, cutting from John's navel to his neck.

John cried out in shock and jerked his head away, but there was no pain.

Kane turned and dropped the switchblade into the metal box with a clink.

"Oh, come on, John. You didn't think it would be that easy, did you?"

John opened his eyes and glanced in the mirror. There was no gaping wound in his stomach. His intestines weren't spilling out. But his t-shirt had been sliced completely through the middle, from navel to neck.

Kane reached out both hands and gripped either side of John's shirt. He pulled his arms apart and the wet, gray fabric ripped loudly. It hung from the collar at John's neck and the sleeves at his shoulders. John's stomach and chest were naked.

Kane paused and stared at John's chest for a moment. He extended one finger and caressed it against his captive's exposed skin. This time, John couldn't repress the shiver.

Kane held his finger in front of John's face. There was a smear of dark red blood on it.

"Looks like I slipped a bit," he said. "I told you not to struggle."

John let out a hard breath. It wasn't a sigh of relief—his current situation made that impossible—but a sigh of reprieve. He was still alive. And as long as he and Sarah were alive, they still had a chance.

Kane knelt beside the metal box and began speaking again.

"Now, like I said, I kind of counted on you not being cooperative. And that's okay, because frankly, I don't like you, Michaels. You've fucked with my program, and that's not something I'm prepared to tolerate. I expected you to be a difficult convert—a challenge—but you just kept surprising me. Like the night with Vernon. You were *supposed* to kill him. *That* was going to be the thing that pushed you over the edge, committed you irrevocably to the program—the thing that made you mine. That was part of the plan. But you fucked that up, too. And John, that's just the *beginning* of why I don't like you. Now, I'm going to find out what I need to know regardless, and if you put up a fight, well, at least that'll keep things interesting for me." He paused to glance up at John and smile. "It'll keep things interesting for you, too."

John watched as Kane removed the items from the metal box. It hurt his neck to keep his chin lowered while his wrists were bound above his head, but he couldn't turn away.

"I told you we've got a basement full of supplies that come in handy when you least expect it. For instance, take these two car batteries." Kane indicated the white and black batteries he had removed from the box, now sitting on the concrete floor at John's feet. "We don't have any vehicles around that require this kind of battery. And yet, we elected to keep a couple on hand anyway. Just in case."

Kane bent down and lifted the jumper cables from the metal box. One set of connections was clamped onto two sponges, each about the size of a fist.

Oh shit again.

He retrieved a set of thick rubber gloves from the box and pulled them on as he spoke.

"But now, I'm really glad we have this stuff here. It gives me a chance to flex my creative muscle. Work on my people skills, you know?"

Kane attached the other end of the cables to the positive and negative posts on the first battery. The other was just a backup.

John lifted his head.

Kane had a backup battery.

"Now John, I'm going to ask you the question again—how long have you been substituting my formula?"

Kane dipped the sponges into the bucket of water. Blue sparks leapt from the ends.

John looked back to the floor. A puddle had formed from when Kane threw the other bucket of water on him to wake him up. John was standing right in the middle of it.

Fuck me.

"Still no answer?" Kane asked as he got back to his feet. He held the sponge connections in front of him like a gunfighter.

"Time to get interesting."

CHAPTER 72

CUTTER PEELED THE PAPER from the double-meat hamburger and tossed the sandwich onto the ground. Walker tore into it, nudging the bun aside with his nose and biting into the meat patties.

Cutter shook his head as he watched the dog eat. Poor mutt was about half-starved. It had been Cutter's fault. After leaving the bank, he had driven the truck to the small patch of trees and grass that represented the town park and sat at the picnic table all day, reviewing the contents of the notebook and file he had retrieved from the safe deposit box. He had read straight through lunch, and he probably wouldn't have thought about supper if Walker hadn't begun to let out those tiny whines. The dog tried to be tough, but hunger sometimes got the best of him.

So Cutter had driven to the tiny Dairy Queen and bought them both burgers. Probably wasn't the best thing in the world for the dog, but Cutter didn't want to drive back to the ranch. He had other places to go that night.

He sat behind the wheel with the truck door open, allowing the cool evening breeze into the cab as he sipped his Coke through a straw. He was still coming to grips with the contents of the folder.

It all went back to Jane Doe.

Seven months ago, when the trucker had come into town and burst into the sheriff's office ranting about the dead girl on the highway, Jim Albright smelled something funny. Just like Cutter had.

The trucker had put the girl's body into the back of his trailer and covered her with a musty old blanket. It was the best he could do, the frazzled man had explained. Sheriff Albright then had the trucker drive him to the spot in the desert where the girl came crashing onto the pavement. The highway had still been wet with her blood, but Jim couldn't discern any clues to the how or the why.

He returned the next morning, after he had taken a full statement from the trucker, and walked around for a couple of hours. Jim hadn't brought Dwight with him. Based on what Cutter could discern from the Sheriff's notes, he hadn't been too keen on the kid joining the department. It didn't seem as if Jim disliked the deputy, but it was also apparent he didn't think the young man had enough experience to be involved with a case like that.

Dwight had been with the department for six weeks at that point, Cutter wasn't sure the kid was even ready for it now.

Sheriff Albright had spent the morning scouting the area. He had even drawn a little map on one page of the notebook. From what Cutter could make out, the highway had run parallel to an embankment for miles. The embankment just happened to be very steep at the point where Jane Doe fell.

His notes indicated the road couldn't even be seen from the other side of the embankment. It sloped up in a gradual rise. And since the pavement ran parallel to it, unless a vehicle was moving along the highway, you could look straight that direction in broad daylight and not realize the road was there. The conservative, block lettering also listed some hunches on why the girl fell into the road.

Albright had theorized that if Jane Doe had been hiking at night, she may have seen the headlights of the oncoming truck in the distance and tried to get to the highway to flag the driver down. But with the angle of the slope at that particular point, she couldn't have known that the road sat at the bottom of a large drop off. Her death had probably been an accident.

But that still hadn't explained what she was doing out there in the first place.

The question seemed to bother Jim Albright then the same way it bothered Cutter now. With no vehicles around, no houses for miles, and no state parks or hiking trails anywhere in the area, it just didn't make sense that a woman would be hiking in the middle of the desert at night with no water and no provisions.

So Sheriff Albright had started taking his notes and asking his questions. He showed Jane Doe's picture to everyone in town. Based on the notes, he had done it on his own. Cutter supposed the sheriff hadn't believed Dwight capable of even helping with that small chore.

Of all the interviews, the only hint of recognition came from Harriet Patterson. Cutter remembered her name from his first conversation with Cal. She put out the one-page newspaper she printed off her computer and charged a nickel for. Apparently, she also handled bookings for the Sonora Community Center.

Harriet said the girl looked a little familiar. That maybe she had seen her around town. Maybe in the community center. According to Albright's notes, Harriet had gone there one day to pick up a paperback she had accidentally left behind and interrupted a meeting with a number of people inside. She said they were a scruffy-looking bunch, but Harriet knew the lady in charge so she thought nothing of it.

Dr. Lilith Regen booked the community center once every few months to hold one of her seminars. Harriet never understood why the doctor would have a one-morning seminar way out in Sonora instead of in El Paso. After all, that had to be where the scruffy people were from, certainly not from around here. But, as Harriet pointed out, Doctor Regen was a psychiatrist and she wasn't, so what did she know? Anyway, Harriet wasn't concerned with the meeting. She just got her book and left.

But the woman in the picture, she just might have been one of the people there at the community center that day.

There had been other notes. Other interviews with names of people Cutter didn't know. It was difficult for him to piece together what Jim Albright had been thinking from his penned entries. There was a lot of information, but there wasn't a key to decipher it.

And there also wasn't an explanation for what the materials were doing sitting in a safe deposit box instead of at the sheriff's office or his house. It was the sort of action someone took if they were afraid of theft, if they didn't feel safe leaving it lying around.

But Jim Albright had been the sheriff. Of all people, why on earth wouldn't he feel safe in his own town?

Cutter flipped to the final section of the notebook, past the interviews and the maps and the notes in the margins. The last pages were blank.

Something belonged there. Those last pages were going to be the place Sheriff Albright recorded his theories, his ideas on what Jane Doe was doing in the desert, hiking so late at night.

Maybe he never had a chance to fill those final pages in.

A sinking feeling eased into Cutter's stomach. He wanted to believe Jim Albright never had an opportunity to complete those pages because he was forced to take his wife to a care facility for Alzheimer's patients. He wanted to believe the sheriff had decided to focus on his wife's needs and elected to leave the Jane Doe case to the state authorities.

But the luggage in the hall closet begged to differ. The presence of the well-traveled Samsonite suitcases plastered with decals of their journeys made it hard to believe the Albrights had gone somewhere without them. And the folder behind the filing cabinet of the perfectly ordered Andy Griffith sheriff's office. And the key behind the cabinet of the immaculate home office.

Something had gone wrong.

Cutter closed the notebook and glanced out the truck door at Walker. The dog was nudging at the pickles on the open bun. His black nose was smeared with mustard.

Cutter hated to admit it, but he needed help. He couldn't make sense of Albright's notes on his own. The names didn't register. The maps didn't register. Cutter simply didn't know the town of Sonora well enough.

He found himself wondering if Dwight or Cal knew about the notebook. Jim's feelings toward the young deputy had been apparent based on his notes (or lack thereof), but there hadn't been any mention of Cal's name. Maybe Cutter could find the help he needed there.

He would ask the burger girl at the Dairy Queen where Cal lived. It was a small town, and Cutter was pretty certain everyone would know where the mayor's house was.

He kneeled from the truck, pulled a handkerchief from his pocket and wrapped an arm around Walker's neck, wiping the mustard off the struggling dog's nose. Even though Cutter hadn't asked for the job, Cal—as the mayor—was still technically his boss. And you needed to look nice if you were going to visit the boss.

CHAPTER 73

DOCTOR REGEN reached out and took Sarah Michael's hands into her own. "It's not your fault, Sarah," she soothed. "I'm not blaming you. Just tell me what happened."

It had been a long afternoon for the two women, but the hours had been fruitful. When Lilith Regen first called her into the private therapy room in the dining hall after lunch, Sarah had been tentative. Lilith knew Sarah had noticed her husband didn't come back from the runs that morning.

The first hour of the interrogation had been slow but deliberate. Lilith talked and questioned and cajoled. She reminded Sarah of the progress they had made over the length of the program, but the woman in the chair across from her had remained silent, electing not to speak rather than risk the possibility of saying the wrong thing.

Eventually, Sarah began to quietly defend her husband. She said that Doctor Regen was wrong. That she just didn't *know* John. That he had changed. That he had said everything would be all right.

An opening. Doctor Regen spent the next two hours wielding her psychological scalpel on Sarah. It was thrilling. Sarah began questioning herself. When she would attempt to defend John on an issue, Lilith would bring up an event from the past that contradicted the defense. Granted, some of the events were embellished or manipulated by the doctor, but that was intentional. It was a practical test of Sarah's mental faculties. When she failed to recognize the embellishments, Lilith knew Sarah had not been off the formula for long. The drugs were still doing their job. That was good.

But she wanted to know exactly what had happened.

"You're not at fault here, Sarah. You're not in trouble. We're a family. Sometimes people make mistakes, but a family forgives. John never forgave you for the accident. He blamed you for the death of your own child...so unfair of him. But I'm not that way. I forgive you for your mistake. I want to help you."

Sarah was nodding. Hints of tears were in her eyes, but she wasn't sobbing. That was a good sign, too. She should feel bad, guilty, but the emotions themselves should cause her as much pain as the underlying causes of those emotions. Sarah should feel the need to cry, but not be able to because she can't remember how.

"You don't understand. It made so much sense when he explained it to me."

Doctor Regen nodded with sympathy in her eyes. *She did understand*, those eyes said. *Tell me all about it.*

"John told me he was running a couple of weeks ago and got sick. He said he threw up on the trail. And then he said that throwing up made him feel better so he started doing it every morning—drinking the supplements and then going to the bathroom to vomit. I thought it sounded crazy. I mean, they're just vitamins, but why would he lie about something like that?"

Lilith squeezed Sarah's hands. "I think we both know the answer to that, Sarah. John knows he's losing you. He knows you've finally recognized him for what he is, and you're now moving on to become your own person. You've found happiness in the program, and John can't stand that. He would say *anything* to tear you away from your new family, to get you back under his thumb."

Sarah's head was moving, but the motions deviated between nodding and shaking. Confusion filled her wet eyes.

"But I'm not going to let that happen to you, Sarah. We're a family, and a family protects its members. Now when did John tell you about all of this? When did he start trying to confuse you?"

"I—I don't know. I mean, I'm not sure. I think just a few days ago." Her words were starting to hitch a little, but she still wasn't fully crying. And even her short-term memory remained foggy. That was very good.

"He told me about it one night, and then he talked to me more once he started tending the garden with me. I wasn't sure I wanted him working out there with me. I remembered all the stuff you and I had talked about, but I couldn't tell him no."

Doctor Regen nodded. More sympathy. *It was tough to say no.*

"He started talking about wanting to escape, and it made sense. It really made sense. I swear."

More nodding. *That John Michaels could be a tricky guy. It was okay.*

"Later—I don't remember exactly when, I don't know—he told me how he made a new batch of supplement drink. Except, he used sugar and salt and food coloring. He said he poured the real vitamins down the sink. I couldn't believe he had really gone through with it—the supplements made me feel good, healthy—and I didn't know what to do. I didn't think I could go to you. Not after all the things John had said. I'm so sorry."

This time Sarah leaned forward, holding tightly to Lilith's hands, and tears did slip out, but that was okay. This was really hard on Sarah, and Lilith knew the pain in her mind must be explosive.

"Sarah, look at me." Sarah's head came up and her teary eyes gazed into Doctor Regen's own. "It's okay. John tricked you. He manipulated you, and he tried to turn you against your own family."

Lilith suppressed a smile. Sarah's memory of the timeline may have been uncertain, but it was close enough. Lilith now knew everything she needed to know. She could relay the information to Kane. He would be pleased. The sun would set soon. And even though it was a few days early, Lilith suspected they would bump up the final phase—the last act—to coincide with the fate of John Michaels. It would be breathtaking, and a great moment for the program.

But the smile, the one she tried to keep from showing, was the result of what was happening right here, right now. Sarah Michaels, turning on her husband. It was the one thing John Michaels believed in—a fact Lilith knew well from her weeks of private sessions with the man. John honestly believed his love for his wife and her love in return would last forever, that it was the one sure thing in this world.

And Lilith Regen was going to take that away from him.

Because that's what the bastard gets for coming between me and Marcus.

"Sarah, you do understand what it is that John tried to do, don't you?"

Another tear ran down Sarah's cheek as she nodded.

"Tell me what he tried to do, Sarah. Say it out loud."

It took her a moment. Her voice hitched as she spoke through the tears.

"He tried to turn me against my family."

Lilith smiled an understated, sympathetic smile. She was so good, sometimes she scared herself. And this was so perfect.

"What does that make him, Sarah?"

A pause. Lilith could see Sarah didn't want to admit it, but she did anyway.

"A traitor."

Sarah's voice was tiny. The quiet whisper of a small child.

"And what do we do with traitors, Sarah?"

Through the tears, her eyes began to focus. She was gaining strength through Lilith's direction. She was finding her way back to the family, back to the program.

When Sarah spoke again, her voice was stronger. It was perfect.

"Kill them."

Lilith Regen paused before opening the door to her barracks. She stood on the concrete slab and watched as Sarah knocked on the entrance to the men's building. The door opened, and Sarah walked in.

The sun had just dipped below the distant horizon. Reds and pinks spilled over the ridge in streaks through the evening sky.

Lilith smiled. Her revenge against Michaels was so perfect. He was going to die tonight, and when he did, the pain he felt would be beyond mere physical agony. He would be put to death by his own friends—by people he trusted—with his faithful wife watching and encouraging the entire event.

Sarah Michaels had come a long way, and Lilith had guided her with an invisible leash. Sarah had even asked if Lilith thought it would be a good idea for her to speak to BJ and Chance ahead of time—to break the news to them about John. They had, after all, been his friends. It would be easier for them to believe the awful truth if John's own wife told them.

Lilith had nodded. *Yes, it would. Why didn't she go do just that?*

And now Michaels' wife was in the men's barracks, planning her husband's death. Lilith entered her barracks and quickly closed the door behind her. The building was soundproof for the most part, but she thought she heard a scream from the basement.

No sense in agitating the rest of the program participants before the big event.

She took a few steps inside. Yes. John Michaels was most definitely screaming.

Lilith smiled.

That's what he gets for coming between me and Marcus.

CHAPTER 74

CUTTER EXHALED A LOW WHISTLE as he turned the wheel and eased the truck into the driveway of the mayor's house. If the mayoral office for Sonora Valley was the smallest building in town, then Cal had certainly made up for it with his home. It was by far the nicest Cutter had seen in the area.

Cal's place sat about ten miles outside of town, off a dirt road just like every other house that wasn't located directly off the highway. It had taken Cutter a while to find the property (it turned out the burger girl from the Dairy Queen wasn't old enough to drive, so her directions had been sketchy), but when he spied the great white house, he knew his first assumption of Cal had been dead on.

There was some money there.

Cutter could hear rocks crunch beneath the truck's tires. The mayor even had a gravel driveway, pretty fancy for this part of the world. The house wasn't enormous—Cutter had seen larger in Dallas and Fort Worth—but for the desert of New Mexico, the place was extravagant. White brick. Columns supporting the roof over the front porch. Cal actually had trees in a yard that also appeared to have real grass. It was getting dark, so it was difficult to tell for sure, but Cutter thought the grass even looked green. A fenced pasture to the right of the driveway held an impressive horse stable.

For Sonora Valley, Cal's house was practically the Ritz.

Cutter stopped the pick-up and cut the engine. He couldn't see any lights on in the house, but the mayor hadn't been in his office so Cutter suspected he had to be here. He opened the door and climbed from the truck, grabbing Jim Albright's notebook and folder off the seat.

Walker poked his head over the side of the pick-up's bed and Cutter scratched the dog behind his ears.

"You wait here," he said. "I'll be back in a few minutes."

Walker let out a small whine in return, a sound Cutter rarely heard from the mutt. Odd. He gave the dog's ears another solid once-over with his fingertips and proceeded up the front steps of the porch.

From the porch, Cutter realized he had been mistaken. He *could* see a light inside. The front door was framed by tall windows on either side—long, thin panes of glass uncovered by curtains or any other obstruction. Cutter could see into the entryway of the house. It led into a long hallway, and at the end of the hall, he could see light falling from a doorway onto the hardwood floor.

Cutter pushed the doorbell.

"Why, Cutter Valentine, what brings you out to this neck of the woods?"

Cal smiled as he shook Cutter's hand and stepped aside, allowing him into the house. Cutter removed his hat as he walked in, just to be polite. It was the first time he had seen the old man without a cowboy hat covering his white hair. The mayor had a bit of a bald spot. His bolo tie was loosened around the unbuttoned collar of his pressed white shirt.

"Well, I hate to disturb you, Cal, but I was hoping I could get your help on something. To be honest, I don't know anyone else I can go to."

Cal nodded. "Of course. Anything I can do."

Cutter motioned his hand toward the light at the end of the hallway. "But please, don't let me interrupt. I can talk while you finish whatever you were doing."

The old man smiled. His dentures were still in. "Sounds fine. I was just getting a little work done this evening."

Cutter glanced around the interior of the house. "You've got a real nice place here, Cal. You must have worked hard to get it."

Cal's eyebrows lowered in seriousness. "You're damn straight on that account, Mr. Valentine. My parents were just kids themselves when they had me so I wound up working through my youth helping support the family."

Cutter nodded. "Dwight told me how much you meant to his mother."

"Yes, sir. Dwight's a good boy, got a lot of his momma in him, God rest her soul. She was almost more like a daughter to me than a sister. I was just out of high school when she was born. You see, Cutter, I got a bit of a late start in life. I never did much except work, but it paid off for me. I built my business in oil and worked my hind-end off to make it successful. And then I sold it when the selling was right. It wasn't always an easy life. I didn't get married till I was in my forties. Didn't have my daughter till I was almost fifty. But in the end, everything worked out all right."

Cutter walked to a framed picture hanging in the hallway. A younger version of Cal was standing next to a girl in a graduation robe. The girl's face was pale against the black gown.

"This her?"

Cal nodded. Cutter could see the pride in the father's eyes even in the darkened hallway. "That's my baby girl. She's done all right for herself. She's a doctor."

Cutter smiled. "That's great. My son is about to graduate from Tech. He's thinking about going to law school...becoming a lawyer. I do what I can to discourage him, but kids will be kids, right?"

Cal chuckled. "That they will, Mr. Valentine. That they will. Let's mosey on back to my office if you don't mind. I just need to wrap up one thing and then you can tell me what kind of help you need."

They walked down the hall, with Cutter glancing at the pictures as they went. The hallways of older folks always seemed to tell the story of their lives. It looked as if Cal had had a good one.

Cal led Cutter through the doorway from which light was spilling into the hall. The room was a home office, much nicer than the trailer the mayor used in town. Dark wood bookshelves lined the walls, filled with plaques and framed newspaper clippings as well as volumes of hardbound books.

Cal sat behind the desk and pulled his chair into it, situating himself to type on the computer keyboard in front of him.

"I'll be with you in just a second," he said. "I just need to finish this and send it. Feel free to look around."

Cutter walked along the shelves, reading some of the articles. Most of them discussed the wild swings in oil prices during the turbulent seventies and eighties. Cutter remembered those days well. The television show *Dallas* had been busy convincing the nation everyone in Texas was rich and owned at least a few oil wells.

He turned his attention to one of the plaques.

Presented to Calhoun Regen for outstanding support of the Midland, Texas, Kiwana's Club.

So the mayor had a last name after all.

Something caught in Cutter's memory. Something from the notebook. Written in conservative block lettering with black ink.

He turned and watched as the old man typed on the keyboard. He used only two fingers. Hunt and peck. It was the same way Cutter typed. It was the way all old men typed. Especially old men who despised all that new-fangled technology and whatnot.

Cal glanced up from the monitor and looked into Cutter's eyes. And he knew. At that moment, they both knew.

In a split second—faster than an old man should have been able to move—Cal's right hand dropped below the desk and came up holding a solid black .357 Magnum.

Damn.

Cutter had let a damn eighty-year-old get the drop on him. Not that it mattered. Cutter hadn't worn a gun on his hip since arriving in Sonora, and he was painfully aware the old man wasn't likely to care that Cutter now wore the heavy iron badge of the Sheriff.

Mayor Calhoun Regen hadn't been included in Jim Albright's notebook of interviews for a reason—the former sheriff had been investigating him. Albright had been an organized man, and he had sensed something was out of order with the mayor.

Because that's what old dogs do, they stick to the only tricks they know.

Somewhere outside, Cutter heard Walker bark, as if to agree with his master's thoughts. Big help.

Cal eased his way out from behind the desk, keeping plenty of space between himself and the former Texas Ranger.

"Oh, Mr. Valentine. Whatever are we going to do now?"

CHAPTER 75

"I DON'T BELIEVE YOU, Michaels! Tell me the truth!"

Kane's hand threaded into John's hair for what seemed the hundredth time and shook his head back and forth. John was too tired to fight it. His head flopped with the pressure. It felt as if the rubber glove was ripping the hair from his scalp.

John was beyond exhausted.

What time was it? What day was it?

He had spent the past several hours slipping in and out of consciousness, and it was impossible to judge daytime from night in the blackness of the basement.

The routine was the same. Kane would ask him questions and touch the soaked sponges of the power cables to John's chest and abdomen. John would scream. He would answer the questions. He couldn't do otherwise. Kane wouldn't believe him. Then the bastard would leave the room for several minutes (or was it hours?) while John fought to retain consciousness. He had lost most of those battles.

"It is the truth! She had nothing to do with it!"

John was screaming, but his words were garbled. He was finding it increasingly difficult to form his consonants. Everything went numb following the shocks. Drool fell from his bottom lip as he yelled. He couldn't help it.

John's body was swinging from the chain to which his wrists were bound with the duct tape. His hands had lost all feeling hours earlier.

He was dripping onto the floor, a combination of sweat and more dousing with the bucket of water. Kane liked keeping John alert for the treatments. The soaked material of John's khaki pants clung to his thighs. He didn't know if they were wet from the bucket or his own sweat or if he had pissed himself during the shocks. He supposed it didn't really matter.

"She didn't know about it. I swear."

His words were quieter now as he defended his wife. John had a gut feeling he would never be leaving the basement, and he had to give Sarah a chance. Convince Kane that he had acted alone. Then, maybe Sarah could somehow escape on her own.

Kane peeled the gloves from his hands and dropped them into the metal box. He folded his arms across his massive chest and smiled.

"You know, John, I still don't believe you. But that's okay. I know you're lying, and believe me, you've impressed the hell out of me. Most men would be selling their mothers to me by now. But you're strong—stronger than I gave you credit for."

Kane paused as he evaluated the man hanging from the chains with the tattered gray t-shirt hanging from his back.

What is he waiting for? John thought. *For me to thank him for the compliment?*

"You're only trying to protect your wife, and that's commendable," Kane finally continued. "But it's also unnecessary. *Whether or not she had anything to do with it doesn't change her fate one way or the other*. And it's all a moot point for you now anyway. You see, Doctor Regen has spent a very productive day with Sarah."

John closed his eyes. *No.*

"She told us everything we needed to know. Isn't that just a big kick in the crotch for you?" Kane leaned in closer. "One thing you should know, John—*I always win. Always.* I respect the fact that you fought the program—you're not the first—but you never really stood a chance."

John's head rolled back. He was in agony both physical and emotional. He had to know. What else did he have to lose?

"What's in the formula, Kane? What's it do? Constant adrenaline high?"

Kane shook his head. Despite the darkened room, John could see the giant was smiling.

"Inquisitive little son of a bitch, aren't you? And that's a good guess, but not accurate. You see, John, you might think that all of your values and morals—all the things that make you the person you are—are part of your heart, your soul, your *inner being*, whatever ignorant philosophy you subscribe to, but the truth, John, the truth is that it's all just a function of the chemicals in your brain—electrical impulses jumping between cells—and the make-up of certain parts of the brain determines your own sense of right and wrong. We've done a lot of research into this, John, and guess what we've found out?"

John hung from the chain in silence.

"Those parts of the brain can be clouded with certain chemicals. We can actually distort the way a person perceives right and wrong—change their entire emotional personality. The adrenaline's just a glandular side effect. We haven't figured out a way to eliminate it yet."

Through the numb haze of John's mind, the program was starting to make sense.

"That's why the required morning runs," he croaked. Another stream of slobber fell from the corner of his mouth. "The drugs would absorb faster on an empty stomach, and we would all just assume the buzz was some kind of runner's high."

Kane lifted an eyebrow. "You are a smart one, Michaels."

John shook his head. Something didn't make sense. "That's why you used people who weren't accustomed to a lot of physical exertion, but why Chance? He ran all the time in the Navy. It doesn't fit."

Kane laughed. It was a terrible sound. "The hillbilly? I've squeezed smarter things out of my ass. Chance doesn't have the self-awareness to recognize something like that, and he's far too trusting. Just like everyone else."

The comment struck a nerve. "But why do it at all, Kane? You drag these people out here to the middle of nowhere just to test your drugs and kill them? Why bother? You could kill plenty of people without getting them high first, and you'd save a lot of time. What is it—just a game to you?"

Kane shook his head slowly. He began to pace the room as he spoke. It seemed John had struck a nerve, too.

"Oh John, you're so shortsighted. The program is far more than just a game. It's a testing ground. It's a way to hone the formula, and to develop the intricacies of emotional manipulation. You have to realize something—if you want to kill ten people, all you have to do is lure them out here, take them away from any reminders of their past lives, dress them alike, take away their individuality, get them to start chanting," Kane paused and smiled. "And then convince them that certain joy is waiting at the bottom of a very steep cliff. They can't jump fast enough."

He stopped pacing and spoke a bit lower, conspiratorially.

"But if you want to kill *ten-thousand* people... Well, John, that takes a little more planning."

John couldn't believe what he was hearing. What had he stumbled into?

"So you spend a few years in the desert, working out the details," Kane continued. "Fixing the little bugs inherent in any great initiative. You screen your candidates, making sure they fit what you're looking for. You test your drugs on people of different ages and races. You try to get a good cultural cross-section so you can test the effectiveness of your spiritually enlightening speeches. What works and what doesn't. It's a long process, John, but one that pays huge dividends in the end. And it's a process we're just beginning."

John's legs were weakening. As standing became more difficult, the amount of his weight supported by the chains binding him to the ceiling increased. His breathing was labored. The effort to maintain the conversation was exhausting, but he kept asking questions.

"So why us? Why Sarah and me? It was obvious from the first day we didn't fit your profile."

Kane began pacing the floor once again. John could tell he was enjoying this. He probably never got the opportunity to boast to an outsider, and John could see that bragging meant a lot to Marcus Kane.

"Several reasons, John. First, there was the matter of the hundred grand. We don't get many wealthy people who apply for the program. Most people who are well off tend to have a lot of connections, a lot of people who would ask too many questions if they went missing, but that wasn't the case with you and Sarah. You'd think you were the Unabomber the way you shunned other people. And while the program does have resources, an extra few thousand dollars never hurts. What can I say? I'm greedy."

John fought to keep his head upright. He was so tired.

"Second," Kane continued, "We had to introduce the family variable into the equation sooner or later. It's a necessity for the end goal of the program. Granted, we hadn't initially planned to bring in family members quite this early, but when Cornelius faxed us your application from Boston, it was too good to pass up." He paused a moment. "The odds of it had to have been astronomical. John, when I got that fax, I thought it was Christmas-fucking-morning."

John's eyes had started to close. When he forced them open, Kane was standing in front of him, leaning in close.

"And do you know why I was so glad to see your name, John? Do you know why I accepted you into the program even though you *didn't* fit the profile?"

Kane moved in until his nose was almost touching John's. His face was a blur in John's eyes.

"I did it because your sister pissed me off, John."

John felt hot spit land on his eyelids as they slid closed. Kane's words rattled in the pain-filled numbness of his mind.

Jennifer.

"No reaction?" Kane's voice sounded disappointed. "Oh well. You're tired aren't you? Go ahead and sleep. I want you rested for what's coming. I want you to be fully aware of what's happening around you."

The words echoed in the growing darkness of John's mind, the deep voice of a nightmare introducing itself before sleep even fully took hold.

"And after you're dead, I want you to know that Sarah and I are going to have a little party right here. I'll string her up the same way you're hanging right now. Like I said before, she's a good-looking woman. I'm sure we'll party for a long time."

The darkness expanded. Kane's words cut agonizing streaks across John's fading mind.

"But don't worry, you won't be far away. I plan on cutting off your head and setting it right over there in the corner. You can watch the whole thing."

The darkness closed, and John lost consciousness.

CHAPTER 76

WALKER'S BARKING was constant, and even though the dog was outside, Cutter still had to raise his voice to be heard over the ruckus.

"Jim Albright is dead, isn't he?"

Cutter already knew the answer but had to ask. Cal Regen merely nodded his head in response, the black revolver not swaying an inch.

"And his wife?"

A sad smile crossed the old man's face as he nodded again.

"I'm afraid so, but Francine had indeed taken to the Alzheimer's, the same thing to which I lost my dear wife. Believe me, Mr. Valentine, I did both of them a favor."

Cutter's eyes darted to his left and right. How could he have let an eighty-year-old corner him with a pistol? There was nothing in the office he could use as a shield, nothing he could use as a distraction. Nothing.

"A favor? Somehow I doubt either Jim or Francine saw it that way."

Keep him talking. As long as possible.

"Oh, you could be right, Cutter. I'm quite certain that dying so suddenly upset Jim to no end. Especially since he was on the verge of uncovering something so big. But alas, fame and fortune were never in the cards for him." Cal shrugged his shoulders.

Cutter took a casual step toward the desk, shrugging his own shoulders and feigning indifference.

"You forget, Cal. I took down The Baptist. I sincerely doubt there's anything that big in Sonora Valley."

A slow smile spread across Cal's face at the remark, wrinkling his eyes and the corners of his mouth.

"Please, Mr. Valentine, you needn't be so transparent. If you want to know what's going on, all you have to do is ask me." He wagged the barrel of the gun in Cutter's direction as he spoke. "After all, I seriously doubt you'll be telling anyone what you hear." Cal paused to emphasize a point. *"I don't care how many cutting horse rodeos you won in your youth, Cutter, you're not that fast."*

Walker's barking had grown louder. Cutter could hear him scratching at the home's front door. The dog must have jumped out of the bed of the truck.

In hindsight, Cutter realized he should have paid more attention to the mutt's judgment the first time they met Calhoun Regen.

"Okay, Cal, what's going on?"

"History," he replied. "History is going on all around us, every day. What we do affects the lives of those in front of us, Mr. Valentine. Most people choose to live out their pathetic existences in the most benign way—eat, drink, watch television, pop out a couple of kids and die. They are not even footnotes in the great book of humanity. Others choose to make an impact. Julius Caesar, Napoleon Bonaparte, Alexander the Great, Adolph Hitler. These are men who refused to merely accept their lot in life, they chose to change the world."

The old man's voice had begun to increase in volume and quiver. Cutter noticed the hand holding the gun was shaking slightly, the finger on the trigger twitching sporadically as he spoke. It was a bad sign.

"So what would you do, Mr. Valentine, if you had the opportunity to cast your lot with one of these men early on? If you could reap the rewards of their vision?"

A pause allowed Cutter into the conversation.

"Hitler's dead, Cal, and so are all the other men you mentioned. Most of them killed by the power they coveted. I don't think I'd want to be included with them at all."

Cal's eyes rolled toward the ceiling in exasperation.

"You have no idea, Cutter. None at all. As great as they were, those men were narrow-minded. They saw power through the eyes of other men, through the eyes of the rest of the world. They wanted wealth and fame and nations subjected to their rule. They were blind to the meaning of true power."

Walker was scratching at the window by the front door now. His claws made harsh screeching sounds as they scraped against the glass. Growls intermingled with the barking.

"The oil business was good to me," Cal continued. "It was hard work, but I made a lot of money and met a great many interesting people. It was almost forty years ago when I first hired a chemical engineer by the name of Hiram Kane. He was different. Went to MIT and Berkley. Eccentric, some might say, but I knew early on what others will find out soon enough—Hiram Kane is a visionary. A shaper of history. Does the name ring any bells yet, Mr. Valentine?"

Cutter furrowed his brow. *Kane*. There was something familiar about the name, but it had been a long time ago.

"Hiram left my employ only a year after he joined my company—moving on to bigger and better things. I could appreciate that. He then gained a bit of infamy in the eighties. Seems he was misunderstood even back then."

A light flashed in Cutter's memory. Hiram Kane. *No*. It couldn't be the same person Cutter was remembering.

Cal must have seen it in his eyes.

"Ah, you do have some recollection. I thought you might, given your years in law enforcement. Anyway, as you may recall, Hiram vanished about that time. Nobody knew where. You can imagine my surprise when he contacted me five years ago and offered to include me in his plans."

Cutter took another step toward the desk as Cal spoke. This time, the old man noticed.

"Ah-ah, Mr. Valentine. I would appreciate it if you would stop moving. Surely you want to hear how this story turns out. It really is quite interesting."

Cutter stopped.

Damn.

"In fact," Cal began, "If I am to continue this revelation, perhaps you should drop to your knees. I believe that would be safer for all parties involved."

"I'm afraid I've got bad knees," Cutter said. Maybe he stood a chance after all. "Especially my left one. You don't mind if I stand, do you?"

Cal shook his head.

"I'm afraid I do mind, Cutter. If it's more comfortable, you can kneel on the one knee. It won't be long. This tale has almost run its course."

Cutter clutched the denim material at his thighs and hitched his jeans up as he dropped to his right knee. It was a very natural, very normal gesture. He even grunted as he lowered himself.

Maybe.

"So you were contacted by a mass murderer. I believe that's where you left off," Cutter prodded.

"Murderer? So narrow-minded. Just like everyone else. No matter, I suppose. Genius is often misunderstood, and make no mistake, Hiram Kane is a genius. And his plan is revolutionary. Our work in the desert is but a small step toward shaping history."

Work in the desert?

"And that's what Jim Albright uncovered?" Cutter asked. "Your relationship to Hiram Kane?"

Cal laughed. "Jim? Heavens no! If Jim had any inkling of how large a thing he had stumbled upon, well, he would have called the federal authorities. I believe he just began to suspect something was going on at the compound. Or perhaps I should say, 'he began to suspect there was a compound'."

Cutter rested his forearm across his left knee. His right was beginning to ache. He really did have a bad knee, but that was just part of being old, something he wouldn't mind continuing to experience beyond this night.

"So you killed him because he got suspicious?"

"Please Cutter, try to see his death as part of the greater good. And for the record, I didn't kill Jim. I know my own limitations. Marcus took care of that little problem for me."

Marcus? The situation continued to complicate.

"I don't believe I know a 'Marcus'," Cutter said.

"Oh, you wouldn't. Marcus is Hiram Kane's son. A likeable young fellow about seven feet tall and three hundred or so pounds. Probably could have had a promising career as a football player if fate didn't have much greater plans in store for him. I do believe my daughter is sweet on him. In fact—"

A loud bang followed by a canine yelp interrupted Cal's thought. Cutter couldn't believe it. Walker was launching himself against the window, trying to get inside, to reach his master.

Cal looked toward the open door of the study for a split second, and in that instant, Cutter took the opportunity to check his boot. The handle of the six-inch Bowie knife was just visible beneath the cuff of his jeans.

Maybe.

Cal turned back toward Cutter.

"Mr. Valentine, I love my house and don't wish to see it damaged by some ill-tempered dog. So I'm afraid I will have to cut this conversation short. You see—"

"It sounds like extortion, Cal," Cutter interrupted. "You're an old man with a lot of money from the oil business. A smooth-talking psychopath like Hiram Kane comes along and tells you how he's going to change the world—all he needs is a little of your help and a lot of your money. Sound to me like you're getting conned."

Cal's eyes turned livid. "I am not getting *conned*, Cutter. I am..." The old man took a deep breath, tightening his grip on the pistol. "You just have no idea. People put their money into the stock market every day, but *this*, Mr. Valentine, *this* is an investment in the future."

Cutter's hand pulled at the fabric of his jeans, easing the cuff up further. He needed just a little more, but he knew that time was almost up.

"A future," Cal continued, "That I'm afraid you no longer share."

The old man extended his arm, preparing to fire, when the crashing sound of shattered glass erupted from the front door and a ferocious growl filled the hallway.

CHAPTER 77

JOHN SLUMPED AGAINST THE COOL WALL of the ground-floor hallway in Kane's quarters. His wrists were still bound in duct tape, but he was free from that cursed hook in the basement. He had no idea how long he had been unconscious before Kane had pulled him from the chain and carried him upstairs over his shoulder like a sack of dry concrete.

Adrenaline had started to feed John's senses as he grew more cognizant of what was going on around him. As he leaned against the wall under the watchful eyes of Doctor Regen, he could hear the voice of Marcus Kane, deep and booming beyond the metal door that led outside. The door was closed. John suspected the rest of the program members must be in the courtyard listening. It was quite a speech. John had never heard the man speak with such raw energy, even during the spiritual awakening sessions. He was pulling out all stops.

Kane must be working his sheep into a frenzy, readying them for the final act.

John wanted the thought to anger him, to motivate him to live, but he was too tired. The harsh reality of his situation had struck him while Kane administered his electrical torture—John had lost. He had just run out of time.

And it was his own fault.

His plan had backfired. John had wanted to ease BJ and Chance into the truth, to develop the intricacies of their escape into something foolproof, but Marcus Kane had stopped that from happening. John never had the opportunity to reveal the details of the escape plan to BJ and Chance, much less offer his friends the final proof about the reality of the program—the proof he hoped would break through the remnants of the chemical curtain and shatter the drug-induced barriers erected in their minds from the formula.

He should have moved the plan along faster. But he hadn't. And now John was going to die.

And Sarah...

John closed his eyes and rested his cheek against the coolness of the cement wall. In a way, he hoped Sarah *had* fallen back under the spell of the program. Maybe then she wouldn't realize the horrible fate that awaited her.

"It's too bad we couldn't have finished your sister this way."

Lilith Regen's voice startled John. His eyes snapped open, and he glared at the hateful psychiatrist.

"It would have been *so* much more satisfying."

Lilith smiled.

The front door burst open, and Marcus Kane filled the doorway. The flames of a massive fire in the courtyard radiated beyond his shoulders.

The time had come.

"Here he is!" Kane's voice boomed in the night. He grabbed John by the arm and dragged him through the door. "This one has attempted to sabotage the family. He has tried to steal away from you the happiness I have promised to provide. Tell me what he is."

John stood on the concrete slab in front of the building under his own power, but Kane's fingers dug deeply into his bicep with a fierce grip, making sure he did not attempt to run. As he surveyed the crowd, John saw the faces of the program members—his friends—glowing orange in the light of the dancing flames. Their eyes were glassy, distant. They wore the same unholy expressions as the night of Vernon's grisly death.

"Traitor."

The word was soft. It was voiced by Teri.

"Traitor."

Echoed by the rest. Maude. Chance. BJ.

And Sarah.

She was standing at the edge of the group. Her eyes were clouded, focused on something far away as she mouthed the word. John wondered if she could even recognize him—the man with the tattered shirt hanging from his neck and countless pink starburst patterns on his chest and abdomen from the electrical burns.

"And what do we do with traitors?"

John dropped his head as he listened to the group whisper their unanimous approval for his death sentence.

"Kill them."

Tears formed in John's eyes. He had heard Sarah's voice among them. He would recognize it anywhere.

He glanced up and looked to Kane on his left and Doctor Regen on his right. The two had turned their attention to him as well. They were both smiling.

"This is a great day, my friends," Kane said. "You are about to find the joy that has been promised you, the happiness that has eluded you for so long."

Kane looked to Maude and Teri, who both returned his gaze with blank eyes.

"Maude. Teri. You have been the most faithful, so you will be first to find this joy. At the beginning of your long journey, I spoke to you of the cliff beyond the women's barracks. I told you to avoid that place because rattlesnakes guarded it. I gave you this order because you were not yet ready. Your gift—your eternal joy—lies at the base of that cliff. You are ready now. The snakes cannot harm you. Nothing can hurt you. So you will run. You will run and not stop. For at the bottom of the cliff is life."

Kane lowered his chin and leveled his finger at the women. They were shifting from foot-to-foot, awaiting his permission, wanting his approval to find that life.

"Now go," Kane uttered.

The two women turned and broke into a run, past the raging fire, past the women's barracks and into the night.

"BJ. Chance." The men's heads turned upward as they stared at Kane, their eyes unfocused. "You men have shown great faith, and you are almost ready for your reward. But the traitor has lived among you for a long time. You must now prove that your souls have not been tainted by his lies."

John watched as his friends nodded. He wanted to believe this must be difficult for them. The formula had been cut off for two weeks. On some level, they had to know this was wrong.

But John hadn't had time.

"You must prove yourselves worthy of the gift," Kane stated. "And there is only one way to cleanse your spirits and prove you are ready to receive your prize."

"Through blood." BJ's deep voice finished Kane's thought. Chance nodded at the statement.

Tears glistened on John's cheeks. He turned his head toward his wife. Her eyes were expressionless, blank. He was right in front of her, and she couldn't see him.

"Then take the traitor. Prepare him for his fate." Kane pushed John from the concrete slab. John put his hands in front of him to break the fall, but his wrists were still bound in the gray tape.

He braced himself for impact, but BJ and Chance each caught an arm and roughly hauled him upright. They spun him around and faced him toward the fire. Before he turned, John could see both Kane and Lilith were enrapt with the proceedings. They were now focusing on nothing but their prisoner and the show they had engineered.

They were enjoying this.

John slumped, forcing the two men to support him. He knew it was over. He closed his eyes and offered a silent prayer for his wife. It was the only thing he could do.

When he opened his eyes, he saw the sundial through the blazing fire.

The sundial.

The sundial was barren. The blade had been removed.

His eyebrows came together in confusion. He snapped his head to the right, toward his wife. With Kane and Lilith's attention centered on their prisoner and away from her, Sarah's expression had changed. Her eyes were clear and sharp. She looked at John and offered a quick nod. And then, John understood.

She had done it.

He loved her so much...and she was one hell of an actress.

John glanced at the two men holding him upright by his arms. Their faces were confused. They were unsure.

John knew what he had to do. Somehow, some way, Sarah had gotten to Chance and BJ. The men knew the plan—the sundial proved that—but with Kane's commanding presence looking down on them, they were wavering.

Sarah had done her part, it was up to John to close the deal.

He looked over his shoulder, toward the giant standing on the slab only a few feet away.

"You don't have to do this, Kane. What's the point?" John's voice was guttural, strained. He sounded like a man desperate to save his own life because that's exactly what he was. And he was counting on one last boast from Marcus Kane.

Kane laughed at John's comment. The great and confident guffaw of a man who knew he had won.

"What's the point?" Kane repeated the question through his laughter, and then his voice lowered. "It's called *pain*, John. *It's what I do.*"

Proof.

John watched the faces of his friends as the last remnants of the chemical cloud lifted from their minds. They were good men. And no matter what Kane and Doctor Regen had tried to do to them, they knew the difference between right and wrong.

Suddenly, John was standing under his own power as both men released their hold on him and turned around, to truly face Marcus Kane for the first time.

The giant's smile turned into a look of confused anger. Something wasn't going according to his scripted plan, and Kane didn't like it at all.

"What the hell is this?" he growled.

John rose to his full height, his body aching from the effort.

"It's called a *hostile takeover.*" Despite the pain, a grin crept into the corners of John's mouth. "*It's what I do, you arrogant son of a bitch.*"

Kane took a step back, and the three men sprang into action. Unable to use his hands, John lowered his head and drove his shoulder into Kane's stomach, turning himself into a human battering ram. BJ and Chance each squared their shoulders and body-blocked Kane in a similar manner.

The quickness and ferociousness of the attack caught Kane by surprise. He was knocked off his feet into the open door of the barracks behind him. BJ wrapped an arm around John's shoulders, pulling him from the building just as Chance slammed the door closed. In a flash, BJ released John, reached down beside the door and grabbed the thick iron blade from the sundial—the blade that Sarah had instructed the men to remove and position by the building just a little while earlier—and slammed the heavy triangle of iron in front of the door, wedging it into the narrow space between the concrete slab and the foundation of the building, just as the metal door pulsed violently outward from Kane's weight.

The door held.

Sarah was already in action. She threw herself headlong into Lilith and tackled her to the ground. She wrapped her arms around the struggling doctor and bear-hugged her, pinning Lilith's arms to her body.

BJ and Chance quickly moved to help. They each grabbed Doctor Regen by an arm and jerked her from the ground. The doctor was screaming something unintelligible over the din created by the repeated pounding of the metal door by Kane's shoulders.

The hinges creaked, but the door still held.

John collapsed to his knees as Sarah rushed over, cradling his head to her breasts. The sweat from his hair darkened her light gray shirt.

"Oh, John, what did they do to you?" she whispered.

He tried to hug her, but the bindings on his wrists made it impossible. She noticed his difficulty and set to ripping great lengths of tape from his hands.

When she was almost finished, Lilith Regen abruptly stopped screaming. And they all heard it. Silence.

Kane had stopped beating on the door, stopped trying to break it down from the inside.

John stood and rubbed his wrists, glancing from his wife to the two men who had just risked their own lives to save his. They were all looking to him.

What now?

John took control.

"Okay, here's what we do."

CHAPTER 78

CAL REGEN spun at the sound of the shattering glass, turning from Cutter and pointing his gun toward the door. With a ferocious growl, Walker rounded the corner of the hallway and burst into the room, determined to protect his master. Slivers of glass were matted into his fur. The dog had a long cut across his snout from one of the shards.

Cutter pulled at his jeans and grabbed the handle of the Bowie knife from his boot as Walker entered the doorway. The blade slipped free of its sheath just as the thundering boom of the .357 filled the room, deafening Cutter.

Walker yelped in pain as the bullet struck him in the chest and sent him spinning back into the hallway.

Cutter's right hand was a blur of motion, whipping the knife at an upward slant as Cal turned and leveled the gun at him.

The throw was perfect. Fatally accurate.

The pistol dropped from Cal's fingers as he raised both hands, fingertips touching the black handle of the Bowie knife now buried to the hilt in his throat. Blood seeped from around the silver blade and dripped onto Cal's white shirt. Confusion and pain washed past the mayor's eyes as he dropped to one knee, then slumped to the carpet with a gurgling sigh.

Cutter's eyes were wide with surprise as he got to his feet. It had been more than a decade since he'd last thrown his knife. It was a parlor trick, something to impress the rookies in training. He walked to Calhoun Regen and regarded the mayor with a cold expression, kicking the gun away from his twitching hand.

"My name never had anything to do with a rodeo."

Cal's eyes darted from left to right in confusion, and then ceased all movement, gradually focusing on something far, far away. Cutter genuinely hoped it was Jim Albright.

Cutter stepped into the hallway, kneeling beside the prone body of his best friend. Walker was breathing in ragged gasps, and a crimson stain was spreading across the hardwood floor.

A small whine escaped the dog's lips. Cutter looked into Walker's face, and the canine pulled back the corners of his mouth. He was trying to smile, trying to be brave for Cutter.

"Dumb dog." He whispered the words to his friend.

Cutter lowered his face to Walker's neck and pushed his forehead into the wet fur. He hadn't cried in years, but the moisture was building in his eyes.

"Dumb, brave, beautiful dog."

He pulled his head back and inhaled deeply. He had never lost a partner in his life, and he'd be damned if he lost this one.

He stood and threw open a door in the hallway. It was a linen closet. Perfect. Cutter found a set of blue cotton sheets and began tearing at them, working quickly. He bundled the material into a layered bandage and pressed it into Walker's chest. The dog winced in pain, but did not pull away. Cutter yanked off his leather belt and looped it around Walker, tightening it snug around his body until it maintained the necessary pressure on the wound.

Cutter squatted, gently maneuvered his arms beneath his friend and rose, cradling the dog against his chest. There was a lot of blood on the floor. Too much.

"Hang on, buddy. You're going to be okay."

Cutter spoke into the dog's ear as he carried him down the hallway. He wished he knew whether or not he was telling the truth.

"Just hang on. We're going to make it."

Cutter stepped out the door of the mayor's house and onto the front porch. He stopped at the sight of Deputy Dwight Owens standing at the base of the steps, pistol drawn.

CHAPTER 79

JOHN MICHAELS was in motion, his exhaustion forgotten.

"Chance, how are we coming with the doctor?"

John remained at the door of the women's barracks, closely watching the building in which Kane was trapped. It had been almost five minutes since the poundings on the door had ceased, and John didn't like the silence at all.

"Done," came the word from inside the quarters.

John spun to see Chance standing to one side of the bunk bed and BJ at the other, both admiring their handiwork. Lilith Regen struggled between them, arms extended, each wrist tied to a metal corner post by the excess of duct tape that had previously bound John's hands. An extra strip of tape covered her mouth. She couldn't move.

"Good work," John said, walking inside and leaving Sarah to stand watch at the door. "I believe you have something we need, Doctor."

John's hand went to Doctor Regen's chest and slipped inside her shirt. She wrenched her head back and forth, shouting garbled noises through the tape. John found the key and closed his fingers around it, yanking it from her neck and breaking the gold chain from which it hung.

John quickly passed the key to BJ.

"Let's go," he said, and the three men and Sarah ran into the courtyard.

"Okay, the situation has changed but our priorities haven't." John spoke quickly, addressing his wife and friends in front of the sundial. It was like he was back in the boardroom, developing strategy and giving orders. Except now, instead of gambling with other people's money, he was gambling with their lives.

"Chance, you're the fastest one here. Teri and Maude have a head start on you, but I know you can catch them. We can't let them run off that cliff."

Chance nodded his understanding. "What about Kane?" he asked.

John put a hand on his shoulder. "I'll take care of Kane. He won't be coming for you. I promise. Now go. Save them."

Without another word, Chance turned and sprinted past the women's barracks and into the darkness. He trusted John completely. John hoped his faith was in good hands.

"BJ, you and Sarah are sticking with Plan A. Get to the shed and take whatever motorcycles or transportation you can find. Follow the road out of here as best you can. Get to a phone. Get help out here somehow."

Sarah grabbed John by the arm. "What about you? I'm not leaving you here."

John wrapped his arms around her and hugged his wife fiercely. The action hurt his blistered chest, but he didn't care.

"I have to occupy Kane. If he breaks out of the barracks, I can't let him go after Chance." He looked into Sarah's eyes. "You know that."

Sarah nodded and leaned in to her husband, touching her lips against his. Her hand found John's and pressed something hard into it. "Come back to me," she whispered.

John nodded in return. "I promise," he responded and pushed the thing into his pocket.

BJ stepped close to them. "What about her?" he asked in hushed tones as he jerked his thumb toward the women's barracks. "I hate to say this, but maybe we should kill her. To be safe..." The words sounded more like a question than a suggestion. He didn't mean it. Thank God. But they had all come so close.

John shook his head. “Don’t say that, BJ. We went too far down that road once, we’re not going to do it again.”

John paused for a moment as the remainder of the plan clicked into place in his mind. “Besides, I need her.”

CHAPTER 80

BJ TURNED THE KEY and the padlock snapped open. He slid it off the metal brace, tossed it onto the ground and threw open the door.

Sarah heard the generator running as soon as they stepped inside the shed. It was quiet. No wonder she had never noticed it before, even working in the garden. She ran her hand along the wall beside the door and found a switch. She flipped it up, and two bare bulbs sparked to life in the ceiling.

The pair quickly surveyed the contents of the shed. A worktable lined one wall and featured a plethora of spare parts and tools. A pair of generators sat next to each other on the ground, only one was running. Expanded metal tubing that attached to the generators and ran to the wall served as ventilation for the exhaust. A small black trailer sat in one corner of the shed, too small to hitch to a truck, but just perfect for either of the two black four-wheeler ATV's sitting there, each with the keys in the ignition.

BJ exclaimed, "Yes!" under his breath and ran to the rolling garage door. He unlatched it and jerked it upward, sending it along the racks running the length of the ceiling.

"Let's go," he said to Sarah, indicating one four-wheeler as he climbed onto the seat of the other. Sarah shook her head.

"I can't," she said. "I can't leave him, BJ. You have to understand that."

BJ stood from the ATV and walked to her.

"Sarah, listen to me carefully. John wants you to go. He has a plan. Now you and I both know he's risking his life, but you also know he's earned the right to do it."

He put both hands onto her shoulders and squeezed them. "Sarah, I've known a lot of people in my life, but I've never known anybody as smart as your husband. And I honestly believe he can make this plan work—whatever it is. I have faith. You gotta have faith, too."

Sarah nodded. He was right. John deserved a chance, and she wouldn't let this be for nothing.

"We're not taking both four-wheelers," she said as she climbed onto the back of the long seat BJ was just on.

"But Sarah—" BJ began.

"No buts," she said. "If John changes his mind, he's going to have something waiting in this shed to get him the hell out of here."

BJ stood beside her, hesitant.

"Please, BJ." She spoke it as a request, but the expression on her face assured him this was the way it would have to be.

"Shit," he said as he climbed onto the seat in front of her and turned the ignition. The engine sprang to life, vibrating beneath them. He switched on the headlamp and the ground in front of the garage door was bathed in white light.

"Hang on," he yelled, and pulled his hand against the throttle. Sarah wrapped her arms around him as the four-wheeler shot out of the shed and sped into the night.

CHAPTER 81

JOHN TURNED HIS HEAD at the sound of the four-wheeler revving and caught a glimpse of BJ and Sarah speeding into the darkness. He stood in the courtyard and breathed a sigh of relief.

Thank God, she's safe. If nothing else, Sarah should be safe.

He glanced toward Kane's barracks again. It was still silent. The quiet sent a nervous quiver into John's stomach. It blended with the numbing pain of his burns.

He walked toward the women's barracks. Toward Lilith Regen. He hadn't lied when he told BJ that he needed her. She had suddenly become a crucial part of his plan.

A loud pop issued from a mesquite branch in the fire. John spun toward the sound and watched as sparks floated into the night sky towards the shining silver moon. It wasn't full yet. Kane had attempted to end his program early. He had been that confident in himself. Maybe that would prove to be a mistake.

John shook his head as he resumed his walk to the women's barracks. This was a huge gamble. He had prided himself for years on his ability to read people. The skill had served him in his career at least as much as analyzing financial statements or negotiating contracts. In the end, it always came down to people. Assessing who they really were deep down inside, and knowing how they would react to a given situation.

John was counting on his assessment of Marcus Kane. In fact, he was risking the lives of those closest to him on it. But he was sure he was right.

He stepped into the women's barracks and stood in front of Lilith Regen. He grabbed a corner of the tape that covered the doctor's mouth, hesitated for just a moment, savoring it, then ripped the tape from her lips.

Lilith screamed in pain.

"You stupid son of a bitch! Marcus is going to kill you when—"

John's hand flashed as he slapped Lilith across the face. His palm left red marks on one cheek.

"Shut your hole, Lilith," he said.

The shock on her face was evident. It was the first time anyone in the program had ever called her by her first name. She was furious, but she remained silent.

"I want you to do something for me, you pale bitch."

John's tone was mocking. He was trying to get a rise out of Lilith, and he knew he was succeeding. He had been cataloguing a mental profile on the good doctor for some time as well, and he knew exactly what buttons to push.

"If your boyfriend ever works up the brains to get himself out of that building, I want you to tell him I'm going east. Tell him I'll meet him on the other side of the pitchfork."

He paused for a moment, finding the perfect tone of derision for his parting comment.

"But tell him that if he has the balls to face me, I'll kill him. Do that for me, will you, toots?"

John spun on his heel and walked toward the door. Lilith couldn't remain silent any longer.

"He'll kill you, you asshole! He'll cut your fucking head off. Do you hear me?"

John never turned around. He marched out the door at the same steady pace. He was glad Lilith couldn't see his face. It hurt to move, and he knew he wouldn't be able to hide his pain for much longer.

He walked through the courtyard toward the men's barracks. He glanced toward Kane's building. Still nothing.

He could hear Lilith Regen's voice echoing inside the women's barracks. She had quite a vocabulary. At least he had been dead-on in his assessment of her. He hoped Kane would follow suit.

Because if there was one glaring flaw about Marcus Kane that John had detected, it was his arrogance. And John was now risking the lives of those he loved on Kane being unable to resist a challenge, to resist the lure of killing the man who had fucked with his program.

John looked up at the moon once more. It was bright. He would be able to run with decent light even after he got away from the blazing fire in the courtyard.

He winced as he took his first jogging step. The jarring motion sent waves of pain through his battered torso. But he could handle it. He had to.

John increased his pace and jogged past the men's barracks, heading due east.

CHAPTER 82

CUTTER STOOD ON THE TOP STEP of the mayor's front porch, looking into the barrel of Dwight's pistol. His only thoughts were of his best friend's blood seeping out from beneath the makeshift bandage. Walker let out a small, quiet whine. The dog was still trying to be brave.

"Sheriff—Cutter, what happened?" Dwight was flustered. His voice was high-pitched, the sound of a panicked nineteen-year-old kid. "I was driving home and thought I heard gunfire. Did your dog get hit? Where's Uncle Cal?"

The questions flew from the deputy's mouth in a jumble. Cutter could see the headlights of the kid's lime green Ford Fiesta, still running in the driveway. He didn't have time for this.

Cutter proceeded down the stairs and walked toward his truck.

"Open the passenger door for me, Dwight. Walker's been hit in the chest."

The deputy holstered his gun and ran toward the truck, opening the door wide before Cutter got there. The kid followed orders well.

Cutter gently lowered Walker onto the seat. The dog winced at the motion, but there was no more whining, just ragged breathing.

Dumb, brave dog.

Cutter turned to face Dwight, who was moving from one foot to the other like he had to pee.

"Cutter, what the hell happened?" Dwight blurted, half-wincing at the sound of himself swearing.

Cutter took a deep breath. He had been wrong about Cal Regen—deadly wrong. He hoped he wasn't wrong about Dwight.

"Your uncle's dead, Dwight," he said simply. There was no time to lie, and no sense in it. He had to get Walker medical attention.

In the harsh glare of the Ford's headlights, Cutter saw the color drain from the deputy's face. The kid was trying to grasp what he had just heard.

"Cal was involved in some bad things, Dwight. He pulled a gun on me. He shot Walker, and he tried to shoot me. I had to do it." Cutter paused as he reached out and put one hand on the boy's shoulder. "I'm sorry. I really am."

Dwight's wide eyes looked into the night. "It's the compound in the desert, isn't it?" he asked.

Cutter cocked his head to the side. "You know about it?" He hadn't been sure if the deputy had any involvement, but he wanted to give the young man the benefit of the doubt. From everything he could gather, Dwight Owens was a good kid doing a tough job for the right reasons. He hoped he wasn't mistaken in that assessment.

Dwight continued to look into the distance. "Uncle Cal had me drive some folks in his van out to this complex a ways outside of town. He said it was for a seminar Lilith was holding." He glanced back to Cutter. "Lilith's my cousin."

Cutter nodded. He had figured that one out.

"The complex was only about fifteen miles outside of town, but Lilith had me drive the van in circles for hours. The windows were blacked out, so none of the people in back could know where we were going. They were all dressed alike."

Dwight paused. "The funny thing is, I drove three different groups of people out there in the past year, but I never drove anyone back out. I asked Uncle Cal about it one time, and he told me to mind my business." His voice grew soft. "I just figured someone else drove them out."

Cutter evaluated the deputy. He knew the kid must be going through an emotional storm right now, and he could tell Dwight was blaming himself for whatever was happening at that compound. It wasn't fully developed yet, but the kid had a nose for law enforcement. He had smelled something funny going on out there, but he had let the matter drop. Now, he would have to live with it.

Dwight refocused his eyes on Cutter. "Sheriff Albright?"

Cutter shook his head.

The deputy lowered his chin. "Something I didn't tell you earlier," he said softly. "I went out to visit the sheriff a couple of days after Uncle Cal told me he was taking a leave of absence. I told you I didn't think the sheriff cared for me much, but I wanted to give Mrs. Albright my best wishes to get well. When I pulled up to the house, I saw Uncle Cal's van pulling away. There was a really big guy at the wheel. I started to follow him and called Uncle Cal on the CB radio. I thought the guy had stolen the van, but Uncle Cal told me to mind my business and go back to the office."

His voice was very soft now. "But I didn't. I went back to the sheriff's house to check on them, but they weren't there. I asked Uncle Cal about it, and he got onto me for not going back the office like he said. Then he told me the Albrights had probably gone to a hospital in the city. The other night, when I heard him tell you he didn't know the sheriff had left town, I knew something was wrong. I just didn't know what."

A low canine whine emitted from the cab of the pick-up. Time was wasting. Cutter felt sorry for Dwight. He honestly liked the kid with the bum hand, but there were more important things at the moment than sympathy. There was a job to do, and there were lives to save.

"Dwight, I'm sorry about your uncle, I am, but we have other things to do right now. There'll be time to grieve later, do you understand?"

He shook the deputy's shoulder. The motion seemed to bring the kid back from the distant place. He was shaking it off, getting back to business. That was good.

"You told me you know where this place in the desert is. Now answer me this—do you believe those people are in real danger? Tonight?"

Dwight took a moment to consider. The kid was evaluating his gut feel. It was an instinct that would be honed over time. Finally, he nodded.

"All right then," Cutter said. The night's priorities had just multiplied. "Can you get to the compound tonight? And give me directions to get there, too?"

Dwight nodded again. "Yes sir, but it'll take a while, especially in my little car."

Cutter shook his head. "You're not taking your car, you're driving my truck. But first, you're taking Walker to Red Mercer's place. You tell Red to do whatever he has to do to help him."

"What about you?" Dwight asked.

Cutter turned and leaned into the cab of the truck. He grabbed a rifle from the gun rack in the back window and set its butt on the ground, leaning the barrel against the door as he spoke.

"Just tell me how to get to the compound as the crow flies." Cutter already had an idea from the maps in Jim Albright's notebook, but he needed specifics.

"Um," Dwight started, visualizing the terrain, "It's actually a lot closer than using the roads. It's about ten miles due west. There's a giant rock formation in the shape of three fingers on the side of a ridge, looks kind of like a big pitchfork. The compound is on the other side."

Cutter nodded at the deputy and leaned into the truck, touching his forehead to Walker's for a brief moment. He whispered something in the dog's ear and gently scratched his neck. Before closing the passenger door, he paused just long enough to open the glove compartment and retrieve something from it.

"What are you gonna do, Sheriff?" Dwight asked as Cutter double-checked that the rifle was loaded.

"I'm going to the compound to save those people. The same thing you're going to do. And stop calling me 'sheriff'."

Cutter reached his hand up to his shirt and pulled the heavy iron badge from its place there. He tossed it to the startled kid.

"Congratulations, Dwight. You just got promoted. I have a feeling you're going to earn that tonight."

Cutter turned on his heel and walked away from the stunned young man. He was heading for the stables.

"But what about you?" came the shouted query from behind him.

Cutter glanced over one shoulder as he walked, not slowing his pace.

"I've already got a job. Now get going."

CHAPTER 83

THE COURTYARD OF THE COMPOUND had been silent for several minutes. Lilith Regen had ceased her screaming struggles in the women's barracks. Only the occasional popping of the fire interrupted the strained serenity.

A deafening impact shattered the quiet. The metal door to Kane's barracks bulged outward, dented from the immense force of the blow. It was followed by another crash. And another.

The fourth collision knocked the mangled door from its hinges, and it flew six feet into the courtyard. The metal blade of the sundial bent back upon itself from the blow.

Marcus Kane stood framed in the doorway, the reinforced Olympic weight bar with three forty-five pound plates at either end gripped in his massive hands. He was sweating. His muscles bulged from the exertion of carrying the makeshift battering ram from the basement. But the door was down now. And Kane was free.

He stepped into the empty courtyard and surveyed his surroundings. The fire still roared, but there was no activity to be seen. He heard Lilith begin to scream his name from the women's barracks. *Help her. She was tied up.*

Kane turned away from the sounds and moved to the shed. One of the four-wheelers was still there.

What the hell?

Kane knew that four of them had turned on him. Four were traitors to the program. Four would die. And John Michaels would be the first.

He had expected the four to take both ATVs and flee to the town. That would have been fine. Lilith's father could have ensured they stayed in town until Kane arrived. And if her bratty cousin had stuck his nose in it, then he could be easily dealt with. It would be a loss for the greater good. Cal and Lilith would understand that. They would probably even appreciate it.

But the traitors had only taken one four-wheeler, and they had left the small trailer behind. That meant no more than two of them had fled.

That was even better. It was like Christmas morning again.

But where were the other two? Who had run away and who had stayed behind? And why?

Let Michaels still be here, Kane found himself wishing. *Please.*

He left the shed and returned to his barracks. There were items there he would need—for the hunt.

Lilith Regen had stopped screaming. It had been too long since she heard Marcus break the door down. And he still hadn't come. That was bad.

Maybe he blamed her for the uprising. Maybe he thought it was her fault that Sarah Michaels had somehow organized it.

That bitch.

Lilith already hated John Michaels, and she now felt a growing rage against his wife. Marcus was going to be angry with her, and it was Sarah's fault.

Kane stepped into the doorway of the women's barracks and Lilith froze. He wasn't wearing a shirt, and the sweat coating his muscles glistened in the firelight. The twin blades were strapped into place on his right hand. His eyes were cold and dark, menacing. He was angry.

Lilith closed her eyes as he approached her.

It was all Sarah Michaels' fault.

She heard Kane's footsteps stop in front of her, but she didn't open her eyes. She didn't want to see.

The sound of a serrated blade tearing through heavy tape filled her ears, and her wrist was tugged with the force. She opened her eyes. Her left hand was free.

Kane moved quickly with the blades and sliced through the gray tape binding her right hand. She winced at his speed, fearing the blade might slip and cut her wrist, but the silver edge never touched her skin. A moment later, both hands were liberated.

She rubbed the feeling back into her wrists and looked up at the haunting face of Marcus Kane. She was afraid to speak.

"Where?" he uttered the single word.

Lilith took a deep breath. "Michaels said he was going east, past the pitchfork. He said to tell you that if you followed him, he'd kill you." She hesitated. "I think he's trying to keep you away from the others."

Kane reached behind his back and produced a silver .32 revolver clutched in his massive hand. Lilith winced again, but Kane didn't seem to notice. He reversed his grip and offered the pistol to her, handle first.

She exhaled as she accepted the gun. Kane leaned down close to her face as he spoke.

"The program is at risk, Lilith," he said. His breath was hot on her forehead. "And Michaels is the cause. I'm going to punish him."

Lilith nodded. She gripped the gun with intensity.

"You are going to take the other four-wheeler out, and you are going to find the rest of them. And when you find them, you are going to shoot them. If you fail, I will be hunting *you*. Are we clear?"

Flecks of hot spittle landed on her forehead, and Lilith nodded.

Of course he was angry. What would you expect?

She lifted one hand up, tentatively reaching toward Kane's chest. He turned and marched out the door.

Damn that Michaels bitch for making Marcus act this way.

She stood at the door, watching her lover as he quickened his pace and began to sprint east, past the men's barracks. He was going to find John Michaels and punish him. Lilith had no doubt about that.

Once Kane vanished into the darkness beyond the fire, Lilith began walking to the shed. She was going to find John's wife and serve up some punishment of her own. Lilith shoved the gun into the waistband of her pants.

Sarah Michaels was going to die.

CHAPTER 84

AS THE FOUR-WHEELER CRESTED THE HILL, Sarah lifted out of her seat. She tightened her grip around BJ's thin waist. The trucker was driving like a bat out of hell, balancing the difficulties of maneuvering across unfamiliar territory at night with the imperative of finding help and bringing it back as quickly as possible.

Sarah and BJ both knew Kane would not stay locked up forever. He would find a way to escape the makeshift prison. And they both knew that when he did, he would go after John.

The road flattened and BJ throttled the bike. Their speed was not as great as it could have been since the four-wheeler had to support the weight of two people, but Sarah had no regrets in leaving the other ATV behind. She couldn't bear the thought of leaving John alone without a means of escape. Just in case.

She realized that leaving the other bike in the shed also provided Kane and Doctor Regen a means to follow them, but it had been worth the risk.

She and BJ just had to find some kind of civilization. A phone. Some method of contacting the authorities and getting them out to the compound.

BJ turned the front wheels sharply as they edged into a corner of the road and the four-wheeler began to slide across the dirt. He eased off the throttle. They would have to take it a little slower. Not knowing the terrain was a serious disadvantage to negotiating the corners and hills. The headlight illuminated only a short distance in front of them, and these vehicles weren't meant for fast riding at night.

Sarah clutched BJ's waist and thought of John. They had suffered through so much together. She didn't want to believe it would end like this. It couldn't.

She wondered where her husband was, and what he was thinking at that moment.

CHAPTER 85

A MILLION THOUGHTS raged through John's mind as he ran. Sweat poured from his body and chilled him as the cool breeze of the night blew against the blisters covering his bare chest and stomach. He wondered if this was what it meant to have your life pass before your eyes. So many thoughts, so many memories.

He remembered the night in college when he and Sarah went skinny-dipping in the lake on the edge of the campus. They had been so afraid of getting caught. Up until tonight, it had been the scariest thing John had ever done.

He thought of his few brief moments with his daughter in the hospital. It was strange. Always before, John recalled those moments as among the worst in his life. The agonizing grief and sick feelings of failure had overwhelmed him. But now, as he ran through the desert, he understood how special those few precious minutes were. He had held Chloe, had felt her kick her tiny foot. And his little girl, although only with them for such a brief time, was the most beautiful thing John had ever seen. He now realized those moments had been the best of his life.

His mind flashed to one of his earliest memories. An older boy pushing John into the dirt at the neighborhood playground, John too young to even know what "bully" meant but old enough to be very scared. His sister appearing from nowhere like an interceding angel. Jennifer was still young. The mysterious and seething anger to which John would grow accustomed seeing in her had yet to mature. That day she was simply big sister. And in the eyes of little brother, she had saved his life.

As John ran, dodging the cactus and rocks by the light of the silver moon, a cold realization dawned on his psyche with unrelenting force.

There was no one to save him now. Big sister had died in this very desert. Now it was his turn. He was going to die. And soon.

It was something he supposed he had known when he first improvised this plan back at the courtyard, ordering Chance to save Maude and Teri and telling BJ and Sarah to go for help. On some level, he knew even then that he was sacrificing himself to save his wife and friends.

He had no chance of outrunning Kane. Even on John's best day, Kane could run circles around him and probably kill him without breaking a sweat. The vivid memory of Kane's blurred fist smashing the tarantula into the door flashed through John's mind.

Even on his best day.

This wasn't John's best day. Far from it. Kane had assaulted him during the morning runs, before breakfast. John had spent the day in physical agony, slipping in and out of consciousness. He had had no food. Nothing to give him the strength he would need to run from Kane, much less do battle with the giant.

John glanced over his shoulder. In the distance, he could barely make out the orange glow from the fire in the compound's courtyard. The rock pitchfork was behind him to his right. He was heading in the direction he had seen the sun rise every morning. Due east.

A cramp bit into his side and he had to slow his pace. A stiff breeze blew the tatters of his shirt from his back. Goosebumps broke out across his chest and arms.

He was going to die.

He had known it when he first decided to use himself as bait for Marcus Kane, but the reality of it hadn't hit him until he was alone. Alone in the dark.

At least Sarah would be safe. That was all that mattered. John regretted lying to his wife at the end, promising he would come back to her. It had been a lie, but a good lie. A necessary one. And she would be okay. Eventually, she'd be all right.

Because Sarah was strong. God knew she had proven that tonight. She and BJ would get away and bring back help. If luck was with them, then Chance could save Teri and Maude and somehow survive this thing, too.

And John, well, he would make it possible. Even if it meant his own death.

He pulled up, stopping his run. His legs were growing weak. Adrenaline had carried him this far, but now his thighs felt like Jello. He knew he could run further—perhaps push himself another quarter mile—but if he collapsed in the dirt, what would be the point?

He turned a slow circle, mentally marking his area. He would make his stand here. A thick mesquite branch lay on the earth to his right. He bent over and picked it up. It was about three feet long and still heavy, even though it was dry. He gripped it like a baseball bat.

It would have to do.

He turned back toward camp, toward the dim orange glow on the horizon. That was the place where he would come from. Kane.

To his left, John heard the lonely howl of a single coyote echoing from the pitchfork. It sent a shiver up his spine. The truth was, he was afraid.

The thing in the dark was coming.

CHAPTER 86

CUTTER DUG HIS HEELS into the sides of the mare, urging the horse to run faster. It had been years since Cutter had ridden a horse, but the reins still felt natural in his hands.

He looked to the heavens and thanked God there were no clouds in the sky tonight as he gauged his direction by the stars. He twitched the reins, adjusting the horse's course.

He had been riding for several minutes, and the mare was working into a lather. It was bad for a horse to be ridden so hard straight out of the gate, but Cutter knew there was no choice.

Something was in the desert. Something bad. And while he didn't know exactly what was going on, it was bad enough that Cal Regen had been willing to kill for it. Cutter couldn't let that happen again.

His thoughts turned to Walker, and he said a quick prayer for his friend's life. Cutter didn't know if the good Lord took a particular interest in dogs, but there was one mutt in Red Mercer's care that Cutter felt deserved a special favor. He mouthed "amen" but an image of Walker's pooling blood on Cal's hardwood floor flooded his mind and Cutter decided to say one more prayer, just in case the first one didn't take.

He hoped Dwight would be okay. A lot had happened to the young man in the past hour. Not many people would be able to handle that kind of pressure without cracking, but Cutter had a feeling the kid could manage. He would have to.

Cutter lowered himself over the front of the horse as the mare galloped forward. He squinted his eyes in search of a rock formation in the shape of a pitchfork.

Despite the illumination of the bright moon, the distant ridges all blended together in a dark horizon. He knew the pitchfork would be impossible to find unless he could see it from the correct angle. Otherwise, it would just be another dark jumble of stone in the distance.

Cutter scanned the horizon but couldn't make out any special formations. He dug his heels into the horse again, urging it onward.

CHAPTER 87

CHANCE COULD HEAR HIS HEART pounding in his ears. His legs were numb and his lungs were on fire, but still, he ran. This was no jog. This was a deadhead sprint for which lives depended on his speed.

He took his eyes away from the ground in front of him for just a moment. He needed to check on Maude and Teri. He had spotted Maude's light gray t-shirt just a few seconds earlier; now, he could just make out the thin form of Teri running about a hundred yards in front of Maude. She was faster than the older woman. The distance between them would make this difficult.

Chance looked back to the ground in time to adjust his step and leap, narrowly avoiding a rock jutting from the ground. That was close.

His legs felt like lead. He had been sprinting the past two miles, and the physical trauma from the effort was brutal. He had developed a cramp in his right calf half a mile ago, but he ran through the pain. He couldn't let the cramp stop him. He couldn't let anything stop him.

Chance still couldn't believe the events of the past few weeks. Even though he failed to get into the program while in the Navy, he had spent his entire life attempting to live up to the values and code of the SEALS, and he had failed so miserably, in so many ways, it hurt to even consider it.

Looking the other way when Denise left the program, not even caring even though he had experienced genuine feelings for her during their time at the program.

Openly encouraging the execution of Vernon. He hadn't liked the rat-man, but that didn't make his murder right.

And what he had almost let happen to John...

He didn't know many things, but one thing of which he was certain—John Michaels was his friend. When things had reached their murkiest point in his mind, when Chance no longer knew the difference between right and wrong, it had been John who started talking to him about the Navy SEALS. It had been John who had forced Chance to wrack his memory to remember the history, the procedures, the code. Just to remember.

John could have walked away. Chance was certain about that. It would have been easier for John to escape on his own, but he hadn't. John had stayed to save BJ and Chance and the others. And now, John was risking his life against Kane in an attempt to let Chance save Teri and Maude. Chance wasn't about to let him down.

He glanced up again. He was getting closer to Maude. Two hundred yards separated them. He could hear the woman's heavy breathing from here. Neither Teri nor Maude had driven themselves in the runs the way the rest of the group had. At first, Chance had been a little irritated at their lack of enthusiasm for the physical activity of the program, but now, that fact just might allow Chance to save their lives.

He sucked in another deep breath. It hurt. It hurt to even breathe. But he would not stop. He wouldn't let John down, and he wouldn't let these women die. Because that's what a Navy SEAL does—he saves lives.

A hundred yards from Maude now. Two hundred from Teri. He was gaining. He couldn't slow down, not even for an instant. The cliff had to be getting close. He had to move faster.

Chance ran the way he knew any SEAL would run, at breakneck speed. He threw caution to the wind, leaping over cactus and rocks rather than running around them. It had been hard the past few days, difficult to remember. But he had. In the end, he knew what it was to be a Navy SEAL, and he realized you didn't have to wear the uniform to live the code.

He looked up.

Fifty yards to Maude.

Suddenly, Teri was gone.

"No!" The word erupted from Chance's mouth, but it was more whisper than scream. He had no breath. Teri was over the edge.

And Maude wasn't slowing down.

Forty yards.

Chance increased his pace again. He couldn't lose Maude.

Thirty yards.

He couldn't lose them both.

Twenty yards.

Chance couldn't see it, but he knew the cliff was immediately ahead of them. If he didn't slow down, he risked not being able to stop himself. He could die, too.

Ten yards.

Chance drove himself forward as hard as he could. He was a Navy SEAL, and he wasn't about to let Maude go.

At two yards, he dove headfirst toward the running woman, arms extending, wrapping around her waist and bringing her tumbling to the earth. Sharp stones cut Chance's right forearm as Maude landed on top of him. They rolled in the dirt.

When they stopped, Chance could swear he heard the sound of rocks flying into empty space from their scuffle. They were that close. Too close.

Chance bear-hugged Maude, pinning her arms to her sides as she struggled to get up. She fought him, animalistic grunts and wheezes coming from her throat.

Chance held her tight. He whispered in her ear, trying to calm her down.

"It's okay. You're going to be all right." It was difficult to speak. He was still breathing so hard. His thighs were alive with pain as blood surged through the aching muscles. His calves were on fire.

Maude's struggles became more sporadic as he continued to hold her tightly against his chest until, finally, she gave up her resistance.

Her body relaxed and sank onto the cool earth. It was over. Chance could hear her ragged breathing as he whispered in her ear.

"Just rest. You're going to be okay. I'm gonna get you out of here."

They lay on the ground for a long while, listening to the updraft of the wind whip against the face of the cliff beneath them. Chance heard a coyote's shrill howl in the far distance. He hugged Maude closer, reassuring her.

As the ache began to recede from Chance's legs, he planned his next course of action. He would hold Maude here for the time being, long enough to assure him that she had calmed down, and long enough for help to arrive.

And then, after John and BJ and Sarah had brought the authorities, and once Maude was safe, he would find a length of rope and rappel down to the base of the cliff. He would recover Teri's body. He would do it because a Navy SEAL never leaves a teammate behind.

Everyone goes home.

CHAPTER 88

BJ EASED OFF THE THROTTLE as the ATV crested the hill. The pitchfork rock formation and the compound were far behind them, and they were miles beyond the perimeter within which the group had been permitted to run during the program. Sitting astride the four-wheeler, neither BJ nor Sarah could believe what they saw on the valley floor below. The moon was high and provided ample light to make out the overgrown dirt road on which they traveled. What now lay before their eyes boggled their minds.

They continued down the hill, BJ steering the four-wheeler along the trail. When they traveled another half-mile, arriving at the thing, BJ brought the ATV to a stop. He turned the handlebars from one side to the other, moving the headlight along with the front wheels, illuminating the area around them.

BJ finally broke the silence. "Can you believe this shit?"

Sarah shook her head as she released her grip from his narrow waist and stepped off the bike. She knew they should keep moving, but this was too unreal.

Based on what they could see from the top of the hill, the trail they were on perfectly bisected the center of another dirt road, but the other road went nowhere. It was in the pattern of a massive figure eight, at least a mile long based on the view from above. The contrasts in the two roads went further. Where the trail leading from camp and continuing straight ahead was overgrown and hardly used, the figure-eight road was clear of most desert brush. It looked like it was driven on every day.

"Look over there," BJ gestured at something in the road. He aligned the headlight to better reveal it.

A single long rock protruded several inches from the earth of the worn dirt road. The rock was three feet in length and ran perpendicular along one of the dirt tracks. If you hit a rock like that going very fast, you'd feel it.

"Coming out here," BJ continued, "How many times would you say we hit a big rock hard enough to knock us out of our seats? A big rock on the left side of the van? Twenty times? Fifty?"

Sarah nodded. "At least," she said quietly. She was reflecting on the ride they had taken at the beginning of the program, from the Sonora Community Center to the compound. It had been so long ago. There were so many twists and turns. It seemed like all they had done was twist and turn for a couple of hours. And hit the same stupid rock.

She turned back to BJ, the glare of the headlight making her squint her eyes.

"You know that this means, don't you?"

BJ nodded. He was a driver by profession. He had already figured it out. It had taken them well over two hours to get to the compound from the town of Sonora, but more than half of that journey had been made looping endlessly around this figure-eight. That explained the level of wear on the road. Doctor Regen had wanted them to believe the program was a hundred miles from civilization. No escape.

But now they knew the truth. They could make it. Help was closer than they had imagined. They just had to find it.

Sarah actually smiled as she walked back toward the four-wheeler. If they could get to town fast enough, maybe they could return with help before Kane could escape. Maybe they could save John's life.

As she straddled the back of the bike behind BJ, she looked up the road and saw them. Coming from the direction they assumed the town lay, a pair of headlights crested a hill and moved toward BJ and Sarah.

Someone was coming.

After a nightmare lasting three months—where the people Sarah trusted to help them had tried to kill them—she didn't know whether to be happy or afraid.

CHAPTER 89

THE COYOTE nervously raised and lowered his front paws as he watched the hunt unfold on the valley floor. The canine eyes shone silver under the light of the moon. His night vision was superb, and he could see everything that occurred below.

He was the runt, the smallest of his pack. At least he had been, when he still had a pack. The coyote had been on his own for several weeks now. He had lost weight from his already thin frame. He had never been skilled at hunting, and he was now forced to completely rely on foraging—picking at the sun-dried carcasses of snakes and eating several spiders he had caught unaware. That was the new life of the coyote. Ever since the thing with no fear killed his brothers that night at the base of the cliff.

The runt had run away. He had fled the thing, the upright that wore claws, and he had not returned to the base of the cliff since. Even when hunger drove him into desperation, enough to begin eating the spiders, he still would not venture back to the cliff, for he was a fearful animal. He was a runt, and that was his nature.

The coyote watched now as the thing with no fear raced along the valley floor. The runt knew a hunt was in progress. He continued to move his front legs, lifting his paws into the air one after the other in excitement.

But the animal was confused. The other upright, the prey for the thing, was no longer running. It had stopped and now stood its ground.

The coyote cocked his head as he watched the strange upright creature. Even from this distance, the runt could see that the prey was nowhere near the size of the predator. And when the prey had run, it did so with a limping gait, not the smooth stride of the predator. The smaller upright was no match for the thing with no fear.

And yet, it had stopped. It was waiting.

The coyote shifted his gaze across the valley floor to the thing in the dark. It was advancing quickly on its prey. It moved with confidence and grace. The thing was the ultimate hunter.

The runt lifted his face and howled at the moon. It was instinct. The hunt was in play, and in this small way, the coyote had joined in.

CHAPTER 90

SARAH AND BJ stood in the middle of the dirt road, illuminated from behind by the four-wheeler's headlight and waving their arms at the approaching vehicle. The decision had been simple. The person approaching was coming from town; hence, the driver could be neither Kane nor Doctor Regen. Therefore, Sarah and BJ would flag the vehicle down and ask for help.

Besides, Sarah thought as she scanned the surrounding desert, *it's not like there's any place to hide.*

As the approaching headlights grew near, they realized the vehicle was an older model pick-up truck. The driver was pushing the vehicle to breakneck speeds.

The two stepped back, afraid the truck wouldn't be able to stop in time, but the driver hit the brakes, dirt and small rocks spraying the trail. A tremendous rattle came from the contents of the truck's bed as the pick-up slid to a stop, angled long-ways in the road.

The headlight of the four-wheeler shone a beam through the settling dust directly onto the driver's door.

BJ and Sarah coughed and waved their hands at the dust, peering along the light. The engine of the truck went silent, and the door opened. A kid stepped out. He couldn't be more than eighteen or nineteen.

"Sorry about that," the young man said as he waved his own hands at the dust. "I'm Sheriff Owens. Are you folks okay?"

Sarah coughed again before replying. "We're fine. You're the sheriff?"

Dwight nodded in response. He thought he recognized the tall man. When he had driven the van to the compound, he hadn't been allowed to speak to the passengers (and they weren't even supposed to see him), but there weren't many black folks in Sonora Valley so he had stuck out in Dwight's mind.

"Yes ma'am. Where's everyone else?" he asked.

The question triggered an avalanche of responses from both the man and woman. They were speaking rapidly, overlapping each other. Dwight tried to keep up.

The others were back at the compound...they had trapped Kane...tied up Doctor Regen...trying to save their friends...

He held up both hands. "Now slow down, both of you." Dwight was shocked at the authority in his voice. He really was the Sheriff of Sonora Valley.

"You're going to be okay. I want you both to stay on this trail. It meets the highway in another seven or eight miles. When you get to the highway, turn left. It's only a couple of miles to town from there. Go to the sheriff's office and wait for me. I'm going to go find your friends. Don't worry, I'll—"

The approaching sound of a small engine revved to high gear interrupted his thought. All three of them turned toward the noise.

A single bright headlight emerged over the distant ridge. It was the other four-wheeler. It bore a single rider, allowing it to move far faster than BJ and Sarah had been able to go.

Sarah took a step toward the pick-up. She spoke in a voice that was barely audible, but Dwight thought he heard, "Let it be John. Please let him have changed his mind."

"Stay behind me," the young man ordered, motioning to the pair with his good hand. BJ stepped toward the hood of the truck to the sheriff's right. Sarah moved to the bed of the truck to Dwight's left, glancing over the side to see its contents.

Despite the situation, Dwight wanted to smile. He was taking control, acting with authority. He was the Sheriff of Sonora Valley. Cutter would be proud.

He squinted toward the fast-approaching headlight. He couldn't make out the identity of the driver.

The four-wheeler sped past BJ and Sarah's ATV before braking to a halt a few feet from the driver's door of the truck, spraying gravel at the young man.

Illuminated from behind by the other four-wheeler's headlight, Dwight recognized his cousin.

Suddenly, he no longer felt in control at all. What was he supposed to do now? He knew Lilith was responsible for what was happening in the desert, so was he supposed to pull his gun on her? Should he tell Lilith about what happened to her father? That he was dead?

Lilith Regen dismounted her ATV. Her normally straight black hair was windblown and frizzed about her head in unkempt knots. Her pale face was ghostly in the white light of the headlights.

Dwight raised both hands toward his approaching cousin. "Now take it easy, Lilith."

"Get out of my way, Dewey." Her voice cut through the air like a knife.

Dwight took a step toward her. He was still the Sheriff of Sonora Valley, and he was going to control this situation. "Lilith—"

Lilith's hand emerged from behind her back in a swift motion as she leveled the gun at Dwight's chest and fired. The impact from the bullet spun him backwards into the door of the truck. He collapsed onto the road without another sound.

"I said get out of my way." Her voice was ice.

Lilith spun toward the front of the truck, aiming at BJ, not allowing him the chance to jump her. Her finger was tightening on the trigger just as the blade of the shovel struck the top of her head. Sarah had swung it in a downward motion with as much force as she could muster, and the sharpened corner of the blade cleaved through the soft part of the back of Lilith's skull—parting her wind-blown hair and penetrating several inches into her brain.

The gun fired. BJ heard the high-pitched whine of the bullet as it whizzed by his head, an inch from his ear.

Sarah released her grip and watched in shock as the shovel remained embedded in Lilith's head, the handle swinging as the doctor dropped to her knees. She squeezed off another shot, this one striking the body of the truck. BJ winced at the sound and skipped away from the dying woman.

The doctor fell forward into the dirt, head rolled to the side, the handle of the shovel smacking flat on the ground. Sarah stood over her. She felt no triumph. If Lilith Regen was free, that meant Marcus Kane was free as well. Out there somewhere. Out there with John.

"I'll be damned."

At the sound of BJ's voice, she turned away from Doctor Regen. She couldn't look at her anymore. BJ was kneeling over the body of Dwight Owens, checking him in the glow of the four-wheeler's headlight.

Sarah dropped to one knee and looked at the young man. There had been too much death tonight. She didn't want to see any more, but she had to check.

That's when she noticed it, too.

The young sheriff was wearing a heavy iron badge—much thicker than the modern badges she had seen on television—and the bullet had struck it square in the center. BJ used his thumb and forefinger to tug on the metal star. The slug from Lilith's gun had imbedded itself deep into the iron, mangling the center of the badge, and had pushed two of the star's points deep into Dwight's chest upon impact, but Sarah could tell the cuts didn't go beyond the muscle.

BJ shook his head, amazed at the kid's luck. Dwight probably had a broken sternum and would be sore for a month, but the badge had saved his life, just as he had saved theirs.

Sarah looked past the headlights toward the horizon from which they had just come. Somewhere beyond was the desert compound. Marcus Kane was out there. And so was John.

CHAPTER 91

MARCUS KANE raced along the desert floor, head ducked low. He was no longer a man. He had become the thing in the dark.

He reveled in the transformation.

His mind was a cauldron of conflict—Kane's boiling rage at the man who dared challenge him battling against Kane's animalistic joy at the hunt. For the hunt was everything. Kane's senses were heightened. His muscles were sinewy death. And his claws were sharp.

Nothing escaped Kane's notice as he ran between the mesquite trees, rocks and cactus. In the distance, he heard the echoing howl of a coyote. The coyote was weak. Kane could sense it from the lilting taper of the cry. But the coyote was meaningless. Nothing else mattered tonight.

Kane flared his nostrils and believed he actually caught a whiff of his prey's scent. He could taste the fear in the air.

Michaels was afraid of him.

As he should be.

Because Michaels had fucked with his program and now he was going to die. Kane was going to cut his fucking head off and throw it into the air. And then he was going to find the rest of the miserable bleating sheep who had dared challenge his domain, and he was going to kill them all. One by one.

The thing in the dark increased his pace, pumping his powerful legs like pistons. He focused his vision on the blackness before him. At long last, he saw the distant form of his prey.

This was going to feel so good.

CHAPTER 92

JOHN SQUINTED in an attempt to focus his eyes through the darkness. He thought he had detected movement. Something in the distance.

Kane.

He adjusted his grip on the thick mesquite branch and found himself again wishing for a place to hide—a way to set up an ambush for the thing in the dark—but John had run through this terrain enough during his time at the program that he knew there was nothing here. Nothing but the surrounding blackness.

So he would make a stand, and he would fight Kane with every waning ounce of strength that remained. He would give Sarah and BJ a fighting chance to bring back help, and he would do what he could to provide Chance some time.

He saw it this time. Definite movement.

John focused his vision and perceived the oncoming form of Marcus Kane, still a shadowy force in the darkness.

Butterflies coursed through John's stomach, but one thought comforted him—he had been dead-on in his evaluation of Kane. The leader of the spiritual awakenings and the driving force behind the program did have a weakness.

Arrogance.

And Kane's vanity, his driving need to pursue John Michaels rather than eliminate the more pressing threats to his program, proved John right.

John watched as the vague rushing shadow began to grow and take shape. Marcus Kane didn't seem to run, he appeared to glide across the desert floor. John knew the man's legs were pumping, just as his own had minutes earlier, but Kane ran with a smoothness and purpose that John had only seen in the animal kingdom.

And he was getting closer.

A lump formed in the dryness of John's throat and he tried to swallow it away. He had no saliva. He was so thirsty.

Of course, this *was* the desert. What could he expect?

Kane was close now. John could see him clearly, and he knew Kane must be able to see him as well. Only another few seconds.

The coyote howled again in the distance, and John shook from the cold chill that started in his stomach and traveled up his spine and into his shoulders. He couldn't help it.

He tightened his grip on the branch once more and realized he could no longer feel his fingers. He was squeezing the blood from them.

Kane was a hundred yards away and not slowing down. The thing in the dark was close indeed. John's thoughts flashed to his sister.

Is this what had happened to Jennifer?

With that, a powerful new feeling swept over John, overwhelming him with its embrace. A warmth, like a palpable wave of sunshine, permeated his body. He was no longer cold. In fact, John could swear he felt swells of heat ripple along his skin, soothing the harsh electrical burns and dispelling the goose-bumps. The butterflies left his stomach. He was at peace.

"Thank you," he whispered to the night. He didn't know if his sister could hear him, but he suspected she was quite nearby.

John's mind was at peace. The fear was gone. He was going to die, but Sarah would live. And his friends would live. Of that much he was now certain.

Kane appeared at the edge of the clearing and stopped. He was breathing hard, but it appeared to be more from excitement than physical exertion. John could tell the giant was truly enjoying this.

"You stopped," Kane uttered. John could sense surprise in his voice. Kane didn't hide it very well. "That was a mistake."

John shook his head. He had made plenty of mistakes in his lifetime. That was, after all, why he was here. But this was not one. Not at all.

"You think that little stick is going to stop me?" Kane asked. He raised his right hand, displaying the twin silver blades that reflected the moonlight. He was trying to goad his prey, make the hunt more fun.

John simply shrugged.

Kane exhaled at the motion, a bestial sigh of frustration that rattled within his throat. The hunt was no longer going as it should. It was time to end it.

Without a word, Kane lunged toward his prey. Acting on instinct, John drew back his mesquite bat and swung it at his attacker in a blur of motion. Just as quickly, Kane raised his left arm to block the blow. The mesquite branch snapped in half against Kane's massive forearm.

Kane smiled.

John released his grip and drew back his fist for a punch. Kane moved faster. The giant dipped his shoulder and jabbed upward with his left fist, catching John in the solar plexus with a crushing blow that lifted him off his feet.

The wind rushed from John's lungs as he dropped to his knees, unable to move. Kane rammed his knee upward, smashing it into John's chin. The impact slammed John's jaw shut, rattling his teeth and sending a wave of light across his vision. He fell backward onto the cold earth, fighting to regain his senses.

Kane stood over his prey's sprawling figure. He heard the coyote in the distance. Kane lifted his head and a guttural howl erupted from his mouth and into the blackness of the night.

He was the thing in the dark. Man no more.

As John heard the nightmarish sound above him, he shook his head, trying to clear his senses. His vision was still doubled, but he knew that was about to be the least of his problems. He moved his hand over the dirt and worked it into his pocket. His fingers touched the thing he was looking for, the thing Sarah had pressed into his hand before leaving the courtyard.

He closed it into his fist and withdrew his hand as the unholy howl of Marcus Kane ceased.

Kane dropped to his knees and straddled him, his hips coming to rest on John's thighs. His weight was enormous. John couldn't have moved his legs if he tried.

Kane cocked his head at the man beneath him and waved his right hand before John's face, as if about to perform a magic trick. The tip of one silver blade scratched the tip of John's nose. John felt his skin slice open at the contact. Kane leaned forward as he began to speak.

"Do you see these, Michaels?" he asked, still flourishing the serrated edges in the moonlight. "These are a part of me. They may not have come with this body, but they should have." He paused, admiring the implement strapped to the back of his hand. "They're beautiful, aren't they? And they work so well. In fact, I think you'll find they are just the right distance apart for your eyes."

Kane lowered the blades to John's eyes. Positioned less than an inch away, they appeared as twelve streaks of silver in John's addled vision.

John let out a loud laugh.

Kane pulled the blades away and stared at the hysterical man pinned to the ground beneath him. Michaels had finally lost it. It was a shame. He had assumed his prey would be stronger, and he hated to give up the hunt so soon. Still, nobody laughed at Marcus Kane, not even a crazy man.

"You want to tell me what's so funny?" he growled.

John allowed his laughter to taper off to a few giggles. He needed another moment to adjust the thing in his hand, to get it positioned correctly.

"It's just that you honestly have no idea," John said.

The comment annoyed Kane. "No idea about what?"

"You have no idea that you've already lost. No clue at all."

Kane's eyebrows narrowed in consternation. His prey was mocking him. Him. *Marcus Kane.* It could not be tolerated.

"You see," John continued with a laugh, "No matter what happens to me, your operation has been exposed. People will come, Kane. People who know your face. Who know Doctor Regen. You'll never be able to complete your great plan."

Kane shook his head in a rage. The laughing madman didn't know what he was talking about. He hadn't lost. The thing in the dark never lost.

John stopped laughing. His expression turned serious as he addressed the man leaning over him. He had the thing from his pocket where he needed it now, wedged between the middle knuckles of his right hand.

"And every time you look in a mirror," John said, his voice deep and purposeful, "You'll remember that I'm the man who beat you at your own fucking game."

That was enough. Kane pulled back his right hand—preparing to plant his blades squarely into his prey's eyes—when John's hand flashed upward, moving faster than Kane would have thought possible. The sharpened onyx arrowhead struck Kane in the cheek, splitting the skin and glancing off his molars, chipping the teeth.

The follow-through of John's punch shredded a six-inch laceration in Kane's face, from his mouth to his ear.

Kane howled in rage, the sound garbling as it passed not only through his lips but also through the mangled hole in the side of his face. He plunged his blades down, driving them into John's abdomen.

John felt the knives enter his body. He felt the small pop when the tips of the blades punctured through the layer of muscle and descended into his organs. He felt an odd pressure inside, like fingers of pure heat squeezing at his stomach.

When Kane ripped the knives free, John felt the million tiny catches as the teeth of the serrated edges pulled against the tendons of his abdominal muscles. The arrowhead dropped from his hand.

His stomach was hot, blending with the peaceful warmth flowing within his body. He closed his eyes. It wasn't so bad. It was going to be okay.

Kane raised his left hand to his face. His fingers touched the hanging flap of skin that dangled along his jaw. He felt the cool night air against his exposed molars. And he felt burning rage at John Michaels.

He leaned down, commingled blood and saliva seeping from his wounded face and onto John's naked chest.

"New rules, Michaels," Kane sputtered. The words were difficult to form and sounded odd coming from his mangled mouth. But he had to say it. Had to let the little prick know just who had lost this particular game. "Whoever lives longest wins."

Kane raised the blades above his head, aiming his finest deathblow. He decided to plunge the knives into Michaels' neck. He imagined that would be the most painful way to die.

John opened his eyes and focused on his killer. He knew it was over, but he really didn't mind. At least Sarah was alive.

He tensed as he saw Kane preparing to drop his fist, preparing to drive the blades to their final home, when a blossom of red appeared at the center of the giant's chest. It was followed immediately by a loud cracking sound, echoing in the distance.

Kane jerked backward, glancing down at the unexpected hole that had opened in his sternum. Confusion washed over his face.

Another bloom of crimson erupted just to the left of the first, precisely over Kane's heart, and was followed by the same distant crack.

It took John a moment to recognize the sound of a rifle.

Kane looked up in uncertainty, searching for the source of the sound, and then slowly dropped to the earth, his powerful body crumpling. The giant came to rest on his side, his legs still draped across John's lower torso.

John was staring into the eyes of Marcus Kane, just a foot in front of his own.

Blood poured from the wounds in Kane's chest and soaked into the thirsty earth. And as the light passed from Kane's eyes, John mouthed the words, the last thing the demon would ever see.

"You lose."

Darkness spread over John's mind, joining the warmth encompassing his body. His senses were leaving him, one at a time. He heard the sound of hooves approaching at a gallop.

Odd. He hadn't seen any horses since he'd been here.

The pain in his belly was just a dull numbness now. It wasn't so bad. None of it was so bad. Sarah was going to be okay. And Jennifer. Not long at all now.

John coughed and it felt wrong. Something moved in his stomach that wasn't supposed to. He guessed getting your abdomen skewered would do that to you.

"Hang on, son. I've got you. Open your eyes for me."

The voice was nice. It had a pleasant Southern drawl to it. It was almost in his ear, but it sounded so distant. John felt a hand on his shoulder, and he realized the owner of the voice was touching him. He forced his eyelids to open, and he saw him.

It was an older man with a big gray mustache. He wore a cowboy hat, and something else. Something on his chest.

John could hear Jennifer's voice, somewhere out there, past the man with the mustache. And it came to him. He took to heart the last advice his sister had ever given him in this life.

REMEMBER.

How could he forget? The thing on the man's chest. He had seen one in a museum, and another in a book. The book he had read just so he could ask Sarah out on that first date.

"Don't quit, son. I'm going to get you out of this. Just don't give up on me."

John forced his eyes open again to look at it once more. It was beautiful, the way it caught the soft beams of moonlight and almost seemed to glow.

The silver star of the Texas Rangers.

EPILOGUE

CUTTER VALENTINE walked along the white hallway trying to breathe through his mouth. He had always hated hospitals, and the harsh, ever-present smell of antiseptic hanging in the air was a primary reason.

He shifted the package he was carrying to his other hand when he located the door for which he had been searching. Room 604. He gently knocked and opened the door a few inches. Sarah Michaels appeared in the space, swinging the door fully open.

Before he could say hello, her arms encircled him in a tight embrace. It was the kind of greeting Cutter had never minded when coming from a pretty lady. He patted her on the back a couple of times as she finished the hug.

When she pulled away, there was a big smile on her face. She turned her head to speak, looking back into the room.

"John, Mr. Valentine's here."

Cutter removed his hat as he walked through the doorway. "Call me Cutter, please. Or even Earl if it suits you better."

The hospital bed was raised to an upright position, allowing John to sit up. He wore the blue gown the hospital had provided, and a plastic IV tube was attached to the back of his hand. He still appeared pale, but compared to the night Cutter found him, John Michaels looked like a million bucks.

"Cutter, then," John said. He wore a smile, too. "Thanks for coming. I know El Paso isn't an easy drive from Sonora."

Cutter nodded. "Well, I heard they moved you out of the ICU so I thought I'd swing by and check on you, make sure you were treating this little lady right."

Sarah sat on the side of the bed next to her husband, cautious of the myriad of plastic tubes. She blushed at Cutter's remark, but the smile never left her face.

"He's treating me right, Earl. I promise."

Cutter paused. He liked the way the name sounded coming out of Sarah's mouth. It sounded mighty nice.

"So what do the sawbones tell you? You going to live?" Cutter extended his hand and shook John's, careful not to unsettle an IV or anything.

John nodded. "Good reports so far. They tell me I'll be shitting in a bag for another six weeks—"

"John!" Sarah scolded him, slapping his shoulder. But Cutter could tell she was being careful. Very gentle.

John grinned at her playful slap. "But the doctors are expecting a full recovery. I owe you a considerable deal of gratitude, Cutter."

Cutter raised one hand. "Just doing my job, but you should definitely be thanking your wife. If she hadn't driven my truck back to the compound to find us that night, I'm not sure how we would have gotten you out of there."

John looked at his wife. There was a lot of love in that look. "I owe her a lot, too," he said softly.

Sarah squeezed her husband's arm and turned back to Cutter. "How's Sheriff Owens doing, Earl?"

A grin creased Cutter's face beneath the gray mustache. '*Sheriff Owens*'. It sounded mighty odd, but that was okay.

"He's sore, but he'll be fine." He paused, reflecting on the young lawman with the bum hand. "Dwight lost an awful lot out there, but I think he found something, too. If nothing else, he'll have a nice scar on his chest with a great story to tell along with it. Should come in handy with his profession."

"And everyone else?" Sarah's eyes looked hopeful at the question. Cutter knew she and John shared a special bond with the other people who survived the program.

"They're going to be fine. They're all spending the next few days under medical supervision here in El Paso, checking for any lingering side effects, but everything seems okay so far. I suspect you'll have some visitors pretty soon. The tall guy, BJ, has already talked about bringing his son out to meet you both as soon as he can."

"Teri?" John voiced her name softly.

Cutter sighed. "We were finally able to track down her parents. The FBI is helping them with funeral arrangements."

"That's good," John said. His face grew serious as he asked his next question. "Cutter, have you figured anything out yet?"

Cutter sighed as he shook his head. "I'm afraid not. So far, the Feds have recovered the remains of more than fifty people at the base of that cliff—the one Chance showed us—but Kane kept his records at the compound clear. There was nothing on the computer, and only a few hard files in his quarters. The mayor's office was a dead-end, too. They ran a tight ship."

"And Doctor Luther, the psychiatrist who referred us to the program?" Sarah asked, her eyebrows raised.

"Missing in action," Cutter replied. "We checked the other two psychiatrists who referred the rest of your group—the one in LA and the other in Oklahoma City—and couldn't turn anything up on them. It's like they disappeared from the face of the earth. Their families don't know anything. Their friends. Their hospitals. Nothing."

He wasn't sure how to tell the couple the rest of the news, or if he even should. He decided to reveal everything. It was important they know. Important because of what he had to ask them later.

"But when the FBI went to your doctor's apartment, the one in Boston, they did find something. There were about three pints of blood soaked into his bed. The doctor had given blood at the office a few weeks earlier, and they checked it against a sample. It was a match."

Sarah inhaled sharply. John's hand found hers and squeezed it, reassuring her.

"They haven't located a body, but it's a high probability he was killed. Same for the others."

John finally asked the question—the one Cutter hated to answer. "Who?"

Cutter dropped his head a little. "We don't know for sure, but our primary suspect is Hiram Kane."

A look of confusion crossed John's face. Sarah's expression mimicked her husband.

"Who?" John repeated the same question.

"Hiram Kane is Marcus Kane's father. I won't lie to you—he's got a file with the FBI that's thick as a phone book. He did some godawful stuff a long time ago and then disappeared. Vanished without a trace."

John was shaking his head. "So, you think he was working with the program?"

"More than that. Based on the short discussion I had with Cal Regen before he died, Hiram Kane *is* the program. And there's something else I should tell you."

John and Sarah both looked apprehensive at the news he was delivering. Cutter hated to be the one responsible for that look—especially after everything the poor couple had been through already—but it was for their own safety.

"Marcus wasn't Hiram Kane's only son," he continued. "Records indicate Hiram had two others. Three sons that he took with him when he disappeared."

The look of apprehension on the Michaels' faces was turning into a look of sickness. This was bad.

"Now we don't know the location of the other two sons, but if Marcus was working with his father on this, then it's possible the others are also." He paused. It was time to ask. "I'd like your consent to put the two of you under federal protection, just until we figure out what the situation is."

The room was silent as John and Sarah absorbed the information they had just received. Finally, Sarah spoke.

"Do you think we're in danger, Earl?"

Cutter took a deep breath. He thought he knew the answer to this, but he couldn't be certain.

"I don't think so," he said. "From what I gathered talking to Cal, Hiram Kane is obsessed with his agenda. I think the doctors were removed because the program had been exposed, and they could have revealed information to the police if they were questioned. That makes me believe Hiram would go out of his way to avoid any contact with either of you. Contact is what the FBI would expect, and after reading his file, Hiram Kane never does what is expected. The man is cold. And I honestly believe he's cold enough to let his son's death go unavenged. That's good for you."

John and Sarah looked at each other and then back to Cutter. They knew he wasn't quite finished yet.

"But..." John said.

"But I don't know for sure. That's just my hunch. And until we find out for certain, I'd like for you to accept the federal protection. Just to sleep better at night."

John smiled. Cutter wasn't sure what brought out the grin on the man's pale face.

"Sleep better at night," John repeated. "We'll do it. But be sure to keep us posted on the progress of the case."

Cutter nodded and glanced out the window. He'd been in the hospital too long. It was time to go.

"I'll let you know how things develop," he said. "I promise."

He took one step toward the door when he remembered the package. He turned back to John, handing him the large envelope.

"Almost forgot. I told you there wasn't much at the compound, just a few files, but I thought you should have this."

John opened the envelope and pulled the manila folder from within. He turned the file on its side so he could read the label. '*Michaels, Jennifer*.'

"That's technically evidence, so you'll need to give it back to the Feds." Cutter paused. "After you've finished with it."

John opened the folder and glanced at the first page, then closed it again. He looked up at Cutter but didn't speak. Sarah said the words for him.

"Thank you, Earl."

Cutter pushed his hat onto his head, and tipped its brim with one finger at the couple. They were nice folks, and though it wasn't going to be easy for them, Cutter thought they were going to be okay.

With a nod, Cutter Valentine turned and walked out the door.

◇ ◇ ◇

The man sitting on the couch was enormous, just an inch shy of seven feet. He was taller than Marcus Kane, bigger. He had been since he had turned eleven—a fact that had annoyed Marcus to no end while they were growing up. The man's massive hand grabbed the remote for the television and turned up the volume.

Silas Kane couldn't believe what he was seeing.

The footage was of a desolate landscape in New Mexico. Yellow police tape and countless officers formed a barrier, blocking the media from the scene. A military-assisted no-fly zone prevented news helicopters from capturing the spectacle. But the intrepid cameraman for this particular station had brought a ten-foot stepladder, and was now straddling the top of it. The picture transmitting from his camera wobbled from his efforts at balance. His view was not perfect, but he was able to shoot clearly over the heads of the police.

Piles of bleached skeletal remains covered the desert floor by the base of a cliff. Human remains. Bones and skulls lay in heaps over the rocks and dirt.

Way to go, Marcus.

Silas Kane had received news of his older brother's death while reading the website of the *Seattle Post-Intelligencer* the previous day.

Marcus had died at the hands of some loser attorney or something like that. Silas decided he might check into it further. Maybe.

Regardless of how he had died, Marcus bit the bullet while chasing the ludicrous dreams of their father. It seemed like such a fucking waste. Not an action Silas Kane planned on repeating.

But the Feds were going to be out there now. Looking. Their father didn't exactly have a discreet past, and the media was going to have a field day with this. That would put pressure on the cops. And that in turn put pressure on Silas Kane to reevaluate his choice of locale.

Way to go, Marcus. Dickhead.

Silas pressed a button on the remote and the television screen went dark. He leaned back on the couch. He needed to think. Needed to figure out where he could go so the cops would have a hard time tracking him. He needed some place big. With a lot of people.

That meant New York or Los Angeles. Because Silas wasn't about to set foot in Texas.

He rolled his head to the side, looking into the green eyes of the young hooker who sat on the couch next to him. She was completely naked.

"What do you think, sweetheart, New York or LA?"

The girl didn't say a word. Her eyes were blank. Silas held her chin between his thumb and forefinger and moved her mouth as he spoke, raising his voice an octave.

"I like New York."

He grinned and pushed his hand against her face. The girl's head flopped at an unusual angle. Her broken neck would no longer support it. Her glassy eyes continued to stare at him.

"New York it is," Silas said, speaking in his regular deep voice.

He rose from the sofa. He had a busy day in front of him. He needed to pack a suitcase and ditch a body in the bay.

◇ ◇ ◇

John Michaels held the folder on his lap in the hospital room. His hands shook as he turned the pages, reading every word in the file. The notes were written in Doctor Lilith Regen's scrawled penmanship.

The file constructed by the madwoman held the answers to so many of the mysteries that had plagued John for years. In the course of two months, Doctor Regen had learned more about his sister than John had in a lifetime. And all she had done was ask.

The case history revealed the truth behind Jennifer's anger—the unfocused rage that had caused her to down an entire bottle of *Nytol*, all forty pills, and brought her into the care of the program. It all went back to the father that John never really knew.

It turned out his father had not been the kindest of men. According to the notes in the file, he drank a great deal and tended to lash out at John's mother with painful regularity. It wasn't long before Jennifer became the secondary target of his abuse. But it was the day their father hit John—striking him hard enough across his six-year-old face to draw blood—that Jennifer had fought back.

At only eight years of age, she had stood in the living room, facing down the drunken wretch that had caused the family so much pain. She told him if he ever laid a hand on her little brother again, she would be going straight to the police. Rather than challenge the resolve of the girl, their father decided to pack up and leave. He didn't need this kind of shit.

The file told the story of that last night, when Jennifer heard their mother beg her husband not to leave. That they would all change. Her and the kids. Even the girl.

Their father hadn't listened, choosing instead to abandon his family. But on that night, seeds of hatred were planted in Jennifer's mind against her mother—the woman who was willing to sacrifice her own children for the company of an abusive louse. Those seeds of resentment would grow, developing deep roots through the course of her childhood. But it would be when Jennifer was sixteen, and her high school boyfriend slapped her in the midst of a disagreement, that the rage would fully bloom.

Tears formed in John's eyes as he read the account.

All that anger. And all that love.

He closed his eyes, trying to remember the day their father had left, but found he could not. He had no recollection of being struck in the face. He had unknowingly suppressed the memory his entire life while his sister had fought against it each and every day. It wasn't fair.

He reviewed the rest of the notes through blurred vision. Doctor Regen's handwriting grew steadily more aggressive as the file progressed. The letters were sharper. The ink bore deeper into the paper. She hadn't been happy with Jennifer's rejection of the program.

When Doctor Regen had tried to use the private sessions as a means to encourage the denouncement of the evil of the outside world, Jennifer had taken an opposing stand. She refused to believe that all of society was selfish and hurtful. There *were* good people out there. Her brother was one of them. She hadn't spoken to him since their mother's funeral, but as the notes transcribed, she *knew* that wherever he was, John Michaels was a good man.

John sniffed as he scanned the notes Doctor Regen had penned along the sides of the interview records. The words were written in a harsh, scrawled pen in bold ink. Some were underlined. Others circled.

Strong-willed. Skeptical. Stubborn.

A hint of a smile crossed John's lips. That was Jennifer all right.

But it was when he reached the final line of the records that the tears finally fell. It was the last word, written in all capital letters.

TERMINATED.

John closed the folder as his wife crossed the room to put her arms around him, cradling him against her. He sobbed, the motion caused him pain from the tubes connected to his body, but he sobbed.

He had spent his entire life resenting his sister for coming up short, but he now realized that he had been so very wrong. In the end, Jennifer had simply done what she always did best. She protected her baby brother.

John Michaels continued to cry for a long time that evening.

He just couldn't stop.

Sarah Michaels lay on the small cot the nurses had brought into the private room. She stared at her husband in the hospital bed across from her. It had been a long evening. Reading the file had been hard on John. Very hard.

But something about it had been good.

She had held him for over an hour, combing her hand through his hair as he sobbed quietly into her breast. Neither of them had said a word. Speaking wasn't necessary. They had found a closeness that words could not define.

He had cried, and she had held him. And when they finally separated, something truly remarkable happened.

After she had stood from the bed—her hand still holding his, cautious of the tubes—her husband did something she had never before seen. He closed his eyes, and fell asleep

In the entire time she had known him, all those years of marriage, John had never fallen asleep before her.

Not once.

As she watched him, his peaceful face lit by the dim bulbs of the equipment surrounding him, she couldn't help but smile.

They were going to be okay.

Despite everything around them that had gone wrong, in the midst of the nightmarish hell that was the program, their love had persevered. They had gone to the desert to find something they had never really lost.

Sarah rested her head on the thin hospital pillow. She could not take her eyes off the man across the room. The man she loved.

And she knew he loved her in return. With all his heart and soul. And that was the only thing that really mattered. Whatever the future held—even if it wasn't going to be easy—their love would carry them through.

They were going to be okay.

◇ ◇ ◇

The man sitting on the end of the pew looked to be in his late fifties. His graying hair was cropped close to his head. He had a large, barrel-chest and even sitting down, he was almost a full head taller than the rest of the congregation.

Hiram Kane was lost in a world of his own. He reflected on the past week as the preacher thumped his Bible and raised his voice to those gathered at the church.

So much had gone wrong in the last few days—ever since Marcus had failed to send his scheduled nightly report. Hiram had known something was awry and was on a plane within an hour, traveling first to LA, then to Oklahoma City. Tying up loose ends.

Boston had been close. He had been afraid word of the New Mexico disaster might have reached Dr. Cornelius Luther before he did. Or worse, the authorities might have learned of Luther's involvement and picked him up. But those were all needless worries.

The Feds acted with their characteristic sluggishness, delaying the crucial questions for the survivors of the program until after they had received medical attention and been given a warm cup of cocoa. It was really sweet.

And Cornelius Luther had no clue. That made it a little easier. The doctor from Boston had always been sloppy anyway—repeating names over the telephone and occasionally trying to place calls that weren't directed through the internet relay centers. Ridding himself of Luther and the others had been in the best interests of the program.

Part of the greater good.

Their deaths had been a loss, but only a minor setback. The desert initiative had already yielded much of the required data. The psychiatrists were on their way to becoming a liability. Besides, Hiram Kane had made lots of friends over the years, and the program had plenty of resources.

But it had still been close. He had been forced to terminate Luther right there in the doctor's apartment in Boston—that left unnecessary potential for evidence—but it had been a risk Hiram had deemed acceptable at the time. The clock had been ticking.

And in the end, it was of little consequence. The authorities would presume Hiram was responsible for the deaths of the psychiatrists anyway, and they would be correct. The program would just have to continue with more caution going forward.

That meant not going after the Michaels couple. Or the Ranger.

Hiram regretted that fact. As a father, he was rather perturbed that his oldest son had been murdered by a business consultant. The Ranger was one matter—that sort of thing was professional—but *John Michaels*?

Marcus had been wrong to accept Michaels into the program in the first place, and in doing so, he had lost his own life and put the program at risk. Losses were to be expected in the greater scheme of things, but Hiram hadn't planned on losing Marcus so soon. But he still had Silas out there somewhere. And he still had his third son.

Hiram reclined on the pew as he listened to the preacher shout the good news to the congregation.

"You feel helpless right now," the preacher was saying. "You feel like the whole world has turned against you. Well, I know your pain."

The man was young and stood just a little over six feet tall. His arms looked impossibly thin as they waved about his slender body while he spoke—a scarecrow in a black suit. The congregation knew the preacher as Jonas Knight, a precaution that was going to pay off in spades now that Marcus had exposed the program.

"But I want you to know there's healing. There is happiness out there. You just have to know where to find it!"

Hiram smiled. Jonas Kane had always been the runt of the family, but he was gifted.

"You find that joy by seeking out the truth, for the truth..." the preacher allowed a dramatic pause to heighten the anticipation. "Shall set you free!"

His youngest son was good. Some would say extraordinary. Jonas was incredibly smart—much more so than the other two boys—and possessed a dedication to the program unmatched by anyone except Hiram himself.

"And you might ask yourself, where is this truth?"

Jonas Kane was also a remarkably talented public speaker. Hiram glanced around the church. They had only begun the Wednesday evening services two weeks ago, and already there were thirty faces enrapt at the words of his youngest son. Just looking at them, Hiram could see that the individuals filling the pews were weak. But eventually, those who were stronger would begin to attend. And in time, even the strongest-willed would be subject to the program. Subject to the truth.

"The truth is in here!" His thin fingers thumped against the black Bible he waved with his other hand.

They would have to grow slowly. The program called for it. It would still be months before they began introducing the formula to the congregation, and it would take a couple of years for the plan to truly reach fruition.

"In here, we read that the world is full of evil!"

Yes, it would develop slowly, but soon they would hold spiritual awakenings every night of the week. Soon their flock would grow.

"And how can you avoid all that pain, all that evil that makes up this hateful world?"

Just a few short years, and he would have his revenge. His triumph.

"You find a guide! Someone who can lead you to the Promised Land! And friends, you've come to the right place."

Hiram smiled to himself as he watched. All the faces in the congregation were following the preacher as he moved from one side of the podium to the other, delivering the message. They were sheep in need of a shepherd, and they looked upon their spiritual leader with reverence.

They could have no way of knowing their shepherd was the son of the wolf.

◇ ◇ ◇

Cutter Valentine slowed his pick-up truck to a gradual stop in front of the small brick house. The woman was kneeling next to the flowerbed along the sidewalk, pulling weeds from among the petunias. Her back was to the road. She hadn't turned around.

Cutter watched her from the truck. She had built quite a pile of weeds beside her. He turned the key and cut the engine. It had been a long drive from New Mexico, and he was tired.

The woman turned at the sound. She had cut her hair. It was a lot shorter now than it had been before. It looked good.

When she saw him, she began to stand. She braced her hands on her knees for support. Old age was blooming, but she carried it well. Now on her feet, she put her hands on her hips, watching the man in the truck the same way he watched her.

She smiled.

Cutter's heart skipped a beat. How could she still have that effect on him after all these years?

Maggie walked to the truck, stopping outside the open driver's window.

"Hey, stranger," she said.

Cutter returned her smile.

"Howdy, ma'am."

He opened the door and stepped onto the sidewalk. Her arms were around him before he could say another word. The hug felt good. Better than Cutter had felt in a long time.

The incidents in the desert had forced him to make some hard decisions. And the drive home from New Mexico had given him plenty of time to think about them.

He came to a conclusion about himself—he could never again become the man he once was. For better or worse, he had changed. But that was what people did. No matter how hard they fought against it, no matter how happy they might be with their lives just the way they are, events and circumstances will change things. The trick is to accept the changes and focus on the good in life.

It was a new trick this old dog had finally been forced to learn.

As he hugged Maggie, he knew it wouldn't last forever. It was a good life, but there were other things Cutter would have to do. Putting the badge back on was a start. He had been officially reinstated to the Texas Rangers (following his "temporary leave of absence") while he had worked with the FBI in sorting out the events in New Mexico. The new job meant new responsibilities.

Hiram Kane was out there somewhere. And he was planning something big. Something big and very bad. Cutter couldn't allow him to succeed with that plan.

Maggie's face moved away from his chest, peering into the cab of the truck. She pulled away from him with a quizzical expression on her face.

"Did you bring home a friend or finally break down and buy a satellite dish?"

Cutter smiled and reached inside the truck, gently rubbing Walker's ears. John Michaels' survival hadn't been the only miracle that night. Red Mercer had managed to pull off a pretty impressive one of his own. The mutt's chest was still wrapped in layers of white gauze, and he wore a large, upturned plastic collar to prevent him from chewing at the bandages. The dog did indeed resemble a furry satellite dish. He looked absolutely ridiculous.

Maggie didn't seem to mind. She reached past her husband and ran her fingers through the short hair on Walker's head, careful not to brush against the healing cut on his nose. The dog's lips pulled back in that familiar canine grin.

Cutter leaned against the truck and watched as his wife talked to his friend. He had come to realize something else over the past few months. His life would never be perfect. He loved Maggie more than anything in this world, but sooner or later he would have to begin the process of tracking down Hiram Kane. Maggie wouldn't be too happy about that, but she would understand. Maggie always understood.

He reached his hand out and touched his wife's new, short hair. It was mostly gray now, just like his own. He loved it. She smiled at him, and kissed his aging hand.

It was never going to be a perfect life, but it was a good life.

Good enough.

ALSO AVAILABLE FROM DEREK BLOUNT

The Second Son
(Book Two of the Hostile Takeover Trilogy)

If you enjoyed *Hostile Takeover*, please note that *The Second Son*, Book Two of the trilogy, will be released in December 2015 (available for pre-order on Amazon in October 2015). Join the mailing list at **derekblount.com** for notification.

The Three Christmases of William Spencer

Hailed as "*a truly beautiful book*" and "*a wonderful gift book for sharing the joy of the season and the meaning of life*", this family friendly tale with elegant red linen hardcover will become a Christmas tradition and find its way onto your coffee table every year.

Purchase your copy on Amazon today or learn more at **derekblount.com**.

A Note from Derek Blount

Thank you for reading *Hostile Takeover*. If you enjoyed the book, please stay tuned for Book Two of the trilogy. *The Second Son* will be available December 2015 (pre-orders begin October 2015). Also, please join our email list at derekblount.com for notifications about future work.

In other "thank you" news...

Thank you to my smart, kind, gorgeous, funny, warm and wonderful wife, Bethany. You are my heart.

Thank you to my parents, who have made me the man I am (whether that's praise or blame is in the eye of the beholder).

Thank you to my sister, Jessica, who told me she loved seeing my name in print. Thanks for looking out for me growing up.

Thank YOU, dear reader, for investing your time with me. I hope our journeys together are always worth your while.